THE SCANDAL OF LORD RANDAL

LAUREN ROYAL

August 2021 Edition
FORMERLY TITLED "LILY"

THE SCANDAL OF LORD RANDAL by Lauren Royal

Formerly titled "Lily"
Originally published in paperback by Penguin Putnam Inc.

Published by Novelty Books, a division of Novelty Publishers, LLC, 205 Avenida Del Mar #275, San Clemente, CA 92674

August 2021 Edition

Cover Art Illustration by The Midnight Muse

Learn more about the author and her books at www.LaurenRoyal.com.

ISBN: 978-1-634691-55-0

MORE CHASE FAMILY BOOKS

For DeeDee Guiver Perkins,
Diena Brennan Simmons,
and Julie Bowring Walker,
who wore hoop skirts with me at the senior prom.

Our friendship means the world to me.

ONE

Trentingham Manor, the South of England
August 1677

E'D FORGOTTEN about her.

Well, maybe he hadn't quite forgotten about her, but he'd certainly put her out of his mind.

Well, maybe he hadn't quite put her out of his mind, but he'd known she was only sixteen. And sixteen was too young, so, being the sort of man he was—an honorable one, or so he liked to think—he'd made a conscious decision not to pursue her.

For the four long years since their last meeting, whenever thoughts of Lily Ashcroft had sneaked into Lord Randal Nesbitt's head, he'd reminded himself she was only sixteen.

But now, Rand realized with a start, she must be twenty.

Focused as Rand was, the priest's voice, reciting the baptism service, barely penetrated his thoughts. Nor did the wiggling month-old child in Rand's arms. Instead of looking at the altar, he gazed at Lily standing beside him in her family's oak-paneled chapel, her sister's other twin baby held close.

Twenty. A lovely dark-haired, blue-eyed twenty. A marriageable twenty.

In all of Rand's twenty-eight years, he'd never really considered marriage, so the notion was jarring.

"Having now," the priest continued, "in the name of these children, made these promises, wilt thou also on thy part take heed that these children learn the Creed, the Lord's Prayer, and the Ten Commandments, and all other things which a Christian ought to know and believe to his soul's health?"

"I will, by God's help," Lily replied softly. Gently, gazing down at the babe in her arms.

Rand was unsurprised. In four years she had changed, of course. But her gentleness, that innate sweetness, hadn't changed. Couldn't have changed. It was what made her Lily.

Ford Chase, Rand's friend—and father of the children in question—elbowed him in the ribs.

"Hmm?" Startled, Rand looked down to the lad he was holding, its bald little head patterned with colors made by sun streaming through the chapel's stained-glass windows. Ford's child, he thought, surprised by a rush of tenderness. Rand's godchild...or at least the tiny babe and his twin sister would be his godchildren once they managed to get through this interminable service.

"I will," he answered, echoing Lily's words and vaguely wondering what he'd just agreed to.

"By God's help," the priest prompted.

"By God's help."

God help him get through this ritual. Mass, and then a lesson, and now this ceremony at the font—Rand felt like he'd been standing on his feet forever. Delivering a two-hour lecture at Oxford wasn't nearly this exhausting. He feared his knees were locked permanently.

He wanted this to be over. He wanted to talk to Lily. Never mind that she'd barely noticed him. He'd arrived at the last minute and had no chance to greet her before this rigmarole all began.

The priest turned a page in his *Book of Common Prayer*. "Wilt thou take heed that these children, so soon as sufficiently instructed, be brought to the bishop to be confirmed by him?"

"I will." Rand and Lily said the words together this time. Their voices, he thought, sounded good together.

"Name these children."

The child squirmed in Rand's arms, choosing then to begin wailing. "Marcus Cicero Chase," Rand bellowed over the cries.

"Rebecca Ashcroft Chase," Lily said more softly and with a smile, even though the girl's cry had joined her twin brother's, seeming to fill the chapel all the way up to its sculpted Tudor ceiling.

Whoever would have thought such small infants could make such a huge racket?

The priest rushed to finish, scooping water into his hand. It trickled through his fingers, running in rivulets down the backs of the two babies' heads and landing on the colorful glazed tile floor. "I baptize thee in the name of the Father, and of the Son, and of the Holy Ghost." He muttered some more words and made crosses on the children's foreheads. "Amen."

Amen. It was over. Well-wishers crowded close. Still holding his squalling godson, Rand turned to Lily.

She was gone.

How could she have disappeared so quickly? Using his height to advantage, he peered over heads. But she'd vanished.

Nearby, Ford held tiny Rebecca and was chatting with an older man. Lily's father, if Rand remembered right. Or rather, Ford was shouting at the man, since the Earl of Trentingham was hard of hearing.

Marveling that his tall, masculine friend looked so comfortable holding an infant, Rand shifted little Marc uneasily. Rebecca had stopped crying, apparently content in Ford's arms, but in Rand's arms, her twin brother still howled.

Glancing around for help, Rand was relieved to see Ford's wife, Violet, moving close. When she reached for her son, Rand gave her a grateful smile. But then he found himself oddly reluctant to hand Marc over. The babe might be loud, but he smelled sweet and had a pleasant, warm weight.

When Violet took him, Marc quieted immediately. Resisting the urge to run his fingers over that fuzzy little head, Rand leaned a hand on one of the intricate carved oak stalls. "I assume you chose his name, Marcus Cicero, for the philosopher."

Violet bounced the lad in her arms, her brown curls bouncing along with him. She looked more motherly than Rand usually pictured her. Did children change people so much? "It was only fair," she said. "Ford had the naming of our firstborn."

"Nicky? Ah, Nicolas Copernicus," Rand remembered. "Well, I suppose it's a better name than Galileo Galilei."

"Ford's other scientific hero?" She laughed, her brown eyes sparkling with humor behind the spectacles Ford had made for her. "Even *he* wouldn't saddle a good English child with Galileo for a name."

"And Rebecca? Who is she named after?"

"No one. I just like it. And there's never been a major female philosopher."

"Yet," Rand added, knowing Violet hoped to publish a philosophy book of her own someday.

"Yet," she confirmed with a nod, clearly appreciating his support. She touched her husband's arm, claiming his attention. "We'd best be heading home," she said when he turned, "or our guests will arrive there before us."

When Ford smiled at her, Violet's return smile transformed her face. Perhaps she wasn't as beautiful as her sisters, Lily and Rose, but she was attractive in her own, unique way, and it had nothing to do with the magnificent purple gown she'd donned for the baptism.

Moreover, it was obvious she made Ford happy. A sort of happiness that glowed from his eyes whenever he looked at her. A sort of happiness neither Rand nor Ford had dreamed of back in the days they attended university together.

It was frightening how much the man had changed.

Ford still held his new daughter, her tiny fist tangled in his long brown hair. Unable to resist this time, Rand skimmed his fingers over Rebecca's dark curls. "So soft," he murmured.

Violet nodded. "All babies are soft."

"I haven't touched a baby since I was a very small child myself."

"Really?" She looked surprised to hear that. "Well, someday you'll have children of your own."

"Perhaps," he allowed. "My favorite truism is 'never say never.' But God willing, should it happen, it won't be too soon."

Her laugh tinkled through the nearly empty chapel. "We really must be going."

"Come along, Rand," Ford said. "I want to show you the water closet I built. It's much better than the ones imported from France."

A smile curved Rand's lips as he followed them out the door. It seemed his friend hadn't changed that much, after all.

TWO

"WHAT?" LILY laughed as her friend Judith Carrington pulled her toward a carriage. "What's so important you couldn't wait until we got to Violet's house to tell me? So important you made me almost drop my niece, not to mention nearly dislocated my arm dragging me out of there?"

Before climbing inside, Lily waved at her parents and sister Rose, lest they think she'd abandoned them. Hers was a handsome family, she thought suddenly. Her father was tall and trim, his eyes a deep green, his real hair still as jet-black as the periwig he wore for his grandchildren's baptism. Her mother and Rose were both dark-haired and statuesque. They looked elegant in their best satin gowns, Mum's a gleaming gold and Rose's a rich, shimmering blue.

Looking at them, one would never guess they were so eccentric.

Her mother waved back distractedly, holding her two-year-old grandson, Nicky, as she busily ushered guests out the door to their waiting transportation.

Feeling Judith's hand on her back, Lily laughed again and lifted her peach silk skirts to duck inside the carriage. "What?" she repeated.

"Oh, just this." Even though they weren't ready to leave, Judith pulled the door shut. Then she settled herself with a flounce. "I'm betrothed."

"Betrothed?" Lily blinked at her friend. "As in you're planning to wed?"

"Well, Mama is doing the planning. But it's ever so exciting. Come October, I'm going to be a married woman. Can you believe it, Lily?"

"No, I cannot believe it." The third of her friends to marry this year. Yesterday they'd been children; now suddenly they were supposed to be all grown-up. "Who will be your groom?" Lily asked.

"Lord Grenville. Didn't your mother tell you she'd suggested he offer for my hand? Father says it's a brilliant match."

Grenville was wealthy, but thirty-five years old to Judith's twenty. "Do you love him?" Lily wondered aloud. She hoped so. Judith was plump and pretty, but even more important, she was genuinely nice. A good friend who deserved happiness.

"I barely know him. But Mama assures me we'll grow to love each other—or get along tolerably, at least." The excitement faded from Judith's blue eyes, replaced with a tinge of anxiety. Her fingers worried the embroidery on her aqua underskirt. "It will all work out fine, I'm sure of it."

"I'm sure of it, too," Lily soothed, reaching across to take her friend's cold, pale hand. She squeezed, wishing she were as certain as she sounded. Lily's parents had promised their daughters they could choose their own husbands, but she knew it didn't work that way for most young women.

Her family was different. The Ashcroft motto—*Interroga Conformationem*, translated as Question Convention—said it all.

The Carringtons, on the other hand, were as conventional as roast goose on Christmas Day. Judith forced a smile and pushed back a lock of bright yellow hair that had escaped her careful coiffure. "Who was that handsome man who stood as godfather?"

Lily sat back. "One of Ford's old friends. Lord Randal Nesbitt."

"Wouldn't it be fun to be newly wedded together, have babies together?" Some of the color returned to Judith's cheeks. "You should marry *him*."

"Wherever did you get that idea?" Lily crossed her arms over the long, stiff stomacher that covered the laces on the front of her gown. "I barely know Rand."

"Rand," Judith repeated significantly, making it clear she'd noticed Lily's familiar use of the name. "What does that matter? I hardly know Lord Grenville, either. And believe me, he doesn't look at me the way *Rand* was looking at you."

"Looking at me?" Lily echoed weakly. She'd hardly looked at him at all. She'd been focused on the cooing baby in her arms, her sister's first daughter. Her first niece. Nicky was great fun, of course, but now she'd have a little girl to play house with, to fix her hair, to—

"Lord, he didn't take his eyes off you the entire time." Judith's lips curved in an impish grin. "Watching him was certainly more entertaining than the baptism."

Lily felt her face heat and wondered if Judith could be right—if instead of watching the ceremony, everyone had been watching Rand watch her.

But surely that hadn't been the case. Why would Rand be interested in *her*? The two of them had nothing in common. Her friend had seen something that wasn't there. "You just have the wedding fever," she said lightly, rubbing the faint scars on the back of her hand. "Besides, if he's interested in anyone, I'm sure it's Rose. They share a passion for languages."

"Ah," Judith said with a smug tilt of her pert nose. "You know more about the man than you're willing to admit."

Ignoring that, Lily leaned to look out the window. But there was a long queue of carriages. They were going nowhere.

"Who's that?" her friend asked, following her line of sight. "The girl in pink, coming out of the barn with your brother?"

"That's Jewel, Ford's niece. Rowan and she have been friends forever."

"What sort of friends? And what do you suppose they were doing alone together in a barn?"

"Goodness, Rowan is only eleven and Jewel ten. Your mind is too much on romance these days. Knowing the two, they were probably planning a prank."

"In a *barn*?"

Lily laughed at the expression on her friend's face. "Over the years, there's hardly a building on either property they haven't used to stage a prank."

Judith looked likely to say more, but the door popped open and her mother poked her head in. "Were you leaving without me, dear?"

"Of course not, Mama." Judith scooted over to make room. "We just came inside to talk."

A large, jolly woman, Lady Carrington wedged herself beside her daughter and tucked in her voluminous coral skirts. Before her footman could shut the door, Lily's striped cat nimbly leapt inside.

Lady Carrington sneezed. "Shoo!" she exclaimed, waving a manicured hand at the hapless feline.

"Beatrix," Lily said softly, "you cannot ride in this carriage."

The cat gave her a hurt look but leapt out.

"Much better," Judith's mother said as the door shut. She turned to Lily. "This afternoon, I'm hoping your father will advise me about flowers for Judith's wedding."

The Earl of Trentingham was nothing if not an expert on flowers. "I'm certain Father will fancy being consulted," Lily assured her.

The carriage began moving at last. "I've my heart set on yellow flowers," Lady Carrington told Lily, "because Judith looks best in yellow. But she wants to be married in blue. What color will you wear for your wedding?"

"Blue is nice," Lily said with a vague smile.

She wasn't ready to think about weddings, and most certainly not her own.

Rose was a year older—her wedding should come first.

THREE

*W*HEN LILY arrived at Violet's house, Rose motioned her into the drawing room.

She gestured toward where Rand stood in conversation. "He keeps looking over here, Lily. He's spotted me." Tall and willowy, Rose made a pretty picture against the drawing room's soft turquoise walls—and well she knew it. She straightened one of her glistening chestnut curls and smoothed her deep-blue satin skirts. "He remembers me," she added confidently.

"Of course he remembers you." Lily glanced in Rand's direction—or at least she intended to glance. Instead, she found herself staring. "You worked together translating that old alchemy book, didn't you?" she added slowly.

How had she managed to ignore him in the chapel? Rand wasn't a man to whom women would be indifferent. His physique was lean and athletic, and his hair, a million mixed colors of blond and brown, was longer than hers and gorgeous enough to make her jealous.

As though sensing Lily studying him, he turned his head while still talking. For a split second, his intense gray eyes blazed into hers.

Or she thought they had. She blinked, clearing her vision. Now Judith had *her* imagining things.

"I've been dreaming about this day for weeks," Rose said, reclaiming her attention.

"The baptism?"

"No, you goose. Seeing Lord Randal again. Ever since I danced with him at Violet's wedding, I've known he's the man for me."

Suddenly Lily remembered that Rand had danced with her, too, at their sister's wedding. Not to mention, of course, that Rose lusted after every handsome, eligible man who crossed her path.

But Lily had to admit that Rand could be the one for Rose. Good looks aside, he was more suited to her sister than most men were. The two of them were both academically minded and shared mutual interests. "I had no idea you'd been thinking about him all these years."

"Dreaming," Rose repeated on a sigh.

"Four years is a long time to dream." Lily cast him another quick glance, then smiled at her older sister. "I suppose he *is* the memorable sort."

Rose looked at her sharply. "You're not interested in him yourself, are you?"

"Of course not!" First Judith, now Rose? Was something in the air today? "Whatever would make you think that?"

"You said he's the memorable sort."

"That doesn't mean I want him. A man like Rand would never be interested in someone like me. He'd want someone like you, Rose. You're both fascinated with languages. Rand and I have nothing in common. And he's too tall." Lily drew herself up to her full height of five-foot-two and figured she stood to about his shoulders.

Looking down at her, Rose snorted. "There's no such thing as a man who's too tall. Will you promise?"

"Promise what?"

"Promise me you won't pursue him. Promise me you won't get in my way."

The entire idea was so absurd, Lily laughed. "I promise. In fact, I'll do better than that. I'll help you land him."

"Would you?" Rose breathed.

"Of course. You're my sister. I love you, and I want to see you happy."

Rose's dark eyes actually misted. "You're so good, Lily. You want everyone to be happy."

"Is there something wrong with that?"

"Of course not," Rose said, and then in the next breath, "What will you do to help?"

Rose would be Rose, Lily thought with an inward smile. "Whatever I can. But you must do your part, too. And that means, for once, not pretending that your head is filled with pudding. I wish I could speak half the languages you do. You're bright and intelligent, and hiding that makes no sense."

"For Lord Randal, perhaps it doesn't, because we have similar interests. But for other men—"

"For any man. Why would you want a man who doesn't value your strengths?"

"You don't understand men, sister dear. Most of them thrive on feeling superior." When Lily opened her mouth, Rose held up a hand. "But we were talking about Lord Randal, who isn't most men—" She broke off, her eyes widening. "Gemini, here he comes!"

As Rand approached, their mother seemed to appear out of nowhere—a habit Lily and her sisters found vexing. Mum gave him a brilliant smile. "Lord Randal. How very nice to see you again." Her brown eyes shone with genuine warmth. "We missed you at my first grandson's christening."

"She means Nicky, my godchild," Rose put in. "I shared the honor with Ford's two brothers."

Rand shrugged a shoulder, a half smile curving his lips. "I was sorry to miss the occasion, but I'm afraid I was in Greece."

"Greece!" Rose laid a graceful hand on her embroidered stomacher. "That sounds like a dream. I would so adore traveling the world. I could make use of all my languages."

Lily did a little mental dance, so happy to see that her sister was doing as she'd suggested—as the entire family had been suggesting for years. For once in her life, Rose wasn't going to hide her brains and pretend to be empty-headed.

It would work, Lily was sure. Rose's bad luck with men would finally come to an end. And then, she couldn't help thinking, with her sister safely wed, she'd feel free to find love for herself.

Mum cleared her throat. "You'll remember my daughter Rose?" she asked Rand. "And Lily, her younger sister?"

"And Lily," Rand repeated, his eyes meeting hers. Capturing hers, like they had four years ago and again just a few minutes earlier.

In all of her twenty years, she'd never seen another gaze as compelling as Rand's. It felt as though he could see right into her, yet not in an uncomfortable way…in a way that warmed her and held her captive.

She'd forgotten about that. It seemed she'd forgotten a lot in those four years.

Rose—bold Rose—reached to touch him on the arm. "Did you ever succeed in translating that alchemy book?"

"*Secrets of the Emerald Tablet*?" He smiled at Lily before shifting his attention to her sister. "Not yet. A fine puzzle it is, very time-consuming, and Ford said that with the sale of his watch patent there was no longer any rush."

At that, Ford broke into their little group. "You certainly took that to heart," he said accusingly. "Four years is a bit longer than I had in mind."

"I'm here now, aren't I?" Rand countered, sounding defensive. "And ready to finish it."

Ford grinned, revealing the heated exchange to have been

nothing more than jesting between friends. "Only because you have nowhere to live."

"That's not true. I have a beautiful new home."

"Half built."

Rand ruefully rubbed his forehead. "The hammering and sawing were driving me insane."

"Rand has commissioned a new house," Ford explained to the girls and their mother. "It was supposed to have been ready by now, so he'd already sold his old one."

"And as a consequence," Rand added, "I've been sleeping in a construction site."

Rose nodded, her face a study in understanding. "Where's your new home, my lord?"

"Rand," he corrected her, having asked them four years ago to call him that. "And it's in Oxford."

"Rand is a professor of linguistics," Ford reminded Rose, although Lily was sure her sister needed no reminding.

But apparently Rose decided to pretend she'd forgotten. "Oooh, my lord, that's so impressive," she cooed, favoring Rand with a wide smile—one Lily had seen her practice countless times in her dressing table mirror.

"A matter of determination and persistence," Rand told her, looking oddly immune to that smile.

He wasn't responding to the old, coquettish Rose. Lily would have to point that out to her sister. Flirtation didn't mesh well with her new, more intelligent image.

"How long will you be staying?" Mum asked him.

"My house should be finished within a week or so—"

"As long as it takes," Ford broke in, "to figure out whether the book indeed holds the secret to making gold. Now, would you all like to see the new water closet?"

"It seems to me," Rand said in the sort of needling tone only a fast friend would put up with, "it's taken you longer to build that water closet than I've spent on the translation." He turned to

Lily's family. "I remember when his brother had water closets installed—"

"Colin," Ford clarified.

"My friend here was so envious. Said he'd design one for Lakefield in no time. That was what, ten years ago?"

"Eleven. Come see." As he talked, Ford led them out of the drawing room, threading his way through the many guests. "I've finished but one so far, and you're a fortunate man since it's in the room where you'll be staying."

Rand went with Ford up the square oak staircase, Rose hurrying to follow. Lily watched her sister's swishing skirts as she and her mother trailed everyone else up the stairs, her striped cat, Beatrix, scampering behind.

Ford reached the landing and headed down the corridor. "Colin's water closets were imported from France."

"They must have been expensive," Rose said.

"Absolutely. But I examined his thoroughly, and they seemed a simple enough design to build myself. In fact, I thought of improvements."

"Of course," Mum put in.

She thought her son-in-law was brilliant. In fact, she'd originally told Violet that Ford was too intellectual for her. Funny how wrong she'd been about that, but it had been just as well. Mum was somewhat renowned as a matchmaker, and although Violet and Ford were perfect for each other, if she'd tried to match them up, their marriage would never have happened.

The three Ashcroft sisters loved their mother dearly, but they were determined to avoid becoming another page in *The Big Book of Weddings Arranged by Chrystabel*.

Lily was watching, in fact, to see if Mum would try to match Rose with Rand. They were an obvious fit, after all, and at twenty-one, Rose was getting rather desperate. When poor Violet turned that same age, Rose had pronounced her an official spinster.

But if Mum tried to push Rand on her, Rose would surely go

looking elsewhere. And Lily would be honor-bound to help. The girls had a long-standing pact to save one another from their mother's matchmaking schemes.

Inside the guest chamber, everyone including the cat squeezed into a tiny room that Ford had hired a man to construct in the corner—while Ford was an accomplished inventor, he was less talented at anything requiring sweat or a ladder. They all gathered around the water closet and peered down at it in wonder.

It was a padded box with a round opening in the top, rather like a closestool. But instead of a removable chamber pot inside, there was a permanent alabaster bowl. "Back here," Ford pointed out, "this copper pipe leads down from it." The pipe disappeared into the wall. "The system works as a siphon."

They all nodded, since he'd explained siphons to them years ago, along with other scientific marvels.

"I suppose it empties into the river?" Rose asked, demonstrating her intelligence.

"It does. And there will be more pipes—eventually all over the house. I mean to put a water closet in every bedchamber. And my laboratory."

Leaning to pick up Beatrix, Lily hid a smile. The man practically lived in his laboratory.

Another pipe ran up from the back of the seat, ending at a tank affixed to the wall. "The water," Ford said, gesturing toward a third pipe that disappeared into the ceiling. "It's fed from a cistern on the roof."

"How does it work?" Lily asked.

"Well, first you use it—"

"No need to demonstrate that," Rose rushed to say.

"Of course not." Though her brother-in-law rolled his eyes, it was a good-natured roll. While Lily suspected there'd been a time he'd disapproved of Rose's forthright nature, those days were long past.

Rose was Rose, and all the family knew it.

"After you use it, you pull on this lever." Ford grabbed a handle attached to the tank. "It releases the water to wash the waste out to the river."

He pulled, and there was a rushing sound. Startled, Beatrix leapt from Lily's arms and streaked from the room. Nearly bumping heads, everyone leaned over the alabaster bowl to watch the water flow down the pipe.

"Goodness," Lily said. "It's wonderful. There's nothing to take out, nothing to clean."

"As though you've ever scrubbed a chamber pot," Rose teased.

"Oh, hush." Lily playfully shoved her sister's shoulder. While it was true they had no lack of servants at Trentingham Manor, that was beside the point.

Used to their squabbling, Ford simply pushed back up on the lever. "When it's clean, you stop the water."

"That's it?" Mum asked.

"That's it," Ford said with a smile. "To deal with the, um, unpleasant odors in the pipes, I've curved the one below the bowl into an S shape. Clean water fills it and forms a seal."

Mum beamed. "Brilliant, as usual."

"Very impressive," Rand allowed.

The demonstration over, they all squeezed through the narrow doorway into the pale green bedchamber. Luggage—Rand's, Lily assumed—sat in a corner. "Why did you build the first one in here?" she asked Ford.

"I wanted to make certain everything worked right before I started punching holes in the walls of rooms we regularly use." He waved them back toward the corridor. "Come along, now. I want to show you the pipes outside, and others are waiting for a demonstration."

"Everyone will want to see it, I'd wager." Rose maneuvered to descend beside Rand. "I wish they'd all leave. I cannot wait to use it."

Rand appeared to be smothering a laugh.

Mum released a sigh but let the improper comment pass. "Me, too," she whispered to Lily as they followed the others downstairs.

"Me three," Lily murmured.

Once outdoors, Ford hurried them through the garden and around the side of the house. Bright new copper pipe shone in the sun, making its way down the white wall before disappearing into the ground. A tidy trail of newly turned earth traced the pipe's path to the nearby Thames.

Amusement glittering in her eyes, Rose raised one perfect brow. "I see you've become handier with a shovel."

"Harry did the digging," Ford said, referring to his ancient man-of-all-work—and apparently either taking Rose's observation as a jest or failing to recognize her subtle sarcasm.

Probably the latter, Lily decided. The man was known to be rather oblivious.

An orange kitten came up and wound around her, ducking beneath her skirts to tickle her ankles. With a giggle, she bent to fish it out. "This is all so very clever," she told her brother-in-law, smiling as she stroked the kitty's fur and felt it begin to purr. "Can you put some water closets in Trentingham, too?"

"And have pipes running down the outside of the house?" Now Rose's perfect brows drew together. "That wouldn't look well at all."

Mum shrugged. "I could accept the unsightliness for the convenience."

"Father would never allow it," Rose said.

To the contrary, Lily doubted their father would even notice —he rarely took note of much beyond his beloved flowers. If a thing didn't grow, he wasn't apt to pay it much attention.

"What's your cat's name?" Rand asked.

Lily gazed down at the ball of fluff vibrating against her middle. "This isn't my cat. I've never seen it before in my life." Still stroking the soft apricot fur, she looked up at Ford. "Is it yours?"

He shrugged. "Not that I'm aware."

Of course, *he* wasn't apt to pay much attention to anything that *did* grow, unless it was some sort of muck in a beaker in his laboratory.

"Cats just come to Lily," Rose told Rand.

He grinned. "They must be able to tell she's the nurturing sort."

Lily's cheeks heated. "I adore animals," she said. "All animals."

"She's the *mothering* sort." Rose sidled closer to Rand.

"Rose," Mum said softly.

But that didn't deter Lily's sister. "Men don't care to be mothered," she purred, laying a hand on Rand's arm and narrowing her eyes until she looked rather catlike herself. "Do they, Lord Randal?"

"I cannot speak for other men," he said tactfully, leaving it at that. In keeping with the careful wording, he gently extricated himself from her grip by crossing to his friend. "Ford, I do believe your other guests are getting impatient."

"And Violet asked if you'd freshen some of her floral arrangements," Mum reminded Rose.

Although Rose enjoyed turning flowers into towering works of art, she looked reluctant to leave Rand's side. "Violet can wait awhile."

"Now, dear, that's not very sisterly." Mum smiled at the men. "Please excuse us," she said as she took Rose by the arm and led her off.

"I must give others the tour," Ford said and followed them.

And just like that, Lily found herself alone with Rand, wondering what she should say.

FOUR

*I*T WASN'T THAT Lily had no experience talking to men. She could hardly remember a time when men—or boys, when she was younger—hadn't pestered her and Rose for precious time in their company. None of them had ever made her nervous. But for some reason butterflies seemed to be battling one another in her stomach.

And Rand's piercing eyes seemed to see it.

He smiled in a way surely intended to set her at ease, gesturing toward three oak trees hung with swings. Two children sat on a broad one built for a couple. "Is that your brother, all grown-up? He was an imp of seven last time I saw him."

Lily smiled. "Yes, that's Rowan. And he may be growing tall, dark, and handsome, but there's still a bit of the imp left in him, I assure you."

"And is that Ford's niece with him? Jewel? She's showing every sign of developing into a beauty." A frown appeared between Rand's eyes. "Do you think they're sitting rather close on that swing?"

Their raven heads *were* rather close together. But Lily wasn't worried. "They're longtime friends, and Rowan thinks of her as a sister. Or a brother, more like."

The two children slipped off the swing and headed toward the house. When Jewel reached for Rowan's hand, he hid it behind his back. Watching, Rand laughed. "Apparently Jewel doesn't feel quite so sisterly towards your brother. And I reckon Rowan will wake up someday and notice she's a girl."

"She's pretty."

"Not nearly as pretty as you."

Lily had certainly received compliments before. But most men were glib, flattery tripping off their tongues with little thought and many flowery phrases. Rand's words were simple and soft-spoken.

And he should be saying them to Rose.

Taken aback, Lily clutched the kitten tighter. The feline squeaked and leapt from her arms, landing by Rand's feet. It looked up at her with a comically hurt expression before scampering away.

Lily stared down at Rand's black shoes, long-tongued with stiff ribbon bows. The heels were black, too, not red as was the fashion. Her gaze meandered up his lean, muscled form, noting that his slate blue velvet suit wasn't dripping with ribbons and baubles. Though well dressed, he wasn't a fop.

Perfect. No wonder Rose was so taken with the man.

When her gaze reached his face, he grinned in a fashion that made her wonder if he'd read her mind. But thankfully he chose not to comment, instead gesturing toward where Jewel was following Rowan to the house—by way of walking atop an eight-foot-high stone wall. "Is that wise?"

"My brother is a monkey," she told him, relieved to be on another subject. She couldn't remember ever eyeing a man before—that was one of Rose's seductive tricks.

Rand began walking toward the formal garden, a charming area divided by low hedges cut in geometric patterns, the flower beds dotted with cheerful reds, yellows, and purples. "Do you suppose Jewel is taking him to see the water closet?"

"Probably. I wouldn't be surprised if they're plotting a way to use it for a prank."

"I would hope not," he said. "I imagine they could make quite a mess."

She wrinkled her nose at the thought. Chamber pots weren't appropriate conversational subject matter, no matter how new and fancy. "So you're staying with Violet and Ford until the translation is finished?"

"I'll be here for just a week or two, until my house is ready. Although I do hope to make good progress on the translation in that time." At the edge of the garden, he stopped beside a long table. "Would you care for some refreshments?"

The selection looked delicious. "Yes, thank you."

He handed her an empty plate and took another for himself. "The house was supposed to be completed long before now, but a friend is building it, and you know how that goes—when something else comes up, it's always easier to put off a friend's job than a contracted client's."

"He doesn't sound like a very good friend," she observed.

"Oh, but he is. We've known each other since we were knee-high lads in dresses. It's just that Kit is very busy, very much in demand. You may have heard of him, in fact. Christopher Martyn."

"The architect? Isn't he working for King Charles?"

"So you *have* heard of him." Piling fruit on his plate, Rand cast her a glance. "I suppose, then, you can understand how another client can take precedence."

"When that client is the Crown, I suppose I can." She selected a wedge of apple tart as they worked their way down the table. "But you're a professor, yes? I'm surprised you can leave Oxford for weeks."

"It's summer," he said blithely. "A four-month break. I usually travel the Continent, looking for lost languages"—he flashed her a lopsided grin—"but I thought I'd stay home this year and settle into my new house."

She followed him into the garden, stepping gingerly since Beatrix had reappeared and was padding along with her, batting at her swishing skirts. "Yours sounds like an exciting life."

"I'm not sure I'd describe it as exciting, but I enjoy my life, yes. It's interesting, and I'm content."

They skirted around a sundial, old but lovingly repaired. Tables were scattered around the garden, surrounded by chairs for the guests. Sitting with Lady Carrington, Lily's friend Judith waved in invitation, her golden curls gleaming in the sun. Lily waved back and started over, but Rand stopped at a tiny square table and pulled out one of the two chairs. "Will you do me the honor?"

"Oh. Yes. Of course." She seated herself carefully, sending Judith an expressive shrug. Judith winked and waggled her brows, obviously misunderstanding why Lily was with Rand.

That was something Lily didn't quite understand herself. It should be Rose here, she thought as Beatrix returned and leapt onto her lap.

"This striped cat is yours, if I'm not mistaken?" Rand took the chair opposite. "However did it find its way here from Trentingham?"

She found herself caught again in that astonishing gray gaze. "Given you asked that question, I surmise you don't know much about cats."

"My father raises dogs," he told her, grabbing two pewter goblets of wine from a maid passing by with a tray. "Big, mean ones who would eat your cat for breakfast."

She laughed. "Surely not."

He smiled at both her and the purring cat. "He adores you."

"Beatrix is female, actually." The feline began hiccuping in a decidedly unladylike fashion. "What made you think she was male?"

"You're a beautiful woman...all males would adore you," he said and bit into a strawberry.

She looked away, hoping he wouldn't notice her choking on a

bite of tart. Ford was coming out of the house, leading another little group around to see the pipes to the river.

Swallowing the cinnamony apples and custard, she turned back to Rand. "Thank you, but being nice is much more important than being attractive. Although Rose is very attractive," she added as an afterthought. "Don't you think so, my lord?"

"Rand," he reminded her. "And yes, Rose is quite attractive *and* being nice is much more important. But *you're* both attractive and nice."

What on earth was she supposed to say to that?

He was impossible.

Her fingers went to trace the scars on the back of her left hand before she realized what she was doing and hid it beneath the table. Rose would love this sort of attention. The two were quite definitely suited.

A sparrow landed on their table, providing a welcome distraction. "Hello, Lady," she murmured and fed it some crumbs from her plate.

Watching her, Rand absently rubbed the ends of his magnificent mane between two fingers. "Are you still hoping to build a home for stray animals?"

After all this time, he remembered her dream. "Very much so," she said, both startled and pleased, but also wondering if he thought her goal childish. She'd been a child when she'd chosen it, after all.

But he seemed to be taking her seriously. "Have you made plans?"

"Of sorts. I'll come into my inheritance next year. I'm planning a simple building so as to have funds left to staff it for a number of years. I'm hoping to obtain donations as well. Eventually enough to keep running it once my money is depleted. And perhaps even build others."

"A solid strategy. Have you thought of having the building donated?"

"I'd prefer it built specifically for my purpose. To convert a house or other building could cost as much as starting from scratch."

He nodded thoughtfully. "Perhaps an architect would donate his services." His eyes twinkled, looking silver in the afternoon sun. "I happen to know one—"

"Uncle Ford!" Jewel came bounding out of the house, her pink skirts flying. "Uncle Ford! Something's happened with..."

Her words faded as she disappeared around the corner.

Rowan flew through the door next and darted after her, pink-cheeked to match her skirts, his mouth hanging open in something akin to horror.

Lily jumped to her feet. "They've done something," she exclaimed as Ford appeared at a run and dashed into the house, shouldering his way past all the guests hurrying out. "I knew it!"

FIVE

"**I** SWEAR, UNCLE Ford, we did nothing." Jewel held her skirts up off the floor while she turned in a slow circle, assessing the destruction. "Oh," she wailed, "look at my chamber!"

Rand gestured at his luggage sitting on the four-poster bed—as opposed to the floor, where it had been earlier. "I thought this was *my* chamber."

"Uncle Ford had it painted green because that's my favorite color. I sleep here when I visit. And now it's all ruined."

Ford poked his head out of the little room in the corner where he was examining his invention. "At least it's clean water," he pointed out defensively.

New water stains on Rand's luggage were the least of the damage.

The oak floor was sopping. The wet went up the walls, the water having apparently been deeper before escaping the chamber and making its way down the corridor and stairs. Most of the ground floor had flooded as well, including all of the beautiful, expensive carpeting that Violet had had specially woven.

But this room, where the disaster had originated, was by far the worst. The pale green bedclothes dripped, the air held a chill, the carpet felt soggy beneath their feet, and Lily suspected that mildew was setting in already.

"We did nothing," Rowan repeated. "We just came up to look, and when we opened the door—"

"Now, Rowan," Lily began, knowing her brother all too well. Especially when he was with Jewel. The girl's father was infamous for playing pranks, and she'd taught Rowan every trick the man had taught her. "Do you expect us to believe—"

"He's right," Ford broke in, apparently having finished his investigation. "It was the fault of my design—a problem with the tank mechanism." Looking rather pained to admit that, he ran a hand back through his long brown hair. "I expect it began flooding the moment I turned my back. I never considered...it never occurred to me..."

"Never say never," Rand interjected dryly.

Jewel went to the window. "Everyone else has gone outside."

"Of course, you goose." Rowan snorted. "The floor is wet all over the house."

"The women wouldn't want to ruin their fashionable satin slippers," Rand added, glancing down at the water-stained shoes on Lily's feet, visible since she was holding up her skirts.

"There are more important things than shoes," she pointed out. "Like Violet's carpeting. She's going to be furious."

"No, I'm not," Violet said, walking in with a squish-squash sound. She went on her toes to grace her husband with a light kiss. "I'm used to catastrophes," she declared with an exaggerated sigh. "Part and parcel of my marriage. Besides, we must only remove the carpets and spread them outside to dry. A few rain-free days and they'll be good as new."

"Are you sure?" Jewel asked dubiously.

"About it not raining? No," Violet said in her practical way. "But they *will* eventually dry. I'm afraid, though, that this room will be uninhabitable for a day or two, at the least." She looked toward Rand apologetically.

"I can ride home," he assured her. "Oxford is but a few hours."

"Wait." Ford held up a hand. "What about the translation? There's no need for you to leave. We'll move someone. The nursemaids—"

"I won't have you upsetting your whole household," Rand interrupted. Unlike the sprawling mansion Lily lived in, Lakefield was a typical L-shaped manor house. Enough rooms to sleep the family, a few servants, and a guest, but that was all.

Ford crossed his arms. "I won't have you leaving. Your house is a wreck at the moment."

A smile twitched on Rand's lips as he pointedly scanned the chamber. Lily choked back a laugh.

"Rowan!" Her mother's voice floated up the stairs. "Rowan, have you and Jewel—" A gasp chopped off her sentence as she stepped into the room. "Heavens, this is—"

"A bloody mess," Ford finished for her. "And my fault, not your son's."

"See?" Rowan said with a grin of vindication. "It's not my fault Lord Randal cannot stay here."

"It's nobody's fault." Rand strode to the bed, his shoes making a sucking sound as he went. "I should probably be home badgering Kit anyway, if the house is to be finished this decade." He reached for his luggage.

"Don't you want to finish the translation?" Ford looked frantic. "We'll find a place—"

"Lord Randal is welcome to stay with us," Mum interrupted with a smile. "We've more guest rooms than we know what to do with."

Lily's mouth hung open. Why, they hardly knew Lord Randal Nesbitt.

But apparently that made no difference to Mum. "You'll be close to Lakefield," she added. They were naught but a quarter-hour's ride down the road. "By tomorrow, perhaps this room will once again be habitable."

Violet glanced around mournfully. "I doubt it."

Looking a mite dubious, Rand set down the luggage. "If I overnight at Trentingham," he said slowly, "I can return tomorrow and help put the place to rights."

"A generous offer," Ford said.

Violet pushed up on her spectacles. "There's no need for Rand to wrestle with soggy carpeting."

"The boards underneath must be dried, lest they warp."

"We have servants to do that sort of thing."

"But if we had extra help—" Ford pressed.

Violet cut him off with a laugh. "Rand can 'help' you in the bone-dry laboratory upstairs, huddled over that ancient alchemy text."

Her husband's expression made clear that sounded good to him.

And so it was settled. Rand would sleep at Trentingham and return in the morning.

Lily supposed it was well done of Mum to offer the hospitality, but she hoped it didn't mean she was trying to match Rand with Rose.

That would ruin her sister's plan.

SIX

*T*RENTINGHAM Manor was teeming with family and friends who had come to attend the twins' baptism, so Rand's addition to the mix was clearly little imposition. But he did appreciate Lady Trentingham's kind invitation. She seemed a true gentlewoman.

Although perhaps a bit overly solicitous.

"Lily, dear," she said as they walked into the linenfold-paneled dining room for supper, "I'd appreciate it if you'd sit beside Rand, since he isn't acquainted with our other guests."

Which would have made sense if Rose hadn't already planted herself on his other side.

"Lord Randal," she gushed, laying a hand on her chest theatrically, her fingertips flirtatiously grazing the skin revealed by her wide, low neckline. "What a pleasure to have you as a dining partner."

"Rand," he corrected her, as he had countless times. So far as he was concerned, *Lord* was nothing more than a reminder of his disturbing roots. He liked to think of himself as a professor now, not a marquess's son. "And the pleasure is mine," he assured her, meaning it. This civilized supper was a lot more pleasurable than riding home to all the hammering and sawing at his house in Oxford.

"Cousin Rose." A gentleman on her other side begged her attention, waving a bejeweled hand at the floral arrangements—enormous vases of colorful posies that graced each end of the table, flanking a towering centerpiece. "Have we you to thank for these beautiful works of art?"

"Why, yes," Rose said warmly. "I'm pleased, cousin, that you're enjoying them." She turned back to Rand, fluttering her eyelashes in a way that tempted him to laugh. "I love arranging flowers."

"They're lovely." They were. She had an artist's eye, a flair for color and balance. He turned to Lily. "Do you work with flowers as well?"

"Oh, no. I've no skill with plants."

Rose shook her head, as though she felt sorry for her poor, talentless sister. "She cares only for her animals."

As if on cue, a sparrow flew into the room and landed smack on the table, right in front of Lily.

"Holy Hades," Rowan said. "Not again."

"Rowan," Lady Trentingham admonished.

"Well, someone should shut the windows."

Rose fanned herself with a languid hand. "With all these people, it would be too hot if we shut the windows."

"Cut the hedgerows?" Her father nodded sagely. "Yes, I've asked the groundskeepers to do that."

No one looked confused or surprised. Apparently they were all well enough acquainted with Lord Trentingham to know that along with his passion for gardening, the man was half deaf.

"Excellent, darling," Lady Trentingham said loudly, flicking crumbs off his cravat. She looked to Lily, who was busy feeding bits of bread to the sparrow. "Not at supper, dear."

Lily sighed. "Go, Lady." She tossed the gray-brown bird a final crumb. "Outside now."

Amazingly, the bird gobbled the last of its feast and then took flight, heading for one of the windows where a squirrel sat on the sill, seemingly watching the proceedings. With a flutter of feathers, the sparrow landed beside the squirrel and turned to tweet at it. The squirrel chirped back, for all the world like they were having a conversation.

Rand had never seen a wild bird that obeyed, let alone a squirrel that didn't run at the sight of humans. He turned to Lily. "You do have a way with animals."

"Oh, there's more to Lily than that," her mother informed him from down the table. "She plays the harpsichord like an angel."

Lily blushed. She looked fetching when she blushed. Of course, she could be wearing rags and scrubbing a floor, and she'd look fetching. As it was, she'd exchanged the water-stained gown for one made of some shiny, pale purplish fabric that hugged her upper body like a second skin.

He couldn't help but imagine the shapely form barely hidden beneath that shimmering bodice.

He dragged his gaze back to her face. His fingers itched to touch the tiny dent in her chin. "Will you play for us after supper?" he asked her.

"Eh?" Lord Trentingham shook his dark head. "Everyone will stay after supper. They've all been assigned rooms, have they not, Chrysanthemum love?"

"Of course, darling." Lady Trentingham smiled her ever-patient smile. "And Lily will play," she told Rand.

"And I shall sing," Rose announced as she reached for some bread, grazing Rand's arm in the process.

On purpose, he was sure.

Rose wanted him. She'd made that clear, in action and words, four years ago and again now. As conversation buzzed around him, he wondered why he wasn't tempted.

Rose was lovely—tall and willowy, with a flawless, creamy complexion, glossy deep brown locks, and eyes so mysteriously dark they could be mistaken for black. A classic beauty. And not a cold one. True, she remained every bit as outspoken and forward as he remembered. Yet Rose had grown up. She was much warmer than he recalled.

But the spark was missing. None of her heat penetrated his heart, while on his right, Lily seemed to burn like a bonfire. Chatting with the guest on her other side, she sensed Rand's gaze and turned slightly to meet his eyes, then looked away to continue her conversation.

"I should like to hear you sing," he told Rose, wondering if she had the voice for it.

She graced him with a smile that revealed fetching dimples. If she were one of Lily's cats, she'd have been purring.

And after supper, when she raised her voice in song, he was indeed impressed. Singing of love, the words flitted from her throat, rich and true.

But Lily's playing was even more splendid. Despite the fact that various relatives were all seated decorously in the cream-and-gold-toned formal drawing room, Rand found himself rising and wandering toward the harpsichord.

While Beatrix dozed on her lap, Lily's fingers flew over the ivory keys, raising magic in their wake. She glanced up and smiled at him, and without thought, he opened his mouth to harmonize with her sister.

> *"Go tell her to make me a cambric shirt,*
> *Parsley, sage, rosemary, and thyme,*
> *Without a stitch of a seamster's work,*
> *And then she will be a true love of mine."*

Only when he finished did he realize that Rose had stopped singing to listen to him. He nodded at her to take the next verse. Back and forth they went until the song ended and the room burst into wild applause.

"Your voice is beautiful!" Lily exclaimed.

His face went hot. "Your playing is exquisite."

Her shrug was as graceful as her music. "I practice often. It's a way to pass the time."

"It's more than that. It's a gift to all who listen." Ignoring all her curious relations, he moved around to hit a key, the single note reverberating through the chamber. "I cannot play."

"I cannot sing."

He grinned. "Gift us with another tune, and your sister and I will accompany it. Together this time."

She thought for a moment, then the jaunty notes of "The Gypsy Rover" took air, his voice rising along with it.

Rose waited until the chorus to join him.

"He whistled and he sang till the greenwoods rang,
And he won the heart of a lady."

Their harmony was flawless, he thought as they sang on. And as the lyrics said, Rand wished he really could whistle and sing and win the heart of a lady.

But regardless of their perfect harmony, it wasn't Rose he was wishing to win.

They sang a third song, and a fourth, and then he lost count. More than once, Lily's gaze locked on his as his voice and her notes blended. They made beautiful music together. For fleeting moments it seemed that he and she were the only ones in the chamber, and from the look on her face, he'd wager it was the same for her.

When the gilt mantel clock struck midnight just as another tune ended, Lily blinked and jumped to her feet, making Beatrix tumble to the floor with an outraged *meow*. "Do you think it's time to retire, Mum?"

"Oh!" Lady Trentingham stood as well. "Rose, you must come with me. We have yet to prepare a room for Rand."

Rose frowned. "I'm sure the staff has taken care of that."

"Not all our special welcoming details." Lady Trentingham turned to her assorted family. "I trust you can all find your beds?" As they began drifting out, she focused on her older daughter. "Come along, dear. You'll need to find flowers for Rand's chamber."

"But Mum—"

"Come along," she repeated, more tersely than seemed to be her nature. "Lily, will you wait here and keep Rand company until his room is ready?"

"I need no flowers," Rand interjected.

"Nonsense. Rose?" Lady Trentingham moved toward the door, herding the last lingering friends and relatives along with her.

The chamber seemed so quiet after everyone had left. And Rand felt odd to find himself alone with Lily for the second time that day.

"Mum," he said, searching for a way to breach the sudden silence. "That's a strange thing to call one's mother."

"I know." Lily's soft laugh broke the tension. Still at the harpsichord, she sat again and began playing, a soothing tune he found unfamiliar. Beatrix reclaimed her rightful place on her lap.

Obviously knowing the piece well, Lily talked as her fingers picked out the delicate notes. "You'll probably have heard that my father raises flowers. Multitudes of them. He named us girls after his favorites—surely you'll have noticed that—and Rowan after the tree. Mum's given name is Chrystabel, but he calls her Chrysanthemum...Mum is short for that." Her fingers stilled. "It's silly, I know."

"Keep playing." He leaned against the dark wood instrument and waited until she did. "I don't think it's silly so much as touching. I take it you're all close?"

"Very."

The single word was uttered so matter-of-factly he knew she took that closeness for granted. But he wouldn't acknowledge the envy that clutched at his throat. He'd long ago accepted that his family was happier without him. And life on his own was just fine. Better, in fact.

When the cat lifted its head, Rand followed its gaze to see a bird land gracefully atop the harpsichord.

"Hello, Lady," Lily greeted softly, her fingers not missing a note.

Confused, Rand ran his tongue across his teeth. "Do you call all sparrows Lady?"

"Of course not. I don't call most sparrows anything. But Lady is special."

"Do you mean..." He focused on the nondescript bird. "Is this the same sparrow that flew in at supper, the same sparrow you fed at Ford's house?"

"One and the same," she said, playing a little bit faster. "I raised her after I found her in an abandoned nest, and now she follows me around. She and Jasper."

"Jasper?"

"The squirrel."

Still playing, she nodded toward the sill. Sure enough, a red squirrel sat there, gnawing on an acorn. Rand supposed it must be the same squirrel that had appeared at supper, although damned if he could tell for sure. Like sparrows, one squirrel looked much the same as another.

To him, anyway.

Beatrix settled back down on Lily's lap, and Lady flew to join her friend at the window. Jasper chattered, his bushy tail flicking up and down. To Rand, it seemed all the animals were watching him. Talking about him.

Under those three sets of eyes, he shifted uneasily. "Are you never alone?"

"Rarely," Lily said blithely.

Rand shrugged. Absurd as it might seem, perhaps it was natural for her to be surrounded by such loyal creatures. He decided to watch Lily instead of the animals. Feeling pleasantly worn-out after the long day, he swayed in time to her music. "What song is this?"

"Nothing, really. Just something I made up."

"You write music, too?" Slowly he lowered himself to the bench seat beside her. "Is there no end to your talents?"

As she scooted over to make room for him, her fingers faltered, then resumed. He smiled to himself, thinking he'd managed to fluster her. Was it the compliment, or his nearness?

He hoped it was the latter. Her nearness set him on fire.

He'd known four years ago that something in Lily Ashcroft spoke to something in Rand Nesbitt. Though he'd tried his best to forget her, his efforts had been for naught.

Beatrix began hiccuping. "I'm not particularly talented," Lily protested. "Your singing is much better than my playing. I've never heard another voice as rich as yours."

Unlike her, he wasn't modest enough to deny a truth. He knew his voice was exceptional, but it wasn't a talent that had been valued in his family. "I've never heard anything like your music," he said. "So we're even. And I hope we'll be able to play and sing together again."

At his words, her hands ceased moving for good. They went limp and dropped into her lap, causing Beatrix to squeal indignantly and leap to the floor. In seconds, the cat had followed her animal friends out the window.

Lily cleared her throat. "If your room at Lakefield isn't ready tomorrow night, perhaps Rose will sing with you again."

She looked so earnest. He fisted his fingers to keep from reaching to touch that adorable dent in her chin. "I don't care whether Rose sings with me again. As long as you play."

"Wh-what?" She shifted, turning to face him, searching his eyes with her wide blue ones. "But you and Rose sing together so beautifully. And she knows languages—not ancient ones like you do, but many modern ones, and—"

"I'm not interested in Rose," he clarified. "But you...I've thought about you for four years."

The breath rushed out of her with a *whoosh*. Her eyes grew bigger and bluer, disbelieving in her fine-boned face. She looked fragile and sweet as an angel.

But Rand was feeling anything but angelic.

Unable to help himself, he leaned in and touched his mouth to hers. His arms sneaked around her to pull her gently against him. Though she hesitated at first, after a moment he felt her yield to the kiss. Her lips were soft and giving, and her skin felt warm, exuding a heavenly scent of lilies.

It made his head swim, made the blood sluice through his veins, made him want to devour her. But he forced himself to hold back, because Lily was innocent. Lily was his best friend's sister-in-law. Lily was his generous hostess's virgin daughter.

When he reluctantly pulled away, her eyes were wider than ever—with shock and something else. Wonder, he thought. Or maybe he hoped it was wonder, even though he damn well knew he shouldn't.

He wanted her—he wanted her with an intensity that heated his blood, an intensity that had taken him off guard, an intensity that had made him reach for her unthinkingly. But this sort of want could lead only to disaster. Lily was no courtier, no world-wise widow, no tart. She was all-too-respectable marriage material.

His room at Lakefield had better be ready tomorrow, because he sure as hell couldn't stay at Trentingham any longer.

Randal Nesbitt had never really considered marriage, and he had no intention of starting now.

SEVEN

*B*REATHLESS, LILY stared at Rand. It had been her first kiss, and no matter that it had been rather chaste compared to those her sisters had described, it had still melted her to the core.

But how had she allowed him to kiss her? Especially considering she'd promised Rose not only to stay away, but to help her win him?

She felt like a traitor.

"My lord," she started.

"Rand," he corrected patiently.

He *was* patient. And he was handsome and brilliant. And although he wasn't the avowed animal lover she'd always pictured for a husband, he didn't laugh at her aspirations; in fact, he encouraged them.

Wouldn't it be fun to be newly wedded together? Judith's voice echoed in her head.

For a moment she dreamed of wedded bliss, of waking every morning to more of Rand's kisses. But then she mentally shook herself. It didn't matter that his kiss had made her heart flip over. It didn't matter that he supported her ambitions.

Rose wanted him. Rose was older and should marry first.

Rose and Rand shared an interest in languages. They both sang like the angels. Such music they could make together, such academic heights they could reach.

But moreover, Lily had made a promise to Rose, and she wouldn't betray her. Not only would she never forgive herself; she just couldn't hurt her sister.

Lily never wanted to hurt anyone. Or anything. Ever.

"Lily?" Rand queried softly.

"You shouldn't have done that."

"You didn't fight it," he pointed out calmly. "In fact, I would swear you participated."

"I...how..." She raised her chin, determined to stop sputtering. She never sputtered. She'd always been comfortable around men, and she couldn't fathom why it wasn't the same with this one. "I couldn't possibly have participated. I wouldn't know how. I've never before been kissed."

He looked pleased at that news. "Well, then, you must have a natural talent."

Her face was turning hot, and she was on the verge of sputtering again when her mother and Rose stepped into the room. Lily couldn't remember ever being happier to see her family.

"Your chamber is ready," Rose announced to Rand, frowning to see them together on the harpsichord's bench.

Rand didn't stand up, so Lily did. Quickly.

Mum's lips curved in a smile. "Come, Rand. I'll show you the way."

He finally rose—rather reluctantly, Lily thought. Still smiling, Mum led him from the room. As the two of them made their way up Trentingham's grand staircase, Lily heard Rand humming a jaunty tune.

Even his humming sounded rich and beautiful.

When that faded into the distance, an uneasy silence descended. Lily dropped back to the bench.

Rose's dark eyes narrowed. "What were you doing with him?"

"Singing," Lily lied, shocked to hear the word pass her lips. She never lied to her sister. She never lied to anybody. "I mean, he was singing. I was playing. We were playing and sing—"

"All right." Rose waved an impatient hand. "As long as you're not going after him. You promised he could be mine."

Despite that promise, Lily bristled. "*He* might have something to say about that."

For a woman who'd so far failed to catch a husband, her sister looked awfully smug. "Oh, I'm sure I can make him want me."

"You know nothing about him. Has it even occurred to you that he might already be interested in someone else?" *Like me,* Lily added silently.

Hopefully?

No, that kiss hadn't meant anything. It had been a mistake.

And Rose wouldn't hear of any obstacles. "You let me worry about other women," she said, apparently unconcerned that Lily might be one of them. "My new strategy of demonstrating my intelligence along with flirtation is going to work just fine."

"Fine," Lily echoed a little shortly, then chided herself. There was no call for such an attitude. Hadn't she already decided her sister was entitled to Rand should she prove able to win him? "About the flirtation—" she began.

"I don't want to hear it. It's not as though you've won a man for yourself. I know what I'm doing."

"Of course you do," Lily said quickly, absently rubbing the faint scars on the back of her hand. Her fingers stilled when Rose's gaze settled on them.

Rose slid onto the bench seat beside her and placed a hand over hers. "No one notices," she said softly. "And it doesn't look bad anyway. After all these years, the marks are almost gone. Honestly, Lily—"

"I know." She turned to grasp both her sister's hands. So what if she wasn't perfect? A few narrow, faded white scars... most people were much more imperfect than that.

And most people weren't fortunate enough to have such a loving, caring sister. Lily still couldn't believe she'd gone back on her promise by allowing Rand to kiss her.

Well, it wouldn't happen again.

"Lily?"

Freeing her hands, she gave Rose a shaky smile as she raised them to the harpsichord. Her fingers began moving over the keys. Music always soothed her. Even when, like now, she chose a melancholy tune.

After a moment, her sister's lovely voice rose in song to match the notes. "Alas, my love, you do me wrong, to cast me out discourteously...And I have loved you for so long, delighting in your company..."

A fitting lyric, Lily thought with an internal sigh. Then she tried to look on the bright side. At least Mum didn't seem to be trying to match Rose and Rand.

They should be happy for small favors.

EIGHT

*R*AND'S BEDCHAMBER was filled with flowers. Lovely arrangements sat atop the bedside table, the clothes press, the washstand. Smiling to himself, he walked around the room, pacing off nervous energy as he skimmed his fingers over colorful, velvet-soft petals.

It was quite obvious Rose excelled at arranging flowers, and while he had been kissing Lily, evidently she'd been busy. And so had their mother, by all appearances, because the dressing table was lined with bottles of scent. *Her* hobby, he suddenly remembered, was making perfume.

No wonder her daughter smelled so delicious.

The small, clear bottles all looked the same—plain with silver-topped stoppers—but the liquids inside them were different hues, ranging from nearly colorless, to yellowish, to brownish. Humming a tune, he lifted a bottle, opened it, and waved it under his nose. Finding the fragrance spicy and masculine, he dabbed some on his face, then sniffed his fingers. Shrugging, he took another bottle. More citrusy, this scent. He patted some on his jaw and decided he liked the first one better.

He shrugged out of his surcoat and tossed it on the bed, followed by his cravat. Despite the long day and the sort of bone weariness that naturally followed, he wasn't at all sleepy. Being here felt too strange, as did his feelings for a certain daughter of the house.

He sat at the dressing table—a lady's dressing table, it was, much too delicate for his tastes—and idly unstoppered another bottle. None of the specific ingredients were identifiable, but this one smelled like it could be used to season a pie. A Christmas pie. He watched himself in the mirror as he slapped some on both cheeks and tried to remember the last time he'd really enjoyed Christmas.

He didn't have fond memories of Christmas, so he moved on to the next scent.

Musky. This one put him in mind of a hot tumble beneath the sheets. Much better than thinking about his family. Since he'd never found himself lacking for female companionship, the fragrance brought a smile back to his face. He layered it over the others, thinking about the last mistress he'd had in Oxford. A pleasant tumble she'd been, but they'd parted last month on amiable terms, she having found another man, one willing to take her to wife. And if she'd left with a bit of regret in her eyes, his own emotions had leaned more toward relief.

He wasn't interested in marriage.

At least, he'd thought he wasn't. Dons, the teaching fellows at Oxford, weren't allowed to wed. Although professors weren't similarly restricted, very few fellows were ever elevated to that lofty stature, especially at his age. Professorship had always been a goal, but he'd never counted on it, never stopped to think about the fact that as things now stood, he could have a wife and children should he want them.

The chamber seemed overly warm. He rose to pace the room, loosening the laces at his neck, untying his cuffs, rolling up his sleeves. Catching a glance of himself in the mirror, he halted. Implacable gray eyes gazed back at him.

Marriage had crossed his mind more than once today, rather

uncomfortably. But whatever could have changed to make him suddenly picture children...a whole family?

His new home, perhaps? It had, after all, five bedchambers. As he and Kit had planned it, had he been thinking, somewhere deep inside, that he might someday want to begin filling all those many rooms?

Hell, no.

Holding Ford's son might have jarred his emotions, but he'd never seen himself as a family man. He had no idea how to raise a child, no good example from which to work. He wasn't ready for that sort of responsibility; perhaps he never would be. The concept of marriage was frightening enough, but children...the mere idea made him shudder.

From the far reaches of the mansion, notes wafted up and through his door. "Greensleeves." A traditional tune, played, he thought, by a nurturing, traditional sort of woman.

Perhaps the only woman who could make him change his mind.

NINE

"**R**OSE, DON'T!" Lily admonished in a whisper.

"Whyever not? It's a kind gesture to see to a guest's welfare." Ignoring her sister, Rose knocked on the door. "Lord Randal?" She raised her voice—and an Ashcroft's raised voice was no timid thing, living as they did with the half-deaf earl. "Lord Randal, are you quite all right? Will you be needing anything more this evening?"

Lily huffed, then caught her breath when the door suddenly swung open. Rand stood there in shirtsleeves, and those rolled up. His forearms looked a healthy brown. The top of his shirt was unlaced as well, revealing a bronzed triangle of skin.

How was it that a professor saw the sun? Didn't academics spend their days secluded in research?

Once again, she found herself staring. Although he was handsome—arresting, even—his wasn't a pretty face. The jaw was a mite too strong, the nose too long, the brows too heavy and straight. But there was something about those eyes, that smile...

"Yes?" he said, amusement in his gaze as he examined her quite as boldly as she'd been examining him.

She released the breath she hadn't realized she'd been holding. "I—"

"I only wanted to inquire as to your welfare," Rose hurried to put in, so quickly Lily wondered if she sensed something between the two of them.

"I'm quite fine," he said, stepping closer to the doorway.

A cloud of scent moved with him. Not a subtle cloud. "Have you been testing Mum's perfumes?" Rose wrinkled her nose. "I apologize, my lord. Evidently one of my mother's creations is less than pleasing."

Very tactful wording for Rose, Lily thought with admiration. She really seemed to be watching herself in this quest to win Rand for a husband.

He waved a hand, releasing another burst of cloying fragrance. "Oh, I've quite enjoyed the perfumes," he assured them.

"I expect you have," Lily said, biting her lip to stifle the smile that threatened. It wasn't a bad bottle, if she didn't miss her guess, but rather an unfortunate mixture of several. "How many scents have you sampled?"

"All of them," he said blithely, rubbing his jaw, then sniffing his fingers. He stepped back, perhaps belatedly realizing he reeked. "I suppose that wasn't such a good idea?"

"One doesn't mix fragrances. That's the perfumer's job," Rose informed him, sounding both intelligent and instructor-like.

A professor should admire that tone, Lily thought.

But he only shrugged. "I did it rather absently, I expect. My mind was elsewhere."

His eyes met Lily's, implying exactly where his mind had been.

"I...I must see to my animals before bed," she stammered, feeling her cheeks heat. Wondering if that was because of his hot gaze or her mention of the word *bed*, she hoped he hadn't noticed her blush. "Shall I order you up a bath first?"

Judging from the way Rand's lips curved—knowingly—he'd noticed. "I expect that would be an excellent idea."

"Go ahead, Lily," Rose said. "Your menagerie needs attending." She waved a graceful arm. "I'll wait here until the bath arrives, so I can see to Lord Randal's comfort."

He looked amused at that, as though Rose was so transparent he could see right through her. "I can see to my own comfort," he said dryly. "But I thank you ladies for your kindness."

Then he caught Lily's gaze and grinned before shutting the door, leaving both girls outside.

TEN

*S*HE'D OVERSLEPT. She never overslept. Moving to the last animal's bowl to fill it with fresh water, Lily yawned, still blinking away the cobwebs of a restless night—a night filled with dreams of silvery gray eyes and warm, bronzed skin.

She looked around the barn, happy that her chores were finished. The enclosures were clean; all the creatures had been fed, splints checked, matted fur brushed out till it shone. In comparison, she imagined *she* looked like something the cat had dragged in, but now that she was done, she would sneak back into the house through a servants' entrance to make herself presentable.

She set down the water pitcher and brushed straw off the plain green gown she'd thrown on upon awakening—then froze when she heard voices outside the barn.

"The knot garden is over there," Rose was saying, her tone honeyed and cajoling.

"Ah, but your sister keeps her animals in here, doesn't she?" Rand countered. "I'd as soon take a peek at them."

And peek in on Lily, too, Lily fancied him adding silently—then bit her lip.

Well, she couldn't control her thoughts, could she? She couldn't help the ideas that jumped into her head, no matter that she didn't really want Rand to be thinking any such thing.

Rose wanted him, and Lily had promised to keep her distance. Moreover, she wanted Rose to be happy. Life was so much more pleasant when the people around one were content.

Light flooded the dim, cavernous building when the double doors opened. As Rand and Rose stepped inside, Lily shoved her unkempt hair farther under the hat she'd jammed on her head to cover it. She managed to resist pinching color into her cheeks.

"Good morning," she said brightly.

Rand grinned. "Yes, it is."

Avoiding Rose's scowl, Lily knelt beside one of the pens to pet a fox cub.

"I've never seen one hold still before." Rand's footsteps crunched on the straw as he walked nearer and crouched close by. "They always run from people. They even run if they catch you watching them from a window."

"This one cannot run." She showed him the small broken leg she'd splinted.

"But she doesn't seem frightened."

"He," Lily corrected. The small fox wagged its white-tipped tail. "And why should he be frightened?"

A spell of silence followed, filled only by rustling and the assorted grunts of animals, as Rand tilted his head and studied her. "No reason," he conceded finally. "You're very gentle."

The tone of his voice made her heart turn over. "Anyone can be."

"Not anyone." He stood. "What else do you have in your care?"

She walked along the pens that crowded a corner of the barn, stopping where a spotted fawn nuzzled her with his nose. "Meet Timothy—"

"Timothy?"

"He looks like a Timothy, doesn't he? He lost his mother." Feeding the baby deer a handful of grass, she leaned to the neighboring pen to lift the cloth draping a deep basket. "And here's a rat—"

"A rat?" He stared at the creature in question, a fat, furry brown rodent that never failed to make her smile. "You would save a rat?"

"Randolph was hurt. But he's recovered quite nicely. I may set him free later today."

"To be eaten by a cat, no doubt."

"Not my cats. My cats are his friends. Besides, it would be cruel to keep him confined when he's well enough to roam." Timothy had finished his treat, so she wiped her hand on her skirts and moved to the next enclosure. "Over here I have a badger, but he's sleeping." She indicated a black-and-white snout poking out from a pile of old blankets. "They're nocturnal, you may know. And little Harold here is sleeping, too."

"A hedgehog?" Rand's eyes radiated amusement.

At the other end of the barn, a door opened. Lily's brother started in, then spotted them and began backing out.

"I'm finished, Rowan," she called. "You can come play with the animals."

"Maybe later." He slammed the door shut.

Rose laid a possessive hand on Rand's arm. "Shall we go see the gardens now?" she asked sweetly.

"Your father's gardens are quite extensive, aren't they? I really must be getting to Ford's house. I promised him help. If I might borrow a mount—"

"Of course," Rose said with a smile. "Our stables are much more impressive than this old barn. And I shall ride with you to show you the way."

"I think I can find Lakefield on my own."

No doubt he could, since Lakefield's lands bordered Trentingham, accessible by both the road and the river. But Rose wouldn't be deterred. "I should like to come along. Perhaps I can help Violet. Twins are a handful."

Lily suppressed a laugh. The twins had two nursemaids, and Rose had never shown interest in helping Violet before. But it was good, she decided, for Rose to appear parental. A man looking for a wife would also be thinking in terms of a mother for his children.

"Well, then," Rand said easily, "we shall have a nice ride. You'll join us, Lily, won't you?"

"I—what?" she asked, taken off guard.

"Lily has yet to eat breakfast," Rose pointed out, having doubtless noticed her absence at the morning meal. She did, at least, tactfully forgo mentioning that Lily wasn't properly groomed for a visit, either. "She can join us later."

"Nonsense," Rand returned. "We'll wait. In the meantime, you wanted to show me the gardens?"

A smile lit Rose's eyes. Lily followed them out of the barn, turning toward the house while her sister led Rand in the other direction.

Mere seconds later, her sister's voice stopped her in her tracks. "Rowan Ashcroft, what on earth do you think you're doing?"

Rose sounded *very* parental. Lily hurried around the back of the barn, arriving just in time to see her brother tug a thin wooden stick through a fold of paper, the friction producing a hiss. As the wood burst into flame, he looked up and gave a grinning answer to Rose's question. "I'm making fire."

The grin vanished as the sliver of wood burned close to his fingers. He dropped it with a yelp.

Rand strode forward to stamp it out. "What is it you have there?"

Rose brushed at her red satin skirts. "It doesn't matter," she said even more parentally. "He's well aware that he isn't allowed to play with fire."

Too parentally, Lily decided. It was one thing to display a

love of children by offering to help Violet, quite another to scold like a shrew. Especially considering Rowan was Rose's younger brother, not her child.

"But what *is* it?" Rand bent closer.

Rowan handed him the paper. "It has phosphorus on it." If Rand looked surprised at hearing a boy of eleven use such a word, Lily wasn't. Rowan spent hours every week in Ford's laboratory. "And this," he said, pulling another of the slim wooden sticks from his pocket, "has sulfur on one end. Ford's friend, a man named Robert Boyle, has discovered that the two together make fire. Phosphorus has a very low burning point," he added importantly.

Although Lily wasn't at all sure what that had to do with making fire, Rand nodded thoughtfully. "Brilliant. May I try?"

"Boys will be boys. And apparently men will be boys, too," Rose said in a tone Lily thought unwise for a woman hoping to marry one.

Lily shot her a warning glance, then turned to her brother. "Did Ford give you these things?"

His face reddened. "He showed them to me. Mr. Boyle is thinking about selling them. It's a good idea, isn't it? I'm thinking he could make a lot of money."

"I'm thinking Ford would be unhappy if he knew you'd taken such dangerous things home." Her brother shuffled his feet. "I'm thinking," she added softly, "that Ford would feel terrible if you burned yourself because he made the mistake of showing you something interesting, believing you were old enough to know better than to play with it."

"I guess I should give the things back," Rowan muttered.

Rand drew the wooden sliver against the paper, smiling as it sparked. "I'll return them." He reached out a hand. "Have you any more of the sticks?"

Rowan dug in his pocket, handed over a few more slivers, then turned and ran for the house.

ELEVEN

*A*N HOUR LATER, Rose banged on Lily's door. "Lily? Lord Randal wants to leave."

Lord Randal again. Excusing her maid, Lily went to admit her sister. "May I suggest, Rose, if you wish to win the man, you might call him by the name he prefers?"

Rose shrugged. "I think Lord Randal has a nice ring to it. But I know you're trying to help, Lily, and I do appreciate it."

Lily wished her sister's words sounded more convincing.

"Are you ready?" Rose added.

"Nearly." Beatrix at her heels, Lily went back to her dressing table to fetch the hat that matched her smart blue riding habit. "Aren't you going to change?" she asked, eyeing her sister's low-cut, bright red gown.

"I like this dress. I told Lord Randal I'd prefer to take the carriage."

"Oh." Lily set down the hat. "Shall I change, then?"

"Good God, why should it matter what you wear? I told you, he's growing impatient. Now, you must let him climb in first—"

"He's the man. He's going to hand us in."

"Just leave it to me. Then you must allow me to enter next so that I can sit beside him. You'll sit across."

"You're trying too hard." Beatrix jumped up onto the dressing table, and Lily stroked her fur. "Just be your usual beautiful, charming self—"

"I cannot leave this to chance," Rose interrupted. "Lord Randal is the only man I've ever truly loved."

From where Lily was standing, her sister's emotions ran more to desperation than love—with perhaps a little lust thrown in for good measure. But she did allow that with all the two had in common, true love was likely to develop, given time.

"Whatever you say, Rose," she said. "I'll follow your lead."

Beatrix went with them and was first into the carriage. Rand, of course, insisted the ladies get in next. He settled himself beside Lily, and for a few awkward minutes, Rose alternately glared at her and aimed flirty smiles at him.

Rand appeared to be avoiding Rose's heated gaze, staring out the window instead. He hummed the same tune Lily remembered from the night before, perhaps in an attempt to fill the silence.

Suddenly Rose sniffed the air. "Sulfur," she said disapprovingly. Parentally. True, she was displaying her intelligence by recognizing the chemical, but hadn't she said men didn't care to be mothered?

Lily nudged her with a foot and gave a little shake of her head.

Perhaps getting the message, Rose looked to Rand with indulged amusement. "While you were waiting for us, did you play with the fire-making things? After you told Rowan you'd return them? Did you use them all up?"

Rand appeared anything but chastised. "What does Ford need with a scrap of paper and a few bits of wood? I'm sure he has more, and I think young Rowan has learned his lesson."

Boys would be boys, Lily thought, then rushed to change the subject before her sister made the mistake of saying that again out loud. "How is it that a marquess's son became an Oxford professor?"

"Yes," Rose put in, "how on earth did *that* happen?" Her tone implied that, regardless of how it had happened, she was hoping he'd go back to being plain Lord Randal, not a professor of anything.

Rand, however, just shrugged. "I'm a second son. An all-but-disowned second son."

"Surely not," Lily said.

"Perhaps not officially, but I might as well be. I couldn't wait to get away from home, and once free, I never wanted to go back."

Even Rose looked genuinely concerned. "Did your parents mistreat you?"

"From what little I can remember, my mother treated me wonderfully, but she died when I was six. My father, well…let me just say that his dogs received more of his attention than I did. He noticed me only when I was in trouble."

Lily imagined him young, fresh-faced, misbehaving. "Were you often in trouble?"

"Mostly just when I tried to expose my older brother's misdeeds. The exalted heir who could do no wrong. Or so my father was convinced. My attempts to prove otherwise were hopeless."

"What did your brother do?" Rose asked. "Was he naughty like Rowan?"

"Rowan?" Rand's expression was one of total disbelief. "Rowan is a saint compared to Alban. The man is downright cruel—or at least he was as a boy. As I haven't been home in eight years, I don't know what he's like now. But though I know people can change, I don't expect Alban has. He's always hated me. He hates a lot of people. There's something evil about my brother."

Eight years. Lily couldn't fathom avoiding her family for eight years. She saw a loneliness in Rand, a loneliness in his eyes. A loneliness she yearned to help him heal.

"Evil," she mused. "Could it possibly have been your imagination? Jealousy on your part? After all, he's the heir, and you were young. Perhaps if you go back—"

"I have no desire to go back. I'm happy with my life as it is. And if you had read Alban's diaries—"

"You read his private diaries? No wonder he hated you!" Despite his distress, Lily was tempted to laugh. If she'd read her sisters' diaries, or Rowan's, they'd be out for her blood, no mercy. Not that any of them kept diaries, but that was beside the point.

To Rand's credit, he turned a dusky shade of red. "It was only because I was hoping to expose him—"

Rose made a rude noise. "Hoping to get him in trouble, you mean."

"Well, he deserved it. And I didn't precisely read them," he said, a bit defensively. "I transcribed them."

Beatrix leapt onto Lily's lap. "What do you mean?"

"I decoded them. He wrote them in secret languages that he devised. Because they were so incriminating."

"And you broke the codes?"

"Constantly. It infuriated him, of course. And I never managed to prove his guilt to my father's satisfaction—he only punished me for invading Alban's privacy. But it did reveal this skill I have for puzzling out languages. I'm sure the old man was as relieved as I was when he gained me early entrance to Oxford based on that talent."

Lily stroked the cat thoughtfully. "And you've stayed there ever since."

"It became my home. I eventually became a fellow and then a professor. I know my father looks upon my profession with disdain. A Nesbitt, working for a living. But I like my life. The university is orderly."

He looked out the window again, his eyes turning hazy.

"At Oxford, the world makes sense."

TWELVE

 O SOONER HAD the carriage door opened than
Ford whisked Rand upstairs to the attic. "How was
your stay at Trentingham?"

"Fine." Rand looked around at the chaotic jumble of scientific
instruments that littered Ford's laboratory. "Is there nothing I
can do downstairs, where the damage—"

"It's all being handled. I'm in the middle of something here—
I'll be with you in a minute." Ford added a noxious-smelling
substance to some cloudy fluid in a beaker. "Fine, was it?"

"Actually," Rand admitted, "it was damned awkward. Will
the guest room be ready for me to sleep here tonight?"

Ford stirred the mess with some sort of stick made of glass.
"If you can live with a bare, damp floor."

"Bare and damp won't deter me."

"Very well, then." Ford nodded. "I'll let this sit until tomorrow. Let me go get the book."

Rand plopped onto a chair and rubbed his face. In two short
days, his placid life seemed to have become overly complicated.
He felt absurdly relieved to be moving back here this afternoon.
Trentingham Manor was a lovely home, but at Lakefield he ran
less risk of finding himself alone with a certain lovely daughter.

He felt much safer here. More in control. Less likely to have stupid things come out of his mouth.

I've thought about you for four years...

"Here it is," Ford said, setting the book on the table and taking a seat beside him.

"It" was *Secrets of the Emerald Tablet,* a small, brown leather volume that appeared to be of little consequence. Ancient and handwritten in a cryptic code, it looked like a simple diary. But it was much more than that. It was purported to hold the key to the Philosopher's Stone—the secret of how to make gold.

Ford had found the book years earlier and brought it to Rand to translate. When the task had proved a difficult one, they'd set it aside for a time. Now Rand looked forward to the challenge.

It would take his mind off another challenge that had much more personal repercussions.

"Awkward," Ford echoed thoughtfully, moving closer with a scrape of his chair. His laboratory was a homely space, huge but hardly luxurious, cluttered as it was with every toy a scientist and alchemist could desire. "My mother-in-law is generally good at setting her guests at ease."

"And her daughter is good at unsettling them."

"Rose?" Ford chuckled. "Although she can be rather forward, I assure you she's an innocent at heart."

"*Rather forward* hardly begins to define Rose. But I meant Lily."

"Lily? Lily soothes those around her. Creatures as well as people. What could sweet Lily possibly do to discompose you?"

Rand met his old school friend's eyes. "She can look at me. That's all it takes."

"Holy Hades," Ford said, borrowing his father-in-law's favorite phrase. "You're falling for her."

"I didn't say that," Rand protested. It was a long way from lusting after a woman to *falling for her,* wasn't it?

His friend's laughter was more irritating than supportive. With a huff, Rand opened the book.

His feelings on the matter seemed to get more complicated by the minute. These cryptic writings would be a hell of a lot easier to figure out.

THIRTEEN

*D*OWNSTAIRS, LILY and Rose had joined their oldest sister in her cheerful, turquoise-toned drawing room. With the three of them together, it felt just like old times.

Almost. Violet, of course, was married now, and a mother of three herself. Although she lived close by and they got together often, Lily did miss the nights when they'd all snuggled in one of their chambers, chatting and giggling away the hours.

She watched Beatrix wander the room, poking her little black nose here and there as she searched for something familiar. Suddenly Lily wished for the old and familiar, too. "You should come home to sleep one night, Violet."

"At Trentingham?" Violet stopped pacing, which meant tiny Rebecca started snuffling. The baby seemed to prefer constant motion.

"I'll walk with her," Lily offered. She couldn't wait to get her hands on her niece.

When Rebecca was settled in Lily's arms, Violet dropped onto one of the turquoise velvet chairs. She lifted her spectacles and rubbed the bridge of her nose. "Why should I stay the night at Trentingham?"

"A sleeping party. It would be like the old days." As Lily

walked back and forth cuddling Rebecca, her gaze swept over little Marc asleep in a cradle. She smiled to see Rose playing with Nicky on the floor, his miniature English warship in fierce conflict with her Dutch one. "I know you rarely let your children out of your sight, but you *do* have nursemaids. They could relieve you for one night, don't you think?"

Violet seemed to contemplate that odd idea for a moment before she grinned. "Perhaps I could find time to read a book."

"No," Lily said, then reconsidered. If solitary time to read was what her sister needed, she wouldn't deny her. "Of course you could read, if that's what you want. But I was thinking we could spend the night together. The three of us, like we used to."

Rose looked up with a wicked smile. "And read *Aristotle's Master-piece?*"

"Not that," Lily said quickly, remembering the hours they'd all spent together stealthily reading the scandalous marriage manual before Violet's wedding.

Lily had found *Aristotle's Master-piece* an uncomfortable combination of intriguing and embarrassing, and she hadn't been sad when the book moved to Lakefield along with her sister. But that had been years ago, when she was only sixteen. The mysteries of the bedchamber, which had seemed frightening and unimaginable then, were easier to imagine now.

In fact, lately her imagination seemed to be working overtime.

Still, dragging the *Master-piece* back out wasn't what she had in mind. "I just thought...I thought it would be nice to talk."

"Bang!" Nicky sailed his ship closer to Rose's. Beatrix's small head whipped back and forth, following the battle. "Bang, bang!"

"Quieter," Violet cautioned. "Your sister's sleeping."

Rebecca had nodded off in Lily's arms. Violet gazed at her daughter tenderly. "Of course I'll come sleep at Trentingham. Someday soon. It will be great fun." Though she sounded enthusiastic, her brown eyes were filled with concern. "Is there something in particular you'd like to talk about?"

"Nothing special. Just...life."

Rose aimed a tiny Dutch cannon. "*I* want to talk about Lord Randal."

The one thing Lily *didn't* want to talk about. Despite her promise, she felt she'd heard her sister gush over the man quite enough. Especially because, regardless of all their plotting, Rose seemed to be making no headway.

"How many times," she said, more peevishly than was her nature, "do you suppose he's asked you to call him Rand?"

"Oh, about a million," Rose answered gaily. "But I like to think of him as a lord. *My* lord."

Lily feared Rand would never be Rose's lord. He'd made it clear, with words and a kiss, which sister he preferred. And while she had no intention of going back on her word by allowing him to get closer, she'd seen nothing to make her believe he'd turn to Rose instead.

She met Violet's gaze, sending her a silent message.

"Has he shown interest?" Violet asked Rose carefully.

Their sister's lovely nose went into the air. "He walked with me in the garden today. He's been very kind."

"Bang, bang!" Nicky yelled. "Aunty Rose, you're not watching. You're going to sink!"

"Quieter," Violet repeated—rather patiently, Lily thought, considering she'd probably heard her sister utter that word a thousand times or more.

Lily lowered herself to a chair, being careful not to wake the baby. "Rand *is* kind," she said, more dreamily than she'd intended.

Beatrix began hiccuping.

"That silly cat." Rose stood, abandoning her ship to the mercy of the English. She narrowed her eyes at Lily. "You made a promise. Are you intending to break it?"

Violet looked between them curiously. "What promise?"

"Well…" Lily began.

"She promised," Rose finished for her, "to stay away from Lord Randal." Her gaze whipped back to Lily. "And to help me win him."

Lily swallowed hard. She'd been helping her, hadn't she? Every way she knew how. "Have you ever known me to break a promise?"

Rose appeared to give that some thought. "No," she said at last. "You always do the right thing."

She said it as though always doing the right thing were a character flaw, which Lily was beginning to think might be true.

And how absurd was that?

FOURTEEN

*L*ATER THAT afternoon, the notes wafting from the harpsichord did their magic as always, transporting Lily from her family's cream-and-gold-toned drawing room to a much more peaceful place.

At the moment Trentingham was far from peaceful. The drive was crammed with carriages waiting to take friends and family home. Uncles and cousins were busy seeing that their things were properly packed and loaded onto the correct vehicles. Children ran through the corridors, their feet pounding on the planked floor as they chased one another in last-minute games.

Lily knew she should join everyone and say goodbye. And she would, after a few more minutes of playing behind the drawing room's thick oak doors. The music was too soothing to resist. Her fingers glided over the keys, picking out a tune of her own creation, one that matched her mood.

Pensive. Confused. Longing—although for what, she wasn't sure.

The door opened, and her mother slid gracefully into the chamber. Mum waited for her to finish. "Dear," she started as the last note faded, "that was lovely, but you really should be—"

"I know, Mum." Lily rose, forcing her lips to curve in a smile. "I'll go make my farewells."

"That's my Lily." Mum smiled in return. "Aunt Cecily could use some help with bringing Lucy and Penelope downstairs." Lucy and Penelope were Lily's small cousins, aged two and three. "I'm afraid all our servants are engaged with the luggage."

"Of course I'll help." With one last wistful look at the harpsichord, Lily quit the room and followed her mother upstairs, looking forward to kissing the two girls goodbye.

But the nursery was empty. "Oh, well," Mum said cheerfully. "Aunt Cecily must have managed to wrestle the little rapscallions downstairs by herself. Come along, then." She turned back to the corridor.

Feeling like one of King Charles's tennis balls being batted back and forth, Lily followed. Then nearly bumped into her mother when she stopped before a door—the door to the room that had been assigned to Rand.

If Lily hadn't already known that, she would have figured it out on hearing the humming that drifted from inside.

Mum knocked and called through the oak. "How is it going, Rand?"

The door opened, and Rand stood there, a shirt dangling from one hand. "It's going well, thank you," he said, stepping back into the room to toss the garment into his trunk. He looked, Lily thought, like he was relieved to be heading over to Lakefield to stay.

Well, she was relieved, too. The less she had to watch Rose fawning over him, the better.

A frown on her forehead, Mum pointedly scanned the room. "Where is the maid I arranged for? Did she never show up?" She turned to Lily. "Perhaps you can assist Rand with his packing."

"I—" Lily started.

"That's my Lily." Without waiting for her agreement, Mum turned to look down the stairwell. "Arabel!" she shouted. "Don't you dare leave without a bottle of perfume!" And before Lily could say anything, she was gone.

Lily shifted her gaze to Rand, suppressing a smile when she saw him roll up a pair of breeches. With a sigh, she walked into the room. "Let me help you with that."

"I can do it myself, although I cannot fathom why the maid unpacked everything. I brought enough for a two-week stay, but not here."

"She wasn't privy to your plans." She took the garment and folded it neatly, thinking it felt a bit scandalous to be handling his clothes. "As soon as some of these people leave, more help will be available."

Lady and Jasper watched from the sill, holding a noisy conversation. "What could a squirrel and a bird possibly be discussing?" Rand asked rather peevishly, then didn't wait for her to answer. "I told Ford I'd be back in an hour. He wants to work some more on the translation."

"Ford will have to understand." She walked over and bent to set the breeches in his trunk. "He can wait."

When Rand didn't respond, she straightened to find him near her. In fact, he was looming over her, near enough that her skin prickled in reaction.

"I cannot," he said, his voice lower and husky.

"What?" She blinked.

"I cannot wait. To kiss you."

A sudden awareness began pulsing through her veins. "My lord—"

"Rand."

"Rand," she whispered. He was so close she could smell him, soap and the faint remnants of all those warring perfumes, all layered over his own unique scent. The scent that was Rand. And he wanted to kiss her. Her lips tingled with the memory of last night's kiss, so innocent and yet so affecting. She wanted that again…that and more.

Rose. She'd promised Rose. She couldn't do this.

She backed up toward the corridor, her gaze darting around the chamber. "The door is open."

He followed her—and reached around her to shut it. "Now it's not."

She backed away more, until she was smack up against it.

"Lily." He followed her again and placed his hands on her shoulders. "I very much wish to kiss you."

Even through the fitted jacket of her riding habit, his fingers felt warm, their imprints sending a rush of sensation through her. Her mouth dried, and she licked her lips. "I very much wish..."

"What?"

She could hardly breathe. "I don't know."

"Yes, you do." His eyes glowed silver, a mixture of confidence and desire. "You want to kiss me, too."

"Maybe. But...I cannot."

"Oh," he said, "I think you can."

And then he proved it.

His mouth on hers was gentle, like it had been the night before. Still, that light touch was enough to make her dizzy. Finding it impossible to think clearly, she reached to wind her arms around his neck. His hands slipped behind her, settling on the small of her back to draw her against him.

He felt warm, solid. She moved even closer and fit her curves to his body. A low groan rose from his throat, and his lips slanted more urgently, coaxing hers to open.

Lily knew about this kind of kiss—she was, after all, the youngest of three sisters. She'd anticipated the day she might try it, with both excitement and some trepidation. It had sounded... well, rather messy and not entirely pleasant, no matter that she'd been assured otherwise.

So it was with some apprehension that she responded to the pressure of his mouth, opening her lips the barest measure. His tongue traced a slow line between, and she shivered and opened wider, giving him what he wanted.

And goodness, she wanted it, too. His tongue invaded further, teasing hers with a heavenly skill that made her weak in the knees. Her eyes drifted closed. Her arms tightened around him, and she breathed in his heady scent, tasting him in return.

Quite suddenly her world seemed filled with him. He tasted glorious. And the mysteries of the bedchamber no longer seemed frightening—not when her entire body thrummed from only a kiss.

At last he gently eased away and rested his lips on her forehead. "I have to leave," he said, the words gruff against her skin.

Lady tweeted from the window, and Jasper answered with a chirp. Lily hadn't heard them while Rand had been kissing her. She hadn't heard or felt or seen anything—except for him.

She was trembling all over. And Rand was right.

"Yes," she said. "You should leave."

FIFTEEN

$\mathcal{I}$T WAS A WEEK later, when Lily was exercising her horse, Snowflake, that she spotted Rand running along the bank of the Thames.

He'd avoided her all that time. Or she'd avoided him. Or both—she wasn't sure. But now, riding toward him, her heart began to race...and it wasn't from the exertion of the gallop.

She slowed deliberately, both Snowflake's gait and her own breathing. It didn't matter that the mere sight of this man set the pit of her stomach to tingling. She wouldn't let him kiss her again.

She'd promised Rose. Never mind that Rose had contrived to visit Violet every day this week and come back reporting she'd seen neither hide nor hair of Rand. A promise was a promise.

Lily was seeing a considerable amount of Rand's hide now. Above plain buff breeches, his loose white shirt was unlaced and open at the neck, the sleeves rolled up past his elbows. Tied back into a queue, his glorious hair streamed on the wind behind him, shimmering in the sun. His unfashionably low-heeled boots pounded along the grassy bank in a rhythm measured and unceasing.

He ran, she thought, like a wildcat, lithe and sleek.

She knew the moment he saw her. There was a telltale stumble in that perfectly smooth motion. And a matching hitch in her heartbeat.

He stopped and leaned over, hands to bent knees, panting hard as he waited for her to ride closer. When she did, he straightened and looked up at her, using a hand to shade his eyes.

His face was flushed; his shirt clung damply to his skin. That piercing gray gaze swept her from her toes on up. When it met her eyes, searching, it seemed almost as though he were seeing her for the first time.

Holding her reins in one hand, she self-consciously smoothed her butter yellow habit with the other.

"Good day, Lily."

She swallowed tightly. "Good day."

"I'm finished running," he said, stating the obvious. But for some reason, she had a feeling he spoke of more than exercise. Moving beside her white horse, he reached to help her down. "Will you walk with me? I like to do that after I run."

There was no harm, she supposed, in walking. But when his hands spanned her waist to ease her to the ground, she felt a disturbing jolt of sensation. And he let his fingers rest there longer than he needed to before he stepped back.

She deliberately looked away, taking Snowflake's reins and looping them over the branch of a scrubby tree.

A sparrow fluttered from the sky and alighted in the sparse foliage. Rand looked up, then raised a questioning brow. "Lady?"

"Yes. She thinks she's protecting me."

"She thinks I cannot defend you without her help?" His laugh sounded strained. "She's insulting my masculinity."

To the contrary, Lily suspected Lady was acknowledging his masculinity—protecting her *from* Rand rather than in spite of him. But she certainly wasn't going to encourage him by telling him that.

They turned and walked along the riverfront, settling easily into a comfortable tempo. Keeping far enough away from him that he couldn't take her hand, Lily focused on the water. Swans glided majestically, and faint laughter drifted from one of the boats filled with people enjoying the summer sun.

"Do you run often?" she asked, then realized she knew the answer.

Here was the reason he looked so browned and healthy, so lean and sleekly muscled. Apparently not all academics spent their days locked away in research.

"Often enough," he said. "It helps me think."

Surprised, she turned her head to meet his gaze. "How can you think while you run that hard?"

"Not during." He smiled, his teeth blindingly white in his heated face. "After. Like now. When my body is pleasantly worn-out and I can feel the breeze cooling my skin."

It had always done that for Rand, the running. It wasn't only the speed. It was the strain of pumping muscles, the sound of pounding feet, the delicious gulps of air rushing in and out of his lungs. The rhythm. It all combined to clear his head—to *fill* his head—leaving no space for worry or concerns. When he was running, he was only running.

And when he stopped, he could always think more clearly. Life seemed simpler. Problems seemed surmountable. For him, it had worked that way as long as he could remember.

But this time, when he'd stopped, Lily had been there. And he'd thought, quite clearly, that he must be falling in love.

The realization had come out of nowhere, as though he'd stumbled on a key and unlocked a cryptic code. His heart had hammered against his ribs. Was still hammering against his ribs.

He wasn't sure he believed in love, wasn't sure he was ready for it. Without his family's help—without anyone's help—he'd made a life for himself. A good life, a comfortable life, a life in which he didn't have to answer to anyone.

A lonely life, a little voice whispered.

"How long have you lived in Oxford?" Lily asked, then watched Rand shake his head as though to clear it.

"Half my life—since I was fourteen. I couldn't wait to get out of my father's house. The man doesn't approve of what I've become, but it suits me better than living under his thumb and following his orders."

"Did he expect you to assist him with his estates?" She knew that Rowan would do that someday, but Rand seemed so independent. Besides, it was different for Rowan. Someday Rowan would be Lord Trentingham, but Rand would never be more than Lord Hawkridge's younger brother. "I can understand why you wouldn't want to do that, or live the life of an idle gentleman. Between your lecturing and your research, you have so much to contribute."

"It's a shame my father doesn't see it that way. I believe my leaving for Oxford was the only thing we ever agreed on. He was as happy to see the back of me as I was to turn it upon him."

He grinned as though that was supposed to be amusing, and she smiled in return. But she sensed a sadness lurking beneath his good humor. There was so much more to Rand than his father was willing to see. So many admirable qualities. And underneath them all, that loneliness she'd glimpsed. That lack of a family who believed in him.

No matter what, she'd always have her family and their support. She'd never realized how lucky she was. Rand had made his place in the world, but he'd done it alone.

No one should have to be alone.

Her heart aching for him, she glanced toward him as they walked and found his gaze fixed to where she was absently rubbing the back of her hand. "How did it happen?" he asked.

Embarrassed, she waved the scarred hand dismissively. "It doesn't hurt anymore, if that's what you're wondering. It happened long ago."

"But how?"

Though he didn't seem at all repulsed, she stared down at the thin white lines. The proof of her imperfection. "A cat. Not Beatrix. And it wasn't his fault—I was teasing him. I learned to respect animals after that. All animals."

"I cannot imagine you disrespecting anything."

Something in his voice made a nervous laugh bubble out of her. "I try," she said, "but I'm far from perfect."

"You're close enough to perfect for me," he said very seriously. He stopped walking and took her by the shoulders to stop her, too, gently turning her to face him. "May I kiss you again, Lily?"

Her pulse skittered. His shirt had dried, and it billowed in the soft breeze. She wanted to lay her palms against the front of it and run them up to feel the warm, tanned skin revealed in the open placket.

But she couldn't. And she couldn't let him kiss her again, either. It didn't matter that her lips seemed to be tingling with remembered anticipation.

She licked them. "Rose…"

A puzzled frown appeared on his brow. "Rose? What has Rose to do with this?"

She hesitated. They were standing beneath a tree, and a flutter of wings heralded Lady alighting above them. But Lady couldn't help her, couldn't protect her.

Only the truth could do that.

Holding Rand's gaze, Lily took a deep breath. "Rose wants you."

His lips curved in a crooked smile, and one hand drifted from her shoulder. He touched a fingertip to the little dent in her chin. "So you're being a good sister, is that it? Let me tell you, Lily, Rose may very well want me. But I want *you*."

He couldn't, she thought.

Maybe he did. But he just couldn't.

His finger traced a featherlight pattern on her chin, making her melt, making her crave his kiss even more. But this wasn't right. She'd promised. She'd broken her promise twice already, and twice was two times too many.

While Lady twittered, Lily struggled to keep her head. "You're so like Rose. You both sing, the languages..."

Her words trailed off. Lady flew to a lower branch.

Rand seemed to consider that line of reasoning for a long moment.

When he finally spoke, his tone was laced with quiet conviction. "Maybe I am like Rose. But I don't want someone *like* me. I want someone to *complete* me."

His voice was so deep, the sentiment so earnest, his eyes on hers so sure. When he leaned closer, when his hand slipped from her chin to curl around the back of her neck, when he lowered his lips to hers...all she could do was surrender.

And surrender felt entirely too good.

Slowly he backed her against the tree, his mouth working its magic. Her lips opened willingly this time, eagerly, her tongue reaching out in tentative exploration. His mouth felt soft but made hers burn with fire. She pressed closer, reveling in the feel of his hard, toned body against her.

Leaves rustled overhead as he moaned, deepening the kiss. An answering sound rose from inside her. His hand tightened on her nape while his other arm went around her, a clear bid for possession. He tasted of Rand, and she sucked in his scent, stronger and more heady following his run.

Her senses reeled, and a ripple of excitement began flowing through her, building toward a crescendo. It made her dizzy, made her knees weak, made her want more.

She arched her neck as his lips trailed down her throat. "Lily," he whispered, her name a damp promise in the sensitive hollow. "I want you."

Her eyes fluttered open.

"You cannot," she said, afraid it was the same for her. She tried to pull away, fought to regain her senses. This was wrong.

"We...we haven't known each other long enough for you to know what you want."

"Four years."

"No," she argued, biting her lip. Tears threatened, but she blinked them back. This couldn't be happening. "Not four years. Not even a month. A few weeks four years ago, and nine or ten days now. Most of them spent apart."

"Well, then," he said quietly, so guilelessly she knew he believed it, "it must have been love at first sight."

Love. The single word made her heart knot and grow heavy in her chest. Feeling his hands against her nape and her back, the humming warmth of his body against hers, she knew, without a doubt, that he really, truly did want her.

And she wanted him.

But Rose wanted him, too.

Blood pounded in her head, filled her ears, rocked her senses. He'd spoken of love—and if he loved her, Lily, then he'd never marry Rose, would he? What was the point of keeping her promise if Rose's hopes were destined to be dashed either way?

For one single moment, she wanted, more than she'd wanted anything in her life, to break a promise to her sister. Then she gasped, appalled that she'd even had such a disloyal thought. Her word meant everything to her.

"I have to leave," she said, echoing what he'd said a week earlier. And she turned toward Snowflake and ran, Lady flying after her.

SIXTEEN

OR THREE SOLID days, Rand did nothing but eat, sleep, work on the translation, and run. And think. And run and think some more.

At the end of that time, he still wasn't sure how—or even if—his feelings for Lily had turned from simple lust to something deeper. The mechanics of falling in love seemed cryptic, as elusive as the symbols in Ford's ancient alchemy book.

But Rand Nesbitt was a man who prided himself on his ability to figure things out.

Leaving Ford's laboratory for supper, he asked, "Do you believe in love at first sight?"

"No," Ford said flatly. "It makes no logical sense."

"Then you didn't feel...with Violet..."

"On first sight?" Ford's mouth twitched as though he were holding back a laugh. "Absolutely not. I thought her rather plain and more than a little odd. Though I cannot imagine why," he added thoughtfully.

Rand followed him down the winding staircase to Lakefield's cozy, burgundy-toned dining room, where Violet was waiting with their children.

She didn't look plain at all—she was practically glowing, as a matter of fact, as she handed one of the twins to a nursemaid. And as for odd, well, if that word didn't describe Ford Chase, Rand didn't know one that did.

When it came right down to it, who wasn't odd, anyway?

He took a seat and waited while a footman set a plate of chicken and artichoke pie before him. "Do you believe in love at first sight?" he asked Violet.

"Of course," she said. "But lust at first sight is more common."

A becoming blush touched her cheeks, making Rand suspect she'd experienced lust at first sight. He felt suddenly—absurdly—jealous, wishing her sister would feel the same lust for him. If his own experience was anything to judge by, lust could be a solid foundation on which to build heavier emotions.

Love. He'd uttered that frightening word, risked baring his soul, offered his heart in his hands...and had it rejected.

Lifting his fork, he shifted his gaze to Ford in an attempt to gauge his old friend as an inspiration for female lust. If he looked hard enough, he could almost understand why ladies might find Ford handsome, but truth be told, what he really saw was the gawky schoolboy the man had been when they'd first met.

Who knew what drove women? Lily *had* allowed him to kiss her three times. Perhaps there was hope for him, after all.

"Why are you asking?" Violet tucked a cloth under Nicky's chin, then pulled his plate closer and put a spoon in his chubby hand. "Do *you* believe in love at first sight?"

"I'm not sure," Rand said. He certainly hadn't until recently. Besides, his first sight of Lily had been so long ago. After all this time, how was a man supposed to remember what he'd felt way back then? In the intervening years, he'd probably built her up in his mind.

And on that flimsy basis, lately he'd found himself daydreaming about a lifetime of wedded bliss. Clearly he was going soft in the head.

Violet speared a piece of artichoke heart. "Of course, love—sustainable love—is dependent on more than physical appearance."

"Which is why," her husband said, "love at first sight is a myth."

"Not at all." Her voice took on the tone of a philosopher waxing philosophical. "Love occurs when something in one person recognizes something basic and true in another. To borrow a term from my mother's perfume-making, call it that person's essence. One would see this essence embodied in everything the other person does—those thoughts, actions, responses, and choices that go to display her values."

"One cannot see all of that at first sight," Ford argued.

"I beg to differ." Clearly enjoying this sort of debate, Violet waved her fork. "One person's essence responds innately to another's—it's not a conscious response, nor one that knows time. Upon meeting a woman, some part of you will notice how she moves, gestures, talks, smiles—how she carries herself in general. Her essence—not only her surface appearance." She focused back on Rand. "Take my sister Lily, for example."

Though the pie was delicious, swimming in rich gravy, Rand nearly choked. "Lily?" He shot a glance to Ford, whom he'd told about Lily in confidence. But his friend avoided his gaze, industriously cutting an already-small-enough bite of chicken.

"Just as an example." If Violet's expression might have revealed ulterior motives, she expertly concealed it while sipping wine. "Lily is beautiful, isn't she?"

Rand sipped from his own goblet. Lustrous mahogany hair, deep blue eyes, that irresistible face and figure...

"I don't expect any male would argue with you about that."

"And perhaps most males would notice that first, but there's so much more to Lily. She makes beautiful music. She's also quite intelligent. One needn't be bookish to be intelligent."

"Did I ever say—"

"Those are all obvious things, but now let's look at her

essence, those values we can see in the way she carries herself and behaves. She's nurturing and compassionate. People feel good around Lily, because she cares. She really cares, about everyone and everything. She's benevolent, she seeks harmony, and above all, she endeavors at all times to make the right choices. The sum of these is what makes her Lily."

"Her essence," Rand murmured.

"Yes!" Beaming, Violet set down her goblet. "And the sort of man who would recognize a kindred essence in Lily, most especially on first sight, would also recognize that she will someday make a wonderful mother." With that, her gaze lovingly went to her babies in their cradles.

And Rand was rendered speechless.

He wasn't sure he could even eat.

He was just getting used to considering love and marriage… fatherhood was another matter entirely.

SEVENTEEN

"*L*ILY, ARE YOU ready to leave?"

"Just a moment, Mum." With a sigh, Lily stroked Randolph's soft brown fur one last time. She'd put it off more than a week, but she knew what had to be done. Setting her jaw, she crouched to tenderly place Randolph on the grass.

Without so much as a thank you, the rat scampered happily into a flower bed.

Lily sighed again and fished Beatrix out from beneath her skirts. "May I take her with us?" she asked as she rose.

"I suppose she'll contrive to come along either way." Mum sifted through the basket on her arm, checking that all her perfumes were in order. "But you must leave her in the carriage. You know cats make Lady Carrington sneeze."

Half an hour later, Lily stood on the steps of Carrington House with her mother and Rose. As Mum lifted the knocker, a sneeze resounded from inside.

"Beatrix is in the carriage," Lily said defensively. Glancing back to make sure, she saw a small black nose pressed to the vehicle's window. Jasper and Lady sat atop the carriage's roof, looking similarly innocent.

The door opened, and a butler ushered them into the

drawing room, where Lady Carrington was waiting with coffee, expensive imported tea, and cakes. Judith sat on a sturdy carved chair, dabbing at her nose with a lace-edged handkerchief.

Mum set her basket on a table and raised the cloth covering. "Your usual blend," she said to Lady Carrington, handing her a bottle of scent. "And for you, Lady Judith, a new blend to celebrate your betrothal. More fitting for a lady of your status."

"It's more spicy," Rose explained.

Judith's eyes widened. "Oooh, may I see?"

Lily brought the perfume to her friend, pulling the stopper out as she went. She waved the bottle under her own nose and smiled before handing it to Judith. "It smells lovely."

Judith dabbed a bit on one wrist and raised it to her reddened nose. "It does. Even all stuffy, I can tell. Thank you ever so much, Lady Trentingham."

"You're very welcome, dear."

Replacing the stopper, Judith stood. "Would you care to see the fabric for my wedding gown?" she asked Lily and Rose. "And the style? Madame left a fashion doll for me to show you."

They followed her up the curving oak staircase.

"I think the dress will be ever so beautiful," Judith said, pausing for a sneeze. "Lord, I'm so excited about my wedding."

"You should be," Rose said somewhat wistfully.

The wedding dress fashion doll reclined in a place of honor against Judith's mauve pillows in her feminine room. "Isn't it lovely?"

"It is," Lily agreed softly. The doll's gown was palest blue with a wide neckline and golden ribbons crisscrossing the stomacher. The underskirt was cloth of gold.

Suddenly, quite unbidden, an image popped into her head—of herself wearing such a gown and standing beside Rand. The blue fabric brought out the hue in her eyes, which were fastened on Rand as she recited her vows. The golden underskirt shimmered, rustling when she moved...

"You're so lucky," Rose told Judith, snapping Lily out of her reverie.

She closed her eyes momentarily, then opened them with new determination. She should be picturing Rose standing beside Rand, rather than thinking disloyal thoughts.

Settling into the window seat, Judith sneezed again. "Pardon me," she said with a sniffle. Then her voice dropped a notch. "I'm lucky about the wedding," she mumbled, "but I'm worried about the wedding night."

Her heart aching for her friend, Lily forgot her own troubles. She sat beside Judith and took her hands. "You'll be fine," she told her with all the confidence she could muster. "All brides are nervous."

"Do you think so?"

"Goodness, I'm sure of it." She slanted a glance to Rose before looking back to her friend. "Do you believe in love at first sight?"

"Absolutely. But I've seen Lord Grenville, and—"

"I didn't mean to pry," Lily rushed to clarify. "I just wondered if you believed. In the abstract."

"Yes. Oh, yes." Judith had always been a romantic. "That's why I—"

"*I* believe in love at first sight," Rose interrupted. "I fell in love with Lord Randal the very first time I saw him."

Despite her worries, Judith grinned. "You fall in love with every man you see."

"I do not," Rose protested. "Only the handsome ones. Like Rand."

Rand, Rand, Rand. Lily rose and paced back to the doll, staring at its pale blue magnificence. She would never feel right wearing a wedding dress before Rose was Lady Somebody.

"There are cakes downstairs," Judith said into the sudden silence.

Lily was all too happy to escape the discussion, but no sooner had they reentered the drawing room than Rose revived it. "Mum," she asked, "do you believe in love at first sight?"

"What nonsense," Lady Carrington said, her chins trembling with indignation. "Love grows between two suited individuals. It was that way for me, and it will be the same for my Judith and Lord Grenville." She brushed crumbs from her mouth and motioned her daughter closer. "Come here, dear. Have a cake."

Judith took two. Evidently her illness wasn't affecting her appetite.

"Mum?" Rose pressed.

Mum set down her teacup. "I do believe in love at first sight," she said firmly. "I experienced it with your father."

Lady Carrington harrumphed.

"Of course," Mum continued undaunted, "dear Joseph took some convincing. I've yet to meet a man who believes in love at first sight."

Lily knew one. One who was trying to convince *her*.

"Nonsense," Lady Carrington repeated as she reached for another cake.

Lily's mother smiled charmingly and changed the subject. "Have you heard the latest?" she asked, lifting her cup. "Two more of my introductions are culminating in marriages. Lady Eleanor Randolph is betrothed to Lord Ducksworth. And you're not going to believe this." She paused to sip for effect. "I've managed to match the eternal bachelor."

Lady Carrington's eyes widened. "You don't mean…"

"Yes." Mum nodded proudly. "Lord Percival Newcombe."

"No!" her friend gasped, a cake halfway to her lips. "To whom?"

EIGHTEEN

"**J**OSEPH**,**" Chrystabel said as she slid into bed beside him that night, "do you believe in love at first sight?"

He came up on an elbow and eyed her warily. "Is this a trick question?"

"No."

"Then no. I don't believe in love at first sight."

"No?"

"Yes? Is yes the right answer? I've never thought about it, my love."

She laughed. He was such a man.

Chrystabel loved the nights, the precious hours spent alone with her husband in their thick-walled bedchamber. Here, where the sound of her voice competed with nothing but an occasional crackle from the fireplace, her Joseph could hear her perfectly.

And he knew how to touch her perfectly, too. How to make her feel perfectly wonderful...

He rolled closer and reached to untie the ribbons that secured the top of her nightgown. "Does this have something to do with Lily and Rand? Are your plans not working out?"

She sighed, delightfully distracted by his fingertips brushing her skin. "I'm certain he desires her."

"Love at first sight?"

"Maybe. Do you remember how he looked at her, even four years ago?"

"No. I don't remember." He slipped the gown from her shoulders. "I'm not sure I even noticed."

Of course he hadn't. He was a man. "Well, it was quite obvious he was drawn to our Lily then, and it's even more obvious now. Surely you've noticed it now?"

"Not really." He lowered his lips to her neck, kissing the sensitive hollow while he worked the nightgown lower.

"Even since I pointed it out?" she asked breathlessly.

"I have eyes only for you, Chrysanthemum," he murmured against her throat. "Only you."

Half charmed, half exasperated, she shivered. "Well, Lily isn't immune to him, either—of that I'm sure. But despite all my efforts to get them alone together, the poor boy isn't making much progress. After I noticed Rand runs every day by the river, I told Lily that Snowflake needed some exercise, but—"

"Poor boy must not have my talents," her husband interrupted, cupping a breast. Making skilled use of his thumb, he pulled back to grin at her indrawn breath. "Are you sure he's good enough for Lily?"

"You're incorrigible," she said. But she didn't remove his hand, instead arching her back in blatant invitation. "I told you, didn't I, that Violet said Lily promised Rose she'd stay away from Rand? Besides feeling bound to that ridiculous vow, Lily is genuinely concerned for Rose. I can see it in her eyes, in her attitude. She's afraid to put her own happiness before her sister's."

"Give it some time, love. She'll come to her senses." He lowered his mouth to where his fingers had been.

"But Rand's house will be ready soon," she choked out on a gasp. "He'll be leaving."

"Give it some time," he repeated against her tingling flesh. "If he wants her, he'll be back. You didn't win me in a day."

Oh yes, she had, she thought with a secret smile as she helped him wiggle her out of her nightgown. It just proved her finesse with men that he hadn't noticed.

NINETEEN

ONCE IN A great while, a man had to get drunk. And it was always better to do that with a friend.

Sitting in Ford's laboratory, Rand stared at a nearly blank piece of paper. He blinked hard to make out the words. "We've been here all night and translated only a single sentence," he muttered, finding himself fascinated, in an odd, detached sort of way, at hearing the slur in his own voice. "We'll never finish. You'll never make gold."

"What's a few more years when these words have been waiting for four hundred?" Ford reached across the cluttered table for a decanter of brandy, impressing Rand when he didn't knock over any of the assorted paraphernalia. He filled Rand's beaker for the third time.

Or maybe the fourth. Rand had lost count.

"So you're in love, are you?" Ford said.

"Maybe. Probably not. I cannot be sure." Rand paused for a sip, trying not to speculate on what chemical concoction the beaker might have held the day before. "I think so."

Topping off his own beaker, Ford nodded. "You're in love."

"She won't have me. It's that older sister of hers. Rose." Rand took another sip—or rather a gulp that he'd intended to be a sip.

"She keeps pointing out how Rose and I are more suited," he complained. "Rose sings and can speak Italian. As though I'm looking for those qualities in a lover." Then another thought occurred to him—one that made the liquor seem to sour in the pit of his stomach. "What if she's only using Rose as an excuse? What if she won't have me because I'm only a professor? She lives in a bloody mansion, and I—"

"Lily's not like that," Ford rushed to interrupt. "She cares about her animals. She cares about other people. She *doesn't* care where she lives."

Rand nodded—slowly, to keep the room from blurring—as he tried to believe that. He almost succeeded. "Then why does she keep bringing up Rose?"

"Guilt," Ford said succinctly.

"Guilt?"

"Look, we all know Rose wants you—"

"Every woman wants me," Rand said with a wide, drunken grin. He was intelligent, he was financially stable, he was charming, he was tall and—from what women had told him—apparently easy on the eyes...and as much as he hated to admit it, he had the title *Lord* in front of his name.

No female had ever turned down Rand Nesbitt.

Then his expression fell. "Except Lily."

"Guilt." Taking his time about it, Ford drained his beaker. "She doesn't want to steal you from Rose."

"Rose doesn't have me. Therefore Lily cannot steal me from Rose." Rand felt inordinately proud of that observation. "Those two statements make rational sense, don't they? And I'm a professor of linguistics, not logic."

"You're brilliant," Ford said dryly. "But you're forgetting something."

"What's that?" Rand asked, marveling at the way the words sounded once they'd left his mouth. *Whazzat.* Had he said *whazzat?*

"The way women's minds work. Or don't, as the case may be. Would you care for some more brandy?"

Rand held out his beaker. "I think I need it."

Ford refilled his own, too, then leaned back in his chair and stretched his long legs out in front of him. "Listen," he said, rolling the beaker between his palms, "it doesn't matter whether Rose has you. The salient point here is that Lily knows Rose desires you, and she's unwilling to hurt her sister by taking what Rose considers hers—never mind that you're not and never will be—because Lily is putting her sister's feelings before her own. She won't allow herself to marry—"

"Who said anything about marriage?"

"Hold your tongue and listen. Lily won't allow herself to marry before Rose, most especially to a man Rose wants for herself."

Rand sipped more brandy as he attempted to absorb that convoluted line of reasoning. He found himself truly amazed. "How the hell do you know all that?"

"Violet told me. And she also said that Lily made Rose some harebrained promise to stay out of her way, which further complicates matters."

"Did Violet give you a solution?"

"She said it was hopeless. But that's where she's wrong." Ford leaned forward, narrowing his eyes as he focused on Rand's. "Listen, my man. It's time for you to take your own advice."

Rand sat up straighter and then waited until the world stopped spinning around him. "Advice? About love? I'm not even sure I believe in it. I've bloody well never given advice—"

"When Violet didn't want *me*, remember? You helped me devise a plan. And it worked."

"I did?" He blinked, trying to recall. "I must have been gloriously drunk."

"You were," Ford assured him. "Now, listen. Seduction was the key. You must make Lily desire you so very much that she doesn't give a damn about her sister. Her lust for you can overcome her loyalty to Rose. If you give it your best, it will work, my friend. Take it from a man with experience."

Rand rubbed the ends of his hair, warming to the idea. It sounded like an excellent plan. And certainly an enjoyable one. He would put it into effect starting tomorrow.

But for now, he felt like he was going to be sick.

TWENTY

*T*HE BURN OF overworked muscles. The sound of his own labored breath. The rhythm of his feet on the turf. All worked to clear Rand's mind...but disturbing thoughts insisted on creeping in anyway.

He'd stayed indoors yesterday, fuzzy-brained and out of sorts, the pounding in his head quite enough without the jarring beat of a run. He hadn't felt up to putting the seduction plan into action, either. It had been years since he'd indulged in drink like that—for good reason. This recent bout would serve to ensure he drank moderately for another decade at least.

Still, he'd managed to make progress on the translation—enough, in fact, that he and Ford had come to the sad conclusion that *Secrets of the Emerald Tablet* held no secrets to making gold. Over the past few weeks, Ford had tested every formula Rand could find, with results ranging from hopeful-but-disappointing to all-out laughable.

Now there were no more formulas. There was no point in laboring to decipher what little was left of the text.

"I'm sorry," he'd told Ford when they'd closed the book last night.

"I always knew this was a possibility. Hell, the mere idea of making gold was too good to be true. I'm sorry you wasted so much time on it."

Rand had shrugged, even that small movement hurting his aching head. "You know I'm always up for a good puzzle, and I enjoyed this one thoroughly. Besides, it gave me a sound excuse to escape all the construction. Kit should be finished by now."

Now there was no reason for Rand not to go home to Oxford. Except Lily.

Today, sunlight sparkled off the Thames, and the fresh air felt good in his lungs. Pounding along the banks, his feet seemed to be saying, *se-duc-tion, se-duc-tion, se-duc-tion.*

He laughed at himself; what a pathetic case he'd become. His next breath was a huge one, drawn in through both nose and mouth, meant to cleanse his body and head. But with it came a faint scent that made alarm slither down his spine.

Fire.

He stopped and turned, scanning the horizon. There it was. Slightly inland and to the west, dark smoke puffing up to smudge today's clear blue sky.

Trentingham was over in that direction, he realized with a jolt of panic.

A moment later he was running faster than ever in his life.

~

*Y*ESTERDAY LILY had awakened with the sniffles and a scratchy throat, so she'd stayed home while Mum and Rose went out calling. Today, she'd awakened coughing and sneezing and could barely drag herself downstairs to tend to her menagerie. After completing her chores and nearly nodding into her breakfast, she'd crawled back into her nightgown and collapsed into bed for a much needed nap, half expecting not to open her eyes again before dark.

But now she lay teetering on the brink of wakefulness,

vaguely wondering what had roused her from sleep. She was tired, so tired her whole body ached, and she could tell from the color behind her closed lids that it was still midday. She rolled over, intending to drift off again, to seek more healing slumber—

Shouts. The stench of burning wood. Her eyes popped open, and she leapt from the bed and rushed to the window, her knees trembling.

Smoke billowed into the sky—light gray, dark gray, menacingly black—and below that, red and orange flames licked upward, rising from what looked like the soon-to-be-roofless barn.

Her animals were in there. Her heart racing, she grabbed a wrapper and struggled into it even as she ran for the door.

TWENTY-ONE

"*Y*OU CANNOT GO back in there, my lord! It's about to collapse! They're only animals! Not worth your life!"

Rand ignored the frantic stable hand's warning, waving him toward the long bucket brigade bringing water up from the river. Coughing, he set down the badger and quickly scanned the small collection of dazed creatures.

The hedgehog, the fawn, a rabbit, a weasel...Lily had said she was planning to release the rat, and he prayed that she had, because he hadn't a chance of finding anything that small in the blinding smoke. But he'd seen a shadow in the grayness...the fox cub, he suddenly realized. The fox cub with the broken leg.

This one cannot run, he heard Lily say in his head. This one couldn't survive without him.

He'd originally raced into the blazing barn because he'd needed to make sure Lily wasn't in there. But once inside, he'd remembered her face, her gentle hands as she cared for her strays. He couldn't leave them to die. Not the ones he'd already saved, and not the fox cub, either.

To more cries of "No!" and "Stay back!" he charged once more into the conflagration. What air remained was hotter than his first two trips, and drier, searing his lungs. Flames thundered, their orange, white, and blue tendrils licking up the wooden walls. Billowing black smoke threatened to blind him.

He stumbled toward Lily's makeshift pens, coughs wracking his body as he peered through the haze, his eyes blurred with burning tears. Frantically he searched the enclosures, finding nothing. The blaze roared all around him, the sound filling his head, battering his senses.

Heat lashed him in scorching waves. He couldn't see; he couldn't breathe; he couldn't stay in here a minute longer.

This one cannot run...

He pictured Lily saying the words, kneeling beside a pen, *right there.* Sucking in acrid air, he reached down blindly, his fingers encountering soft, trembling fur.

And then he was on his way out, the cub a gasping, hot bundle in his arms, both of them searching for cool, healing air. Just as he cleared the door, a mighty crash sounded behind him, and for one terrifying moment he seemed surrounded by raining sparks.

Then there was light, and he could breathe, and someone was pulling the cub from his arms. "Oh God, oh God, oh God," someone cried, whacking him on the back. It made him cough more, and he tried to twist away, to run away, but he only stumbled. His eyes were still streaming and he couldn't see, but whoever it was followed him.

"You're on fire!" she screamed, and it was Lily's voice, and he stood still and let her beat upon his back until at last she stopped.

"Oh God," she said again and took him by the hand to pull him farther from the flames. They both collapsed to the ground. Rand rubbed his eyes, feeling grit, his head swimming in a haze of smoke and unreality.

He blinked until his vision cleared. He and Lily gazed at each other, ash and soot drifting around them and settling slowly to earth like a dark, eerie snowfall.

"You saved my animals," she whispered, quiet tears rolling down her cheeks.

"You saved *me*," Rand croaked through his raw throat. Still coughing, he reached a hand behind to touch his back, but it didn't hurt enough to be burned.

"It was your hair." Lily coughed, too. "Your hair was on fire."

He reached higher then, to the ribbon that bound the queue he wore when he ran, and it was still there—but the hair below it felt wiry and crumbled in his fingers.

"I'm sorry," she said, coughing some more.

He shrugged, still feeling dazed. "It hardly matters. It will grow back." They both coughed together. "Did the smoke get to you, too? Or are these sympathy coughs?" he said with a weak smile, then frowned, peering closer, finally noticing how she looked. "You're wearing a nightdress. You're ill, aren't you? Rose is at Lakefield now, as usual, but she failed to mention you're ill. You'll catch your death—you shouldn't be out here."

Her cheeks flushed pink. She took the robe clenched in her fingers—the one she'd used to beat out the flames—and draped it over herself. Once white, it was streaked gray and black from his hair. "You shouldn't be here, either," she said. "What are you doing here?"

"I was running and saw the smoke." His head cleared, and suddenly he realized the fire was still raging. "Go inside, Lily. Lie down. Your animals are safe." Even now, a couple of women were busy moving them to the stables. "I need to help here."

He pushed to his feet and came face-to-face with Lily's mother.

She laid a gentle hand on his arm. "You should go inside, too. You've done enough."

"But the barn—"

"It's hopeless, and the rest is under control."

Rand turned to see. Although the bucket brigade was still operating full force under the direction of her husband, the men weren't fighting the fire, instead drenching the surrounding area to prevent its spread. The barn itself—or what was left of it—was burning merrily despite their earlier efforts.

Lady Trentingham forced a wan smile. "It was old and needed replacing. So long as no one's hurt, it's no great loss. Come inside. I'll fetch some water so you can rinse off the soot." Without waiting for his agreement, she hurried toward the house.

His hands were coated in black, and he wanted to wash his face. Imagining he looked like hell, he reached to help Lily rise. The sunshine was dimmed by the veil of smoke overhead, but not so much that he couldn't see the outline of her body through her thin white nightdress. He thought it wise not to mention that, however. She sneezed twice during their slow progress to the house and looked even worse than he felt.

Well, her poor red eyes and nose did, anyway. The rest of her looked magnificent.

By the time they stepped indoors, Lady Trentingham had a basin and towels set up in the drawing room. She ushered them both inside, handing Rand a clean white shirt and Lily a fresh robe and a pair of shears. "I must see that ale is brought to the men," she said and rushed off.

Lily looked shocked to be left alone with him, but Rand was too tired to care. She hurried into the robe and belted it tightly at her waist. He pulled the ribbon out of his hair, then looked down at his grayish shirt, noticing all the tiny black holes where sparks had singed it. With a shrug, he began to strip it off.

Her mouth dropped open, but she didn't avert her eyes.

Seduction, he remembered.

Hoping she was enjoying the view, he pulled the shirt over his head and turned to the water.

TWENTY-TWO

*L*ILY'S GAZE WAS glued to Rand's back, watching the muscles ripple as he washed all the black soot off his hands and arms, then his face and neck. She'd never seen a man's bare back, unless she counted Rowan's, but he was still just a boy. And Rowan's back didn't look like Rand's, either; it looked rather like her own or Rose's. Rand's tapered from wide shoulders down to narrow hips, and every muscle was defined beneath the taut skin.

Feeling her fever rising, she dropped onto a chair.

Drying his face with a towel, he turned. "Why did she give you scissors?"

"Hmm?" Swallowing hard, she tore her gaze from his chest and looked down to where her fingers, white-knuckled, gripped the shears. "I suppose she thought you'd want to cut off the burned part of your hair."

"Oh. That makes sense." His voice sounded huskier than normal—from the smoke, she imagined. But whatever the reason, the deep words seemed to vibrate right through her. He tossed away the towel and grabbed her father's shirt. "Will you cut it for me?"

"Me? Cut your hair?" Her breath was coming short. He

dropped the shirt over his head and tugged it into place. Though it was a bit small, it did cover him sufficiently.

She couldn't decide whether she found that a relief or disappointing.

"Well, I cannot cut it myself, not and make a good job of it," he said reasonably, shoving the bottom of the shirt down into his breeches. For some reason, watching that made her breath come even shorter. "Most of it's on the back of my head," he added.

"It? Oh, your hair. Yes. I suppose it is." She began to clear her throat, but when that hurt, she coughed instead. "Sit down, and I'll do my best to cut it."

"I cannot." He indicated his filthy breeches and the cream-colored upholstery. "Can you stand?"

She did, noticing her knees felt shaky. Her illness must be worsening. Her arms felt weak when she raised the scissors and began snipping off the scorched hair. It smelled terrible and looked awful.

"I'm so sorry," she said from behind him, mourning the gorgeous mane.

He shrugged, the shirt tightening across his wide shoulders. "It was my only vanity. It's probably as well that it's gone. I'll have more time for my work now that I won't be caring for it."

She laughed, glad he wasn't cross. And her animals were safe. Her heart lightened as she carefully snipped. "Why?" she asked.

"Why what?"

"Why did you risk your life to save them? You don't even like animals."

"I don't *dislike* animals, and I'd certainly never want to see any creature suffer. Just because they're not my reason for living doesn't mean I don't care."

"Oh." It sounded so simple when he put it that way. So reasonable. So Rand. And she wanted to say that animals weren't *her* reason for living, either—that people, especially special people like him, were much more important.

But she shouldn't be saying something like that, because he might get the wrong idea. And then she might be tempted to break her promise to Rose, and then—

"But if you want the God-honest truth," he continued, "I wasn't thinking of the animals when I saved them. I went in looking for you, afraid you might be trying to save them yourself. And then, when you weren't there—" His voice broke, and he cleared his throat. "When I rescued those creatures, I was thinking of you, Lily, and how you'd feel if they perished."

She stopped snipping and started shaking. He'd saved animals for her, risking his life and losing his hair in the process. He couldn't...she couldn't...

"Lily?"

"I'm almost finished." She drew a deep breath and made a few more cuts. But it was hard to concentrate, because she was afraid she'd just fallen in love with Rand Nesbitt.

She hadn't seen him in a week—a week spent craving his kisses, a week spent searching her soul. A week spent at war...a ceaseless battle between her own growing feelings and her loyalty to her sister. A sister who was getting more and more annoying in her seemingly hopeless pursuit of Rand.

And this—this impossibly selfless, wonderful thing that he'd done for her—was threatening to push her over the edge. Push her, for the first time in her life, into breaking a promise. Rose would never forgive her, but that hardly mattered, because even more important, she would never forgive herself.

He turned and met her eyes, and she feared her knees might buckle.

"Are you finished?"

"I think so." She sneezed, and then coughed, and then gave a long, deep, miserable sniffle. "Yes, I'm finished."

"You should go to bed, then. I'll walk you to your chamber."

"Rand, you cannot."

"Of course I can." He took her arm and started marching her

toward the staircase. "You're ill and I'm exhausted. I can assure you nothing untoward will happen."

Truth be told, she was glad for his support as she trudged up the steps. Beatrix appeared and followed behind. "Thank you," Lily said primly when Rand had delivered her to her door.

"Go on, get in bed."

Supposing he wouldn't leave her alone until he saw her settled, she sighed and picked up the cat, then climbed under the covers, still wearing her wrapper. "Thank you," she said again.

Rand remained standing on the threshold. "May I come in?"

Lily's heart hitched, and Beatrix began hiccuping. "That would be quite improper."

"Your mother left us alone."

"She does things like that. Mum has never been overly concerned with propriety." When she sneezed, embarrassingly loudly, Beatrix leapt to the floor. "At least so long as others are not around to observe."

"Ah," he said, "I remember. The Ashcroft motto. *Interroga Conformationem*, Question Convention." He glanced down to where Beatrix was ribboning between his legs, rubbing against his smudged boots. "What the devil is she doing?"

"She likes you."

"Why?"

Lily shrugged. "Why not?"

"I'm a dog person." In an attempt to get away, he sidled into the room, apparently forgetting that Lily hadn't granted permission. Bored by his disinterest, Beatrix scampered out the window to join Jasper on a tree branch right outside.

Rand immediately strode to the window. "There's ash drifting in," he said as he slammed it shut. When he turned, he stood stock still and looked around.

Lily followed his roaming gaze, trying to envision her bedchamber through his eyes while she dabbed her stuffy nose with a white-on-white monogrammed handkerchief.

White carpeting covered much of the dark oak floor. Her bed

was hung with white lace panels and piled with plump white pillows. More white lace draped the windows. Her dressing table and washstand boasted white marble tops.

"It's very virginal," he finally said.

She blushed, then grimaced, knowing her cheeks now matched her red nose and eyes. She watched him wander to the mirror above her dressing table. It was framed, of course, in white.

He stared at himself, skimming his fingers along the bottom of his hair, which now stopped short of his shoulders. "Do I look bad?"

"No. Only different. You...I suppose you could wear a periwig," she added, hoping he wouldn't, although most noblemen did.

He turned from the mirror. "I think not," he said tersely.

She nodded, absurdly relieved. Even now, Rand's hair was too pretty to cover up, all those shimmering colors mixed together. Long hair or short, he looked utterly handsome. So handsome her throat tightened just looking at him, and it was sore, so that made it hurt, and anyway, she couldn't tell him how handsome he was, because that might give him the wrong idea.

He'd worried that she might have been in the barn. He'd saved her animals. She was afraid she might love him, for all of that and for so much more.

What on earth was she supposed to do now?

Nothing, she reminded herself. She'd made a promise. One that was getting increasingly harder to keep.

"I'm tired," she said. "Could you possibly leave now?"

He didn't. Instead, he walked over and leaned down and set his lips on hers, claiming her mouth in a gentle kiss.

Hot already, she melted into the heat of the caress. His lips tasted of Rand, but also of the smoke he'd encountered rescuing her strays.

When he drew back, he looked blurry, and she blinked her eyes to clear them. "How?" she asked in a daze.

Completely uninvited, and apparently forgetting his stained breeches, he shoved aside white lace and sat beside her on the bed. "How what, sweetheart?"

She blinked again at the endearment. "How can you kiss me when I'm so ill and ugly?"

"You're not ugly." He grazed his knuckles along her heated cheek. One finger trailed from the little indent in her chin to trace the ruffle edging her wrapper. Then it slipped beneath, and beneath her nightgown, too, skimming the swell of a breast.

No man had ever touched her there, and it felt marvelously scandalous. Her skin prickled with excitement, and her head swam with more than fever. Despite being hot, she shivered.

"You'll always be beautiful to me," he said in a way that convinced her he meant it.

And he wanted her. She remembered that. She'd been thinking about that all week, at times even getting cross—her, Lily, cross!—with Rose for so stubbornly standing in her way.

But Rose would never, ever forgive her...

"I missed you," she blurted out without thought. "This past week, I've missed you."

Rand's fingers stilled as he gazed at her, the deliberate seduction forgotten.

Had anyone else ever missed him? Really missed him? He seriously doubted it. He and his closest friends, Ford and Kit, could spend months apart—years, even—without truly missing one another.

For Lily to miss him seemed a great gift. An honor he could only hope to deserve. He wanted her more than he'd thought it possible to want another human being.

"I missed you, too," he said simply, because he couldn't think of a way to put it better. He leaned to kiss her again, hoping his lips would tell her what he couldn't seem to put into words. Feeling the heat in her skin, he made it a chaste kiss, but no less heartfelt.

He pulled away before the need pulsing through him drove him to try something he might regret.

"Oh, Rand," Lily said on a sigh...and then, "Oh, Rose," in a pained whisper.

Refusing to register the rejection in her eyes, he gave her another gentle kiss. "I'll come see you again tomorrow afternoon, Lily. I hope by then you'll be feeling better."

The plan was working; he was sure of it. Despite the fact that three sets of eyes watching from the tree outside the window made him more than a bit nervous, he walked away humming.

TWENTY-THREE

*T*HE NEXT DAY, Lily was feeling somewhat better and refused to stay in bed. Having always believed that looking better made one feel better, she chose a pretty periwinkle gown. When her maid dressed her hair, she asked her to wind silver ribbons through the curls to match the trim on her dress.

None of this, of course, had anything to do with the fact that Rand had said he'd be paying a call.

As her maid was finishing up, Rowan wandered in, looking much worse than she felt. His black hair stuck up in places, as though he'd been plowing his fingers through it, and his eyes appeared dark and haunted.

Lily nodded permission for the maid to take her leave, then turned to face her brother. "Rowan, what's wrong?"

"I'm just..." He came closer and began playing with a perfume bottle on the dressing table where she was seated. "Did you tell Father and Mum about the fire-making things I took from Ford's laboratory?"

"No, of course I didn't." She rubbed a hand over the back of his head, smoothing his hair where he'd mussed it. "That was between us."

His narrow shoulders relaxed, then tensed again. "How about Rose? Did Rose tell them?"

"Not that I know of. Why are you so worried about this? It was a mistake, and you learned not to take things, didn't you? Everyone makes mistakes."

The bottle made a rhythmic noise as he ran it back and forth on the marble tabletop, its gold painted designs glinting in the sun from the window. "I thought...well, I thought maybe Father and Mum would think I started the fire with the fire-making things. But I didn't have any of those things, I swear. I gave them all to Lord Randal, and I haven't taken any more from Ford's laboratory. Truly, Lily, I haven't." His hand stilled as he met her gaze in the mirror. "I...I just don't want anyone to think the barn burned down because I was playing with Mr. Boyle's fire-making things."

"Nobody thinks that. Has anyone said that to you?"

He shook his head.

"Nobody is blaming anyone for starting the fire. These things happen, and we're all happy that no one was hurt. It was an old barn that Father was planning to replace anyway."

He looked relieved—almost—before he resumed playing with the bottle, making circles this time. "You know what you said about making mistakes? How everyone makes mistakes?"

"Yes, everyone does." Goodness, did she know. She may have made the worst mistake of her life promising Rose.

"Well, I made one," Rowan said. "A really bad one. I thought something would be funny, but it wasn't. It went wrong, and it wasn't funny at all."

Her promise had gone wrong, too. Horribly wrong.

But knowing her brother, she was sure his mistake had been nothing like hers. Lucky for him, he wasn't old enough to make such a monumental mistake. A mistake serious enough to ruin his whole life.

She put her hand over his, stopping the motion. "Was it a prank?"

Not looking at her, he nodded.

"Sometimes," she said, "we don't think things through before we do them." She hadn't thought at all before making that promise. Not for one moment. If she'd stopped to think, maybe she would have said no.

"But I feel terrible, Lily."

She raised a hand to turn his face gently toward her, meeting his regretful green gaze. "If it was truly an honest mistake, you cannot let it make you feel so terrible. Just learn from it and act differently in the future. This mistake—did anyone get hurt?"

He shook his head violently.

"Then don't be too hard on yourself. You shouldn't suffer for the rest of your life because of one simple mistake."

"Are you sure?"

"I'm sure."

"Don't you even want to know what happened?"

"No. It's between you and your conscience," she told him, glad to find he had one. Her brother was growing up. Besides, it had only been a misfired prank. "Do you want to tell me?"

"No." He smiled, a true smile. "You're right. I shouldn't suffer for the rest of my life. I think I'll ride over to Benjamin's house and see if he wants to go fishing."

"You do that," she said. And with one more grin, he was off, knocking over the pretty bottle in his mad rush to leave.

She righted the blown-glass container, wishing she could right her own wrong so easily. Hers had been a simple mistake, too, an honest mistake. A promise she'd made impulsively, never dreaming it would come back to haunt her.

Rand would be here this afternoon, and she hadn't the faintest idea what she'd say to him. But he wouldn't arrive for hours yet. Feeling restless but not up to anything strenuous, she decided to closet herself in the drawing room and pass the time with some soothing music.

As the chiming of the gilt mantel clock struck noon, Parkinson ushered her friend Judith inside.

"Keep playing," Judith said with a wave of one plump hand. She walked closer and brushed her fingers over a bright new flower arrangement that Rose had set on a small table beside the harpsichord. "What's this song?"

"I'm not sure." Her fingers flying over the keys, Lily smiled. "Rand hums this sometimes."

"It's cheerful."

"I thought if I could work out the notes, he might enjoy hearing it, whatever it is. He told me he would visit this afternoon, so—"

"Visit you in specific?" Judith looked delighted. "I knew there was something between you. Has he asked your father for your hand?"

"No!" Lily's fingers stilled, the abrupt silence a statement all its own. "You know I've been told I can make my own decision," she said quietly. "And Rose wants him."

She couldn't tell Judith about the promise, because suddenly she was embarrassed she'd even made it. But how could Rose have asked it of her? Like earlier in the week, anger burst forth, and she tried her best to push it back down inside.

Judith sat beside her on the bench. "You look sad," she observed. "What do *you* want, Lily?"

"Does it matter? Rose is older." Lily coughed. "She should wed first, don't you think?"

"Nonsense. Not if you're in love." Judith paused while Lily coughed some more. Her tone turned melancholy. "I would give anything to be in love with Lord Grenville."

Maybe Judith was right. If Lily truly loved Rand, should she suffer all her life because she'd made a simple mistake? What had she told Rowan?

But unlike Rowan's mistake where no one had been hurt, breaking her promise would hurt someone. Someone she loved dearly, even though she was cross with her now.

Lily gazed at her friend, tears welling in her eyes for them both. Then she gave an enormous sneeze—a sneeze that made the flowers beside the harpsichord quiver.

They both laughed as she pulled a handkerchief from her sleeve and noisily blew her nose.

"Lily," Judith said. "I'm so sorry I made you ill."

"It was worth it to see your wedding gown." Wiping her eyes, Lily smiled. "You're better now?"

"Much. I was really very ill for only a single day. The next day I was a little better, and the day following that, I was almost good as new."

"Well, I was very ill yesterday, and I feel better today, so tomorrow I shall be good as new, too."

"You're so nice." Judith's golden curls swished as she shook her head, her voice laced with admiration. "How do you do it?"

Lily shrugged. "I'm not all that nice." She didn't feel all that nice, not inside, not when she was so cross with Rose.

"Yes, you are. Most folks wouldn't be so charitable if a friend made them ill. But you're always ever so nice."

"It's the only talent I have, being nice," Lily said. "Violet is intellectual, and Rose is a brilliant linguist and has an artistic touch with flowers. I'm just nice." When her friend stared at her disbelievingly, she bristled. "It's what I am, Judith. If I wasn't nice to everyone, I'd be nothing."

"You're not nice to everyone," Judith argued.

"I'm not?" The two words came out faint and forlorn. Lily swallowed hard, ignoring her sore throat. "I try to be nice."

"You're not nice to *you*," Judith told her impatiently. "You put everyone else first."

"But that's the *nice* thing to do."

"You're so worried about everyone else's happiness, I think you forget about seeing to your own. Stop being so nice, and I think you'll be happier." Frowning, Judith glanced out the window. Her eyes widened. "There he is now."

"Who?"

"Rand." Judith blushed. "Lord Randal, I mean. Lord, he's handsome. What happened to his hair?"

"Did you not hear our barn burned? While he was rescuing my animals, his hair caught fire, and he had to cut it." Lily rose and went to the window, just in time to see Rand slide off his horse—and be greeted by her sister.

"He saved your animals? Oh, Lily, that's so romantic."

"It was very kind." She watched Rose laugh and take Rand by the hand, leading him toward the small redbrick summerhouse. Though he looked confused, he shrugged and went along.

Lily froze for a moment, feeling betrayed. By Rose? By Rand? Then she told herself not to be silly—Rose probably just wanted to show him something. Perhaps she was working on some flower arrangements in the summerhouse. And Rand certainly had no obligation to avoid Rose—not after Lily had repeatedly refused his suit.

Then Rose turned to say something to Rand, and Lily saw her face. Animated. Too animated for languid Rose.

"Something's up," Judith said beside her.

Exactly what Lily had been thinking.

"Come along." Judith took her by the arm. Firmly. "We're going to investigate."

"Investigate?" Lily stared at her friend. "You mean *spy* on my sister?"

"She would spy on you in a heartbeat." When Lily didn't budge, Judith turned her to face the window. "Look. They're both gone. She's taken him into the summerhouse." She pulled on Lily's arm. "Come along. You cannot tell me you don't want to hear what's happening."

Since Lily couldn't honestly tell her that, she went. She felt like a sorry excuse for a sister, spying on Rose, but she couldn't seem to help herself.

By the time they made it outside, they were both running. When they stopped before one of the round summerhouse's four doors and Lily reached for the latch, Judith closed a hand over her fingers. "Wait," she whispered. "Listen."

"Judith!" Lily protested, her voice hushed but fierce. "There's spying, and then there is *spying*. I refuse to—"

And then she was *spying*, after all—riveted in place by the conversation that drifted from inside.

TWENTY-FOUR

"*I*'M FLATTERED, my lady," Rand's wry voice came through the door. "But as it happens, I've set my sights elsewhere." He sneezed. "Pardon me. I seem to be coming down with something. Where are those flowers you wanted to show me?"

"Gemini! They seem to have disappeared." Lily heard Rose's practiced laugh, a tinkling, feminine sound. "Perhaps a kiss might compensate for the loss?"

On the other side of the door, Lily was so aghast she could find no words to express her feelings. "Poor Rand has caught my illness," she whispered irrelevantly.

"How is that?" Judith whispered back. As Lily blushed, her friend's pale blue eyes widened. "Oh, my Lord. He kissed you, didn't he?"

"It's not a crime. Besides, what makes you think he kissed me? I caught your illness without kissing *you*."

"I can see it in your face," Judith declared. "You—"

"Hush. I cannot hear." Lily wondered if Rand and Rose were kissing.

No. Rose was talking. "I wonder," she mused in a speculative tone, "if the lady you've set your sights on has ten thousand pounds to bring to a marriage. It seems to me a mere professor could use that sort of money. A windfall like that would allow you to live the gentlemanly life you were born to."

Judith's mouth dropped open. "Lord, she must be desperate," she said over whatever Rand replied. "I cannot imagine—"

"Hush!"

"And I wonder..." When Rose paused, Lily imagined her running a seductive hand down Rand's arm. Or worse. She was relieved when her sister continued talking. "I wonder what my father, who is out in his gardens as always, would do if he found us alone in here together, hmm?"

Lily gasped. "That's so unfair to Rand, threatening to trap him like that! She's the one who lured him in there!"

"Unfair to *him*?" Judith's whisper came through gritted teeth. "How about *you*, Lily? Is Rose not being unfair to you?"

"Goodness, Rose would never hurt me on purpose! We love each other. But she's so focused on herself I doubt she's even considered I might be seriously interested in Rand."

"Well, then, it's about time she found out," Judith said, and with that, she flung open the door.

Since Rand was opening it at the same time, Judith fell into his arms, landing with a thud against his chest. He took the time to steady her before stepping away. "Pardon me, my lady. I was just leaving."

"Thank you, my lord," Judith said dreamily.

And a little inanely, Lily thought. She stepped into the summerhouse to join them. "This is my best friend," she told Rand, "Lady Judith Carrington." She turned to Judith, not at all sure she liked the dazed look in her friend's eyes. "And this is Lord Randal Nesbitt."

"I'm pleased to make your acquaintance," Rand told Judith pleasantly. "But I'm afraid I must take my leave."

"No." Judith seemed to regain her senses, casting a glance to where Rose stood in the shadows. "It's Rose who's leaving." She marched over and took Rose by the arm. "Come along, Rose."

Rose planted her feet. "I'm not finished talking to Lord Randal."

Slender Rose was no match for Judith's solid build. "Oh, yes, you are." Undeterred, Judith tugged her through the door.

"You're supposed to be my friend," Rose protested loudly as she found herself dragged through the gardens.

"I *am* your friend." Judith's voice was getting fainter. "And as your friend, I insist on saving you from further embarrassing yourself."

Their voices faded. Lily and Rand were left alone. The cool, shaded summerhouse seemed filled with an expectant silence.

Rand sneezed.

"I'm sorry," they both said together.

He cracked a smile. "What are *you* sorry for?"

"I'm sorry you had to put up with my sister's nonsense."

"I'm sorry you had to overhear it."

"I'm sorry I made you ill."

His smile widened. "Ah, but I'm *not* sorry I kissed you."

"I'm sorry you're not kissing me now."

"I'm sor—what?"

He blinked and took a step closer, and she rushed into his arms.

Whatever had been holding her back had suddenly vanished, like the moon on a cloudy night. Promise or no, Rose didn't deserve Rand, not after she'd called him a *mere* professor. Not after she'd tried to bribe him and then trick him into marriage. If Lily had thought she was cross with her sister before, now she was really learning the depths of that emotion.

But she didn't want to think about Rose now. Not when Rand was right here, holding her close, not when she finally felt free to touch him without feeling like she was betraying her sister.

She raised her hands to his face, feeling the slight roughness on his cheeks. She slid her fingers into his hair, the short strands soft and slippery as silk. He wore no fragrance but just smelled like Rand. Clean and warm. His scent made her head swim, more enticing than the costliest perfume.

She went on her toes to press her lips to his, but couldn't quite reach. He was so tall, and she was too short.

"I never dreamed *you* would ever come to *me* for a kiss," Rand said, sounding stunned. "Shall I meet you halfway?"

She laughed, the noise joyous to her own ears. Her heart felt light enough to escape her chest and float away. Rose had put Rand in a very awkward position, and Lily had overheard it, and somehow, that had changed everything.

When their lips finally met, the moment felt like a gift, an instant that would live in her heart forever. The kiss sang through her veins, and Lily knew for certain she was in love.

She could no longer deny that she wanted this man more than she'd wanted anything else, ever.

She parted her lips, inviting him in, sinking into the velvet warmth of his caress. What started out sweet and tender turned reckless and hungry, his mouth slanting over hers, his tongue sweeping inside, making her dizzy. A happiness burst in her—a happiness that made her feel as though she could touch the stars in the sky.

He kissed her eyes and her cheeks and her chin, the wild pulse in her throat, the skin revealed by the wide neckline of her silver-trimmed gown. Her hands sneaked beneath his midnight blue surcoat and around him, skimming his thin cambric shirt to feel the sleek muscles she'd seen yesterday. Her legs threatened to buckle under her, and she pressed herself closer, wanting more.

She'd felt something, a magical something, from the first time this man had touched her. Now, suddenly, the kisses weren't enough. Her heart beat madly, and she ached for more of his touch. When he began easing down her bodice, instead of protesting, she arched, wordlessly offering herself to him like some forbidden fruit.

Rand knew the moment she gave herself over. He sensed desire singing through her body, heard need in the soft moan that escaped her lips. At that moment, he suspected she'd let him take her right there on the hard brick floor.

And at that moment, he also knew he couldn't do this. He dropped his hands and stepped back.

They gazed at each other, their unsteady breathing the only sound in the small, round building.

He wanted her. He wanted her so much that he hurt. But he would wait. Because his need for her now went beyond the physical—even more than he wanted her body, he wanted her heart.

Love. Ford was right, this had to be love. It wasn't a comfortable emotion, but it was there, and it wouldn't be going away. Rand needed Lily—her sweetness, her faith in him, the way she made him feel—more than he needed to breathe. And he wanted, more than anything, to make her feel cherished in return.

He couldn't remember ever putting anyone else first, before himself. It could only be love, no matter that he'd believed it would never happen for him.

Never say never, he thought with a rueful laugh.

Readjusting her gown, Lily looked flushed and beautiful—and disconcerted. "Why are you laughing? Why did you stop kissing me?"

He couldn't explain it. The plan had been working. He and Lily were bound by a certain something—magnetism, Ford would call it—that he'd never felt with any other woman. He could win her, he knew, with the plan.

With seduction.

He was glad it had worked for Ford. But the plan, both times, had been conceived in a drunken haze. And the sobering reality was that no matter how much Rand's body begged him otherwise, seduction was not the way he wanted to win Lily.

Strong as it might be, there was so much more between them than lust. When she agreed to be part of his life, he wanted that decision to be made with her head and her heart, not just her body.

He moved closer but kept some necessary distance by placing his hands on her shoulders. "I want you to play a song for me."

"Pardon?" Unsure she'd heard right, Lily searched his intense gray eyes. Her senses were still spinning. Her knees were still weak.

"I want you to play a song. On the harpsichord. And I'll sing."

"Now?"

"Now. Right now. In your family's drawing room. Will you do that for me, Lily?"

She nodded, too confused to bother asking why. Right now, there was little he could ask for that she would refuse.

He took her hand to leave, but before she could even register how good it felt to have his fingers linked with hers—before they cleared the door—her father walked in.

"Have you seen my ironclad spade?"

Struggling to control her heart rate, Lily took a deep breath and quickly scanned the dim summerhouse. There was no spade. There wasn't anything in here, in fact, save the narrow wooden benches attached to the circular wall.

"It's not here, Father. Why don't you ask the head gardener?"

"Hmm," he said. "I was hoping it would be in here. Perhaps I should ask the head gardener." Muttering to himself, he turned and left.

Rand sneezed, using his free hand to block it. "Pardon me," he said.

"You *are* falling ill."

He shrugged. "Your father didn't hear your suggestion."

"I never expect him to hear anything. If he does, I consider myself lucky."

"He wouldn't have said a thing had he found me alone with Rose, would he?" Sounding incredulous, Rand raised their still-joined hands. "He didn't even notice I was here."

"Well, what did you expect?" Lily grinned. "You're not a flower."

TWENTY-FIVE

*I*N THE FICKLE way of summer, the sky had clouded up while Rand and Lily were in the summerhouse. Beatrix, Lady, and Jasper appeared and followed them back to the house. Claiming he didn't want an audience, Rand maneuvered to get through the door without allowing them inside.

The animals went around and entered through one of the drawing room's windows instead.

Lily sat at the harpsichord and arched her fingers over the keys, then hesitated. Her nose was dripping. She pulled the handkerchief out of her sleeve and dabbed.

"Go ahead," Rand said. "Blow."

Love, she supposed, meant being able to blow your nose in front of the man. So she did, even though she was no timid nose-blower.

It didn't seem to scare him away. In fact, in the middle of her blow, he sneezed again, and then he fished a handkerchief out of his pocket and blew his own nose, too.

"We're wrecks," Lily said, thinking it felt strangely wonderful to comfortably share an illness. She faced the keyboard again. "What do you want me to play?" She suspected the tune she'd been practicing for him wasn't what he had in mind.

He thought for a moment. "Do you know the one that starts 'Let's love and let's laugh'?"

Like so many popular songs, it had no title, but she did know it. She nodded.

He leaned against the harpsichord. "Then play it, please."

When she did, his gaze locked on hers as he began to sing.

> *"Let's love and let's laugh,*
> *Let's dance and let's sing;*
> *While shrill echoes ring;*
> *Our wishes agree,*
> *And from care we are free,*
> *Then who is so happy, so happy as we?"*

Although there were three more verses, he stopped singing, still holding her gaze. She played a few more bars and then stopped, too.

For a moment, the room was so quiet she could hear the clock ticking on the mantel.

"Did you hear that, Lily?"

He wasn't referring to the clock. "The words?" she wondered. *Let's love.* Could he mean...

Her heart skipped a beat, and she nearly missed what he said next.

"The words fit us, don't they? But no, I didn't mean the words. What did you *hear*?"

"What did I hear?" she echoed faintly, feeling confused. But her heart began pumping a little faster. "It sounded good. *You* sound good. You have a wonderful voice."

He stepped closer. "But my voice doesn't sound nearly as good alone as it does together with your music. It doesn't sound as complete." His gaze still held hers in thrall. She could lose herself in those eyes. "I want that with you, Lily. I want you to provide the melody for my songs. And I, the words to your tunes."

He seemed to be talking about more than music. Her blood rushed even faster. Did she dare to hope she could hold on to this newfound happiness?

"Don't say anything," he said, still watching her. "Not yet."

Lady chirped in the window, and Jasper chattered, and Beatrix wound around Rand's legs.

Yet he had eyes only for Lily.

"I'm just a professor," he said.

Rose's thoughtless words had affected him. Hurt him. For a moment, Lily felt a degree of anger toward her sister she hadn't thought possible. "Rand, you aren't *just* anything. Not to me."

He slid onto the harpsichord's bench and shifted to face her, taking her hands. "I want you to listen. I *am* just a professor. I live in a house. Once it's finished it will be a very nice house, but just a house all the same, not a mansion like Trentingham. And it isn't perched on land that stretches as far as the eye can see. It sits in the middle of a town with other buildings all around it."

Was he asking her to marry him, or explaining why he couldn't? "I don't care—" she started.

He stopped her by squeezing her hands. "I'm a second son. I may have the word *Lord* in front of my name, but that's only a courtesy title. I'll never sit in the House of Lords like your father. I could attend court if I wished, and London balls, but the fact is, I don't. Or I haven't," he corrected himself. "I'm willing to go to such events if doing so would please you, as long as it's not during term time."

This *was* a prelude to a proposal. Her breath caught, and she coughed in reaction. "I don't care," she repeated. "Rand, I—"

"I'm not finished." He coughed, too, then furrowed his brow, as though he was trying hard to remember everything he wanted to say. "You should know that I earn a nice living. But you should also know that it's been years since the marquess supplemented my income."

"The marquess?"

"My father. But like I said, I do well enough." When his gaze swept her gown, she felt as though he were disrobing her with his eyes. "I expect I can afford to dress you in the lovely manner to which you're accustomed," he added with a grin.

She smoothed her periwinkle skirts. "I'd wear sackcloth to be with you," she said quietly. "You just sang of love and laughter. Money cannot buy that. Besides, I do have a marriage portion. Three thousand pounds."

Three thousand pounds was a more than respectable dowry, considering the average shopkeeper earned less than fifty pounds a year. But Rand didn't look as though he cared, as though the money mattered at all.

At their feet, Beatrix started hiccuping, and he leaned to pick her up. "What of your animals?"

It was startling to realize she hadn't considered them, even more startling to see Rand—an avowed dog person—with her cat on his lap.

He absently stroked Beatrix's striped fur. "I do have a garden," he started; but then a corner of his mouth curved up in a rueful half smile. "Well, I don't expect your father would consider it a garden, but I've a patch of land behind my house. I can ask Kit to toss up a shelter of sorts...but it won't be the grand animal home you've been envisioning."

The fact that he cared about her dreams made tears prick in her eyes. "It sounds perfect, Rand, enough for the strays I have now. And once I come into my inheritance... well, I always envisioned building here at Trentingham, anyway. I can hire local people to care for the animals." It was what she did for the weeks when she and her family went to London, and the employment, however temporary, had always been appreciated. "Perhaps I'll be able to visit—"

"Of course you will. Oxford isn't far, and I expect you'll want to see your family often."

"A positive statement," she observed, risking a tiny smile. "Does that mean you're finished trying to talk me out of..."

She couldn't say the rest of it. He hadn't, after all, formally asked her to marry him. And the possibility was so shockingly new to her, she hadn't yet thought it over. So she let the words hang there, waiting.

It seemed like forever.

"Yes," he said at last. He squeezed her hands again and leaned near, until his mouth nearly touched hers. His eyes were so close she could see flecks of black and steel blue in the gray. His breath teased her lips, making them tingle. "Since I've apparently failed to talk you out of it, what do you say, sweetheart? Can we play and sing together for the rest of our lives?"

His words were calm and measured, as though he were proposing a business arrangement.

But his heart was in those amazing eyes.

Unlike Rose, Lily admired Rand's success in the face of his family's disapproval. That strength was one of the things she loved about him—through good times and bad, a woman could depend on a man like Rand. But she knew him better than Rose did. She knew that beneath the self-sufficiency lurked a hurt little boy who needed someone to hold him.

Did she want to be that someone? Was she willing to do it at the expense of her sister? Could she, for the first time in her life, be selfish enough to put herself first?

She remembered Rose's behavior in the summerhouse and knew the answer was *yes*.

And she didn't even have to say it. He read her response in her eyes, and both joy and relief leapt into his.

Then their lips met, and her heart took flight. She'd never thought she could feel such happiness. He was everything she'd wanted, and she hadn't even known it. He kissed her over and over, and she wished he would never stop.

A part of her wondered if this was really happening, because it felt like a magical dream. A fantasy come true.

When he finally pulled away, he uneasily eyed the assorted creatures who'd been watching. Appearing startled to find Beatrix on his lap, he set her atop the harpsichord. "I certainly hope they don't expect to witness our wedding night," he said wryly.

She blushed and laughed, then laughed even harder when they both began coughing.

Life was wonderful, even with a stuffy nose.

TWENTY-SIX

*W*HEN LILY AND Rand told Mum they had news for the family, her eyes sparkled with delight.

"Since your father's already in the gardens," she said, "why don't you find him and then wait by the twenty-guinea oak? In the time it would take me to explain why I want him to come inside, I can gather everyone else and meet you there." A wide smile on her face, she hurried off.

It didn't take long to find Lily's father, who happened to be weeding a flower bed near the oak, using a hook and a forked stick. Lily decided to let him continue puttering.

She and Rand waited beneath the tree. "I should have told Rose first," she suddenly realized, knowing her sister was going to be devastated. A stab of sympathy took her by surprise.

Rand shot a glance to her oblivious father before wrapping an arm around her waist. "Because of your promise?"

"You knew?"

He squeezed, drawing her closer. "Your mother would never forgive you if you told your sister first."

"True," Lily murmured, realizing a second truth: She didn't want to tell Rose first. She didn't want to deal with her own anger or her sister's.

"Hey." He tilted her face up and touched a finger to the dent in her chin. "You're supposed to be happy right now."

"I am," she said and smiled.

Next Rowan hurried out to meet them under the gigantic oak. "Benjamin couldn't fish," he said with a pout. "Mum said you have something to tell us?"

"Yes," Lily said, "we do."

"So what is it?"

She tweaked his nose. "You'll have to wait for everyone else."

With a small huff of impatience, he leapt to catch the lowest bough that branched off the huge, twisted trunk.

"It's a big tree," Rand commented, looking like he didn't quite know what to say to Lily's little brother. She supposed that living at a university, he hadn't much experience with eleven-year-old boys.

"Zounds, it's bigger than big." Rowan swung back and forth, looking up at the cloudy sky through the canopy of leaves. "This tree has been here for more than three hundred years. And Father says we must never chop it down, even though it destroys the symmetry of his gardens."

"Symmetry." Rand raised a brow. "That's a big word for a lad your age."

Hauling his feet up, Rowan crouched on the big branch and began climbing. "I know," he said proudly, his voice drifting from above. "What does it mean?"

Rand and Lily both laughed.

"What's that?" Father demanded, noticing all of them at last. Lily laughed even harder, her amusement ending in a volley of coughs.

"It means balanced proportions," Rand said loudly enough for even her father to hear.

"Ah, symmetry," Father said. "You know, I've been advised to chop down this twenty-guinea oak for the sake of symmetry."

Amid more laughter, Rand moved closer to Lily's father so

the man could hear him better. Rand was patient with him, she thought. Not many men would be.

Yet another reason to love Rand Nesbitt.

He raised his voice. "Why do you call it the twenty-guinea oak?"

Father smiled, always eager to answer that question, eager to tell the story that Lily had heard countless times. "A passing timber merchant once offered me ten guineas for the wood, saying it was quite the most enormous tree he'd ever seen."

"Ten guineas, not twenty?"

"I'm getting to that," Father said. "Well, the truth was, I'd been thinking of chopping the old boy down anyway, seeing as it impairs the symmetry of this garden. But I'm not one to act too rashly, you see, and so I told the merchant I'd like to think about his offer overnight. Next morning, bright and early, the fellow was at my door, increasing his offer to twenty guineas." Father waved the long, pointed fork in his hand. "I figured that if the wood's value could increase by a hundred percent overnight, the tree was an investment worth keeping."

Rand laughed out loud, and Father grinned. Lily was glad they seemed to get along. But her smile faded when her mother arrived with Rose and Judith.

The gray sky might be threatening a gentle summer rain, but Rose's expression looked like thunder.

Fresh sympathy tightened Lily's sore throat.

Rowan dropped from the tree. "What is it? You can tell us now. Is it something happy?"

It was, for her and Rand. Lily felt like her emotions were riding a seesaw, but she couldn't help the smile that returned to her face. "Lord Randal has asked me to marry him."

Suddenly everyone was talking at once.

Mum threw her arms around her. "I knew it! Congratulations, dear."

"Can Jewel come to the wedding?" Rowan asked.

"No," their mother said. "Jewel is related to Violet's husband, not Lily's." She kissed both of Lily's cheeks, then pulled back and winked. "Even though I didn't arrange the marriage, I wish you every happiness." Not one to stand on ceremony, she turned into Rand's arms next. "Welcome to the family."

"Thank you," he said, hugging her back rather awkwardly. Lily gave him credit for trying, knowing her family could be overwhelming.

Rowan tugged on her gown. "Lily?"

She kissed his forehead, laughing when he blushed and pulled away. "Jewel may attend," she told him, "if her parents agree." She wanted her brother to be happy, too, and after all, it was *her* wedding. She ought to have a say in the guest list.

Her wedding, she thought in a daze. It still didn't seem real.

"What's all this?" Father asked.

Rand cleared his throat and raised his voice. "With your permission, sir, I'd like the honor of wedding your daughter."

"If you know my daughter well enough to wed her," the earl bellowed back, "you know she's not about to ask my permission. None of my flowers ask me before doing anything."

"We can all hear, darling," Mum reminded him. But he had Lily wrapped in a hug and wasn't paying attention. When he released her, he turned to shake Rand's hand.

"Well done," he yelled, and Lily just smiled and shook her head. If Rand could get through this day with her family, she reckoned he would learn to fit in just fine.

Judith tapped her on the shoulder, her pretty face lit up with a grin. "We're going to become old married ladies together!"

Lily gave her friend a hard hug, wishing Judith could be as happy about her own wedding. "Let's get married before we worry about growing old."

"Yes," Rose said, "*I'm* the one who's old."

Finally, having put it off as long as she could, Lily turned to her sister.

Rose's dark eyes were black with fury. "How could you?" she asked.

How could she *what*? Lily wondered.

What did her sister mean by those three words? How could she break her promise? How could she marry before her older sister? How could she steal a man her sister wanted? How could she be so selfish as to see to her own happiness?

All of it, undoubtedly, Lily thought with a resigned sigh. But while her heart ached for her sister's pain, and she regretted her part in causing it, she refused to accept the guilt.

Rose had no right to ask for that promise. She'd never had a prayer of winning Rand. Some things weren't meant to be.

And others *were* meant to be, like Rand and Lily.

Wanting to explain, Lily took her sister's arm to draw her aside.

Rose shook her off. "Don't touch me. You promised." She did move away from the others, though, closer to the oak. "How could you?" she repeated.

"Because I love him, and I should never have promised, and I couldn't *believe* the way you treated him in the summerhouse—"

"You said you'd help," Rose interrupted through gritted teeth, "and then you told me to do the wrong thing on purpose." As she talked, she advanced on Lily, backing her into the oak. "I went over to Lakefield every day to try to assist with that translation, but he wouldn't even hear of it." Mindful of everyone else, she spoke in a harsh whisper, but her face was right in Lily's, her eyes flashing fire. "I always knew showing my intelligence was the wrong way to win a man!"

The rough bark bit into Lily's back, and she hit her head against it, trying to get some distance from Rose's vehemence. "No, it isn't," she protested. "It's the right way. Rand was just the wrong man."

"Oh, I don't want to talk to you!" With a swish of her skirts, Rose crossed her arms and turned away.

Shaking, Lily walked back to the others.

"I think we shall have a picnic tomorrow to celebrate," Mum said brightly. "With champagne."

Rowan made a face. "No champagne."

"You don't have to drink any," Lily said woodenly, rubbing her head where it hurt. She looked up at the sky and wished she felt more like celebrating. "It will probably be raining anyway."

"Nonsense," Mum said. "If it rains tonight, it shall be clear and beautiful tomorrow."

"A picnic sounds very nice." Shooting Rose a concerned glance where she still stood near the tree, Rand moved to wrap an arm around Lily's shoulders. "Thank you, Lady Trentingham. And I should like to invite your family to Oxford the day after that. Lily should see her new home. I'll give you the grand tour, and you can all stay overnight. I've no furniture yet in my house, save in the one room I've been using to sleep, but an inn lies directly behind it."

"An inn," Rowan breathed. "May we go, Mum?" He looked more excited about the journey than he had about the champagne—or the marriage, for that matter.

"We've stayed at an inn only once since Rowan was born," Mum explained to Rand, "and he was too young to remember." She smiled at her son. "Yes, Rowan, I expect that we can go. I should like to see where my daughter will be living. And Rose always enjoys traveling, don't you, Rose?"

She looked to Rose, but Rose wasn't there.

Lily turned just in time to see her march up the portico steps and slam into the house.

"I'll go after her," Judith said sympathetically.

"No, I'll talk to her." Mum started toward the house, then paused to look back at Lily. "Don't worry, dear. You've done nothing wrong, but she's hurting now, and I can't say I really blame her. She'll come to terms with it sooner or later."

"I hope it will be sooner," Lily said with a sigh.

Despite her love for Rand, if her own sister couldn't be happy for her, she wondered if she could be truly happy herself.

TWENTY-SEVEN

"*WELL*, Chrysanthemum," Joseph said as she crawled into bed that night, "your daughter is betrothed as planned. Are you happy?"

"Happy? I'm not sure who's more miserable, Rose or Lily. Or me."

Rand and Judith had left. Rose had taken supper in her room. Chrystabel had spent over an hour trying to soothe her, then another trying to convince Lily that her sister wouldn't hate her the rest of their lives.

Rain pattered on the window, spelling doom for her picnic, and a headache was brewing, relentlessly hammering her temples. She hated when everything didn't go the way she'd planned.

"Roll over," Joseph said. "I'll rub your back."

She did, snuggling into the feather mattress and sighing when his hands began to work their magic. For a spell she just lay there, letting his fingers knead away her tension.

"Better?" he asked after a while.

"Getting there." The pounding in her temples was fading to a mere annoyance. "I'm afraid Lily might change her mind."

"No, she won't." He rubbed circles on the small of her back. "She's in love."

"You finally noticed?"

Running his thumbs down her spine, he snorted. "I haven't the talent you seem to possess of discerning a person's feelings by the look in his or her eyes. I know she's in love because you told me."

"Ahh." The sound was half agreement, half bliss. "Lily is feeling very badly, though, that Rose is hurting. I'm afraid she'll break the betrothal because her sister is unhappy. Choose her relationship with Rose over Rand."

He trailed his fingertips lightly down her legs. "Have you no sympathy for Rose?"

"Of course I do. She's my daughter, and I ache for her. Although she had no right to bind her sister to that ridiculous promise, I understand that she feels betrayed. And yes, her words in the summerhouse were unwise, but I don't believe for a minute that our Rose is truly that calculating. I suspect she sensed Rand slipping away and acted unthinkingly, out of desperation. Alas, our Rose never has been one to think before words leave her mouth. But she doesn't truly love Rand, and Lily does, which is why I'm worried that Lily...um...Joseph?" One hand was sneaking under the hem of her nightgown. "That's not my back."

"Is it not?" he asked, his voice a study in innocence. "I expect I should rub up higher." He did—higher on her bare legs. "I'm sure Rose will recover."

"Of course she will. She'll be after another man by next week. Which is why I'm more concerned about Lily at the moment." She paused, listening to the soft rain, her body beginning to tingle as Joseph reached even higher. "I hope it's still raining tomorrow," she said suddenly.

"Hmm...?" While his fingers sent pleasure spiraling through her, he began kissing the back of her neck, little kisses that made her shiver. "Won't the rain destroy your picnic?" His warm breath stirred the baby hairs on her nape.

She flipped over to look into his eyes. "Lily and Rand will still picnic. In the summerhouse. Alone. There isn't room for all of us in there, as you know…but it would be a shame for them to miss their betrothal picnic."

Moving over her, he blinked. "Chrysanthemum, you know what happens when two people in love are left alone."

"Exactly," she said, curling a hand behind his neck. "And after that, there will be no more thoughts of ending the betrothal, will there?"

"My love, you have a devious mind."

"And you adore me for it," she assured him, tugging him close for the kiss they both craved.

TWENTY-EIGHT

*T*HE SOFT drizzle of the night before had given way to real rain today, but Rand borrowed Ford's old carriage and rode to Trentingham even though it was obvious there wouldn't be a picnic.

He was surprised when Lady Trentingham came to meet him, carrying one of the new umbrellas imported from France. As he climbed down, she stepped closer than he would have expected and held the contraption over both of their heads. "Come along!" she said. "My skirts are getting wet."

Obediently he walked beside her, feeling silly under the expanse of oiled canvas. Only women carried umbrellas—only wealthy women, come to that. Rich or poor, men wore hats and got drenched. "Where are we going?" he asked.

"To the picnic, of course." Both her hands clenched on the curved ebony handle, she hurried him through the gardens. "Lily was so disappointed that it was raining, I decided to set up the picnic in the summerhouse. I was nearly finished when I heard your carriage arrive. Here we are." She stopped before one of the four arched oak doors.

He opened it, blinking at the dimness beneath the dome. It was empty—of people, in any case. Though it was a bit hard to tell in the gloom of the dreary day, there seemed to be items inside that hadn't been there the day before.

"Go on in," she told him, shifting the umbrella to one hand to fish a little paper package out of her pocket with the other. She gave it to him. "Light the candles. I'll go fetch Lily."

As she went back through the gardens, almost but not quite running in her fashionable Louis heels, he unfolded the package and found a few more of Mr. Boyle's fire-making things. He drew one of the sulfured sticks through a fold of the paper and began lighting candles.

There seemed to be dozens of them spaced out on the benches along the wall. After nearly tripping over something in the center of the summerhouse, he decided to skirt the perimeter instead.

When he was finished, the little circular chamber was alight with a cheerful glow. Plenty enough to illuminate the "picnic" Lady Trentingham had set out on the benches. Platters of fruit, bread, sliced cheese, and sweets. A bottle of champagne and two goblets.

Only two?

And the thing that had almost tripped him turned out to be a pallet set in the center of the brick floor. He stared at it, dumbfounded, until Lily blew in through the door, wearing a summery apricot gown that belied the rainy day.

Lady Trentingham stood on the threshold, the front of her umbrella dripping onto the bricks. "Well, then, I'll leave you two to enjoy your picnic."

Rand glanced at Lily, but she looked as confused as he felt. "Where is everyone else?" he asked.

Lady Trentingham waved a hand. "Unfortunately, there's not enough room." She didn't look particularly sad about that. "I didn't want you and Lily to miss your betrothal picnic, but the summerhouse is rather cramped, don't you think?"

"We could take everything into the house," Rand suggested.

"Or we could get rid of this." He indicated the pallet, which covered most of the floor.

"Heavens, no. It wouldn't be a picnic in the house. Nor if you're sitting upright on a bench, now, would it? And unlike the grass in my husbands's gardens, the bricks are entirely too hard to make do with a blanket or rug."

While that was true enough, Rand eyed the pallet warily. Although there were no covers or pillows, it reminded him too much of a bed.

A bed he'd be tempted to use.

Lily was an earl's daughter, a sheltered country girl. He respected that. He respected himself for doing the right thing yesterday. For not seducing her before they were wed.

"Don't you think we should have a chaperone?" he asked her mother.

"Of course not." Her laughter sounded a bit forced. "You're betrothed, and it's the middle of the day. Besides, you have Lily's menagerie to watch over you."

He hadn't noticed them wander in after her, but now he looked around. Lady was perched up in the rafters, Jasper was under a bench, and Beatrix was winding between his feet.

They would likely make very good chaperones, Rand thought wryly.

Since he had run out of protests, Lady Trentingham wished them a good picnic again and took her leave. When the door banged shut behind her, all was quiet save for the sound of the rain on the copper that capped the domed roof.

For a moment Rand just gazed at Lily. "Were you *that* disappointed to miss the picnic?"

"What are you talking about? Mum said *you* were disappointed."

They both began laughing.

It felt good to laugh, Rand thought. His life had been all too serious up until now.

He removed his wide-brimmed hat and set it on a bench.

"So, do you picnic in here often?" he asked, reaching for a strawberry. He popped it into his mouth and moved the platter to the pallet.

"Never." She pulled a grape off a bunch, but stood rooted in place. "It really *is* too small, as Mum said. When we entertain in the garden, though, we sometimes use it to shelter the food. And my sisters and I like to come out here in the summertime. It's a nice place to sit and read or play a game. If you open all four doors, the breeze flows through, yet it keeps the sun off our faces."

He moved the platters of cheeses and sweets. "Preserves your lily-white complexion, does it?"

She smiled at his play on words. "When we were young, Violet and Rose and I could spend days in here. We used to take playing cards and lay them out end-to-end on the floor to divide the space into pretend rooms. Then we'd play house."

"Divide it into rooms?" He stopped setting up the picnic in order to eye the small area. "They must have been minuscule."

"When you're tiny, even little spaces feel large." Her grin widened, but she looked awkward, tracing the scars on the back of her hand as though she didn't quite know what to do with herself.

"Come and sit by me," he said, drawing her down beside him on the pallet. She tucked her legs beneath her, her movements graceful as a swan.

Lady Trentingham had neglected to supply any tableware, so he broke an apple slice in two and fed half to Lily, enjoying the way her eyes widened as his fingers brushed her mouth. "It sounds as though you had a happy childhood here at Trentingham."

"I did." She swallowed, concern darkening her eyes. "Was there no happiness in your childhood at all?"

"Oh, yes, until I was six. Then my mother died and my father changed. Or maybe he'd been that way all along, but I hadn't noticed. Mother had always been there for me, perhaps taking my part...I was young...I don't remember." He shook his head. "I remember only how it felt after she was gone."

"Lonely," Lily said softly.

He nodded, thinking that loneliness was a feeling he'd carried with him for far too long. But now, with her, it was gone. "I don't feel lonely now."

Her smile was a little bit sad. "Do you never see them, then?" she asked. "Your father and your brother? Or hear from them? Ever?"

"Not in the last eight years." He'd thought that if he forgot about them the anger would disappear, but there were others at Hawkridge he'd done an all-too-good job of ignoring as well. Like his endearing foster sister, who had followed him around with hero worship in her eyes. "But my father has a ward, a girl named Margery Maybanks who was brought to our home as an infant. She writes to me sometimes."

Not nearly often enough, and he missed her. Of course, that was his fault. Reading news of his family made ripples in the nice calm life he'd made for himself—so much so that he often went months before answering Margery's letters.

"Does she tell them about you, then? Does your father know you're now a professor?"

"Oh, he knows. According to Margery, he said that just went to prove I never belonged in his privileged world."

Her heart leapt into her eyes. "I cannot imagine what it would be like if my parents weren't proud of my accomplishments. And my sisters and brother, too. That's what family is all about, why we need them around us."

"I've done all right without family."

"Because you didn't have one," she said stoutly. "But you will now."

Rand's throat seemed to tighten. Her support meant the world to him. Although he'd decided long ago that his father and brother could go to the devil, he'd never realized how important it was to have someone who cared.

Lily crumbled some bread for the bird and the squirrel and broke up some cheese for the cat. "I thought you'd be deathly ill today. I was certain you'd send your regrets, and here you are, all recovered it seems."

"I'm surprised I fell ill at all. You'll find I'm of a strong constitution—perhaps it's all the running."

Rand watched warily as the animals came closer to claim their portions. When Beatrix climbed right over him, Lily laughed.

"How is Rose doing?" he asked, pouring more champagne. He dropped a strawberry into Lily's. Watching the drink fizz, he remembered the first time he'd tried this new beverage, at Ford and Violet's wedding.

Lily sobered and took a big gulp of the bubbly wine. "Rose is very cross with me."

"I'm sorry to hear that. Violet told Ford you'd never consent to wed me, for fear of hurting your sister." He raised his goblet in a toast. "I'm glad she was wrong."

They drank, solemnly, gazing at each other over the goblets' rims—and Rand's heart seemed to swell with unaccustomed emotion. Setting down both their goblets, he gathered Lily into his arms.

She surprised him by pressing her lips to his in a kiss both sweet and seductive. He wondered if he'd ever get used to her coming to him for kisses. His heart melted as he kissed her back, thanking the Fates for sending her to him.

Rain pattered on the roof far above. "I love you," she said quietly.

"I know," he returned, his voice filled with husky wonder. Until now, he'd never realized that love could make him whole. Never realized a part of him had been missing.

She filled that gap, making him complete. And now he wanted to show her how very grateful he was that she'd come into his life to make that incredible difference.

He shrugged out of his surcoat before easing her back on the pallet, snuggling his body over hers. When he kissed her again, she released a blissful sigh. He kissed her mouth and her forehead and her throat, trailing his lips over her soft, fragrant skin. The scent of lilies. For the past few weeks, just a whiff of that scent had sent his pulse to racing, and now he could hardly fathom that he was here all alone in a summerhouse with his sweet Lily.

Well, nearly alone. Midkiss, he cracked open an eye to find three creatures watching. As though daring him, Lady pecked at more bread and then took flight, landing right on his head.

He jerked up, breaking the kiss and sending the bird fluttering to a bench. "Do you think we could put them outside?"

"Hmm?" Lily's lids fluttered open, the blue of her eyes hazy, dreamy.

"Your animals." He swept them with an uneasy glance. "Could we just…lock them outside for a while?"

She blinked. "It's raining. They'll get wet."

"They're animals, for heaven's sake. So what if they get wet?" But she looked determined, so he added, "Never mind."

Maybe if he closed his eyes he could ignore the fact that they were there. He did that and went back to kissing Lily. She felt so warm against him, and so soft, her curves melding to his body, her mouth tasting so *right*. He wished he could kiss her forever.

Or at least his head wished he could kiss her forever. Other parts were telling him that would never be enough.

"When shall we be married?" he asked the next time he came up for air.

Looking flushed and a little bit flustered, Lily levered herself back to a sitting position. "Violet and Ford were wed two weeks after they became betrothed, and—"

"Two weeks?" Still lying on his side, Rand leaned up on an elbow. He propped his head on one hand and reached to play with a lock of her hair. "It won't be easy, but I suppose I can survive that long."

"That long? Mum has been complaining about that rushed

wedding ever since. She wishes to make a proper job of it this time. Six months, she said—"

"Six months! I cannot wait six months."

She smiled. "Neither can I. That is why I talked her into six weeks."

"Oh. I suppose six weeks is survivable."

"It will pass quickly enough. I'll be busy with wedding plans, and you with your house. We'll be married before Michaelmas term starts in mid-October. And I hope that in the meantime Rose will come around..."

Her voice trailed off sadly.

"You're not having second thoughts, are you?"

She took a minute to answer, a minute during which he held his breath. "No," she said at last. "Not really."

The words had come too slowly, too reluctantly. Rand's heart hitched. "Lily—"

"I'm *not* having second thoughts," she repeated and then launched herself at him, knocking him back to the pallet as she crushed her mouth to his.

He kissed her and laughed, sheer joy mixed with relief. But something inside him had shifted. All at once, even more than he wanted to show her how grateful he was that she'd come into his life, he wanted to make her his. Permanently.

Six weeks suddenly seemed a long, long time.

With a wistful sigh, he pulled away before things could go any further. Lily's little sound of frustrated disappointment matched his own feelings all too well. He sat and reached for another strawberry. "Does she always hiccup so much?" he asked, indicating the cat.

"No. Or at least she didn't used to. It's odd the way she's been doing that lately." She pulled off her shoes and reached beneath her skirts to untie a garter.

Rand blinked. "What are you doing?"

She rolled down a stocking. "Do you usually wear shoes to picnic?"

"I don't usually picnic," he said dryly. He'd allowed little time for idleness in his life. As her other stocking came off, he swallowed hard. "You're not going to take anything else off, are you?"

"No," she said quickly; then her eyes glittered. "Unless you want me to."

Oh, he wanted her to, all right. He forced a laugh. "Your mother shouldn't have left us here alone."

"Perhaps not." She looked down, then raised her lashes slowly, revealing a steadfast blue gaze that pierced him to his soul. "But I'm glad for it," she added in a breathy whisper.

Rand was finding it hard to breathe. He sipped more champagne and watched her stretch her bare feet out before her, fluffing her skirts over her legs and allowing him a glimpse of slim ankles.

Her actions were innocent, he was sure. But innocently seductive.

She wiggled her pretty toes. "Oh, that feels so much better." Leaning forward, she smiled. "Let me help you with your boots."

Not sure he could stand her help, he tugged them off before she had a chance. She smiled knowingly, as though she were aware of her own allure and his resulting discomfort.

Maybe Lily wasn't as innocent as he'd thought.

"Have a nun's biscuit," she said. "They're my favorites." She handed him one of the round treats. "You look hungry."

He was, but not for almonds and lemon. A nun's biscuit, of all things. Just what he needed: a vision of chaste nuns while the woman he loved was tempting him to sin.

He bit into the sweet, crisp biscuit, then tensed when she reached to wipe stray crumbs from his mouth before replacing her fingers with her lips.

Lily's mouth was sweeter than any biscuit he'd ever tasted. It was all he could do to keep from tearing her gown off then and there. As it was, he found himself drawing her down to the pallet again.

Or maybe she drew him down. He wasn't sure. And lost in the moment, in the pleasure of her mouth on his, he didn't care. For several long, heady minutes, his world was he and Lily and the incredible wonder of two people made for each other.

Until he felt sandpaper rubbing his toes. "What the devil—"

She laughed, a sound of pure merriment that drowned out the rain. "Beatrix, stop licking Rand's feet." Leaning on an elbow, she held up a bite of cheese, and the cat wandered over to take it with its delicate pink tongue.

At least it *looked* delicate. "I thought it would feel wet," he said. "And soft."

"Has a cat never licked you?" Lily laughed again. "Beatrix seemed to find you so delicious, I'm tempted to taste your toes myself."

That would be his undoing. Just imagining that scenario made the aforementioned toes—and other parts of him—prickle with awareness.

He sat up and shoved the rest of the nun's biscuit into his mouth, and then, for good measure, began humming a distracting tune.

Only it wasn't nearly distracting enough.

TWENTY-NINE

*L*ILY SMILED to herself. That song again. She'd almost worked out how to play it, and she looked forward to the surprise.

But not right now. Now she only wanted more kisses.

Rain beat on the roof above, blending with the tune that wafted from Rand's throat. The sounds combined to create a rhythm that went right through her, mirroring the excitement that thrummed through her body.

Despite the wetness outside, the summerhouse was warm and snug. Candles flickered all around them like stars, seemingly working magic. Although, in all honesty, she wasn't sure whether this cozy wonderland was Rand's doing or her mother's, the romantic ambience worked on her all the same.

Or maybe it was just Rand. Ever since he'd first touched her, she'd burned for more. For everything. For weeks she'd denied it, but now they were going to be wed.

Everything had happened so fast. Only yesterday she'd thought of Rand as Rose's, but now, miraculously, he was hers. And she wanted him with a fierceness she'd never even imagined. A fierceness that completely took her by surprise.

Six weeks. It seemed like forever. She moved closer again and pressed her lips to his.

The humming stopped. "Oh, Lily," Rand said, but his words sounded more like a groan. She worried for a moment that he was cross, but he didn't seem cross. He didn't push her away. Instead, he curved a hand around the nape of her neck and deepened the kiss.

The lips that had been soft and gentle earlier were urgent now, more fervent. He kissed her until she felt breathless, senseless, his mouth trailing down to play in the sensitive hollow of her throat.

His lips felt so good against her skin. His tongue drew warm circles on her flesh, moving lower, delving closer to the cleavage revealed by her low neckline. Her heart raced faster as new sensations rippled through her, not only where his mouth teased her, but other places, too. An ache was building inside her, a most strange and wondrous feeling.

Wishing to make him feel the same way, she reached to unknot his white cravat.

Rand lifted his head. "You cannot do that," he murmured.

The lace-edged fabric came untied, and she began drawing it from his neck. "I want to do to you the same thing you're doing to me. I want to make you feel—"

"You *cannot*."

She stopped, stunned by the vehemence of his words, the steely gray of his eyes. "Why?" she breathed.

"Because if you do," he said very slowly, "I fear I may not be able to keep from doing more."

Was that all? She smiled as the cravat slid free.

"Lily—"

"Rand." Her mouth feeling suddenly dry, she licked her lips. Her heart pounded so loudly she feared he could hear it above the rain and her own harsh breathing. Rising to her knees to face him, she caught his silvery gaze. "I want you to do more. I want *you*," she clarified, echoing his words from weeks earlier.

Now she really knew what he'd meant.

His smile looked painfully forced. "You're going to have me. We're going to have each other. In six weeks."

"I want you *now*." As her fingers went to loosen the lacing at his neck, she watched his eyes widen in shock. She'd never felt like this before—like a wanton, truth be told. And she was every bit as shocked as he—shocked not only at her boldness, but at the desire that raged through her, sweeping clear her resistance and all her inhibitions. She'd never imagined feeling free enough to offer herself to a man.

But then, she'd never before been in love.

He just stared, dumbfounded, while she opened the placket of his shirt and put her mouth to his skin as he had to hers, tasting him, faintly salty and musky, a heady flavor that was his alone.

"Lily." He raised her face and touched a finger to her chin, looking wistful. When Jasper hopped from the bench to the pallet, his bushy red tail flicking up and down, Rand swallowed hard, then sighed. "Even your menagerie disapproves."

"What on earth are you talking about?"

"You're truly bent on seducing me, aren't you? No matter what your animals think."

"They're not thinking, Rand. They're just watching."

She felt a shudder run through him. "I don't like it."

Under other circumstances, she might have laughed. "The animals watching?"

"Yes." He gave her a light kiss before his face set in determined lines. "Your parents wouldn't like it, either."

"The animals watching?" she repeated, nonplussed.

"Yes. I mean, no." He looked deliciously flustered. "I mean they wouldn't like *this*." He yanked her against him and kissed her again, hard.

She let herself slide into the demanding caress. He plundered her mouth, tasting of strawberries and champagne and Rand.

When at last he let her go, she found herself trembling with ill-contained desire.

"My parents kiss all the time," she informed him shakily. "They would certainly like it. As a matter of fact, Mum told all us girls we should make sure to kiss a man before we marry him. To ascertain we're well matched in that area. And she's an accomplished matchmaker, so I'm sure she knows of what she speaks."

Despite everything, Rand's lips quirked in a half smile. "It isn't the kissing they wouldn't approve. It's what it will lead to should you insist on going any further. Your parents certainly wouldn't like that."

He quite obviously didn't know her parents.

"Violet was born seven months after they wed. And she wasn't a particularly undersized baby."

His forehead furrowed in confusion. "What?"

"They didn't wait, Rand. And I don't see why we should, either." She watched his jaw drop open as she continued. "We'll be married in six weeks…but I want you now."

He shut his eyes momentarily. "If you say that enough times, I'll begin to believe you."

"How many times?" she wondered. "Will five or six more do? A dozen? I want you now, I want you now, I want—"

He silenced her with another kiss, a kiss so fierce she wondered if perhaps he'd given in. But when he drew back, he gazed at her, gauging her—and also gauging his own power to resist, she guessed.

Then slowly his fingers moved to unfasten her stomacher, and her heart soared. She'd won. She wanted this. She burned for him.

And besides all that, if they made love now, then later, on her wedding night, she wouldn't have to worry about—

"Are you certain?" he asked, his voice low and earnest, his eyes more intense than ever, his fingers fumbling on the stomacher's tabs. He glanced down, then dropped his hands. "I'm undressing you, and you're not stopping me."

"No." She took his hands and brought them back to the stiff, embroidered garment. "I'm not."

His hands didn't move, just rested lightly against her front. Her pulse skittered. Beneath his fingertips, her breasts felt firm and overly sensitive.

A silence stretched between them. His expression steadied and grew serious. "You do know what you're asking?"

She nodded. "I want you to make me yours."

For a moment—one split second in time—everything stopped. The rain, the animals' chattering, Lily's pulse. When it all started again, she found herself locked in Rand's arms. He pressed his lips to her forehead, a caress so cherishing it made her heart twist painfully in her chest.

At last he pulled back, his fingers returning to her stomacher, less tentative this time. Her own fingers fluttered up to untie his cuffs. Beatrix hiccuped louder. The stiff stomacher made a soft *plop* as Rand dropped it to the pallet.

Beneath where the stomacher had been, Lily was laced tightly into her bodice. As Rand untied the bow, then went to work on the laces, his gaze strayed to watch Lady flit from the bench and land gracefully beside them.

Awkwardly, he cleared his throat. "Are you sure we cannot put them outside?"

"You cannot tell me they're really bothering you."

He couldn't back down now.

Suddenly feeling frantic, she tried to free his voluminous shirt from where it was tucked into his breeches. All she wanted, it seemed, was to feel Rand's skin against her own. He seemed covered with so much fabric. Yards and yards of the frothy white stuff, all standing in her way.

With a pained chuckle he pushed her hands away and drew the shirt off over his head. One smooth, lithe motion that revealed all that warm, tempting skin, reminding her of the day in the drawing room when he'd removed his shirt to wash off the soot from the fire.

Only this time, she could touch him.

She did, running her hands up his chest, feeling the taut skin and the muscles underneath. With a small moan of pleasure, she shifted forward and spread her bodice wide. A soft gasp escaped Rand's lips as she pressed herself against him, the gossamer material of her chemise the only barrier between their upper bodies.

She released a long, languid sigh. "Heaven," she murmured.

"Not even close." Rand lifted the heavy bulk of her double-skirted gown over her head, bringing her chemise along with it…and baring her to his hot gaze.

She'd always anticipated feeling shy and embarrassed in this moment, but with Rand she felt gloriously free. She pressed against him once more. His hard chest felt warm against her nakedness—warm and sensuous as silk. Her breasts tingled, and the ache inside her spread.

"Heaven," she whispered again.

"Not yet." His fingers were frantically unlacing his breeches. He rose quickly to push them down and off, but before she could get a proper look he'd dropped to kneel again before her and reached to pull her close.

His arms went around her, and they met, skin to skin, from their shoulders to their knees. His hands splayed on her bare back, pressing her closer. Down low she could feel a hardness, a hardness that made her blood race, a hardness that told her he wanted her as much as she craved him.

"Heaven," she breathed. "This is really, truly heaven."

"Sweet Lily, you have no idea."

As Rand eased Lily to the pallet and came down beside her, Beatrix's hiccuping intensified. Lady twittered. He swept them with an uneasy glance.

"Rand?" Lily whispered.

Tearing his gaze from the creatures, he kissed her quickly,

wildly, then bent his head to let his lips trail down her throat. A hot stab of lust lanced through her. And love. It was all mixed up together, in her head, in her heart, in her body so aware she felt if Rand just kissed her once more she'd explode.

But he didn't kiss her. Instead his mouth skimmed her breasts and then fastened on one rosy peak. Warm. It felt warm and damp, unbelievably exquisite. Her hands threaded into his hair as he licked his way to her other breast and suckled there until she arched toward him. When he swirled his clever tongue, desire shot to somewhere deep inside. Her fingers fisted in his hair. Suddenly she felt the sensations were more than she could bear.

"Now, Rand."

He chuckled, sending low vibrations through her. "Slower is better, love. We've a long way to go before—"

"*Now.*"

His head shot up. "Don't you like this?"

"I like it too much." Her breath was coming short, and her entire body sang with an awareness she'd never imagined.

But besides all that, the anticipation was killing her.

It had been four years since she and her sisters had huddled here in the summerhouse, secretly reading *Aristotle's Master-piece*. The *Master-piece* had said making love would hurt the first time, and for four years, she had worried about that.

Now it was about to happen, and she wanted to get it over with. She wanted to enter her marriage free of this fretful anxiety.

"Please, Rand, join with me now."

He hesitated.

"Please."

She held her breath, watching while he shut his eyes and swallowed hard. "Sweetheart—"

"*Please.*"

He kissed her once, softly, then opened his eyes and nodded.

Lily's heart pounded, excitement blending with fear as he

began moving over her. Instinctively she raised her knees. Supporting himself on his elbows, Rand took her face in both hands and kissed her while he eased his way between her legs.

He settled against her, fitting there like they were made to go together. An incredible urgency radiated from where his body was poised to enter hers. Her blood pumped faster.

Beatrix let out a long, loud meow.

Rand broke the kiss and froze, only his eyes moving—darting between the cat and the squirrel and the bird, all scattered across the summerhouse.

"I cannot do this," he gritted out. His eyes settled back on Lily, holding her captive. "I cannot do this with them watching."

Passion burned in that gray gaze.

"Oh, I think you can," she murmured with a soft smile. And deliberately she raised her hips, welcoming him into her and at the same time bracing for the pain.

It was sharp, so sharp she cried out. Still holding her face, Rand whispered senseless endearments, raining little kisses all over her cheeks.

"I'm sorry," he whispered.

But the pain was fading already, rapidly becoming an ache of another kind...an ache so exquisite she found herself straining against him in hope of easing it.

He kissed her mouth, and then, still holding her gaze, he moved in her.

A gasp of wonder escaped her lips.

"This, sweet Lily, is heaven," he said.

She couldn't seem to speak at all.

Then they moved as one in a duet as old as time, a perfect harmony that went far beyond music and words. Slowly and then faster, the feelings building to a crescendo, higher and higher until Lily erupted in pleasure so intense she was half convinced she really was glimpsing heaven. Up and up, flying higher yet when she felt Rand go with her.

At long last, she drifted back to earth. Rain still pattered overhead, but more softly now. Across the summerhouse, the animals had quieted. Beatrix had even stopped hiccuping.

Lily opened her eyes to the magic of candles winking in the dimness. Rand was still pressed close, his heart beating in a cadence to match hers. He lifted his head to find three creatures staring at him, and with a groan, he buried his face in the crook of Lily's neck.

A soft laugh rippled from her. "You managed," she said. "With the animals watching."

"Ah, yes." His words vibrated against her throat, sounding amused. "But I hope they're not expecting a repeat performance. I'd just as soon not have an audience next time—not that this time wasn't good."

"It was heaven. I saw heaven."

"Did you?" He kissed her nose, her mouth, then leaned up and shot her a smile. "Please don't tell me you saw cherubs playing harps."

"No." She laughed again. She'd never expected to laugh at a time such as this, but it felt right.

Everything with Rand felt right.

"No cherubs," she whispered. "Only you."

THIRTY

$\mathcal{I}$T TOOK THREE carriages to get to Oxford. A valet and two maids rode in the first, along with all the luggage. The second held Chrystabel and Joseph.

"Do you suppose the children will be all right alone?" she asked.

He laughed. "Three of those 'children' are in their twenties. Relax, Chrysanthemum. It seems like years since we've had a carriage to ourselves. Come over and sit on my lap."

Smiling, she did. It *had* been years. But their offspring, with the exception of Rowan, were finally grown. "I love you," she said.

"I love you, too." He kissed the top of her head. "And I can hear you without all the chatter."

She settled against his warm form, using his body to cushion her from the jarring ruts in the road. It was a calmer ride than many, though, the landscape mainly gentle green slopes. Cattle roamed, grazing aimlessly. "Ah, this is nice." Chrystabel snuggled closer. "I wonder how everyone else is doing."

"You worry too much, Chrysanthemum."

She sighed. "I'm just wondering what happened yesterday. If anything."

"If anything? Two young people in a summerhouse…"

"One of them was sweet Lily."

He snorted. "The other was a healthy male. I used to be a healthy male, which means I know of what I speak."

"You still *are* a healthy male," she protested, knowing he wanted to hear it and also thinking it was true. He was only forty-six, after all. "But regardless, Lily remains worried by Rose's attitude, not that I can blame her. I must figure out a way to get Lily and Rand off alone together some more. Much more."

"Hey." He tilted her chin up and placed a kiss on her lips—a somewhat bouncing kiss due to the ride, but a nice one nonetheless. "Can I entice you to forget about our children for a while? Here I've succeeded in getting *us* off alone together…why aren't we taking advantage of it?"

Conversation was abandoned in favor of blissful sighs.

~

*T*HE THIRD carriage wasn't nearly as peaceful.

On one of the upholstered benches, Rand sat beside Lily, holding her hand. Across from them, Rose glared at their linked fingers while Rowan chattered, excited about his first trip to Oxford.

"You've never been?" Rand asked.

"Never."

"Neither have I," Lily added.

"And you, Rose?" Rand asked, trying to bring her into the conversation.

"No," she said shortly, still glowering.

He squeezed Lily's hand, knowing her sister's disapproval was hard on her. Remembering their encounter in the summerhouse yesterday, he could only be glad it had happened. Lily would have no thoughts of changing her mind now. Perhaps the seduction hadn't been planned or honorable, but he couldn't be sorry, not when it had bonded her to him as tightly as a book to its cover.

At least he hoped it had, he thought suddenly, relieved when her fingers squeezed back. After all, she could be with child. Although that was one thing he *didn't* hope for—not yet, anyway.

Of course, he knew the potential consequences of what they'd done, of what he expected they'd do over and over in the months and years ahead of them. And when children came along, he was certain he'd love them as much as he loved Lily. But he'd prefer some time alone with her first. He was just getting used to the idea of being a husband; he felt woefully unprepared for fatherhood as yet.

"Do you know," Lily said, dragging his thoughts back to the conversation, "we've never been much of anywhere besides London and the area that surrounds Trentingham. Oh, and Tremayne, but not for years."

"Tremayne?"

"A castle and lands our family owns near Wales. We stayed there during Cromwell's Protectorate, and again in '65 when the Great Plague was a threat. Now that Grandpapa has passed on and Father become the earl, Rowan is Viscount Tremayne."

"Are you?" Rand asked Rowan, smiling when Lily's brother nodded and puffed out his narrow chest. "Well, then," he told the boy, "you're certainly more important than I. I'm a mere lord."

"You're important," Lily protested sweetly.

Across from them, her sister groaned.

"Have you never been out of Britain, then?" he asked Rose.

"No," she said as shortly as before.

"None of us have." When the carriage jounced in and out of a rut, Lily jostled against Rand. "Where have you been?"

"Oh, Spain, France, Italy, Greece...I'll take you those places, and more."

Rose smirked. "She won't be able to talk to anyone."

Rand's concern for Lily's sister was rapidly transforming to annoyance. Deliberately he dropped Lily's hand to wrap an arm around her shoulders, pulling her closer. "I'll be happy enough to communicate for Lily."

The look in Rose's eyes told him she hadn't missed the declaration of possession—not that he found that surprising. Rose might have her faults, but he'd never considered a weak intellect among them.

They fell silent for a while.

Lily watched out the window. She rubbed the scars on her hand, determined not to let her sister's bad temper spoil this special day. As they descended toward Oxford the grazing land gave way to water meadows, and now the road was peppered with charming houses, each with a lovely, well-tended garden.

Rand began humming, that same old tune, somehow both quiet and cheerful at the same time. Lily's mind drifted, and she touched her fingertips to her lips, imagining them tender and a little bit puffy like they'd been yesterday after Rand's kisses. She'd gone to sleep last night with one hand on her mouth and awakened that way, too, lying abed too long this morning while she recalled every exciting moment of their time together in the summerhouse.

Sharing herself with Rand had been an incredibly amazing experience, and it couldn't have been wrong—not when they'd pledged their hearts. But she'd thought of little else since, and now, sitting beside Rand but unable to kiss him, to really touch him…she thought she might very well go mad.

Whenever she remembered what it had felt like to lie next to him, to have him within her, her entire body tingled. And it seemed she was remembering constantly. Now that she was no longer worried about the pain, she could hardly wait to lie with him again.

She squirmed on the seat, ordering herself to concentrate on the scenery as they crossed a river and entered Oxford. "Oh, look." She smiled at a beautiful square bell tower built of mellow stone. "It looks so old."

"Charmingly old, I hope." Rand's fingers tightened on her shoulder. "I hope you won't mind living here."

"It's beautiful," she breathed.

"We're on Magdalen Bridge, and that tower is part of Magdalen College. It was built by Cardinal Wolsey. Every May Day since 1501, the college's choir ascends the tower at dawn to greet the coming of spring with hymns."

"Oh," she said, "I imagine that must be lovely." Beyond Magdalen, they passed through the low-arched East Gate, and then they were within the city wall, its battlements interspersed with turrets. Towers of Oxford's many other colleges rose to punctuate the horizon, monuments to centuries of education.

Among the huge buildings of the university, townspeople lived and worked in smaller homes and shops under steep, sloping roofs. Few people walked the streets, but those that did looked prosperous, unlike in London where the poor slept in the gutters. "It's a quiet town in the summer months," Rand said, "but it will be bustling come October, full of students in their billowing black gowns."

"Can we climb all the towers?" Rowan asked, nearly bouncing on the seat.

"Sit still," Rose muttered.

"Not *all* of the towers, but certainly one or two," Rand promised. "I'll take you all on a walking tour later."

Following instructions Rand had given the coachmen earlier, they turned onto New College Lane, a narrow street that ran between New College and Hart Hall. Behind a small rectangular courtyard, his new house rose three stories, the left side still cloaked in scaffolding.

"Here we are," he said, somewhat unnecessarily given that the carriage had stopped behind the one holding Lord and Lady Trentingham.

The door opened, and the driver lowered the steps. Upon

exiting, Rand waved at Lily's parents, noting that they looked particularly happy and, in Lady Trentingham's case, perhaps a bit flushed.

Smiling to himself, he prayed to find such long-lasting companionship with Lily.

Looking lovely in a cornflower blue traveling gown, Lily stepped out and stared up at the rows of Palladian windows. "It's very big!"

"Did you think I'd expect Lady Lily Ashcroft to live in a cottage?" he teased. But his heart warmed to see she approved of her home-to-be.

He followed Rowan to the scaffolding, reaching a quick hand to grab the boy's arm. "No, you don't."

"Holy Had—I mean zounds, I just wanted to climb it."

"It doesn't appear at all safe for young men," Rand said. "Come, let me see if I can find Kit. I'll introduce you all—and find out why he hasn't finished as promised."

A workman came out the front door, burdened with two buckets of paint. He smiled and bowed awkwardly. "Lord Randal."

"Henry. How goes the job?"

"All but done. Mr. Martyn should return soon. He was called away—"

"Of course he was," Rand interrupted. "Isn't he always?" With a short laugh, he waved the man and his paint toward the scaffolding and ushered Lily's family inside the house.

Even though Kit was off-site, the interior swarmed with industrious men, a testament to the man's skill as a builder. "The house is designed in the classical style Kit favors," Rand explained as he led the Ashcrofts through an impressive entry and into the first chamber, a drawing room where a man was noisily installing a marble fireplace surround. "I admired many homes like this while touring Italy, so when he started sketching elevations of what he had in mind, we found ourselves in complete accord."

"It looks different," Lily's mother observed. "Plainer than other homes, but somehow more elegant, too."

"Kit and I designed it together." Rand clearly loved this house; Lily could hear the pride in his voice. "I wanted the decorative elements understated, not so grandiose as in most new homes today. And Kit has an eye for grace and balance."

"Come along!" Rowan yelled.

A bundle of energy after having been pent up in the carriage, he directed a whirlwind tour through the main rooms and the kitchen—no matter that he didn't know where he was going. Upstairs, he led them all on a merry chase down a narrow hallway between the five bedchambers.

"We designed the house with corridors," Rand explained, "so there's no need to go through one room to get to another."

Since the master bedchamber was the only room in the house with any furniture, their footsteps and voices echoed in the empty spaces. When Rowan had finished racing in and out of every chamber, he slid down the slick new banisters to the bottom. The others followed more sedately and gathered in the entrance hall on the ground floor.

"It's beautiful." Lily hugged herself and smiled, looking slowly around the square, high-ceilinged room. She loved all the architectural details, the niches built into the walls, the light that streamed through the many large windows to brighten the interior. Rather than being covered with heavy, dark paneling or a riot of intricate carving, the walls were smooth plaster.

"All white," Rand pointed out with a grin. "Virginal. Like your bedchamber."

Thinking she was virginal no more, she blushed and looked up at the classic coved cornice around the ceiling. "Will the walls be staying all white?"

"I don't expect so. My last house came furnished and decorated in a style that never quite felt like home, but I hadn't any idea how to fix it. For this one, I was planning to hire someone to choose fabrics and furnishings and wall coverings. But now that I have you—"

"She'll leave it all white," Rose interrupted.

"Rose," her mother started.

But then someone walked in, silencing Rose more effectively than Mum ever could.

Lily turned to see what had captured her sister's attention. Or rather, who. Dressed in deep blue velvet with white linen and lace, the man was tall, lean, and had the carriage of someone used to being in charge. His hair was black, his eyes a unique mixture of green and brown.

A very pleasing mixture.

"My house is still unfinished," Rand said without preamble, but Lily could tell he wasn't really cross. His long-suffering sigh was just for show. "What might be your excuse this time?"

"Will King Charles do?" the man asked, a lazy smile curving his lips. Those unusual eyes narrowed. "What the hell happened to your hair?"

"A fire," Rand said without elaborating. He turned to Lily's father, raising his voice. "Lord Trentingham, may I present Christopher Martyn, distinguished recipient of the Procrastinating Architect Award."

Lily's father smiled vaguely; then his ears seemed to perk up. "*The* Christopher Martyn?"

Kit bowed. "At your service, my lord."

"Atchur—?"

"Lord Trentingham is hard of hearing," Mum said warmly as she walked over to pull Rowan down from a ladder. "You'll need to speak up."

But apparently Kit didn't need to speak at all. Father stepped closer. "I'm looking for an architect to design one of those newfangled greenhouses—"

"Lord Martyn is busy," Rose broke in loudly. "Working for the *king*."

"I'm not a lord, my lady. Just plain Mr. Martyn. Although Kit will do."

Rose looked very disappointed to hear that, and Lily took perverse pleasure in thinking her sister couldn't call the man Lord against his wishes. Having decided she didn't always have to be nice, she was turning out to be rather bad.

But it felt better than she'd expected.

Rand performed the rest of the introductions, and then, while Kit took over explaining the details of the building, he drew Lily aside.

"What do you think?"

"I think Rose likes your friend Kit."

"That's not what I meant." He tapped her on the chin. "What do you think of the house? Will you be able to stand living here?"

Feeling wickeder by the minute, Lily pretended to consider. "I saw only one master chamber. I'm not certain that's acceptable."

He looked a bit startled. "When the plans were drawn up, I was expecting to live here alone. But it's a large enough room, don't you think? Wouldn't you rather share—"

"Let me see," she interrupted. "You're asking me to give up living with my moody sister in the dull countryside and move to this busy, academic town...hmm...and then I'll have to sleep with you every night." Watching his alarm turn to amusement, she grinned. "It sounds perfect."

"What about your menagerie?"

"Though I've yet to see the garden, I'm sure it will do fine." Perhaps it wouldn't be ideal, but it would be much, much better than living without Rand. Even suffering her sister's distemper was better than living without Rand.

Why hadn't she been able to see that all along?

"Are you certain?" he pressed, moving closer. He ran his hands up her arms until they were resting on her shoulders.

Out of habit, she shot a glance to Rose, but she really, truly didn't care what her sister thought. She, Lily, deserved happiness, too. "I've never been more certain of anything in my life."

Rand looked like he wanted to pull her against him and kiss her then and there. And she wouldn't have minded, even right in front of Rose.

But Kit interrupted. "Oh, Rand, you have some mail."

Rand was still gazing at Lily. "Later, Kit."

"One thing looked important. A missive from Hawkridge."

"Hawkridge?" That succeeded in seizing his attention. He jerked his head around and squinted at Kit. "I *never* hear from my father."

THIRTY-ONE

"NEVER SAY never," Lily said softly.

And Kit burst into laughter.

"What?" she asked, half distracted by Rand's distress but unable to ignore his friend. "What's so amusing?"

"That's Rand's saying. He's been dogging me with that phrase ever since we were wee lads."

"I think my mother used to say it," Rand said absently. "Where's this letter?"

Kit nodded. "I've been collecting your mail as it comes in. I'll get it."

"I expect we should all go upstairs to my bedchamber." Rand led the way while Kit went off to fetch the mail. "It's the only room where we can sit."

Even there, the seating was lacking. Rose took the single chair at his desk, while Rand waved the rest of them toward his enormous bed, a heavy oak four-poster with hunter green hangings. "I'm sorry there are no other chairs," he said, perching himself on a carved wooden chest. "All my furniture is in storage, and in any case, it needs replacing." He forced a distracted smile. "I'm hoping my new wife will help with that."

"I'll be honored to." Lily sat beside him. "And I promise not to choose white."

"Nothing white?" Rose looked incredulous. "Nothing at all?"

"White isn't a good color for a home with children," Lily said, feeling her cheeks flood with heat.

Why had she mentioned children? Surely nobody knew what had happened in the summerhouse. They couldn't tell just by looking at her, could they?

Her heart seized when she saw her parents exchange what seemed to be a knowing glance. But then Kit came in with a stack of accumulated mail, and her attention was drawn as Rand reluctantly took it.

He flipped through the letters and slowly pulled one out. "Here it is." Forgotten, the rest of the mail fluttered to the floor.

Kit bent to retrieve it. "You didn't believe me?"

"I was hoping you were wrong." Rand shrugged as he broke the seal. A big, black one. Then he just sat there with the paper in his hands. "Word from my father cannot be good."

Lily scooted closer. "Perhaps it's not from your father, Rand. Could it be from his ward instead?"

"I've yet to answer Margery's last letter. And she doesn't use the Hawkridge seal."

"Does your brother never send letters?"

"Alban has nothing to say to me." He stared at his name on the front. "No, this is the marquess's writing."

At last he unfolded the paper. As he scanned the single page, an expectant silence descended on the room. Impatient, Lily leaned to see the letter. The writer had a heavy hand. The ink was dark and decisive.

She looked up to Rand. His face matched the plain white walls, all the color drained, his eyes lifeless.

"What is it?"

Both his hands dropped to his sides, the paper dangling from one. "Alban has died," he said disbelievingly. "At the hands of another man."

The air left Lily in a rush. She knew Rand had harbored no love for his brother, but if she felt this shocked, she could only imagine how the news made him feel. Unsure what to say, she reached for his free hand and quietly laced her fingers with his.

"I'm so sorry," her mother murmured.

"What—" her husband started.

"Hush, darling." Mum laid a firm hand on his arm. "Rand's brother has died."

Rand shook his head as though to regain his senses. The paper crackled when he waved off the sympathy. "I never liked the man, so condolences are unnecessary. But it seems I'm now my father's heir—and the old goat wants to see me at once."

"You're going to be a marquess?" Rose looked between him and Lily, her eyes dark with envy. "The Marquess of Hawkridge? And what are you now that your brother is gone? The Earl of Something?"

"The Earl of Newcliffe," Kit said. "But none of that matters."

Rose's expression said it mattered quite a bit, as well as displaying disdain that a commoner like Kit wouldn't think so.

Releasing Lily's hand, Rand stood and began pacing. "I've no wish to be a marquess. Or even an earl. I like my life."

"Your life may not have to change, Rand. Or at least not right now." Lily watched his agitated movements, feeling helpless to soothe him. He looked like a penned animal. She suspected that if it wouldn't be so impolite, he'd leave Kit and her family here and set off running through the streets. "How old is your father?"

"Only fifty-two," he admitted. "And last I saw him, healthy as a horse."

"Well, then…"

He waved the letter again. "He wants me at Hawkridge. He expects me to leave the life I've built and learn how to run his damned estate. I don't want to do that. I've been happy with my life here…" He finally stopped pacing and turned to meet Lily's gaze. "I'm even happier with my life now."

Mum rose from the bed. "Then you should go tell him that. Both of you."

Although Lily was surprised by the idea, she still felt a prick of hurt when Rand said, "Both of us? I think not."

"Both of you." Mum sounded determined. "Since you've pledged yourself to Lily, and she to you, the two of you should face life's difficulties together. And in any case, Lily should meet her future father-in-law."

"Why? If I have my way, she'll never meet him at all."

Lily rose and moved close to him. "Rand..." Much as she loved and admired him, his relationship with his family was one area she thought could see improvement. Especially now that his "family" was just his father.

Glancing around at her own family, her heart ached for him. Now, more than ever, he needed a reconciliation. Whether he knew it or not.

"Of course I want to meet your father," she said softly. "He's part of what made you the man I love."

His gray eyes turned hard as steel. "Whatever I've made of myself, it was despite him, not because of him."

Feeling like she was becoming less nice by the minute, she set her jaw. "I'm coming with you."

Silence reigned for a span of time, an unspoken battle of wills.

When Rand finally sighed, Lily took that as agreement. "Shall we leave immediately?"

Tempered by her loyalty, the steel in his eyes softened. "No, we'll leave tomorrow. Today we'll tour Oxford and you'll all stay the night at the inn as planned. The letter was written early last week; my father can wait another day." He folded the paper as he addressed Kit. "This turn of events will give you a few more days to finish."

A gasp came from Rose. "A few more days? You two are going to stay at Hawkridge overnight? Together?"

Rand's lips curved in a wry smile. "Together with a staff of a hundred, the meanest dogs in England, and my very formidable father. He's a marquess, if you'll remember."

And Rose, Lily reflected, was unlikely to forget that.

"It's entirely proper," Mum said. "Lily and Rand are betrothed, and I'm certain there will be chaperones aplenty."

Father frowned and reached for his pouch. "Who needs a loan of twenty?"

"No one needs any money, darling." Mum patted his cheek. "Our Lily is going to visit Rand's family, that's all." She, for one, didn't look the least displeased with the developments. She turned back to Lily and Rand. "I'm glad you'll be staying until tomorrow, though. Rowan would hate to miss his tour, wouldn't you, Rowan?" She glanced around. "Rowan?"

Lily quickly scanned the chamber, although given the lack of furniture there was certainly nowhere to hide. "He's not here, Mum. Did he even come up with us?"

A moment later, they were all fanning out through the house. Knowing her brother well, Lily headed straight downstairs. Her heart lurched when sounds of a crash came through the front windows.

She hurried outdoors to find Rowan sprawled on the ground, splattered with white paint from a bucket lying nearby, its contents splashed all over the bare dirt. Above him, the scaffolding tilted at a crazy angle.

He swiped at his face, only smearing the paint more. "Zounds, that thing is rickety."

She paused long enough to shout back through the door. "I've found him! He's outside!" Then she turned to him, a hand to her still-racing heart. "Rand told you it was dangerous. Where's the painter? You shouldn't be out here alone. You shouldn't be out here at all."

Rowan shrugged. "I'm all right." He pushed to his feet—or rather, he tried to. "Ouch!" he hollered and collapsed back to the dirt.

She rushed to kneel beside him. "Is it your ankle?" She tugged off his boot.

"Ouch!" Unmanly tears sprang to his eyes. "It hurts. This is God's reckoning for my stupid mistake; I just know it."

Gently she probed his ankle, relieved to find no indication of a break, although it was swelling rapidly. Her pulse calmed. "Yes, I suppose you should have listened to Rand," she said sympathetically, still exploring the injury.

"Rand? What does Rand have to do with this?"

"Rowan, what are you *talking* about?"

"Ouch!" he wailed. "The barn!"

"The barn?" She released his foot and glanced up at his paint-stained face. "What about the barn?"

His cheeks flushed red under the splatters. "I told you about the barn."

"Told me what?"

"About the prank, and how it went wrong, but I didn't have any of Mr. Boyle's fire-making things...it was a mistake," he finished weakly, obviously realizing that although they'd talked about mistakes, he'd never admitted to starting the fire.

Or not in so many words. She should have realized, though—she liked to think she was clever enough to put two and two together. But she'd been focused on her own problems, her own mistakes, her love for Rand and her promise to her sister.

Shock and anger made her voice shrill. Rand could have died in there—as it was, his hair had burned. "You set it? You set the fire?"

"No, I didn't set it." Rowan looked half guilty, half petrified, his face gone white as the paint. "It just happened. I was trying to—"

"Rowan!" Mum called as she raced outside. "Dear heavens, you're covered in paint!"

Rowan just stared at his sister, silently willing her to stay quiet.

When he didn't say anything, Mum shifted her attention to Lily. "Is he hurt? Is something wrong?"

Lily watched Rowan swallow hard. Inside her, a sense of duty battled with sibling loyalty. By not telling Mum, was she as good as a party to the crime? The fire was a serious thing, not some minor offense like straying too far from home on a fishing outing with a friend. Rand and her animals could have perished in that fire. Or someone else.

But in the end she held her tongue. The Ashcroft offspring had never been tattlers.

"Nothing's wrong. Rowan's fine." She pushed to her feet, the anger draining away. Everything *was* fine, after all. "His ankle is hurt, but he's otherwise unharmed."

Rowan shot her a grateful glance, but he needn't have worried. He was her brother, and his secret was safe with her.

THIRTY-TWO

*A*FTER MUCH fussing by all concerned, it was determined that Rowan had only sprained his ankle.

Rand shook his head at Lily. "I thought you said he was a monkey."

"I should have said he's an accident-prone monkey. At least this time no one will have to stitch him up."

"Would you like to see my scars?" Rowan asked, past his fright and cheerful as ever.

Rand declined, and Rowan didn't remain quite so cheerful when he realized he wouldn't be able to walk around Oxford, let alone climb any towers. Since Lily's father had been to Oxford before, he volunteered to stay behind with his son. The rest of them left the two playing draughts in the common room of the Spotted Cow, the inn behind Rand's house where they would return to stay the night.

"King me!" Lily heard Rowan yell as they walked out the door, much later than they'd originally planned. Knowing that her family's raised voices would ring through the inn from now until they left the next day, she imagined the proprietor would be happy to see the backs of them tomorrow.

Their walking tour started at Wadham College, where Rand

had begun his years here at Oxford. The college was on Parks Road, around the corner and down one street from his house. "You really live in the center of things," Lily remarked.

"We will, yes." Clearly trying hard to set his troubles aside, he took her hand as they all crossed the smooth green lawn toward Wadham's elegant facade. "I hope you'll like it here."

"I love it already. This town feels so peaceful and alive, all at once."

"Wait until it's teeming with students." He nodded to the porter at the stone-vaulted gateway. "Good afternoon, Dickerson."

"Afternoon, Professor Nesbitt."

Rand led Kit and Lily's family into a graveled quadrangle. "Do you not go by Lord?" Rose asked.

"Too pretentious. Besides, I *earned* the title Professor."

"But now you're an earl."

Lily saw Rand's jaw set. "Here, I'm a professor."

It seemed he was determined to keep it that way. Not that Lily minded, but she wondered what sort of a struggle he'd be up against tomorrow. And she could tell, from the tenseness in his body, that in spite of his valiant effort to ignore the letter he was worried about it, too.

She looked around the quadrangle at the stately stone buildings, built in Oxford's traditional Gothic style. All was quiet now, but she smiled as she imagined students hurrying to meet with their tutors, young Rand and Ford among them. "The architecture matches the old colleges, but somehow it looks new."

"Only Pembroke is newer," Kit said. "Dorothy Wadham built this college in 1610."

Rose's eyes widened. "A woman built Wadham? I thought Oxford was strictly for men."

Rand nodded. "It is—even the servants in the colleges are all male. But as Nicholas Wadham's widow, Dorothy carried out his wishes. There are portraits of them both in the hall and statues just outside it. Come, I'll show you."

Gravel crunched beneath their feet as he led them across the quiet quadrangle. The figures made a striking composition framing the door, King James on one side and the founders on the other. The statue of Nicholas Wadham was holding a model of the college.

"He never actually saw it," Rand said. "They began building after his death." He tugged the heavy door open. "Go in. The hall is beautiful."

While the others went inside, he held Lily back, leaning close. "With the exception of your parents," he murmured, "I've reserved each of you separate rooms at the inn."

His breath felt warm by her ear. "Hmm?" She turned her head to steal a quick kiss.

Evidently liking that, he gave a low laugh and kissed her again. "I have no intention of staying home alone all night long."

A frisson of warmth shimmered through her. "Do you not?"

"If I happen to wander through the alley and end up outside your window, I trust you'll let me in?"

The mere idea sounded wicked and wonderful. "I can hardly wait," she whispered, her body thrumming already.

"Lily? Rand?" Her mother's voice drifted from the hall.

Lily sighed. "We should go inside."

Wrapping an arm around her waist, he pulled her close and gave her one more kiss for good measure—a kiss that left her light-headed. "Until tonight," he said softly, turning her toward the door.

Feeling boneless, she let him walk her into the hall past an entrance screen of exquisite Jacobean woodwork. She gawked at the great hammerbeam roof before her gaze dropped to the portraits of the founders. Nicholas Wadham wore a tall black hat, Dorothy a flattish cap and an uncomfortable-looking neck ruff. "They look formidable," she said.

Mum smiled. "I've heard tales enough of the pranks here to suspect they're disapproving."

Rose spun in a circle, taking in the solemn stained-glass

windows and the long rows of tables with candelabras spaced down their middles. "I cannot picture Ford here."

"He came three times a day," Rand assured her, "dutifully wearing the required robe. Ford Chase was never one to miss a meal."

Rose laughed, looking more carefree than she had in weeks. As they exited the hall, Lily noticed Kit slanting her sister a sharp, appreciative look. Well, she always had been a beauty, so long as she wasn't scowling.

Rand took them to the chapel, so they could see its magnificent east window depicting Jonah's whale, then turned to lead them out of the college.

"What's this?" Rose asked, stopping by an unassuming door to stare at four lines of lettering crudely carved into the wood.

Rand smiled. "When King Charles slept in that room one night, the Earl of Rochester wrote that."

"He didn't." Sounding wickedly intrigued, Rose read aloud.

> *"Here lies a great and mighty king,*
> *Whose promise none relied on.*
> *He never said a foolish thing,*
> *Nor ever did a wise one."*

Their collective laughter rang through the empty quadrangle.

"Charles must have been livid," Mum remarked.

"To the contrary," Rand said, "he found it quite amusing. He claimed his words were his own, while his deeds were those of his ministers."

In high spirits, they left Wadham and walked the unpaved streets. Lily already loved this city, a city so steeped in tradition that new buildings were built in old styles. She nearly burst out laughing when she noticed Lady flitting along from tree to tree, then glanced around and found Beatrix stalking them in the shadows. She decided to keep quiet about that, given that Rand was uneasy around her constant companions. But her heart sang to see that her animal friends would be comfortable here in Oxford, too.

Of course, that was assuming she and Rand ended up living here.

"The Sheldonian Theatre," Kit announced. They all stopped to gaze up at the cupola atop its domed roof. "A friend built it," he added, sidling closer to Rose. "Christopher Wren. His first large public building."

Rose failed to look impressed with either the building or Kit's friendship with the celebrated architect. "I've met Mr. Wren," she said. "He came to my sister's wedding."

Seemingly undiscouraged, Kit tried the doors and looked disappointed to find them locked. "The ceiling inside is amazing."

Rand nodded. "It's painted to look like the sky."

"But that's just ornamentation." Kit leaned against the double doors. "The ceiling itself is a wonder of advanced construction, designed with no columns to spoil the view. An apparent defiance of gravity, because Wren contrived all the weight to be supported from above."

"It's a beautiful building." Lily paced its columned front, enjoying the tour but wishing she were alone with Rand. "What is it used for?"

"Ceremonies, mostly." Rand caught up to her and took her hand, that small meeting of flesh making a shudder run through her. Perhaps sensing it, he slipped his thumb inside to tease her palm. "Matriculation, graduation, and the like. And the university's printing presses are housed in the basement."

"Can you see," Kit put in, "the street-level windows that let in light? Wren greatly values natural light. He told me he based this building on the Theatre of Marcellus in Rome."

Despite Rand's quite effective attempts to distract her, Lily didn't miss the admiration in Kit's voice. Or the touch of longing. "Have you seen the Theatre of Marcellus?"

"Sadly, I haven't." He gave a self-deprecating shrug. "I aspire to study the great buildings on the Continent, but I'm afraid I'm hopeless with foreign languages. I have nightmares of never finding my way home."

"Rose has an excellent head for languages," Lily told him.

Her sister swung to glare at her. If looks could kill, Lily thought, she'd be deader than the sculptured heads on the railing around the building.

"What's that?" Mum asked, pointing to something up high in a transparent attempt to smooth things over.

"The Tower of the Five Orders," Kit said enthusiastically. "It's the most unusual structure in all of Oxford."

He led them through an archway, a short tunnel through a plain building, and into an open quadrangle. The buildings surrounding it were more imposing than the austere exterior would suggest. Many doors gave entrance, each with a Latin inscription in gold letters on a blue background.

Rose turned slowly, translating them all. "Grammar and history, logic, rhetoric. Music, arithmetic, geometry, astronomy. Philosophy." And at the far end, "School of Medicine, School of Law, School of Theology."

"Those three are the superior schools," Rand explained. "Before attending any of those, one must pass each of the other schools first and receive his Master of Arts."

Kit wandered closer to Rose again. "You *are* good at languages."

She shrugged, but looked pleased. Kit was making inroads, Lily thought. Flattery was one sure way to Rose's heart.

He cleared his throat as he looked to their mother. "You asked about the tower." It was a wondrous sight in the otherwise rather sobering surroundings. "The Five Orders display the different styles of classical architecture, distinguished by differing columns, bases, and pedestals. From the bottom to the top, oldest to newest, we have Tuscan, Doric, Ionic, Corinthian, and Composite."

Rose looked more interested than Lily would have expected. "Who is sitting up there?"

"The statue? King James. Can you see that he's holding a book? The Bodleian Library is behind you—it receives a copy of every new book ever published. As for the rest of the building..."

Lily listened with half an ear as everyone gathered around to hear Kit talk about the Gothic carving and pinnacles. Bells began ringing from the various towers of Oxford's many colleges, their chimes all different yet harmonious. A beautiful sound. A sound she looked forward to hearing day after day, night after night, when she lived here with Rand, alone in their lovely, brand-new house.

For both their sakes, she hoped everything would work out so they could.

As though sensing her thoughts, he moved closer. When he took her hand again, excitement churned in the pit of her stomach. Though it was growing dark, it would still be hours before he could come to her, hours before they could properly kiss.

She wished she could kiss him properly right now. Or rather, *im*properly.

Goodness, it was fortunate her family was here in this otherwise empty quadrangle, or else she feared she might shove Rand to the grass and start ripping off his clothes.

One day in Rand's arms and she was turning into a shameless wanton!

THIRTY-THREE

"*L*IE STILL," ROSE muttered. Wishing she were sharing the bed with Rand instead of her sister, Lily rolled onto her stomach and rearranged her pillow. "I'm just getting comfortable," she said peevishly.

They'd arrived back at the inn to find a very apologetic proprietor. Apparently one of his clerks had miscalculated and rented out one too many rooms, leaving one too few for Lily's family. The most logical pairing, of course, was Rose and Lily together. Rand certainly wouldn't be able to join her here, nor could she join him—at least not without creating a scandal when Rose saw her leave.

Her body throbbed with newfound lust. She'd never imagined how it would feel to want a man, to wait all day, anticipating the night... and then end up aching and alone. It was torture.

Thinking she couldn't wait to be married, she flipped onto her back and sighed. At the foot of the bed, Beatrix sat up and meowed.

"Lily, will you *please* lie still?"

"All right. I'm sorry." She had to stop thinking about Rand. It had been a long time since she'd shared a bed with one of her sisters—since Violet had lived at home and the three of them had spent nights sharing their secrets. She had a whole lifetime ahead of her with Rand, and this night with Rose should be fun. Perhaps they could regain some of the closeness they'd recently lost.

"Kit is very nicely put together, isn't he?" she asked into the darkness.

"He's handsome enough," Rose admitted in a vast under-statement. "It's unfortunate he's not titled."

Lily turned over again to search her sister's face in the dim light from the fire. "He's a famous architect. Goodness, he gets commissions from the king himself! I imagine he can afford to live in a grand style. Why should it matter that he's not titled?"

"Of course it matters." Rose averted her gaze, staring up at the old oak beams in the ceiling. "Violet is a viscountess, and you —soon you'll be a countess and eventually a marchioness. Why should I settle for less?"

"You're the Earl of Trentingham's daughter, which means you could marry a guttersnipe and you'd still be Lady Rose. Besides, if you love a man, it's not settling."

"Well, I'm not in love with Kit, am I? I've barely met the man, and I've no intention of getting to know him better when he's not what I want." Rose rolled away, presenting Lily with her back. "Go to sleep. You have a journey early in the morning."

End of discussion. Lily imagined she could feel Rose's cold calculation rolling off of her in waves.

So much for growing closer.

Deprived of conversation, Lily's thoughts drifted back to Rand. Over the next quarter hour, she tossed and turned, trying to ignore her body's cravings and failing utterly.

"Go to him," Rose finally said.

"Wh-what?"

"Go to him. I won't tell Father or Mum or anyone else. Just go, so I can get some sleep."

"Rose, I—"

"I'll never like the fact that you won him, but it's a fact none-theless. Go, Lily."

"I—" She wanted to. Oh, how she wanted to. But it wasn't as though Rand were in the adjacent room. "I'd have to walk outdoors alone in the dark of the night. It isn't safe."

Her sister snorted. "It's fifty feet down an alley. Should anyone approach you, Beatrix will draw blood with her claws, Jasper will nip off the poor soul's toes, and Lady will peck out his eyes. Just go."

Lily didn't have to be told again. Nerves scrambling, she slid from the bed and began throwing on her clothes. "Thank you, Rose."

"You'd do the same for me."

"Thank you anyway." The Ashcroft siblings had always stuck together, but Rose's willingness to cover for her said louder than any words that Lily was well on her way to being forgiven.

She was relieved. And grateful.

But mostly, she was on fire.

THIRTY-FOUR

"*L*ILY?" CLEARLY shocked to find her on his doorstep, Rand opened the door wider, then blinked as her three animal friends scampered in past him.

Lily stood on the front step, shivering in the chilly night air but enjoying her surprise. The expression on Rand's face was priceless. The rest of him looked delicious, his hair tousled from sleep, his body wrapped in a dark brown brocade robe tied loosely at his waist.

She wanted her hands on that body. "May I come in?"

"Oh." He blinked. "Of course." Holding a candle with one hand, he wrapped his free arm around her shoulders and drew her inside. As he shut the door, he eyed the assorted creatures. "How the devil did they get to Oxford?"

"I told you, they follow me."

"They follow you," he repeated dryly, as though that explained nothing at all. "What are *you* doing here?"

"I missed you." She moved closer and slipped her arms beneath the silk robe. It was her turn to be surprised when she felt nothing but bare skin. She skimmed her hands over his back, smiling to herself when he bobbled the candle. "I came to talk about tomorrow. Your father—"

He hushed her with a quick kiss. "I don't even want to think about the old goat, let alone talk about him."

"I was jesting." She molded her body against his, feeling altogether wicked and wonderful. The house smelled of new wood and paint, and Rand smelled of warmth and temptation. "Since you couldn't come to my bed, I decided to come to yours."

His eyes widened, a new glint in the warm gray. "Well, then," he said, his voice turning velvet-smooth as he gazed down at her, "shall we go up to it?"

She suddenly realized what she'd said and how forward it must have sounded. Rose would say something like that and hold her head up, but Lily had just shocked herself speechless.

The look on her face must have amused him, because his lips twitched as he drew her hands from beneath his robe, raised the candle, and motioned her toward the stairs.

Her cheeks burning, she preceded him up the steps.

"I cannot believe you're here," he said from behind her matter-of-factly, as though she hadn't just proved herself a wanton.

"Rose told me to come."

"Rose?"

"Yes, Rose. She couldn't stand my tossing and turning." Lily paused on the bedchamber's threshold. As she stared at Rand's bed, the wicked feelings faded. There was a big difference between sliding into passion in a summerhouse and showing up on a man's doorstep in the middle of the night.

Placing a gentle hand on her back, he urged her inside. "I was tossing and turning myself. Couldn't sleep, so I was puzzling out some old text." He pushed aside a jumble of papers to set the candle on the desk by the door. "But Rose?"

"She's accepting us, Rand." Her gaze was still fastened on the bed. The forest green hangings were pulled back, the sheets invitingly rumpled. "She may not be happy about it, but at least she's coming around. She's not going to hate me all our days."

"I'm so glad."

At the sound of the door slamming shut, she jumped and whirled to face him. "What was that?"

"They're outside."

She put a hand to her racing heart. "Who?"

"Your animals." He grinned. "They cannot come in here. But they're not out in the rain. There's no need to worry—"

"You're impossible." Now that the bed was out of sight, safely behind her back, she was feeling amorous again. She went closer and went on her toes for a kiss. "The animals really don't care."

"*I* care." He kissed her forehead, not her mouth. "This time I don't want any distractions." His hands on her shoulders, he slowly backed her up. "This time is going to be different." He kept going, his thumbs caressing the sides of her neck, inciting a delicious shiver. "This time—"

The backs of her legs bumped into something.

The bed.

"This time," he concluded, "we'll do it *my* way."

It was a high four-poster bed with two steps leading up to it. Rand lifted her by the waist and sat her atop the feather mattress.

She swallowed hard. "*Your* way?"

"My way. Slow and easy…"

The way he said that made her suspect there would be nothing easy about it.

Her suspicions were confirmed when he began removing her shoes. Slowly. And untying her garters. Slowly. And rolling down her stockings. Slowly.

Those hot cravings she'd been feeling—the ones that had driven her to run here, the ones that had prompted her to slide her hands under Rand's robe, to brazenly tell him she'd come to his bed—were returning at an alarming speed.

"Rand?" He looked like he was concentrating very hard, his gray gaze intent on what he was doing, his fingers tracing featherlight patterns on her skin. She quivered. "Do you think you could go a little faster?"

"We did fast yesterday. I told you, I intend to go slow."

"But why?" He was driving her mad. "If we go fast," she argued, "maybe we'll have time to do it twice."

His hands fell away from her as he burst out laughing. She crossed her arms, indignant, wondering which upset her more: him laughing at her expense, or the fact that he'd ceased touching her.

Then he smilingly shook his head and said, "Good heavens, I love you." And she wasn't upset at all.

The laughter lingered in his eyes. "My sweet Lily. You seduced me in the summerhouse, but it's my turn tonight. And if you're good, we'll do it twice."

"If I'm good?"

"If you let me do it my way."

His way was exquisite torture. It took him ages just to remove her clothing, and he managed to graze every bit of her skin along the way. By the time he finished, there wasn't an inch of her that wasn't tingling with anticipation.

At last he stood beside the bed and shrugged out of his robe, his body gilded by the dim light of the single candle. He had a runner's long sculpted muscles, all shadowed in stark relief.

She could see he was ready to take her, and she was more than ready to be taken. She licked her lips and raised her arms to him, holding her breath when he eased her onto her back and moved over her.

"Lily." He felt so warm, his weight supported on his elbows, his fingertips dancing on her face. Barely touching, just enough to make her skin tremble in response. "Lily, you make me burn."

"Rand—"

"Hush." His lips grazed her ear, lightly, lightly. Pleasure rippled through her, and heat pooled in her middle. He took an earlobe into his mouth, sucking softly, and the room seemed to spin, rattling her senses.

"Rand—"

"Hush. Be good." His lips trailed down her neck, a warm swath of sensation. He rolled off her to lie next to her, tracing her waist with teasing fingertips while he bent his head to taste her breasts. It was too much at once, especially when he swirled his tongue around one rosy peak and then bit it gently.

She gasped, feeling it harden in response. Feeling *him* harden against her thigh. She reached down and wrapped her hand around him, eager to find what he felt like...warm velvet over steel. Her heart racing, she moved her fingers experimentally, and his moan made her blood race even faster.

When a scratching came at the door, his moan turned into a groan.

"It's only Beatrix," she whispered. "Ignore her."

He did. His talented mouth on her breasts roused a melting sweetness within her. He nibbled her neck while his hand moved to tease her legs, up and down their length, coaxing them apart, trailing between. His fingertips skimmed her thighs, and currents of desire rippled through her.

Then he kissed her until she was breathless, until she was senseless, until her entire world was consumed with the taste and touch of him. And all that long time his fingers worked closer to where she ached, until they were almost there.

Almost.

Lily touched him everywhere she could reach. He was so very male, his body gloriously hard compared to her softness. Her breathing quickened when his did; her heart pumped faster when she felt his pulse respond to her touch. But his hands and mouth on her remained slow and steady.

A sound of surprise escaped her lips when he rolled her onto her stomach. "Hush, Lily," he said. "Be good."

It was frustrating, because she couldn't touch him now, not really, not the way she wanted to. Her hands fisted at her sides. She felt his lips on the soles of her feet, warm and damp and ticklish, and was astonished to find her whole body was so sensitive. He nipped along her calves, paid homage to the backs of her knees, and nibbled the insides of her thighs, pausing in his upward journey to rain kisses across her bottom.

The ache was becoming unbearable. She squirmed and heard a low chuckle in response, his lips on her skin making the sound vibrate right through her.

Tiny pecking sounds came through the door.

Rand froze. "Lady?"

"Mmm-hmm." Lily came up on her elbows. "Ignore her."

Beatrix's scratching joined the pecking as Rand eased her back down to the sheets. "They seem unhappy. Maybe we should let them in."

"They're fine." She turned over and cupped one of his cheeks with a hand, loving the masculine roughness. "Ignore them. Please."

He smiled, a smile so darkly sensuous it made her breath catch in her throat. He turned his head and kissed her palm, a warm press of his lips as he held her gaze with his. "Be good, now," he said, rolling her back onto her stomach. He climbed over her and straddled her thighs. "I'm not finished."

She sucked in a breath. He was there, hard between her legs, nearly where she wanted him. His fingers danced over her back, massaging, tantalizing, teasing. She quivered beneath him, dying to have him inside her, feeling him there so close.

For a moment—a moment that felt like forever—he raised his hands. Lily waited, waited, her heart beating so hard she was sure he could hear it. Then she felt the sliding tickle of her hair as he swept it to one side, felt him lean forward and place a shivery, soft kiss to her nape. Felt his chest hard and warm against her back, felt his breath wafting over her.

Felt the cool air as he drew away…

…felt his tongue on the base of her spine, a long, hot swipe all the way to her neck.

She trembled uncontrollably and heard little taps on the door.

Jasper, hitting something against it.

And then Rand's heavy sigh. "Maybe we should—"

"Ignore them!" she cried, twisting under him, writhing until she managed to get faceup, until she half sat and grabbed him by the shoulders to pull him down upon her. "Ignore them and kiss me!"

He did, parting her lips, tasting of sin and seduction. She'd asked for kisses, and he kissed her. For what seemed an hour, he only kissed her. He kissed her and kissed her, hot kisses that spoke of possession.

She could touch him now, and she did...until his breath sounded as harsh as her own, until their hearts pounded in tandem, until she thought she might scream...until he rolled to his side, taking her with him, and slipped a hand between her legs.

He cupped her and then stilled.

Feeling an incredible urgency, an indescribable ache, she arched up against his fingers, waiting, waiting, waiting...

And he finally moved his hand.

Slowly. Too slowly. Over and over. And over and over, stroking her with exquisite tenderness, until she heard little cries and realized they were hers, until she wondered if one could die from this overwhelming need...

And then he slipped a finger inside her.

"Rand," she breathed. It was too much. Too, too much. The world spun crazily. He drew out, a dazzling glide of sensation, then plunged in again, making her hips lift off the bed. Again. Again and again until she thought her heart might burst from the pleasure.

And then it did. It burst into countless little pieces, and they hadn't even come back together yet when she felt him move up and slide into her as he covered her cry with his mouth.

He felt so perfect, joined with her, filling her, that tears came to her eyes. When he moved, they moved together. A dance of love, slow and measured and then fast and frenzied, until she burst again, this time taking him with her.

The candle guttered across the room, and the chamber went from dimness to darkness. Lily heard scratching and pecking and tapping, but she was blissfully limp on the bed. "Ignore them," she whispered, the words barely passing her lips.

Feeling his way in the blackness, Rand pressed a kiss to her slack mouth. "You sound tired." She heard a smile in his voice, a smile of pure masculine pride. "Do you still want to do it twice?"

"Oh, yes," she said on a sigh.

"I'm glad to hear it, sweet Lily."

Twice, she thought, would never be enough. But she needed some time to recover first.

As his tongue traced her lips, she decided five minutes would do.

THIRTY-FIVE

"**Y**OU LOOK VERY nice, Rand," Lily said the next morning.

Rand blinked. Standing outside the inn while they waited for the rest of her family, he'd been lost in thought, rehearsing in his head the upcoming interview with his father. Now he focused on her, noticing that her pale green dress was quite lovely. The underskirt was white, the stomacher and sleeves sprinkled with little white rosettes.

Very demure and aristocratic. His father would approve.

"Thank you," he said with a smile. "You look very nice, too."

She moved closer, sweeping him with an appreciative glance. "You look even better than at the baptism."

A special occasion, that baptism, and he'd dressed the part. His smile widened at the memory. But the smile turned wry as he suddenly realized he'd dressed for his father today, even going so far as to have hied himself off to a barber early this morning to have his hair properly trimmed.

Ruefully he ran two fingers along his freshly shaved jaw. After all these years, he was still trying to impress the old goat.

The thought stuck in his craw, and he briefly contemplated returning home to strip off his dove gray velvet suit in favor of one of the wool ones he usually wore. But they were running late already.

As was typical with the Ashcrofts, he heard them before he saw them. Along with the family came a valet and two maids and an incredible amount of luggage considering they'd left home for just one night. The trappings of nobility could be cumbersome, to say the least. It took a good bit of time to get everyone and everything settled, during which Rand was reminded why he'd never wanted to be a marquess.

The ride to Trentingham was a loud one with similar rigmarole at the other end. Rand breathed a sigh of relief when he and Lily finally set out for Hawkridge alone.

"How far is it?" she asked, leaning against him in the carriage.

"Not very. A couple of hours downriver."

She glanced up at him, looking surprised. "I wonder, then, why I never met you before Violet's wedding. I thought I'd been to every house within a day's driving distance with my mother and her gifts of perfume."

"There were no women at Hawkridge," he reminded her. "My mother died before you were born. And there were all those years you were at Tremayne, remember? Far away near Wales. Then, soon after you returned, I left for Oxford."

"But surely your father entertains."

"Not since the death of my mother. Even Christmas at Hawkridge is a rather dreary affair, with more attention paid to servants and tenants than any real celebrating."

"It sounds dismal," she said, rubbing the scars on her hand, her eyes apprehensive. "However did you make friends?"

"It wasn't easy." He'd met few young people during his years at home. "If Kit hadn't lived so nearby, I likely wouldn't have had any friends at all."

Lily's apprehension faded, replaced by a look Rand could describe only as resolute. "Well, if we end up living at Hawkridge, things will change."

Rand very much doubted that, but he did allow that Lily had a better chance of influencing his father than he did. He suddenly realized what a good catch she was for a man such as himself: an academic who, until recently, had borne a courtesy title only.

The Earl of Trentingham's daughter. He'd never considered her status before, since he didn't care about such things, but Lady Lily Ashcroft was the sort of wife the Marquess of Hawkridge would approve. He wondered if her mother had been thinking in that direction when she'd insisted Lily come along. He was beginning to suspect Lady Trentingham was a very cunning woman. But he liked her.

Lily yawned and laid her head on his shoulder. "Sleepy?" he asked.

"Mmm-hmm. But yesterday was nice."

He knew she meant last night, but pretended to misunderstand. "Oh, yes, it was very nice. Up until I received the blasted letter and Rowan fell off the scaffolding."

"It was nice after that, too," she protested.

And he realized it had been, even without counting their very nice encounter in the wee hours. "You're right," he said. "The afternoon went very smoothly, all considered. Your parents didn't let Rowan's prank ruin everything. They didn't seem cross."

"Events occur. You take them in stride."

His family hadn't. "They also don't seem upset that you're marrying a professor."

"You're an earl now, too."

"But I wasn't, and they never seemed to care."

"They trust my choice. Besides, they admire you and what you've done with your life."

He'd sensed that. Just walking around the city with them, he'd felt perfectly comfortable. He'd felt like he belonged. "You have a wonderful family."

"My father is half deaf, my mother is an unrepentant gossip, my brother thinks tricking people is a laudable achievement, my sister lusts after the man I love—"

"They're wonderful," he repeated. "You're all so close."

If he'd been envious of that closeness, yesterday had changed that. Because they'd accepted him as though he were one of their own. To them, he wasn't a disappointment.

They were the family he'd never had.

"I'm the luckiest man in the world," he said in a voice made husky by unfamiliar emotion. A day with Lily's family had made clear what he'd missed out on all his life: the laughter, the friendly bickering, the love, that amazing unconditional acceptance.

He wanted, more than ever, to create a family like that with Lily.

In no time at all—or so it seemed to Rand, who'd as soon it took forever—their carriage was turning away from the Thames and rolling up the wide drive to Hawkridge Hall.

"Oh, it's lovely," Lily said softly.

Rand couldn't help thinking she'd probably rather live here, in a mansion on the bucolic banks of the river, than in a smaller house smack in the middle of Oxford.

His gaze swept over the three-story redbrick building. Although its symmetrical H shape was typical of houses built this century, the house was atypical in size and appointments. And the marquess spared no expense to keep it that way. The windows had been replaced since Rand moved away, now the new sash style with double-glazed glass. The mansion was the height of contemporary fashion.

But it sickened him. He had few happy memories of this place.

"It shows no signs of damage," Lily remarked. "Yet your family supported Charles in the war, did they not? How is it that Hawkridge escaped Cromwell's wrath, and so close to London, no less?"

"We have my mother to thank for that. Publicly, she was

great friends with Oliver Cromwell and went so far as to entertain him here. Privately, she was an important member of the Sealed Knot."

"What was that?"

"A clandestine organization that aimed to restore Charles to the throne. The members had secret names; my mother was 'Mrs. Gray.' When I was very young, she traveled to the Continent several times as a courier. Many letters went back and forth, always written in code."

"Ah, I see where you inherited that talent for deciphering your brother's diaries."

He grinned. "My mother even concocted an invisible ink that they used. In the Sealed Knot letters, Cromwell was 'Mr. Wright.' While on the surface she supported him, all along she was plotting his downfall."

"She must have been quite a woman."

"She was clever and principled and beautiful. And I suppose she made this home beautiful, too," he added, knowing, in a detached way, that it was. "But I don't want to live here."

"I, too, would prefer to live in Oxford," Lily assured him, sounding sincere.

He hoped she meant those words, because he meant to fight to keep his current life. And with her on his side, he had some hope he'd accomplish that goal. The marquess was sure to adore her.

"But I'll be happy living wherever you are," she added as the carriage rolled to a stop.

He pulled her close for a kiss. "Thank you for that." He dredged up a smile. "All right. Let's get this over with."

He was helping her down from the carriage when the mansion's arched front door yawned wide. His father stood in the opening. The man's gaze swept Lily from head to toe, then swung glaring to Rand.

"What took you so long?" he asked. "Your brother is already buried."

Just hearing that tone of voice, Rand felt, for a moment, like the small boy who'd always quavered in the face of his father's disfavor. The frosty gray eyes missed nothing, assessing him as they used to—and with no more approval. If Rand had harbored an unrealistic hope that the loss of the marquess's elder son would make him look anew at his younger one, those dreams were dashed.

Never mind how carefully he'd dressed; Rand felt slovenly under that gaze. For that moment he was ten again, pining for the man's love, willing to do almost anything to gain that elusive acceptance. But whatever he'd tried had always been for naught, and today was no different.

And he wasn't that small boy anymore.

Patience, he told himself. There was no point in starting out confrontational. The marquess had asked why he'd taken so long, and he would give him a civil answer.

He was opening his mouth to explain that he hadn't been home to receive mail when the man added, "And who the hell is she?"

THIRTY-SIX

*P*ATIENCE FLED, chased away by stunned disbelief. Rand lifted his chin and wrapped an arm around Lily. "This is Lady Lily Ashcroft, the Earl of Trentingham's daughter. We're betrothed and plan to marry soon."

The marquess's shoulders tensed beneath his jet-black velvet suit. "You'll marry her over my dead body."

For a moment, Rand wished he could arrange that.

Though he could feel Lily quaking beside him, her spine remained straight. He met the man's cold gray gaze with one of his own. "Might I request you get to know the lady before you forbid our marriage?"

"My lord," Lily added in a tone both respectful and steady, "I'm from good family, and I am in love with your son."

The marquess's expression didn't soften. "Then you will make him an excellent mistress," he snapped, and turned to go into the house.

"That's enough!" Rand called after him dangerously.

But the stubborn man didn't even glance back.

Appalled, Rand turned to Lily. "I'm sorry."

"It doesn't matter." Her voice was quiet so as not to be overheard, but determination laced every word. "He won't keep us apart."

Rand hadn't known his sweet Lily had so much steel inside her, but he was supremely grateful to find out. "He won't," he agreed, matching her confidence outwardly.

But he knew that no matter how misguided his father's reasons, the man would fight to the bitter end. The Marquess of Hawkridge always got his way. Together, Rand and Lily would have to make sure this time was the exception.

Servants were milling around them, handing down luggage and carting it up the steps. Rand was surprised to find he still recognized most. They smiled, and he did his best to smile back as he drew Lily up the two sets of stone steps and into Hawkridge's imposing great hall.

Arms crossed, the marquess waited inside, eyeing the luggage sitting on the black-and-white marble floor. His expression of disapproval had given way to disbelief. "She cannot be thinking to stay the night."

Rand set his jaw. "Lily and I are betrothed. If she leaves, so do I."

The marquess thought on that a moment, but he'd always been a man who knew which battles were worth fighting. He beckoned to one of the waiting maids. "Etta, put her in the Queen's Bedchamber. For now," he added ominously. After pausing a moment for effect, he also added, "Randal, you'll join me in my study." Without waiting for agreement, he turned to leave.

The maid curtsied and touched a hand to the white cap that covered her gray curls. Rand blinked in shock. His old nurse had been demoted to a housemaid.

"Nurse Etta—" he started.

"You'd best go," she warned, though her voice was kind. Her gaze strayed to the marquess's stiff, retreating back. "I'll take care of your lady."

Lily went off with her head held high. Rand headed for the

study, hoping she'd find the Queen's Bedchamber a comfortable place to wait.

The room had acquired the name years earlier, shortly after it had been redecorated for a visit by Queen Catharine of Braganza, King Charles's wife. Though Rand hoped Lily would feel honored to be assigned the chamber, he knew the truth: His father meant her to be intimidated. In anticipation of the queen's using it, the room had been fitted out in a way meant to display the marquess's power.

It also—by no coincidence, Rand was certain—sat as far from Rand's own chamber as physically possible. In the opposite wing, on a different floor.

In another move meant to intimidate, the marquess sat behind his desk, which rested on a raised dais toward the back of his study, and waved Rand toward a chair on the lower level.

Rand dropped onto it, sat back, and crossed his arms. Looking up at his father this way used to make him feel like a contrite child, but he'd come too far to fall for the old goat's tricks.

The marquess was one of the few men Rand knew who wore a periwig every waking hour of every day, even tucked away out here in the countryside. When that gray gaze settled on Rand, he braced, waiting for his father to make mention of his uncovered, chopped-off hair. Then he chided himself. It had been too long for the man to recognize the difference. Or he hadn't noticed. Or he simply didn't care.

Or all of the above.

The marquess wasted no time on preliminaries. "Your brother, as you know, had been betrothed since childhood to Margery. I swore to her father they would marry the day she turned one-and-twenty. That happens to be next week. I intend for you to fulfill that pledge."

Rand felt as though the air had been knocked out of him. He closed his eyes for a moment, then forced them open, a failing attempt to appear unruffled.

Margery. How could he have forgotten how these developments would impact Margery?

"Where *is* Margery?"

"In London. I sent her to obtain a proper wardrobe for
mourning. She returns tomorrow." The marquess lifted a quill,
pristine white lace falling back from his wrist. "I expect you to
greet her as befits a husband-to-be."

"I cannot." Rand had washed his hands of the marquess long
ago. He wasn't responsible for the man's twenty-year-old agreement. "I'm sorry for Margery, but I'm pledged to Lily."

Not to mention he'd bedded her as well.

"My honor is on the line," the marquess continued, breezing
over Rand's refusal. "And the family wealth is at stake."

Looking toward the heavens for patience, Rand waved an
arm, the gesture encompassing the overblown glory that was
Hawkridge Hall. "I cannot imagine how the family wealth could
be in jeopardy."

For once, his father looked almost uncomfortable. "I've never
had any reason to discuss family finances with you. But you may
as well know that I mortgaged the Hawkridge lands to raise
funds for Charles."

Rand knew he meant Charles I, not the current King Charles,
and that the funds had gone to support the king's side in the
Civil War. The money would have been lost along with the
battles, but William Nesbitt had been and still was a loyal Royal-
ist. That he'd done such a thing was hardly surprising.

But his next words were.

"I was on the verge of ruin when Margery came into our
lives."

Margery. Rand pictured her young upturned face, her delicate features framed by the palest blond curls. Between her
sporadic letters, he hadn't thought of Margery often—he'd
avoided thinking of anything at Hawkridge for years—but when
he had, they'd been fond thoughts. He thought of her much like
a sister.

Never, ever as a potential wife.

"I'm wedding Lily," he repeated. "Soon."

For heaven's sake, she could be carrying his child.

The marquess dipped the quill and began signing papers while he talked. "As Margery's guardian and eventual father-in-law, I've managed her extensive lands along with Hawkridge's for twenty years. The loss of those lands and income would be devastating, leading to eventual bankruptcy."

One of Rand's hands reached up to find the ends of his once-long hair, then fisted and dropped to his lap. "Surely you exaggerate."

"I do not." The marquess flipped a page.

Rand figured the man's half attention was calculated to make him feel worthless, but it wasn't going to work. He wouldn't *let* it work.

"Should you refuse to marry Margery," his father continued, "her land will be lost to us, and all of Hawkridge will suffer." At last, he looked up. "All, Randal."

All.

Not only what was left of the family, but the old family retainers. Etta and the other servants. The tenants, the villagers—everyone who depended on Hawkridge for their livings.

Rand knew his father was preying on his sympathies. The old man bore no great concern for the people—he worried for himself, and himself alone. But knowledge of the marquess's machinations did little to mitigate the effect of the threat.

Rand rubbed his palms on his velvet breeches. "I don't care," he said, afraid that he did.

A man didn't turn his back on people who relied on him.

The marquess's expression remained stony and resolute. He signed the paper in front of him, the scratch of the quill loud in the awkward silence.

"Lily has a dowry," Rand said. "Three thousand pounds."

"Three thousand wouldn't begin to make a dent in Hawkridge's needs." The page crackled when he flipped it to look at another. "You may leave now. I have much to do. We'll discuss this again tomorrow."

Rand was dismissed. He rose and walked to the door, then turned back. "Perhaps tomorrow you'll come to your senses."

Though it had often cost him dearly as a boy, he never had learned to resist getting in the last word.

THIRTY-SEVEN

FOR THE FIRST few minutes she was left alone, Lily wandered around the magnificent Queen's Bedchamber, alternating between worrying about what Rand and his father were discussing and marveling at the exquisite furnishings.

She supposed the queen really had graced this room at least once, for it certainly looked like it had been decorated for royalty. Even Lily, whose own family home was worth gawking at, found this chamber astonishing.

The enormous state bed, hung with costly cloth of gold, sat on a raised parquet dais behind a balustrade in the French style. Great poufs of ostrich feathers crowned each of the bed's four posts. The ceiling was elaborate painted plasterwork, the furniture gilt wood. The walls were hung with rich tapestries, and the marble fireplace boasted gilded crowns over the chimneypiece and on the piers.

But above all, the position of the room demonstrated its status. Beyond its windows, as in a royal palace, the gardens and avenues spread out in perfect symmetry, from this, the exact central vantage point.

However, Lily had little inclination to gaze upon

Hawkridge's gardens. Her own father's were much more impressive. And while she had no doubt she'd been shown to this chamber in the hope it would convince her of the marquess's wealth and power, having fought Rose—and herself, she admitted—for Rand, she wasn't willing to give him up easily.

Along with the other priceless furnishings, the Queen's Bedchamber contained a lovely rosewood harpsichord. No matter the marquess's intentions, he really couldn't have assigned her to a more perfect room. Smiling in spite of her heavy heart, she sat down to play.

And that was where Rand found her half an hour later.

For a moment, or maybe longer, she'd managed to lose herself in the music. But one look at Rand's face brought her crashing back to reality.

"It didn't go well," she said. A statement, not a question.

He dredged up a smile—a weak, obvious effort. "Everything will be fine. I need to think. I need to…to go off by myself. Sometimes I do that, and I just wanted to let you know."

"All right." But she stood, reaching to catch the stool when she nearly knocked it over. "Where are you going?"

"I just need to run."

"I'll come along—"

"Alone, Lily. I'll be back soon." He took a step closer, close enough to meet her lips with his own. A soft, apologetic kiss. "I promise."

She searched his eyes, her fingers brushing the slight roughness on his cheek. "May I walk you out of the house?"

He shrugged, then silently peeled off his surcoat and tossed it on the bed. His cravat followed. As he strode from the room, he began rolling up his sleeves.

She hadn't taken him for a moody sort of man, but then, she admitted to herself, in truth she hardly knew him. But she knew she loved him. And if he needed some time to himself, how could she begrudge him that? It wasn't as though he were asking to go to another woman.

She followed him from the chamber and down the massive oak staircase, another feature of the mansion that had clearly been built to impress. Beneath the handrails, pierced wooden panels were carved with armor, cannons, muskets, spears, and lances. Trophies of war, their details highlighted by gold and silver leaf.

A display of force and power.

"What did your father say?" she asked Rand, watching his shoulders tense beneath the thin white cambric of his shirt. "Is he demanding you leave Oxford to live here?"

"That minor detail hasn't even been discussed yet." He sighed and paused, waiting for her to catch up. "He's forbidden our marriage."

She ordered herself not to panic. Rand sounded nothing if not resolute. And his father couldn't really prevent them from wedding, could he? They would wish for his blessing, of course, but as a last resort, they could always elope. Especially given that Rand claimed to care little for his inheritance.

As he resumed his descent, she reached for his hand. "Why?"

"My brother was to wed my father's ward, a woman named Margery Maybanks. I told you about her, didn't I? The marquess expects me to honor that commitment."

"Would you not make a poor substitute? She loved your brother, not you."

A short, harsh laugh tore from his throat. "Oh, I doubt she loved Alban. Aside from my father, I'm aware of no one who did." At the bottom of the staircase, he headed across the great hall toward the front door. "Margery's father saved the marquess's life in the Battle of Worcester, and the marquess promised him a boon. A few years later, on his deathbed, the man made his claim: that the marquess raise his motherless newborn daughter here and marry her to his heir on the day she turned one-and-twenty."

A footman opened the door, and they stepped out. After the dark tones that dominated Hawkridge's interior, Lily blinked in the sunshine. "And now you're the heir." She tugged on Rand's hand until he stopped and turned to face her. "Can you refuse?"

"I *have* refused. But…there's more."

"What—"

He hushed her with two fingers on her lips. "Let me think, Lily. I'll return soon." He bent to replace his fingers with his mouth, but after a quick kiss, he ran off around the corner of the house, his boots loud on the cobbled pavement.

His gait looked determined. She followed slowly, rounding the corner in time to see him cross a lawn and disappear into a tangle of trees. A wilderness garden, perhaps. It seemed to be more planned than the woods that bordered Trentingham, with man-made paths cut through it.

She would honor his request for solitude. She had little interest in the gardens, and should he look back, she didn't want him to think she was tailing him. Instead, she wandered around the perimeter of the house, vaguely following the sounds of barking dogs.

On the west side of the mansion she found a yard, bordered by several small buildings. A bakehouse, a stillhouse, a wash-house, a brewhouse, a dairy. She peeked in the diamond-paned windows of the last, seeing milking pails, pans, skimming dishes, and strainers. Inside, a young woman was bent over a cheese press. She straightened and gave Lily a puzzled look, then offered a tentative smile. Lily thought she would have been pretty if her poor face weren't covered in smallpox scars.

As she walked away, her fingertips went to her own smooth skin. Would Rand still love her if she succumbed to the pox?

She rubbed the scars on the back of her hand, telling herself not to be silly. She would love him no matter what disfigurement he might suffer, for better or worse, as the marriage vows said. And when she locked her eyes on his, she knew, for a fact, he felt the same.

Behind the dairy, another fenced yard was teeming with the

dogs she'd heard earlier. Despite her worries, a grin spread on her face. She gathered her skirts to climb the rails.

"They're dangerous," someone said, not unkindly.

She turned to see Etta, the older woman who'd shown her to her room. Etta bore smallpox scars as well, but not nearly as many as the milkmaid, and her large green eyes and curly gray hair made Lily think she had probably been lovely as a young woman.

"I've been sent to look for you," Etta explained.

"By whom?"

"The marquess. He wishes to know your whereabouts."

"Well then, tell him I'm playing with the dogs," Lily said, amazed at her own boldness.

Why, Rose would scarcely recognize her. Loving Rand had given her that newfound strength.

A smile twitched at the corners of Etta's mouth. "If you won't mind my saying, my lady, nobody plays with those dogs."

Lily turned and looked again. They were huge dogs—mastiffs—and there were more than a dozen. But she'd never met a dog she didn't like. Or even more important, one who hadn't liked her.

"Well, then," she said blithely, "it's about time someone *did* play with the poor creatures."

And ignoring Etta's gasp, she bunched her skirts and climbed over the fence.

THIRTY-EIGHT

$\mathcal{W}$HEN RAND returned from his run, he headed straight for his old room to wash his face and change his shirt. Then he went in search of Lily. Hoping to hear soothing music as he approached the Queen's Bedchamber, he was dismayed to find the room empty.

Damnation, he should never have left her alone. If the marquess was even now interrogating her…

Rand's stomach went queasy at the thought.

Steeling himself to go find out, he grabbed his surcoat off the bed and shoved his arms into the sleeves. He slipped his cravat back around his neck and strode over to a massive gilt-framed mirror to tie the neat knot he knew the marquess expected. In his rush, his fingers refused to cooperate. He swore at himself.

"Trouble, my lord?" The mirror reflected a woman poking her head through the doorway.

"Hmm?" He turned and, seeing it was Etta, experienced an absurd rush of nostalgia. She'd aged, of course, and she was newly scarred since he'd last seen her, though not too badly. She seemed shorter than he'd remembered. But the placid green eyes were the same.

Those were eyes one could count on. He hadn't thought

about Etta in years, and he felt a wave of shame for that. But he hadn't wanted to remember the people here who'd cared for him.

The people who could be hurt if he failed to figure something out.

"Oh, please don't call me *my lord*, Nurse Etta. You're supposed to call me Randal in a stern tone of voice."

When she laughed, it wasn't an old lady's laugh—it was the one he remembered from his childhood. Nurse Etta may have been stern when it was required, but most times she had been kindly and good-natured.

"Then don't call me Nurse Etta." She came close and took over tying the cravat. "My word, that makes me feel as though I'm still responsible for you three young hellions." She smiled up at him, looking much like the younger woman he remembered, despite the smallpox scars. "I've been plain Etta for years."

"How did that happen?"

"Why so disapproving?" Finished, she patted his chest and stepped back. "When Margery grew into a young lady, I faced the choice of finding another household with small children elsewhere, or taking a different position here. Your father was kind enough to let me stay on."

He'd never expected to hear the words *your father* and *kind* in the same sentence, and his expression must have shown it.

"Circumstances change, Randal," she added in that old Nurse Etta tone of voice. "It's up to us to accept them and move on."

He suspected those words were directed to him and his current situation, but he didn't want to hear them right now. "I'm looking for Lady Lily."

"A lovely young woman." She bustled over to the bed and began straightening a coverlet that didn't need to be straightened. "She's outside playing with the dogs."

"What dogs? You cannot mean...no..."

She plumped a pillow, then looked up. "Yes. The marquess's dogs."

That was worse than learning Lily was with his father. His heart pounding, Rand headed outside at a run.

But when he reached the enclosure, he told himself he should have known better. He stood for a moment just watching. Lily was fine, if covered in dog slobber. In fact, she seemed to be in her element.

She had a fawn-colored dog fetching a short stick and a brindle dog playing tug-of-war with a longer one. Two more dogs seemed, miraculously, to be waiting their turns for attention. Another few were simply ignoring her, but that in itself was a wonder.

Some of the hounds stood as tall as her shoulder, and they were all trained to fight, bred mainly for their fierceness. Except the marquess, everyone on the estate was wary of the beasts, Rand included.

Thinking it might be more dangerous than running into a burning barn, he climbed into the enclosure and wove his way through the excited animals to Lily.

She glanced over at his approach, then focused on the brindle dog. "Let go," she commanded. The canine dropped his end of the stick, ending the playful tug-of-war.

Rand was unsurprised. Animals always listened to Lily. "Thank you for your patience," he said, drawing near.

She shrugged, clearly unhappy that he'd run off. But she seemed unwilling to make trouble, either. She tossed the shorter stick and watched the fawn-colored dog chase after it. "I understand," she said quietly.

Hurrying back with the wood, the mastiff sideswiped Rand and made him stagger. The mass of these beasts was amazing; not a one of them weighed less than he did. "This isn't really safe," he told her. "They're very aggressive."

"Balderdash. They were starving for attention." With a swipe of its huge pink tongue, the hound licked her smack on the face.

She tossed the stick again. "You should put some thick, knotted rope in here. They'd enjoy playing with it, chewing on it. And that tree is a hazard." She waved toward one corner. "Those apples are exactly the right size to get lodged in their throats. I'm surprised none of them have choked."

He shifted on his feet. "I'm sure my father knows what he's about. He's been breeding the monsters for years."

"Monsters? I thought you said you were a dog person."

He felt himself turning red. "These don't count. I prefer the small, fluffy sort."

Reclaiming the stick from between the dog's big teeth, she appeared to be suppressing a laugh. "Have you ever had a small, fluffy dog?"

"No. But I used to look at these and wish for one."

"They can be meaner than these. We shall have to try to locate a sweet one for you." She dropped the wood to the ground and finally met his gaze. "So tell me the rest."

"Can we get out of here first?"

"I suppose." She patted a couple of hounds on their heads before bunching her skirts in a hand. As she climbed the fence, the dogs began howling. When Rand went to follow, one beast whacked him with its tail, a stinging blow he half suspected was deliberate.

He supposed he deserved it.

When they were safely beyond the fence, he took Lily's face in both hands and kissed her, relieved when he felt her melt against his body. "I'm sorry for running off," he told her. "It's a bad habit."

Apparently having forgiven him, she smiled. "I hope it's your worst."

"Oh, it is, I assure you. Other than this one oddity, I'm a perfect companion."

"*Those* are perfect companions." She gestured toward the dogs. But she was still smiling. "Tell me everything."

Feeling better than he had in hours, he slipped an arm

around her waist and walked her into the gardens. "I don't care what my father wants, Lily. I won't give you up for anything. *Anything.*"

She snuggled closer against him. "Tell me the rest. Your father has pledged to marry Margery to his heir, and now *you* are his heir. What else?"

"Margery's a commoner, but an heiress. She inherited a vast estate. Land that my father has been managing for twenty years."

"And?"

"He claims that Hawkridge will bankrupt without the income from that land. He contends he was close to losing every-thing when Margery came along. He said he mortgaged Hawkridge to the hilt to support Charles during the war."

"Would he have?"

"What?"

"Risked his estate for the king?"

He blinked. "Of course. Did your father not do the same?"

"It was my grandfather at the time. And no." Her father's daughter, she plucked dead leaves off the hedges as they walked. "Grandpapa sent money, but no more than he felt he could spare. And he never went off to fight, nor did he send his son. While we waited out the war and Protectorate at Tremayne, they were both right there along with us. Grandpapa always said he valued family above the monarchy."

A different way of thinking, but Rand liked it. "I suspect the marquess would have called him a coward. But if *he* hadn't gone off to war, he would never have been indebted to Margery's father. And I wouldn't be in this mess today."

"*We* wouldn't be in this mess," she corrected gently. "We'll find a way out together."

In that moment, his love for her increased tenfold. He couldn't remember when anyone had supported him so uncon-ditionally. In order to persevere, he'd always needed to find the strength within himself. But now he could depend on—

lean on—Lily. Those narrow shoulders were deceptively strong.

In the shade of a spreading tree he stopped, turning her toward him to meet her mouth. "I love you, Lily Ashcroft," he murmured against her lips.

"And I, you." Her hands slipped under his coat, and she leaned back to look up at him. "What else? There's more, I can tell."

"You're a dangerous woman." He chuckled and kissed her on the nose before sobering. "The maid the marquess assigned to you, Etta…"

She frowned and took his arm to resume walking. "She's a kind sort."

"She used to be my nurse, and yes, she's very kind." He hadn't expected to find anything he cared for here at Hawkridge. Or anyone. "She—and others—made my childhood here bearable."

A bee buzzed over their heads, then flew off. "You worry for them," she said with the sort of compassion that made her Lily. "Not for your father, not for Hawkridge the estate, but for Hawkridge's people."

"The old family retainers."

"And the tenants and villagers, too, I imagine. There must be dozens of people who depend on Hawkridge for their livelihoods."

"Hundreds." Pulling her close, he buried his face in her fragrant hair. "Oh God, Lily. As much as I don't want to jump to the marquess's command, as much as I cannot imagine giving up my hard-won professorship, as much as I cannot stand to think of losing you—absolutely *won't* consider losing you—"

His voice broke.

"You also cannot imagine letting all these people down," Lily finished for him, drawing back.

Capturing his gaze, she caught his hands in both of hers. *Devastation.*

There was no other word to describe the way she felt. A hole had opened in her middle, a bottomless pit, sucking every shred of her newfound happiness into its void.

Tears threatened as she squeezed his fingers, trying to draw strength from his very bones.

He pulled one thumb from her grip to rub it over the scars on the back of her hand. She searched his eyes, dark gray with pain. "There must be another way," she said. He looked so steady. He was her rock. Rocks did not up and disappear. "Besides meek acceptance of your father's dictates, there *must* be another way."

Clearly wanting to believe her, he nodded—but he didn't look convinced. "I meant what I said, Lily. I won't give you up for anything. But I ran, and then I walked, and yet I couldn't think—"

"There's my marriage portion." She drew him to sit beside her on a wooden bench.

"I told him about that," Rand admitted, looking guilty.

"As you should have. It will be yours as soon as we wed."

With a gentle hand, he pushed her hair off her face. "I don't feel as though it necessarily should be. I didn't earn it. Everything else I have, I've earned."

"It's the way the world works, Rand. I vow, you're one of the few men I've met who wouldn't run to the altar for that sort of money." Yet more proof he was special. "What did he say?"

"He said, and I quote, it 'wouldn't make a dent in Hawkridge's needs.'"

She nodded, unsurprised. Three thousand pounds was a respectable sum for a dowry, but a man of the marquess's stature wouldn't face bankruptcy for a lack of that amount. "Do you expect an additional ten thousand would make a difference?"

He blinked. "Ten thousand?"

"My inheritance. I've told you about it, remember? Grandpapa left me ten thousand pounds—"

"*Ten* thousand pounds?" The look on his face made her realize she'd never mentioned the amount, only discussed what she planned to do with it. "I never thought about…I remember now that Violet was left that much money, but she's the eldest… it never occurred to me…"

Sudden understanding stole over his expression.

"Is *that* what Rose was talking about that day in the summer-house?" he said, looking incredulous. "Her inheritance? I assumed she was counting on her dowry and planning to wheedle the rest out of your father. I never for a minute believed she'd actually deliver on such a sum."

"Not even Rose makes promises she cannot keep," Lily said, feeling a fresh stab of guilt when she remembered her own broken promise. But it was a little stab, because she knew she and Rand belonged together, and because she also knew that all her anguish of the past few weeks was inconsequential compared to what they were facing now. "Yes, we were each left ten thousand pounds. The money won't be mine until I turn twenty-one, but perhaps…no, I'm *certain* my father will allow me to have it early. We can give it to your father, to save Hawkridge, and then we'll be able to marry."

Rand looked stunned. "You had plans for that money. You were going to build a home for stray animals. And use the rest of your funds to run it for many years."

She swallowed a lump in her throat. "So I'll find another way," she whispered. "I love animals, but I love you more."

His eyes grew suspiciously glossy. She'd never seen a man cry. She moved onto his lap, kissing those eyes, his nose, his cheeks. "How much is Margery's fortune?" she asked.

"I don't know. Maybe more. But if the marquess cannot save Hawkridge with thirteen thousand pounds, he's not the man he pretends to be." When he kissed her back, she felt his lips curve into a smile. "It should certainly keep Hawkridge from ruin and set it on the road to recovery, and then I'll be able to persuade him to bless our marriage."

She smiled, too, and kissed him again, thrilling when he deepened the caress. She would never get enough of this, enough of him. Her worries fled and her head was filled with only Rand.

But then a thought intruded and her heart plunged. She broke the kiss. "What about Margery?"

"What *about* Margery?"

"We need to consider her, too, don't you think? After all, she just lost her betrothed, and she's expecting to marry you."

He tensed for a moment, but then relaxed and kissed her again. "What my father expects and what Margery expects are two different things. She hasn't seen me in eight years. I'm certain she will think me no great loss. With her fortune, she can find herself a much better man. Someone important."

"You're an earl," she reminded him. "And someday you'll be a marquess."

"But at heart, I'm a professor." He skimmed a finger over the dent in her chin. "That you would offer me your inheritance…" His eyes glazed over again. "It's overwhelming. And in the face of that generosity, I just know that everything will turn out fine."

Lily wished she could be so confident.

THIRTY-NINE

$\mathcal{L}$IKE THE REST of the house, the dining room was beautiful. Lily had glimpsed an enormous, lavish banqueting hall upstairs, but this chamber was much more intimate.

As Rand walked her in, her heels clicked on the two-toned parquet floor. She stopped to run a hand over the patterned design on the walls, surprised to find it was gold stamped on brown leather. "It looks like gilded wood!" she exclaimed.

"The leather is supposed to absorb the smells of food."

She'd never heard of such a thing. "It's lovely. All of Hawkridge Hall is lovely."

"It's a lovely prison," he muttered back darkly. "It was my prison for fourteen years, and I've no wish to return."

In opposition to the prison that was Hawkridge Hall—a prison designed and paid for by his father—the Oxford house was one-hundred-percent Rand's. A symbol, Lily suspected, of his hard-won independence.

"I want to live in your new house, too," she assured him. Kit had told her that he and Rand had spent months designing it before the cornerstone was laid, because Rand had wanted every square foot to be perfect. And it was. "It's so modern, so simple and classic compared to this mansion. And so empty. I'm so looking forward to filling it over time, making it ours." She was about to add more when Rand's eyes widened in alarm. She swung around to see his father. "Oh! Good evening, my lord."

"My lady," he grunted. "Shall we be seated?"

Lily wondered how much the man had heard as they all took their places at the oval cedarwood table, the marquess seating himself at the opposite end from his son.

There were eighteen matching caned chairs around the table in this "family" dining room, and in Lily's opinion, a family sat together to better enjoy each other's company. At least *her* family did. Mentally shaking her head, she took a chair beside Rand rather than one in the middle—then pretended not to notice when two footmen had to scramble to move her table setting.

Being not so nice was feeling better and better.

Supper was an awkward affair. The marquess was dressed in black mourning and seemed offended that Rand was not. Other than a few minutes of desultory conversation about the man's beloved mastiffs, Lily couldn't get him to talk about anything. Both she and Rand were reluctant to bring up Margery or marriage, so the time passed mostly in silence punctuated by the clinking of Hawkridge's custom-designed silverware.

Though the house was magnificent, there was something about it Lily didn't like. Something dark and forbidding. Maybe it was the deep colors on the walls and all the somber, oak-framed paintings. Maybe it was the studied formality. Or maybe it was just that she'd never been anywhere before where she'd felt so very unwelcome.

When the meal finally drew to a close, Rand pushed back his chair. "Lily plays the harpsichord beautifully," he said as a sort of invitation.

"I have work to do," the marquess replied and left the room.

While Lily wished Rand and his father would act more like a family, in truth she felt mainly relief. "When are you going to tell him about my inheritance?" she asked.

A footman entered to clear the table, and Rand cleared his throat. "Would you care to walk in the gardens?"

Holding her tongue, she went with him outside.

He led her through the more formal gardens and into an area of grass walks lined with hornbeam hedges and field maples that enclosed many small, private gardens. The late-night summer sun was sinking, but not yet so low that she couldn't see and appreciate the beauty of the individual compartments, each of which contained not only a variety of rather wild-growing plants, but also a surprise. Some hid copies of famous statuary, one offered a sundial, and another a cozy bench for two. The one Rand led her into held a tiny round gazebo.

A narrow seat curved around the inside. The structure was so small that when they settled across from each other, their knees touched.

Rand reached to take Lily's hands. "We won't be overheard here. He has spies."

"Spies? I don't think—"

"You always look for the good, sweet Lily," he interrupted. "And you don't know him," he added, leaning close to press his lips to hers.

The warm caress set butterflies to fluttering in her stomach. She wondered if he'd come to her tonight in his father's house. Part of her was horrified at the notion, but another part, a much larger part, hoped very much that he'd risk it.

Now that she knew, really knew, what it could lead to, it seemed a single kiss was all it took to set her blood on fire.

She struggled to pull herself together. "When are you going to tell him he can have my money?"

Lady flew into the gazebo's opening and landed at their feet, but Rand didn't seem to notice let alone recognize the bird. His hands tightened on Lily's. "I'll tell him tomorrow. After I talk to Margery."

It was the first hint she saw that he suspected this might not all work out as planned. Suddenly her stomach wasn't filled with butterflies. More like lead.

What if Margery wanted to marry him? Rand had said Margery had been raised right here at Hawkridge. With him. Was it such a stretch to believe she might have come to love him?

He was, after all, utterly lovable. Generous and caring, strong and successful, self-sufficient where it showed, but with that hurt little boy hidden inside. What woman could truly know him, as Margery must, and not wish to wrap him in her arms and heal that hurt?

And with both Lord Hawkridge and Margery against her, would she, Lily, stand a chance?

She tried to search Rand's eyes, but the light was failing outside, and here in the gazebo it was even darker. "What if she wants to marry you, Rand?"

"She won't."

"But what if she does?"

He scooted around the circular bench until his thigh rested against hers, feeling warm even through their clothes. "I'm marrying you. No matter what the marquess wants. No matter what Margery wants. I love you. *You*, Lily. And do you realize… you may even now be carrying my child?"

A tiny gasp escaped her lips. She *hadn't* realized. Of course, she'd known it was a possibility, but she hadn't thought about it. She'd had no time. It had been only twice, over two short days, and so much else had happened…

And at the time, she'd been sure they were marrying anyway, so it hadn't really mattered.

But now it did.

She laid a hand on her middle. "Oh goodness, Rand, what if I am?"

"We'll love it, of course. Her." He grinned, his teeth gleaming white in the night. "She'll have dark hair and gorgeous blue eyes, just like you. In truth I'd rather have some time alone with you first, but if a child comes, well, it would be meant, would it not? And we'll love her—"

"You've thought about this a lot, haven't you?"

"I have, in the short time since we first loved. I'll admit the idea took some getting used to, but—"

"But what happens if you have to marry Margery?" Panic was rising in Lily's chest, into her throat, a lump that seemed to be choking her.

She stared blindly at the ground between their feet. Her family motto might be Question Convention, but that didn't mean she wanted to be so unconventional as to raise a child alone.

"Can you not see?" Rand touched her chin, that special spot that usually made her shiver, but not now. When she didn't look up, he sighed. "Lily. This is the best thing that could happen. If you're with child, the marquess will have to allow us to marry."

She wished she could believe that, but the Marquess of Hawkridge didn't strike her as the sort of man who felt he *had to* do anything. She tried to swallow the lump, failing miserably.

Rand slid a hand into her hair and tilted her head until she met his eyes. "Stop worrying. Your money will save Hawkridge and ensure everyone's future. We'll marry and live happily ever after."

She hoped so, and when he kissed her, she believed him for a moment. But when he stopped, she couldn't help wondering if he was wrong.

Her life so far had been happy and uneventful, like one of the baskets her sister used for flower arrangements, perfectly woven. Was this where it would unravel? Was losing Rand the price she would pay for disregarding her sister's feelings? For breaking a promise? For being selfish instead of nice?

"Now," he said, his tone changing to one that implied the matter was settled, "since the marquess is uninterested in entertainment, will you play the harpsichord for me alone?"

"In my bedchamber? I don't think your father's household would feel that's proper. You said he has spies."

He laughed as he drew her up and out of the gazebo, linking his arm with hers. "There's a second harpsichord in the north drawing room. But I will come to you tonight. In your bedchamber. And damn the spies."

Crossing the gardens, she laughed, too.

Things couldn't be as dire as they seemed. She and Rand were just too perfect together.

FORTY

*U*PSTAIRS IN Hawkridge Hall, the second
harpsichord was even more beautiful than the first, all
inlaid with different colored woods.

"Johannes Ruckers," Lily breathed, reading the name painted
above the keyboard.

"You know him?"

"Not personally." She grinned at the mere idea. "But Flemish
harpsichords are said to make the most beautiful music, especially those built by the Ruckers family."

"Try it," he said, seating himself in an amazing chair that was
gilded, silvered, and painted in marine colors to suggest
dolphins sporting in the ocean.

She sat on the petit point stool and ran her fingers experimentally over the keys, enjoying the rich sound of the rare
instrument. A small smile curved her lips as she launched into
the tune she'd been practicing.

Rand smiled in return, tapping a toe in time to the music.
Until he bolted out of the chair. "Where did you learn *that*?"

She continued playing. "I taught it to myself. Worked it out, I
mean. As a surprise for you. It's the tune you often hum,
isn't it?"

"Do I?" His lips twitched. "Perhaps I do, from time to time."

He hummed along for a few bars, then leaned an elbow on the harpsichord and set his chin in his hand. His head was nearly level with hers, his eyes commanding her to look up.

"What?" she asked.

He grinned. "Do you know the words?"

"Does it have words?"

"Most assuredly."

"Well then, sing them, won't you?"

"Start over at the beginning," he said with an enigmatic smile.

When she did, he began singing.

> *"Come my honey, let's to bed,*
> *It is no sin, since we are wed;*
> *For when I am near thee by desire,*
> *I burn like any coal of fire."*

Rand's voice was so rich that Lily found herself transfixed. She didn't register the actual words. Just the tone, the depth... the sound seemed to go right through her, into her, warming her.

She couldn't care less where she lived, she thought dreamily. Hawkridge, Oxford, a hovel...if only Rand would sing to her every night, she'd be happy all her days.

He raised a brow. "This next verse is yours."

Her fingers still picking out the jaunty tune, she smiled. "Even if I knew the words, I cannot sing. You sing it."

"Hmm..." He raised his voice an octave and warbled a bit as he continued.

> *"To quench thy flames I'll soon agree,*
> *Thou art the sun, and I the sea,*
> *All night within my arms shalt be,*
> *And rise each morn as fresh as he."*

Lily giggled at his game attempt to sound like a woman. She caught a few of the words and thought she knew why Rand liked this song. The woman wanted to spend the night in the man's arms—and goodness, did she identify with that.

"The final part is supposed to be sung together," he said.

"Is it?" She continued playing, her fingers flying over the keys. "I'm listening," she said, determined to pay attention to the lyrics this time.

One of his boots tapped in rhythm as he waited for the right place in the music.

"Come on then, and couple together,
Come all, the old and the young,
The short and the tall,
The richer than Croesus,
And poorer than Job,
For 'tis wedding and bedding,
That peoples the globe."

Lily's fingers stilled as she gasped. "Couple together? Wedding and bedding? Whoever wrote a song about *that*?"

"Anonymous. He writes a lot of songs." The mischievous glitter in Rand's eyes belied his mock-serious tone. "Are you scandalized?"

"Yes. No." She laughed at herself—no need to play coy with Rand. "Well, maybe I'm intrigued. Would you know more songs like this one?"

"This one is mild—the couple is married, after all." He raised a roguish brow. "I know hundreds, most of them much worse."

"Hundreds?"

"Well, I cannot remember them all. But I have a book."

"A *book*?" What a sheltered life she'd led. "Someone wrote these down?"

His eyes sparkled with undisguised mirth. "Oh, yes, with the music and all. The book is called *An Antidote Against Melancholy*, and I understand it sells very well. Let me see if I can remember another."

He hummed beneath his breath for a while, then he nodded.

> *"As Oyster Nan stood by her tub,*
> *To shew her vicious inclination;*
> *She gave her noblest parts a scrub,*
> *And sigh'd for want of copulation."*

Lily gasped again and felt heat rush into her cheeks. Feeling both a bit naughty and more lighthearted than she'd have thought possible earlier, she began picking out the simple tune while he sang another verse.

> *"A vintner of no little fame,*
> *Who excellent red and white can sell ye,*
> *Beheld the little dirty dame,*
> *As she stood scratching of her belly."*

He stopped there.

"That cannot be all," she protested, still playing and insanely curious as to how the story might end—not to mention what titillating words might be used to tell it.

Rand walked behind her, knelt down, and slipped his arms around her waist. Sweeping her hair aside, he nuzzled her neck. "Do you want to hear the rest?"

She could but nod.

He sang softly by her ear.

> *"From door they went behind the bar,*
> *As it's by common fame reported;*
> *And there upon a Turkey chair,*
> *Unseen the loving couple sported;*
> *But being called by company,*
> *As he was taking pains to please her;*

I'm coming, coming, Sir, says he,
My dear, and so am I, says she, Sir."

She stopped playing and turned on the stool to face him. "Now," she said, "I'm scandalized."

"Are you? You're pink." He grinned. "I like you scandalized."

"I want to see the book."

He laughed, clearly tickled by her reaction. "It's packed away with everything else I had to store from my old house. You'll have to wait until we move to Oxford."

The playfulness suddenly drained out of her. "Will we?"

"Yes." He rose, pulling her up with him. "Yes, we will. Tomorrow I'll talk to Margery, and then to the marquess. And then we'll reclaim our lives. I want no part of this." He waved an arm, encompassing the mansion, the estate, the title —everything.

"I just want you," she said. "No matter who or where you are. Professor, earl, marquess, Hawkridge, Oxford...I don't care. I care only that we're together."

He searched her eyes for a long, tense moment, and then he yanked her against him and crushed his mouth to hers.

This was what mattered, she thought wildly—this heat, this overwhelming need. This longing to share bodies and lives. *Where* was just a tiny, insignificant detail.

His tongue swept her mouth, a declaration of sheer possession. She pressed against him, her arms going around him, beneath his coat, scrambling to get under his shirt. With a groan, he broke the kiss and lifted her into his arms.

The Queen's Bedchamber was just around the corner. In no time at all, he was laying her on the cloth-of-gold coverlet and reaching for the tabs that secured her stomacher. Her heart hammered beneath where his fingers were feverishly working. Her entire body tingled with anticipation.

And then she realized.

"Rand. We cannot."

His fingers didn't even falter. "We cannot what, love?"

As he tossed aside the stomacher and reached for her laces, she sat up and pushed at his hands. "We cannot risk starting a child. If we haven't already, I mean. Your father...what if he doesn't agree to our plan? What if Margery doesn't? What if you have to marry her, Rand?"

"Bloody hell." His hands went limp, and he dropped to sit beside her, jarring the mattress with his sudden weight. After a moment, he turned to look at her. "Nobody can force me. Not even the marquess. You're going to be my wife."

"But what if—"

"I'll never let you go."

"Never say never," she quoted softly.

The light went out of his eyes.

They were silent a long while, their breathing sounding harsh in the still room.

"No," he said at last. "This time I say never."

She drew a deep, steadying breath, then nodded. She had to believe him. Their love was too strong not to find a solution.

Still...

"I'd feel better if we waited," she whispered. "But if you could just hold me tonight..."

He wrapped her close.

FORTY-ONE

"*L*ILY?" RAND whispered into the darkness.

No answer.

How could she sleep? He'd been restless all night, holding her tight, savoring her soft warmth and at the same time gritting his teeth against the need that raged through his body.

Sleeping with Lily—only sleeping—was proving the most exquisite torment. Worse, he wasn't sleeping at all. His mind kept turning over all the possibilities, all the ways their plans could go awry.

When he'd left Hawkridge at fourteen, Margery had been all of seven. Visits during his university years had been sporadic and infrequent—he'd preferred to spend school breaks with Ford's family when possible. His last time home, he'd been twenty and Margery thirteen.

He'd known Margery the child. He'd been acquainted with Margery the girl. But Margery the woman was a stranger.

What if he were wrong? What if Margery the woman *did* want to marry him? She'd lived under the influence of the marquess all these years...

Something shifted at the foot of the bed. At first he thought it was Lily's toes, but then a warm little weight settled across his feet and began vibrating.

A cat. He'd lay odds it was Beatrix, somehow found her way here to Hawkridge. And he'd wager his new house that if it weren't so dark, he'd see Jasper and Lady on the windowsill.

He had a cat on his feet. And its lily-scented owner in his bed. He wasn't sure which made him more uncomfortable.

Then Lily moved against him, and he was sure. More than sure. "Bloody hell," he murmured.

"Hmm?" came her sleep-slurred voice. "Is something wrong? Are you feeling badly?"

"No, just frustrated." He half chuckled, half groaned. "Are you sleeping?"

"I was," she said with a patient sigh, adding guilt to his list of discomforts. "Are you worried?"

"Of course...not."

She rolled over to face him, touching fingers to his face, sweeping hair off his cheek. "Everything will turn out fine."

Her eyes looked black in the darkness but earnest nonetheless. "How do you know?"

"You told me. And I believe you." She gave him a sleepy kiss before her head fell back to the pillows. "Sleep, Rand. I'll still be here in the morning."

Cradling her close, he stared into the interminable night. Margery would be here in the morning, too.

~

*L*ILY SAW NO indication that spies had reported last night's sleeping arrangements to Rand's father. He'd breakfasted before them—Rand had risen late—and closeted himself in his study. Neither did he appear when Lily and Rand heard a vehicle roll up the drive and hurried outside to meet it.

As they stepped onto the cobbles, a footman swung the carriage door wide, and an oval face appeared in the opening.

Dressed in black mourning, Margery looked dazed. She was a pale woman, ethereal almost, and Lily imagined that her recent ordeal had made her even more so. It wasn't every day a woman lost her betrothed to violence.

Lily could hardly conceive of how she'd feel should such a thing happen to Rand. To be planning a life and have it snatched from her so suddenly...well, she was certain she'd look pale, too. Margery currently stood in the way of Lily and Rand's happiness, and Lily had been half expecting to resent her on sight. But now she could feel only sympathy.

Even in her grief, the woman was beautiful. Her hair, so light it was nearly white, framed her face in perfect curls. Her flawless skin looked translucent, and her eyes were a startling deep green. Set off by Margery's pale loveliness, they looked huge. And very, very disturbed.

Lily's heart went out to her...until the woman spotted Rand and her delicate face lit up. Then Lily's heart plunged to her knees instead.

Rand helped Margery down the carriage steps, where she promptly burst into tears, wrapping her arms around him and burying her face in his shoulder.

Lily stood by while the man she loved awkwardly patted the other woman's back. "Margery. Ah, Margery."

"Randy," Margery choked out, gripping him harder.

He'd told Lily that Margery hadn't loved Alban, but it was obvious she did love Rand. Watching them together was more than Lily could bear. She tapped him on the shoulder. "I'll be playing with your father's dogs."

"Lily—"

"No. You need to talk. If I'm not with the dogs, look for me down by the river."

Resolutely she walked away, hoping she wasn't walking out of Rand's life.

FORTY-TWO

"*R*ANDY."

Despite the worried look on Lily's face, and Margery's obvious distress, Rand smiled at her use of the childhood name. Life might have been miserable back when he was known as Randy, but it had also been simpler. And this woman had never been part of the misery.

"Margery." He squeezed her shoulder, feeling responsible for her happiness, the same way he'd felt when she came to Hawkridge as an infant when he was seven. "Whatever's wrong, we'll make it right."

It seemed the old bonds were still strong, like with so many others on the estate. How could he have ignored them all these years? And if the worst came to transpire, could he walk away again, abandon them in their need?

He knew he couldn't.

"Shall we go inside?" he asked her.

With an obvious effort, she controlled her tears. "Is your father at home?"

"He's in his study."

"Then no. I'm not ready to see him. Can we just walk?"

232 | LAUREN ROYAL

"Of course." One arm around her shoulders, he drew her toward the gardens. As they rounded the corner of the house, his gaze drifted toward the dog enclosure, but he didn't see Lily.

Heading toward the grassy paths where he'd walked with Lily last night, he sighed. He wouldn't lose her. That was unthinkable. But for now, he had to concentrate on Margery. She needed him, too.

"I'm sorry for your loss," he began carefully.

"Alban?" To his shock, she practically snorted. "It was a relief to see him put into the ground." She dashed the wetness from her eyes.

"Then...you're not crying because of him?"

"Dear heavens, no." She took a deep breath, looking better already. Some color was returning to her cheeks. "Alban was a cruel man. He was cruel even as a boy; surely you remember that." She shuddered, perhaps remembering things that Rand would rather not know. "I never wanted to marry him."

"Then why did you agree?"

"It was my father's last wish. Not that that stopped me from begging to get out of it. But Uncle William would hear none of it."

The marquess wasn't really her uncle, but she'd called him that since babyhood. To Rand, it had always sounded too friendly a name for the man.

In a sheltered area between two rows of trees, she stopped. "Randy..."

When she hesitated, he turned to her and smiled. "No one calls me that anymore, you know."

Her own smile was wan, but there. "Shall I call you Professor? Or, oh, how could I have forgotten? My lord earl." She executed an absurd, formal curtsy.

"Rand will do," he told her, glad to see the old Margery peeking through all the misery.

"Rand, then," she repeated, growing serious again. "I shall

try to remember, but you'll have to remind me if I forget. Rand…
I…are you aware that Uncle William expects me to marry *you*
now?"

"He's told me as much," he answered, suddenly apprehensive.

She resumed walking, absently trailing one hand along a
hedge as she went by. "Who was that woman with you?"

"Lady Lily Ashcroft, the Earl of Trentingham's daughter."

"She's very beautiful."

"I think so." He watched her elegant fingers skim the leaves.
Margery was beautiful, too, but in a fragile sort of way. She was
taller than Lily and not as fine boned, but Margery would never
allow dogs to slobber all over her. She wouldn't climb fences or
laugh at ribald songs, either. Margery could be flirtatious and
saucy, but beneath it all, she was a very proper young woman.

Well, she'd been raised in the Marquess of Hawkridge's
household, Rand reminded himself. It was a wonder she had
any spunk left in her at all.

She stopped again. "Why is Lady Lily here?"

"She…ah…well, when I received the summons from the
marquess, it said only that—"

"Are you in love with her?"

He met her gaze. There was no sense in lying—the truth
would surely be obvious anyway. "Yes," he said. "I am."

"Thank God."

He blinked, nonplussed. "Pardon?"

"I don't want to marry you, Randy. I mean, Rand." A small
smile curved her lips, then faded. "I didn't want to marry your
brother, and I don't want to marry you. I love you like a sister.
Not a wife."

"You have no idea how relieved I am to hear that."

"Oh, I imagine you're just as relieved as I am to hear it from
you." Turning to walk back toward the house, she slanted him a
sidelong glance. "Did you truly believe I love you that way?"

"I didn't think so," he said. "But I wasn't sure, and many wed for alliance, not love, and the marquess wanted—and Lily worried—"

He stopped, humiliated to find himself babbling.

When a student babbled, he accused the ninnyhammer of being unprepared. Which Rand was, at the moment. Woefully unprepared to deal with this—love, pressure from his family, responsibilities he'd never wanted nor thought would be his...all of it.

They reentered the formal gardens, the gravel crunching beneath their shoes. "Well," he said in an attempt to lighten the mood for both of their sakes, "you cannot blame me for wondering if you might, after all, be besotted. I did, if you'll remember, grace you with your first kiss."

That earned a good-natured smirk. "I don't remember 'grace' being an applicable description. And if I recall correctly, it was *your* first kiss as well. You seemed to be concerned about going off into the world an inexperienced man." Her green eyes perhaps a bit more lively than before, she glanced over at him. "Have you gained any experience, Randal Nesbitt?"

"Oh, in the past fourteen years I've kissed a woman or two. And you?"

"Besides your odious brother at his insistence?" She looked as though the memory made her gag. But then her features softened. "I'm in love with Bennett Armstrong."

"Bennett Armstrong?" He frowned, trying to remember. "Is he not a scrawny boy of ten?"

In spite of her despondency, a little chuckle bubbled up. "He was when you left. He's four-and-twenty now. And not scrawny, I can assure you."

Her dreamy gaze told Rand she had the same feelings for Bennett that he had for Lily. Or a shred of them, anyway. He had a hard time believing most people lived with these strong emotions.

He attempted to picture a grown-up Bennett Armstrong. "His father is a baron, yes?"

"Bennett is the baron now. His father died when the smallpox raged through the county. Three years ago, that was."

That explained Etta's new scars, and the ones he'd seen on other old family retainers. "You never wrote me about the smallpox."

Margery shrugged. "I didn't think you'd care."

He *hadn't* cared, not then. Guilt ate at his insides.

"Bennett is a wealthy baron," she continued. "His father left him gold and estates. I'm certain my own rich but untitled father would have been pleased to see me happily wed to such a man, no matter that Bennett isn't an earl like Alban. Like you," she corrected herself. "Yet I argued with Uncle William until I was blue in the face, and he refused to let us marry." As they drew closer to the house, Margery's feet dragged. "And now there's the complication..."

She seemed reticent to continue. He stopped her with a hand on her arm. "The money? He told me about that. The way the marquess sees it, this is a matter of honor and finances. Love doesn't figure into the equation."

"Money doesn't figure into it, either." She frowned. "I told you, Bennett is a wealthy man. With land, and—"

"It's not your wealth the marquess is concerned with, but his own."

They'd reached the edge of the garden, and Margery plopped down on a bench. "What do you mean?"

"Didn't he discuss this with you?"

"No. I'm female. And that aside, the man tends to be dictatorial."

With a sigh, he sat beside her. "You're a master of understatement," he said and explained about Hawkridge's dependence on her property and the repercussions of losing that income.

"No wonder he didn't want to admit it!" Margery burst out when he was finished. "He kept mumbling about honor and the promise to my father. And now, of course, since it happened, he has the perfect excuse to refuse Bennett—"

"Lily," Rand interrupted her, "has a solution for Hawkridge's finances."

"Does she?" Margery blinked. "But it doesn't solve—"

"She has an inheritance coming. Ten thousand pounds. Plus another three thousand from her marriage portion. That ought to be enough to set the marquess on the road to solvency, and then everyone can wed whomever they want."

Margery toyed with her black skirts. "No, Randy," she started.

"What the devil?" He'd heard a bark from the direction of the river.

There in the distance he saw Lily toss a stick, and a big, wet mastiff jump into the water to retrieve it. Beatrix sat nearby, placidly watching. Apparently the monsters didn't eat cats, after all.

"What are you looking at?" Margery asked.

"Lily." The hound scrambled up the bank and shook violently, spraying her with water that left big dark splotches on her light blue gown. He laughed aloud. "She's playing fetch in the river with one of the marquess's dogs!"

The sight of her, being so very Lily, lightened his heart. She caught him watching and waved. Waving back, he turned to Margery. "I must go tell her you want Bennett, not me. She'll be so happy."

"Rand—"

"Later, Margery." She looked so distressed. "Stop worrying. We'll make it right." Sudden impulse made him lean and give her a quick, chaste kiss on the lips. "For old times' sake," he said lightly, rising from the bench. "Was it better than last time?"

He was gratified to see the ghost of a smile return. "Perhaps. But not as good as Bennett's."

"No? I'm not sure whether I'm happy to hear that or gravely

insulted." He grinned. "I need to talk to Lily; then we'll speak with the marquess."

He started off.

"Wait, Rand, there's more—"

But he was already walking away, and Lily had spotted him. Whatever else Margery wanted to talk about could wait.

FORTY-THREE

*T*HE SMILE FROZE on Lily's face.

He'd kissed Margery. On her mouth.

He'd walked with his arm around her, too. Lily knew that, because although she'd been playing with the dog, she'd kept half an eye on Rand and Margery the entire time.

Or at least while they were visible. For a while they'd disappeared into the hedge- and treelined gardens. Had he kissed Margery there, too? In the little round gazebo where she and Rand had kissed last night?

He was going to marry Margery.

As Lily watched him come closer, she decided she wouldn't make a fuss. Because she was nice. Because his father wanted it this way, and if all the parties agreed, there was no point in fighting fate. Because Margery had known Rand for twenty-one years, while Lily had known him just a few weeks.

Then suddenly she was in his arms, and she wondered how she could have thought any of that. His mouth was on hers, hot and needy, and the whole of her responded. She slipped her hands inside his open surcoat and pressed herself close. Her heart raced; the blood rushed through her veins. And it was the same for him, she was certain.

Nothing had changed between them.

By the time he pulled away, her senses were spinning, her knees wobbly and weak. And although he was smiling, he looked as shaky as she felt. His heart was in his compelling gray eyes, there for her to see.

Perhaps fate would tear them apart, but it was clear as the cloudless sky that it wouldn't be because Rand's feelings for her had changed. And although she wanted an explanation for why he'd kissed Margery, she wouldn't ask, because she didn't want him to know she'd doubted him.

Still smiling, he brushed at his damp coat and plucked his wet shirt away from his body.

The sight of that shirt molded to his body made her swallow hard. "I'm sorry," she said. "I'm afraid Rex has soaked me through." The dog was panting at her feet. She bent to grab the stick and tossed it arcing over the water, watching the mastiff gleefully splash in to fetch it.

Looking every bit as gleeful, Rand swung her back to face him. "It's all right. I'll happily risk more wet to claim another kiss." Involuntarily she swayed toward him, but this kiss was short and light. "Margery doesn't want to marry me," he said with an even wider grin.

"Are you sure?"

"She's in love with another man. A local baron named Bennett Armstrong. My brother's death was a relief to her, since it freed her from their betrothal."

"Then why was she weeping?"

"The marquess has refused Bennett's suit. Because he wants her land and income, of course. But now, with your inheritance..."

"It should work out for all concerned."

"Thanks to your generosity, yes." The dog emerged and shook, soaking them both, and Rand laughed and lifted Lily by the waist, swinging her in a wide circle.

When he finally set her on her feet, he kissed her again

soundly and then gripped both her hands. "Tonight," he said, his voice heavy with meaning, "after all this is settled, I'll come to you."

And they no longer needed to worry about conceiving a child. As her entire body responded to that thought, her fingers tightened on his.

Then she noticed Margery walking toward them.

"You must be Lily," Margery said. "It warms my heart to see how happy you've made Randy."

Lily blushed to the roots of her hair. Margery must have been sitting on that bench, watching, the entire time. And if she hadn't approached now, Lily might well have begun stripping Rand out of his damp clothes.

Well, not really, but she'd wanted to. What a creature of lust she was becoming!

Margery looked wistful.

"I hear you've found a love of your own," Lily told her.

"Yes, I have." Margery's expression softened, but just for a moment. "Randy—I mean, Rand—we must talk. There's something—"

"What the hell are you doing with my dog?"

They all turned to see the marquess storming down the path to the river. Beatrix scampered up a nearby tree to join Lady and Jasper where they sat on a branch, chattering nervously. Lily's heart pounded.

"Don't worry," Margery whispered. "He might bellow like a bear and insist on his own way, but he's not a man to do physical violence."

"I beg to differ," Rand said tightly, making Lily wonder anew what his childhood had been like.

As his father drew near, he looped an arm over her shoulders, a clear message of possession. The tall, formidable marquess stood before them and glared down into Lily's face. "Well?"

Although Lily had always been nice, she'd never been shy. "I was only playing with Rex, my lord. He seems to enjoy it."

"Rex?"

She shrugged. "He needed a name. I assure you, I've done him no harm."

He whistled to the dog, which obediently ran over. "His name is Attila," he said, grabbing the chain around the animal's neck. "And like the rest of my mastiffs, he's a valuable fighter. He'll sell for a top price once he's fully trained—that is, if he doesn't die of a chill first." His fist was white-knuckled on the links. "My dogs do not play."

Lily drew herself up to her full height of five-foot-two. "Perhaps they should. As they don't seem to get a lot of human attention, some toys would be a welcome addition to their enclosure. Knotted rope, as I told Rand." Rand's hand tightened on her shoulder in warning, but she ignored it. She refused to be intimidated by the man she hoped would be her father-in-law. "And you'd do well to uproot the apple tree in there—the fruit is of a size to be a choking hazard."

Surprisingly, the man looked thoughtful if still fierce. "These dogs are meant to accompany soldiers at war. They get plenty of human attention when I train them—to kill. But perhaps some toys might not be amiss. Knotted rope could well promote fighting amongst themselves, which would help keep them in shape."

It wasn't exactly what Lily had in mind, but it was something. And he was no longer ignoring her.

He turned his attention to Margery. "When did you arrive?"

She exchanged a look with Rand. "Mere moments ago, Uncle William."

"Good. We'll talk over dinner. It's long past time we settled your betrothal and marriage. In the meantime, come along. You need to make yourself presentable. The meal will be served in one hour."

He swung on a heel, taking Margery's arm to pull her along with him, the dog trotting on his other side. Lily stared at the man's stiff, retreating back. Margery needed to make herself presentable? Lily had rarely seen a woman so pristine. She glanced down at her own water-and-mud-stained skirts with dismay.

Rand came around to face her and lifted her chin with a hand. "You did well," he said admiringly.

She fluffed at her filthy blue gown. "If he believed Margery needed grooming, he must think I'm a veritable fustilug."

He pressed a tender kiss to her lips. "He wasn't looking at you; he was listening. Miraculously. And he only said that to Margery as an excuse to drag her off. He doesn't want us talking and figuring a way around his plans."

"But we will, won't we?"

"Absolutely. He's unaware of your inheritance. And although he's stood firm on her betrothal, it seems Margery doesn't fear him. Perhaps he's softened in his old age."

He didn't look like he actually believed that, but Lily drew hope from his words. "An hour," she said. "I'll need that time to bathe and change."

He shrugged out of his surcoat and handed it to her. "Take this inside for me, will you? I'm going for a run."

"A run? Now?"

"I'll just have time." His fingers worked the knot in his cravat, then stilled as he met her gaze. "It's just a run, Lily. I like to do that. To—"

"To think. I know."

Then why did she feel shut out?

Not understanding, he smiled as he handed her the lace-trimmed linen. "Thank you. I'll see you at dinner."

All through her bath Lily told herself that Rand's running didn't equate to running away—at least not from her. By the time Etta laced her into a fresh peach gown, she almost believed it.

FORTY-FOUR

"JEROME, YOU may leave us now. And inform the others they are not to enter the dining room unless I ring."

The aging footman bowed and backed away, looking grateful to escape as he shut the door behind him. Rand watched his father pick up his fork and stab a piece of buttered and sugared turnip. The staff was still wary of the man's moods, he thought with an internal sigh. If employment were easier to come by, he imagined most of the old-timers would have left long ago.

"Now," the marquess said, looking pointedly at Rand and then Margery. "You're both here. It's time to seal this betrothal and get on with our lives."

"My lord," Lily started.

"No." The man waved his fork. "You're not part of this family, my lady, and there is nothing you can add to this discussion."

She shared a look with Rand, then set to silently picking at her food.

Seething, Rand lifted his goblet. "You're wrong," he said tightly. "Lily does have something to contribute—an inheritance that she's prepared to put at your disposal in exchange for your blessing on our marriage. Ten thousand pounds, plus her dowry, which brings the total to thirteen. I believe that adds quite a bit to this discussion."

Regardless of the fact that it was an enormous sum of money, the marquess barely blinked. "And where do you suppose that leaves Margery? Your foster sister, promised to my heir on her father's deathbed?"

"Free to marry Bennett Armstrong." Rand sipped smugly.

The man's face turned red as his fork clattered to his plate. "Bennett Armstrong?" he bellowed. "I've forbidden that name to be mentioned in this house!"

Seeing Lily shudder beside him, Rand reached to squeeze her hand.

It seemed Margery, however, was used to this sort of tirade. "Uncle William—"

"Don't 'Uncle William' me, young lady. I've raised you like my own daughter, and I would think you'd have accepted by now that no amount of pleading on your part will make me consider marrying you to a murderer."

Rand's jaw dropped open. "Murderer?"

Margery turned apologetic eyes on him. "I tried to tell you, but you wouldn't listen."

"Bennett Armstrong is a murderer?"

"No!" Margery said at the same time the marquess snapped, "Yes!"

When Lily gasped, Rand tightened his hold on her hand. But his gaze was fixed on the marquess.

"He murdered my son and heir," the man said. "And I intend to see him hang."

FORTY-FIVE

"BENNETT IS NOT a murderer!" Margery burst out. "He did it in self-defense!" She turned to Rand, her eyes frantic. "Alban came after him in the first place."

But all Rand could absorb at the moment was that the man Margery wanted to marry had killed his brother. The hows and whys were beyond him. *And where does that leave Margery?* the marquess had asked. Where, indeed? Even Rand could understand his father's unwillingness to wed his ward to the man at whose hands his own son had died.

Lily's money wasn't going to solve all their problems, after all.

"My Alban," the marquess said, glaring at Margery, "was not a man capable of killing. *Your lover* murdered my son in cold blood. Of course he would claim otherwise, and I've no doubt that a besotted, addlebrained female like you would believe him."

"Alban *would* kill," she shot back. "I saw him kill, time and time again. A rabbit, a lamb. My very own cat when she pounced on him as he was forcing me to kiss him."

Lily hid her face in her hands, and Rand reached to rub her back.

"It's Bennett who's incapable of killing without just provocation," Margery added.

"And he doubtless considered a man determined to wed his lover as 'just provocation.'" The marquess pointed his knife at her, emphasizing each syllable. "Unfortunately, with only his word against a dead man's, I don't have enough evidence for an arrest. Yet. But I intend to get it."

"He's offered a reward for information," Margery told Rand in a voice made high by rising panic. "A hundred pounds."

Lily looked up at that. "A *hundred* pounds?"

"A hundred pounds," Margery repeated, her eyes filling with tears. "Bennett's as good as dead."

Rand couldn't find it in himself to disagree with her. To do so would be a lie. A footman wouldn't earn a hundred pounds in ten years, let alone a groom or coachman or maid. For that kind of money, someone would come forward with damning evidence, honestly acquired or not.

The marquess wielded a lot of power in this small piece of England, and if he meant to see Armstrong hang, Rand had no doubt he would accomplish it.

Plainly seeing the truth in Rand's eyes, Margery let out a pathetic moan and rose from her chair, rushing to kneel at the marquess's knees. Her black gown pooled around her. "I beg you, Uncle William, don't do this. I'll have no will to go on should Bennett die. Let him live long enough for me to prove his innocence."

"Impossible," the man snapped, "given that he's guilty."

She gazed up at him, the tears overflowing, making tracks down her pale cheeks. "Then you'll be killing me along with him."

Just then, she looked entirely too capable of doing herself in, and Rand watched, amazed, as the marquess's features softened with compassion.

But it wasn't long before they hardened again. "He's not dead yet, girl, but I mean to see him pay for murdering my son.

In the meantime, should the two of you think to plan anything, I'll be sending a contingent of men to keep the whoreson under house arrest."

A bell sat by his elbow, and now he raised it and jingled it fiercely, as though venting his frustration on the sterling silver might help him obtain vengeance.

"Jerome!" he called, and the man rushed in.

In moments, it was done. A dozen men were on their way to surround Bennett Armstrong's home.

An hour later, Rand, Lily, and Margery were on their way there, too.

FORTY-SIX

*L*ORD BENNETT Armstrong's house was smaller than Hawkridge Hall and Trentingham Manor, and from the mishmash of styles and the way the house sprawled this way and that, Lily surmised it was older than Hawkridge and Trentingham as well. Sections looked medieval, other parts Tudor, still other portions modern. But regardless of all that, it was obviously the home of a wealthy man.

Each of the three doors had one of Hawkridge's men assigned to guard it, and two more men were posted on every side of the house—in case Lord Armstrong tried to lower himself from a window.

At first, the guard at the front door had no intention of allowing their party to enter. But Rand remembered the man, and soon he was pumping his hand and asking after his wife and children. Rand swore on his mother's grave that he wasn't there to break Lord Armstrong out, and—since the man had apparently adored Rand's mother—in no time at all, they were ushered into the dark, paneled house.

That, Lily knew, was because of Rand's innate charm. She also knew it was because he still had strong ties with the people at Hawkridge. Strong ties that would make it impossible for him to return to Oxford if doing so meant the folks left behind would suffer.

A butler directed them to a study, where they found Lord Armstrong writing a letter.

"Bennett!" Margery streaked across the chamber and threw herself at him. "Oh, Bennett, Uncle William means to see you hang!"

"I know, love." He cupped her face in both his hands. "I was just writing to my uncle with instructions of what to do should that come to pass."

"Oh, Bennett."

With a heartfelt groan, he crushed his mouth to hers, kissing her as though he would never let her go. Margery cooperated fully, running her fingers through his longish dark hair and wrapping her arms around his middle. As Lily watched, Margery worked her hands down Bennett's body, pressing herself against him.

Rand's jaw dropped. "Apparently she's not as proper as I thought," he whispered to Lily.

"Hmm?" She knew she shouldn't watch, and in truth, she felt like a peeper. But seeing them made her want to do the same with Rand. And sadly, with the new developments, she felt nearly as desperate as the other lovers looked.

Well, at least Rand's life wasn't in danger. Only their lives together. She turned and pretended to study a shelf of books, trying to convince herself that things weren't that bad.

At last the couple parted and Lord Armstrong noticed Rand and Lily. His pale green eyes widened. "Randy? Is that you?"

"I'm called Rand these days." He strode forward to shake the man's hand. "And this is my betrothed, Lady Lily Ashcroft."

She curtsied, trying to dredge up a smile. "Lord Armstrong."

Although his gaze didn't make her melt like Rand's did, he was quite good-looking. He managed a grim smile in return. "Let's not stand on ceremony," he said. "I've known your intended all my life. Call me Bennett, please."

"Oh, Bennett." Margery's bottom lip quivered. "I thought that while I was gone, Uncle William would come to his senses. But if anything, he's become even more determined."

"I've seen evidence of that," Bennett muttered, striding to a window to glare down at the guards.

"He's offered a hundred pounds for information that leads to proving your guilt."

"Bloody hell." Bennett shut his eyes, then opened them and sent Lily an apologetic glance. "Pardon the language, my lady."

"I've heard worse," she assured him. "Is there no way to prove your innocence?" She didn't know him, most especially whether or not he might be innocent, but she was praying he was. Clearing him as an acceptable husband for Margery seemed the only hope for her and Rand.

But Bennett just gave a helpless shrug and dropped back onto his bulky wooden desk chair. "There were no witnesses."

Rand began pacing. "Tell me what happened."

Bennett pulled Margery onto his lap and played with a lock of her pale hair while he talked. "I was hunting and, as sometimes happens, had become separated from my companions. Alban rode up almost immediately, as though he had been following and waiting for such an opportunity. He dismounted, pointed a pistol at me, and accused me of plotting to steal his bride."

Rand turned and leveled him with a stare. "Were you?"

Bennett looked to Margery for help. She met Rand's gaze. "Your father wouldn't allow us to marry, so we were planning to elope. I have no idea, however, how Alban could have found out."

"Alban had his ways," Rand said darkly. "So then what happened?"

Bennett's swallow was audible from across the room. "I dived off my horse to knock the gun from his grasp, and it went off. Then he drew his sword, and I panicked. Alban was known for his swordsmanship, and he wasn't looking for a duel of honor—he'd made it clear he wanted me dead. I swiped a stout branch off the ground and bashed him over the head. He went down like a sack of flour."

Rand still paced. "And he was dead."

"Dead as a doornail, I'm afraid. I didn't mean to kill him—I could have shot him if I'd wanted that. I was hunting and had a musket, after all. But I wasn't sorry. He didn't deserve my Margery—he treated her abominably."

"Don't you see?" Margery slid off Bennett's lap and went over to Rand, halting him with a hand on his arm. "It was self-defense. If he hadn't done Alban in, Bennett would've been dead instead."

"But how to prove it?" Lily asked.

"I don't know." Margery looked toward her pleadingly. "But you must help me find a way."

"We will," Lily promised softly.

Rand had too many problems for Lily to burden him with her own, but without her sisters here for support, she'd been feeling adrift and alone. She and Margery had a common goal. Together, with Rand's help, they would fight to keep their men.

The two women shared a sad, understanding smile, and Lily felt a little bit better.

FORTY-SEVEN

*T*HE MARQUESS failed to appear for supper that evening, claiming a backlog of work due to Alban's demise. He took a tray in his study instead.

But later that night, when Rand, Lily, and Margery were passing the hours in the north drawing room, Lily playing gentle tunes while Rand and Margery sat nearby and puzzled over what could be done, the marquess appeared in the doorway. Lily's fingers stilled on the keys, leaving an expectant silence.

"No matter what you believe," the marquess said, addressing himself to Margery, "I have raised you like my own daughter and care for you as though you were. Your pleas haven't fallen on entirely deaf ears."

Rand saw Margery's heart leap into her eyes and felt his own heart leap as well. "Yes?" he asked when she appeared unable to speak.

The marquess swung his cold gray gaze on him. "I have a plan to spare her lover's life."

"Thank heavens," Margery breathed.

"Thank me," the man snapped. "The truth is I know better than to make this offer. You should be thankful I have a soft heart."

Rand bit back a retort. The marquess had claimed he cared for her as a daughter. For Margery's sake, Rand hoped the man believed a daughter should be better treated than a son.

She rose, her black skirts trembling as she slowly approached the doorway. "What is your plan, Uncle William?"

The marquess straightened. "On your twenty-first birthday, one week hence, you will wed my son."

"Oh, no—"

"Oh, yes. Should the two of you fail to marry, your lover will hang. Should the wedding take place, I shall see that he is granted a commutation of sentence and transported to the colonies instead." He paused, drawing breath. "May God forgive me my weakness," he said to no one in particular, then turned and strode from the chamber.

As one, the three of them released their breaths.

"This is unconscionable," Rand gritted out.

Margery's face was even paler than usual. A pure, bloodless white. "We must marry," she whispered, casting an apologetic glance to Lily. She focused back on Rand. "We must marry to save Bennett's life."

FORTY-EIGHT

*M*ARGERY TOOK a few faltering steps toward Rand, then dropped to her knees at his feet. "We must marry." She clutched his ankles. "We must."

A dazed expression on his face, Rand reached for her shoulders and raised her to stand. "There must be another way."

Unable to believe this turn of events, Lily watched as Margery searched Rand's eyes, her own green eyes frantic. She gripped his hands in both of hers. "But will you? To save his life? Tell me you will. From my earliest memories, I looked up to you, Rand. You were my big brother who could do no wrong. You won't let me down, will you? Tell me you'll marry me to save Bennett's life."

Though a muscle in his jaw twitched, he nodded. "I won't doom another man to die. But there must be another way."

Tears streaming down her face, Margery hugged him, hard. Then, without another word, she ran from the room.

Lily released a deep, shuddering breath. "Rand—"

"I've never seen her this selfish." His gaze swung from the empty doorway to Lily. "She didn't for a moment consider how *I'd* feel about this marriage. Or you."

"I'd feel the same way if your life were threatened. I'd ask anything of anyone."

After a moment of thought, he nodded. "I'd do the same for you. But there must be another way for Margery and Bennett. I won't lose you."

She walked closer. "A man's life is at stake."

"There must be another way."

It was becoming a litany, one Lily wished she could believe. "Does your father truly wield such power?"

"I'm afraid so." Rand took her elbow and began walking her toward her chamber. "You must realize that outside of London there is little if any provision for due process of the law. If the Marquess of Hawkridge wishes Bennett dead, he can make it happen. Is it not the same for the little area of the world where your father is the lord?"

Reluctantly she nodded. "I suppose it is. But I've never seen him wish anyone dead. Life at Trentingham is generally peaceful." A peace she hadn't expected to miss, a peace she'd even equated with boredom at times.

Oh, to live again that blessed, boring peace.

"Life at Hawkridge has never been peaceful," Rand said ruefully, stopping in front of the Queen's Bedchamber. "But I hope to take you away from here to where we can live in peace. Soon."

He opened the door. Inside, a fire was already lit and several candles burned merrily, but the room still seemed an empty void.

"Oh, Rand." She turned into his arms.

He held her tight for a long, long time before he extricated himself. "Sleep well," he said softly, then turned and walked away.

Unable to watch him leave, she stepped into the chamber and shut the door behind her. Then leaned back against it, fighting the nausea that threatened when she thought of her happiness slipping away.

256 | LAUREN ROYAL

Just that morning, she'd stood with Rand by the river, laughing, hugging him, so very glad to learn that Margery was in love with another man. *Tonight*, he'd said, *after all this is settled, I'll come to you.*

In that moment, it had seemed that life would be perfect after all. But now, instead of coming to her, he had walked away.

To go to Margery instead? She thought not. She was far past any insecurities where Rand's love was concerned.

But he was an honorable man, and she knew, without a doubt, that if it meant saving Bennett's life, he'd marry Margery instead of her.

FORTY-NINE

*I*N HIS SMALL chamber, Rand sat on the bed to tug off his boots. *There must be another way,* he repeated to himself over and over as he pulled off his stockings and crushed them into balls that he threw across the room with an anger he hadn't felt since he'd last lived in this damned house. He shrugged out of his surcoat and yanked at the cravat at his throat, throwing those across the room, too. He wished he had something to break, but his chamber had been stripped of all but the furniture some time in the fourteen years between when he'd left for Oxford and now.

There had to be another way.

He was loosening the laces on his shirt when a soft knock came at the door. Thinking it must be Lily, his heart gave a little hitch. He wanted her. Oh, how he wanted her.

And he couldn't have her, not now. But neither could he turn her away. Fighting with himself, he hurried to open the door.

Margery stood there instead.

She was still wearing the dull black gown, the clothes the marquess had sent her to London to obtain to show the proper respect for his dead son. Her eyes red-rimmed, she twisted her fingers together. "There's something else I need to tell you."

Though her tone sounded dire, Rand just sighed. "Come in, Margery."

He shut the door and led her to sit on the room's only chair, struggling to appear sympathetic. It wasn't that he didn't care, but he'd had about all the anguish he could take—and despite her obvious distress, he couldn't imagine anything that could make this situation even worse.

Until he heard her next words.

"Rand...oh, Rand, I'm with child."

He dropped abruptly to sit on the bed. "God, Margery." Hardly sympathetic, but he was too shocked to know what to say. No matter that Lily might be in the same way, this was Margery, his baby sister, Margery...

Looking even more miserable, she laid a hand on her still-flat middle. "No one else knows except Bennett. It's why we'd planned to elope. I tried to obey, Rand, truly I did, but I just couldn't marry Alban knowing I carried Bennett's child. Alban was...he would have killed it," she said flatly.

Rand could imagine that all too well. "Well, he cannot kill it now," he said in a way he hoped was soothing.

"But I still..." Again, her eyes filled with tears. "Oh, Rand, will you raise it as yours? I know it's a lot to ask, but we can hope it's a girl so it won't be your heir, and—"

"We're going to find another way." Rand's head was suddenly throbbing. "It won't matter if it's a boy or a girl, because the child will be raised by its father."

"But *what if*, Rand?" Apparently she was quite past believing that. "Uncle William is planning our wedding for seven days hence. What if we're forced to marry? Will you raise this child as yours? I could have hidden it from you, tried to make you believe it *was* yours, but—"

"You're not like that, I know."

And he also knew there was no chance he'd ever fall for such a ploy, because if, heaven forbid, he was forced to wed her, he wouldn't be sharing her bed.

He would never again lie with anyone but Lily.

Margery stood and wrapped her arms around her middle. Slow tears trailed down her pale cheeks, leaking from eyes that looked hopeless. "*What if*, Rand? Will you be a true father to this child?"

"Of course I will," he said simply, because there was nothing else he could say.

But he would find another way...because there was nothing else he could do.

Nothing.

FIFTY

*C*LAD IN HER nightgown with her hair in one long plait, Lily huddled under the covers of the giant state bed.

Just hours earlier at Bennett's house, she'd thought she and Margery had made an unspoken pact, come to a wordless understanding that they would fight this problem together. But perhaps that wasn't true; perhaps it had been her imagination. Because if a silent promise had indeed passed between them, Margery had broken it already.

Not that Lily blamed her. As she'd told Rand, were his life at risk, she'd do anything for a chance to save him. But that truth didn't ease the distress of realizing that, other than Rand, she had no allies here at Hawkridge at all.

Although Beatrix cuddled with her, she'd never felt so alone in her life.

Was she fated to be alone forever?

There must be another way, Rand had said over and over, as though he could make it so by repetition alone. But Lily was unconvinced. It seemed that no matter what solution they came up with, his father would shoot it down.

For a long time she lay awake, stroking Beatrix's downy fur

and watching the shadows made on the walls by the all-too-cheerful dancing flames of the fire. Rand had no love for this house, and as much as she always tried to look on the bright side of things, she couldn't help but think that in this case he was right. Although it was beautiful, there seemed something evil about Hawkridge, something that made her skin crawl. She didn't like being alone in this room.

She hugged herself for a long while. Then she climbed out of bed and slid a wrapper over her nightgown.

A few minutes later, she knocked softly on Rand's door. He came to answer, wearing just breeches and a shirt that was open at the neck and cuffs. He looked as sleepless as she.

"Rand? May I just sleep here?"

He gathered her close. "I'm not sure," he said with a sad little chuckle. "Last night was torture for us both." Tilting her chin up, he pressed a gentle kiss to her lips. "I'm afraid, sweetheart, that for me, you're too much of a temptation."

A heaviness settled in Lily's chest. She stared down at his bare feet. No matter what he said over and over, he wasn't convinced that everything would work out. Or else he would want her in his bed, and damn the risk of conceiving.

"Oh, Lily..." He slipped his hands under her wrapper, settling them on her hips to pull her close. His fingers seemed to burn through her nightgown.

She raised a palm and placed it against his chest, inside the open placket of his shirt, where his bare skin was brown and warm. "Rand..." Shutting her eyes against the pain in his, she went to her toes for a kiss. Though his lips on hers felt achingly familiar, the caress didn't bring the relief she was seeking.

The kiss was hot and desperate and set her heart to pounding, but it failed to make her forget that, barring a miracle, he was going to marry another woman.

He reached blindly to unravel her plait, his eyes still closed and his mouth still locked on hers. A pathetic little moan escaped her throat as she wondered if this was the last time she'd feel the loving tugs of his fingers freeing her hair, the last time he'd claim her lips with passionate abandon.

Finally, with a heartfelt sigh, he broke the kiss and swung her up into his arms.

"We cannot," she said.

"There are other ways, Lily." He deposited her on his small childhood bed and looked down on her, tenderly finger-combing her hair into a halo around her head. "Ways we can be together that don't carry the risk of getting you with child."

"But we cannot." When he stretched out beside her, she turned to meet his eyes. "You shouldn't even be kissing me. Don't you see? We cannot be together this way, knowing you might marry Margery. It would be wrong."

He looked away, staring up at the underside of the serviceable blue canopy. No Queen's Bedchamber, this—no silk for Rand Nesbitt at Hawkridge Hall. His room was barely more than a closet.

"Yes," he agreed at last. "It would be wrong."

She lay back and ran a trembling hand through her hair. What if she was already with child? She had no doubt now that it would make little difference to Rand's father—he was determined his son wed Margery. She would have to hope her womb was yet empty.

But she couldn't find it in herself to wish for that. If fate decreed that Rand's child was the only piece of him she could ever have, she would take it along with the consequences and be happy for the privilege.

"I don't like it here," she whispered into the silence. "This house. I cannot sleep in that room alone."

"Stay with me, then," Rand said. "I'll be the perfect gentleman, although it will probably kill me." He snuggled against her, releasing a strangled groan. "And tomorrow, I'll take you home. I don't like this house any more than you do, and I've things to take care of in Oxford."

FIFTY-ONE

RAND SET THEIR luggage by the carriage and, leaving two outriders to deal with it, headed into the house to fetch Lily.

"You'll be back, I presume? A week from yesterday?"

Rand pivoted to see the marquess standing outdoors, holding two dogs by their chain collars. "Yes, I'll be back," he forced through gritted teeth, hoping against hope that he'd be arriving with a solution to this dilemma.

"Sit," the man told the dogs. "Stay." He climbed the steps to Rand. "Margery told me you're willing to wed her in order to save Bennett's life. She's very grateful."

Rand had nothing to say to that.

"Son," the marquess started—and when Rand visibly flinched, the man sighed. "I suppose I deserve that. I just wanted to say I'm impressed that you're willing to do the right thing and marry the girl. It's admirable, considering you had other plans."

Rand consciously unclenched his jaw. "Lily is more than plans; Lily is my life. And your approval means nothing to me. I don't need the admiration of a man who ignored me all my childhood."

With that, he turned to head upstairs, but the marquess

caught his arm. "I'm...I'm sorry for that." Rand stared, unable to believe the word *sorry* had passed the old goat's lips. He opened his mouth to voice another retort, but the man rushed on. "I was thinking, last night, about you and Alban and Margery."

"And how you liked the two of them better than me?"

"Yes," he bit out. "I did. I'm not proud of it, but there's the truth. I always blamed you for your mother's death. Whenever I looked at you, I was reminded, and—"

"Her death? However did your twisted mind come up with that? I wasn't even home when she died!"

"Exactly. You'd run off somewhere, as was your habit in those days. She died searching for her precious younger son."

Rand felt like all the air had been sucked right out of him. *Run off, as was your habit.* "She died searching?"

"She raced off on Queenie, her mare. The animal failed to clear a fence. Broke two legs and had to be put down. Your mother broke her neck."

"I..." Afraid his legs would give out, Rand retreated in search of somewhere to sit. The backs of his calves finally bumped into a hall chair, and he collapsed onto it.

He stared at the black-and-white floor between his limp, spread knees. "I never knew how she died. I just came home and she was...gone."

The marquess followed him, looking down on him. "No point in telling a boy of six," he said in clipped tones. "If I was wrong to blame you for her death, at least I wasn't daft enough to accuse you out loud."

Rand looked up. "No. Instead you ignored me, mistreated me, drove me from your home—"

"And you managed to survive regardless. And"—the man shifted on his feet—"to make a life for yourself."

Rand Nesbitt's many accomplishments meant less than nothing to the Marquess of Hawkridge. "Not a life you'll ever approve. In the world where I belong, I'm called Professor, not *my lord*."

The man's jaw tightened. "You're an earl now and will someday be a marquess. That's another matter we need to discuss. Which we will, just as soon as you wed Margery and set up residence here."

"I have no intention of living here. I'm not in such a hurry to put myself back in range of your disapproval and abuse."

"I've said I was sorry," the marquess muttered. He glanced through the open door. "I've dogs to attend to."

"By all means," Rand said, waving him off.

The man always had valued his dogs over his son.

$\mathcal{T}$HE RIDE TO Trentingham was awkward.

Rand was subdued, and Lily had difficulty trying to sustain both sides of the conversation. The worst of it was that for the first time since the baptism, she found herself wracking her brain to find anything to discuss. Their ease with each other was gone, their relationship changing already.

It was only two hours between the estates, yet the time passed like the carriage's wheels were mired in mud. Though Beatrix rode inside, her warm softness on Lily's lap failed to provide any comfort. When they finally rolled up before the manor, she couldn't wait to get into the house.

Was it but three days since she'd been home? A day in Oxford and two at Hawkridge. In that short span of time, her entire life had spun upside down.

Just inside the door, Mum met her and wrapped her in a hug. "That was a short visit."

Lily clung to her mother for a moment, inhaling her familiar floral scent. "It felt like a lifetime." When she pulled away, she looked around as though seeing her home for the first time. So light and bright, the staircase off the entry fashioned of classical white balustrades instead of heavy, dark carved wood. The atmosphere warm and loving, not cold and full of resentment. "It's good to be home."

Concern flooded her mother's brown eyes. "Do you not like Hawkridge Hall? Will you not want to live there?"

"Oh, Mum, it seems I won't be living there even if I did want to!" Here, finally, was someone who cared. Lily had felt invisible at Hawkridge Hall—no, worse than invisible. A burden to Rand and *persona non grata* to everyone else. "Things have changed—"

Spotting Rand standing in the doorway, she broke off.

"Rand." Though Mum smiled at him, the expression in her eyes said she knew something was wrong. "How very nice to see you again. You'll stay for supper, won't you? Or does your father expect you back at Hawkridge this afternoon?"

"No," he said dully. "I'm going home to Oxford for a few days."

"The sun sets late this time of year, so you can stay for dinner, then, at least."

He shrugged as though he didn't care. "I'm going for a run," he said to Lily, already struggling out of his surcoat. "I'll be back in a while."

"No," she said. "Oh, no."

As he turned and walked away, Mum laid a gentle hand on Lily's arm. "I can see that things didn't go well with his father. Leave him be, dear."

"No." Lily started toward the door. "I've let him be quite enough. I'll be back and explain later."

"Lily!" Mum called.

But she was already out the door and down the steps.

FIFTY-THREE

"*W*AIT!" LILY called.

But Rand didn't, even though she was sure he'd heard her. To the contrary, he shoved his coat and cravat into the carriage and then began to run, putting more distance between them.

She hurried past blue and yellow flower beds in her high Louis-heeled shoes. Hoping she wouldn't twist an ankle in the soft grass, she wished she hadn't dressed so fashionably this morning.

The shoes and the lavender gown with the heavy overskirt had been a final attempt to impress her future father-in-law. If she wasn't so upset, she'd laugh at herself for her characteristic optimism. The fact was, there was nothing she could do to make the man like her. He wanted his son to marry Margery, and that was that.

He'd probably sent up a cheer when he saw her climb into the carriage and ride away.

Lily had never really disliked anyone in her life, but she disliked Rand's father immensely. Not for the way he treated her—he didn't know her, after all—but for the way he treated Rand.

Rand. There he was, crossing the bridge to the other side of the river.

"Rand!"

Thanks to living with her father, Lily knew how to make her voice carry. But although Rand stopped running, he didn't stop altogether, instead pacing determinedly along the far bank.

Hopping on one foot and then the other, she pulled off her shoes and left them jumbled on the daisy-strewn lawn. Then she picked up her skirts and ran—across the grass, over the bridge, along the path with the river on one side and grazing fields on the other.

Her face heated and her lungs burned. She developed a searing stitch in her side. But she wouldn't stop running.

She would never give up on Rand Nesbitt.

In the woods beyond, she spotted him in the distance and pushed herself to close the gap. "Rand," she called breathlessly.

He slowed, stopped, and turned, looking defeated. "You'll cut your feet," he said in a dead voice.

Panting, she looked down to the forest floor, littered with twigs and leaves. Her silk stockings were torn, which was no surprise, but she hadn't noticed when it happened.

"I—don't—care," she said between gasping attempts to catch her breath. She bent at the waist, hugging the pain in her side. "All I care for, Rand, is you."

If she'd hoped he'd melt at those words, she was disappointed. "Sometimes," he said, "I need to be by myself. Can you not leave a body alone?"

"I've tried that. It hasn't worked."

"I need to think. I cannot think."

She straightened and met his gaze. She had something she needed to tell him, and she knew he needed to share something, too. A piece of the puzzle was missing—the piece she suspected had made him run. "We can think together. Maybe two heads are better than one."

His jaw tensed as though he were forcibly holding back

words. He crossed his arms, shutting her out. His gaze drifted up to the canopy of leaves overhead.

The solitude he wanted would solve nothing. "I'm staying here, Rand. I won't leave you. Do you hear me?" She shouted it to the trees. "I won't leave you, no matter what your father says!"

Slowly he lowered his eyes. "Do you believe in fate?"

"I believe you're *my* fate."

"Oh, Lily." He shook his head, opening his arms. "Come here."

His arms felt so good around her, so solid and sure. He kissed her, kissed her until she was more breathless than she'd been from running, until she felt boneless and light-headed. He put one-hundred-percent of himself into the wordless promise of that kiss.

And she knew, without a doubt, that whatever it was that made him run away, time after time, had nothing to do with a lack of love for her. Perhaps he simply didn't know how to share. He'd spent so very much of his life on his own.

Well, she'd show him how. Two heads *were* better than one, two hearts even stronger.

When he finally drew back, she searched his intense gray eyes. "What happened? It's something else, isn't it? Besides Margery and your father's ultimatum?" He tried to look away, but she moved to the side, keeping her gaze locked on his. "What happened?" she repeated. "What new complication has arisen to pile on top of the others?"

He sighed, looking reluctant to confide in her.

But at least he didn't run.

With both hands, she propelled him toward a stump and pushed down on his shoulders until he sat. "Tell me," she said.

He gathered her onto his lap. Leaves rustled overhead, and a sparrow fluttered from one branch to another. Lady, found her way back home. Jasper blinked his little squirrel eyes at them, then darted up a tree. Lily rubbed her scarred hand and stared at her stockinged toes, waiting.

"The marquess," Rand said at last, "has claimed he had an excuse for the way he's treated me all of these years."

"You were a child. There was no excuse."

"He blamed me for the death of my mother."

"What?" She shifted to face him. "How did she die? You never told me."

"I never knew. It seems, as a child, I had a habit of running off." He paused as though waiting for her to agree or to chide him. When she didn't, he went on. "I was six when it happened. She couldn't find me and went out looking."

"And died?"

"A riding mishap. She broke her neck."

"Oh, Rand." Sensing his pain, she wrapped her arms around his neck and buried her face in his shoulder. "It wasn't your fault."

"I'd disappeared."

"You were six. You weren't responsible for her accident. It could have happened another day, another time—"

"But it didn't." The guilt rolled off of him in waves. "It happened when I ran off. I killed her."

She lifted her head. "No. You're not to blame."

"My father thinks I am. I left her, and she died. And look at me. I'm still running off and hurting the people I love."

She offered him a wan smile. "I believe I just put a stop to that. And Rand, you didn't kill her. Your father saying so doesn't make it true. You were six years old. Events happen. This one was tragic, but you cannot believe it's your fault."

"My father believes I'm to blame."

"Not really," she argued. "Or he'd have voiced that blame aloud long ago. And he never did, did he? Or you would have known how she died before now."

He appeared to consider that for a moment, and Lily felt a

little of the tightness ease from his body. "You won't convince me the man is good," he finally said.

"No, and I wouldn't try. His treatment of you was unpardonable, but perhaps natural, for all that. He was hurting—"

"Hurting?" Rand interrupted in a tone of patent disbelief.

She nodded. "He must have loved her very much to react in such a strong manner, even if it was wrong."

"Love? I cannot picture that man in love. I doubt he even believes in such a fine emotion."

She decided to drop that for now. "Regardless, he was wrong to treat you that way. Not only because you were—are—his child, but also because—"

"I was only six," he finished softly, as though really hearing that for the first time.

"Yes, you were only six."

An invisible burden seemed to roll off his shoulders, and he sat there a long while, silent, rubbing her back.

"I need time to think," he said at last.

"About your mother?"

He shook his head, a slow, mournful motion. "About Margery. I cannot marry her, loving you. I cannot. And yet...can I condemn another man to die?"

Of course he couldn't; he wouldn't be the man she loved if he could. Lily swallowed hard. "Would it make it any easier if I told you I'm not with child?"

His hand stilled on her back. "What do you mean?"

"I...I awakened this morning, and..." She felt her cheeks flood with color. She'd never discussed anything like this with a man, but she'd known since this morning that she had to. She'd run all the way out here to tell him. "My courses are upon me," she said quietly. "I'm not with child."

"Oh," he said; then his arms wrapped around her and held her close. "I'm sorry."

"Are you? Truly?" Her first feelings this morning had been of sorrow, although she knew she should have been relieved. And truthfully, a large part of her *was* relieved. "Your father, you know—it would have made no difference. We had no hope of using it to our favor."

"I know. But...well, I was picturing her already. She looked like you. I'd be the first to admit that mere days ago I'd have quailed at the thought of fatherhood, but now that I've had time to get used to the idea, damn if I wasn't looking forward to it."

"I was picturing a boy. A gray-eyed boy with long, dark gold hair."

His lips curved in a half smile. "Twins. They run in your family, don't they?"

Despite everything, she had to laugh. "If you'd seen my sister heavy with twins, you wouldn't wish that on me. Besides, it's Ford's family that runs to twins. Surely you know he's a twin himself."

"Ah, yes. Kendra." For a moment, Rand looked far away, lost in the past. Then the faint smile faded from his face and he hugged her even tighter. "One child, twins, triplets—I don't care, so long as they're ours. More than anything, Lily, I want you to have my children."

"Oh, Rand, I want your baby, too." She laid a hand over her empty womb, thinking about what might have been, what might never be. "There must be another way," she said, using his words. "You're right—we both need to think."

He put his bigger hand over hers. "Not now. I'm sorry, but I must go to Oxford. I need more clothes, and other—"

"I didn't mean you're never allowed to go off alone. You'll think in Oxford, and I'll think here."

By unspoken agreement, they rose and began walking in the direction of Trentingham. Rand took her hand. "After Oxford, I must go back to Hawkridge. It's my only hope of finding any evidence to free Bennett. He said he was hunting with a party; one of the other men might have seen something. Or someone else. If need be, I will interview every soul in a ten-mile radius."

Leaves crunched beneath Lily's stockinged feet, and when a

twig snapped with a loud *crack*, Rand swept her up into his arms. She linked her hands behind his neck. "I shall come and help you."

She saw the telltale hesitation, felt the slight tightening of his arms before he decided to come out with it. "Let me talk to my father first. You'll be but two hours away, and I'll come for you, I promise, once I ascertain you'll be accepted."

His gray eyes pleaded for her to understand, and she did, but it was frustrating to feel so helpless.

"Trust me on this, sweetheart," he said softly.

"If I think of anything that could help, anything at all, I'll come to you," she warned him as they emerged from the woods.

In the soft grass that lined the banks of the river, he set her on her feet and pressed his lips to her forehead. "I wouldn't want it any other way," he murmured, the words a damp promise against her skin. "We're in this together. Never doubt that, my love."

FIFTY-FOUR

*D*INNER WAS A subdued affair.

Bacon tart was usually one of Lily's favorites, its flaky crust and sweet almonds contrasting with the salty meat, but today she only picked at it while she listened to Rose grill Rand about the latest developments. For once, Rose didn't seem jealous about Lily's betrothal—in fact, Lily would wager her sister was glad she wasn't the one in this predicament.

Mum looked very sorry that she'd insisted Lily go along to Hawkridge, although as Lily pointed out, her absence wouldn't have changed anything.

"It would have spared you some discomfort, dear," Mum said.

But that didn't matter to Lily. The reward for that discomfort had been more time with Rand—precious time that could turn out to be their last.

Afterward, Lily saw him out to his carriage. "If you think of anything," she told him, "anything at all—I want to know. And if I think of anything, I'll send word to you at Oxford."

"I may not be there long enough for word to reach me. Fewer than six days remain until the wedding. I need to get back to

Hawkridge well before that if I'm to find evidence enough to prevent it."

"Then stop here on the way. Please. It won't cost you but half an hour, and I may have an idea—"

She broke off when his lips descended on hers.

The kiss was wild, desperate. It made her mouth burn with fire and her senses reel dangerously. She knew, without a doubt, that she would never find this with another man—and the truth cracked her heart.

When he finally broke the kiss, he crushed his forehead against hers, his eyes closed. "God, Lily, this cannot be the end for us. It just cannot."

"It won't be." She kissed him again, softly, before drawing back. "You'll stop by on your way to Hawkridge?"

He opened his eyes and nodded.

"Then I'll see you in a few days," she said, suspecting those days would be the longest of her life.

Rose, however, wasn't going to let her mope around.

"I think tonight we should have our sleeping party," she said when Lily reentered the house.

Lily rubbed her face. "Whatever are you talking about?" She wasn't interested in any sort of party, especially tonight. Tonight she just wanted to crawl into her bed, curl up, and think hard about how Bennett's innocence could possibly be proved.

If he even *was* innocent...but she had to believe he was. It was the only chance she and Rand had.

"The sleeping party, remember?" Rose put a hand on Lily's arm, her eyes dark with concern. "You said Violet should come over to sleep. And I think we should invite Judith, too. She's your best friend—she'll want to hear what's happening. I'm going to write notes to both of them and ask Parkinson to see they're delivered."

Before Lily could protest, Rose was off.

For a while Lily stood in a daze, then she went upstairs and changed into a more comfortable gown. She didn't need to impress anyone here at Trentingham.

By the time she caught up with her sister, messages had been sent to both Violet and Judith, and Rose was in the kitchen talking to Mrs. Crump, their cook. "Fruit, nuts, bread, and cheese. And some nun's biscuits," she said, "since those are Lily's favorites. We need it all ready to take to her room at nine o'clock." Spotting Lily, she turned and smiled. "We don't want to starve during our sleeping party."

Lily hadn't realized her sister could be so efficient. Or kind— especially considering the broken promise. "Why are you doing all this, Rose?"

A flush touched Rose's cheeks. "You told Rand that two heads are better than one. Well, four would be even better, don't you think? Perhaps tonight we can hit upon a solution."

Lily wasn't sure she felt up to what Rose had planned, but she sincerely appreciated the sentiment. "Thank you," she said, "for caring."

"Don't be a goose," Rose said with a wave of a hand. "You're my sister. Now, we'll need some nice flower arrangements for the supper table and your chamber. I'd best get busy."

As Rose hurried away, Lily looked after her in wonder. It seemed her sister was back to normal, but she couldn't figure out why.

A soft drizzle began to fall outside, turning the world gray and dismal to match Lily's mood. Violet and Judith both arrived in time for supper, and the whole story was told again. By the time they all made it up to Lily's room for their sleeping party, laden with a decanter of wine and the refreshments that Mrs. Crump had prepared, Lily was exhausted to the point of numbness.

She collapsed crosswise on top of her white coverlet. "I'm afraid you're going to have your party without me."

Violet set down a bowl of fruit and reached a hand to help

her sit. "I'm sure you're tired," she said sympathetically, settling beside her on the bed. "But we have a mission to accomplish."

Even in her state, Lily couldn't help but notice the faint circles under her oldest sister's eyes. "You look rather tired yourself."

"Two babies will do that to you," Violet said with a tender smile. But it faded as she watched Lily lay a hand on her abdomen. "You'll have children, too, Lily."

"We just have to put our heads together and come up with a brilliant idea," Rose said as she sat herself on Lily's other side.

The three of them against all the injustice in the world.

"Why?" Lily couldn't help asking Rose. "Why all of a sudden are you willing to help me wed Rand Nesbitt?"

"The Earl of Newcliffe," Rose corrected her, but not unkindly. "And as to why…well…" Her cheeks reddened. "This afternoon, when I saw how miserable you were, and Rand, too—well, it made me realize I'd never loved him like that. I only wanted him because he's so handsome."

"And titled," Violet reminded her, leaning across Lily to send their sister an arch look.

"Well, that, too. I *do* want someone of consequence, you know. But Lily and Rand—they belong together."

"Thank you," Lily whispered. How bittersweet it was to have her sister finally approve at the same time her betrothal was falling apart.

Seated at Lily's dressing table with a platter of bread and cheese, Judith stopped eating long enough to release a languid sigh. "You and Rand are so romantic."

Lily eyed her friend thoughtfully. "You look happy."

"I am." Judith's pale blue eyes shone. "I've spent some time alone with Edmund—I mean, Lord Grenville—"

"You'd never been alone with him?" Rose interrupted.

Buttering bread, Judith blushed. "Well, it's not exactly proper, I know, but Papa managed to talk Mama into allowing it. I was so very unhappy, not really knowing Edmund and thinking I might never come to love him."

Lily began filling four goblets with wine. "So what happened?"

Judith looked up, her cheeks flushed with wonder. "He's ever so marvelous. The sweetest man. I cannot imagine why I expected to fall in love at first sight. It takes getting to know someone, don't you think? What a man looks like doesn't matter as much as what he's like inside."

Rand, Lily thought, was wonderful both inside and out. She would never find another man so perfect.

She handed Judith a cup. "So what is Lord Grenville like inside?"

"Thoughtful. Kind. He answered all my questions and listened when I answered his. He loved his first wife dearly, but he was ever so sad that she couldn't give him any children. More than anything, he wants children. And I...I want to give them to him."

"Have you considered," Rose asked, "that the failure to have children might be due to some lack on *his* part?" It was just like Rose to say out loud what other women would only wonder silently. "After all," she added, "he's thirty-five." She said *thirty-five* as though the man were likely to topple over and die of old age at any moment.

"That's not so ancient!" Judith burst out defensively. Lily's sister blinked, clearly taken aback, but Judith went on. "Do you know, Rose, that someday you will be five-and-thirty, too? And for your sake, I hope by then—"

She broke off, leaving the rest of the sentence unspoken. But they all knew what she'd been about to say.

I hope by then you'll have found a husband.

"Well," Rose said stiffly. "I hope for *your* sake that Lord Grenville's childlessness wasn't due to his own shortcomings. I expect you may gain some enlightenment when you discover whether he's skilled in the bedchamber."

"I can assure you," Judith said just as stiffly, "that his child-lessness had nothing to do with his skills. He's a *very* good kiss-er." A hunk of cheese halfway to her mouth, she paused and glanced around as though waiting for them all to express shock. "Are you not scandalized," she finally asked no one in particular, "that I allowed him to kiss me?"

Violet laughed. "No, we're not scandalized. As a matter of fact, Mum always advised us to kiss a man before assenting to marriage. After all, it's a lifetime commitment, so it's a good idea to assure you're compatible in that area."

"Oh," was all Judith said.

In fact, Lily thought she looked a mite disappointed they didn't think her a fallen woman.

"I'm so glad you're happy," she told her. "I imagine that now you're really looking forward to your wedding."

"Oh, yes," Judith breathed.

Lily wished she had her own wedding to look forward to instead of dreading Rand and Margery's. Five days now. While she was thrilled for Judith, for some reason her friend's newfound happiness made her own situation seem that much more miserable.

Judith handed her a nun's biscuit. "Have you kissed Rand?"

Biting into the sweet almond and lemon treat, Lily nodded and left it at that.

"She's done much more than kiss him," Rose said, waggling her brows.

Feeling her face flood with color, Lily gasped. In Oxford, Rose had promised not to tell. She glared at her sister. "You have no reason to believe such a thing."

Rose's dark eyes widened as she got the message. "Gemini, I was only jesting."

Lily brushed sugary crumbs off her skirts while she thought of a way to quickly change the subject. "Remember that song I was practicing for Rand? The one he's always humming?"

"What of it?"

"It has naughty words. And he knows others, too. He has a whole book of them."

"A book?" Rose licked her lips. "Did you read them all? Or play them?"

"Only a couple that Rand remembered. The book is in Oxford."

Rose looked very disappointed.

"Could you mean *An Antidote Against Melancholy*?" Violet reached for a strawberry. "Ford has that book."

"In your library?"

"No, upstairs, mixed in with all of his dusty science tomes and various books from when he attended university. I've looked through that songbook—it *is* very naughty," she added with a grin.

Lily sipped her wine. "How funny that he and Rand would have the same book."

"Perhaps it was required reading at Oxford," Judith quipped, eliciting titters from Lily's sisters.

"Let's send for it," Rose suggested. The glitter in her eyes belied her solemn tone. "It sounds educational."

Violet laughed but scribbled a note to Ford. They sent a footman to deliver it and instructed him to wait and bring the book back. "Now," she said, "while *we* wait, we must solve the problem at hand."

Lily went over the whole story again, all the depressing details. Then they tossed around ideas. But every solution proposed, no matter how promising at first, turned out to be flawed, impossible, or downright ludicrous.

As it appeared more and more that Lily's situation was hopeless, the suggestions became fewer and farther between, until an hour later they finally fell into a heavy silence.

Violet slipped off her spectacles and polished them on her skirts. "Egad, we're a woebegone bunch. This is supposed to be a party. We'll discuss this again later, but for now, let's see if the songbook has arrived."

Soon they were in the drawing room, giggling, the book propped up on the harpsichord where they could all see the words while Lily read the music.

"Play this one, Lily," Rose said, her dark eyes wide. She began singing.

"Let her face be fair,
And her breasts be bare,
And a voice let her have that can warble;
Let her belly be soft—but to mount me aloft,
Let her bounding buttocks be marble!"

They'd brought the wine with them, and Judith gulped hers, looking shocked. "I cannot believe men sing songs like that!"

Amusement twitched Violet's lips. "Oh, women sing songs like that, too."

"They don't," Judith said.

"They do." Violet reached over Lily's shoulder to flip some pages, then stepped back. "'The Nurse's Song.' Play this one, dear sister." She sang along with Rose.

"My dear cockadoodle,
My jewel, my joy,
My darling, my honey,
My pretty sweet boy!
To make thee grow quickly
I'll do what I can:
I'll feed thee, I'll stroke thee,
I'll make thee a man."

The Ashcroft sisters laughed, but Judith gulped more wine. "I don't understand. To make thee grow quickly?"

"It's the man's yard the song speaks of," Rose said.

"His yard?" If anything, Judith looked even more confused.

Rose waved a hand. "The man's...you know."

For all her forthrightness, Lily thought, Rose was still innocent.

"I vow and swear," Rose continued, "you must read *Aristotle's Master-piece* before you get married."

Now Judith gasped. Although she knew the Ashcroft sisters had all read it, the book was considered scandalous. A desperate look in her eyes, she turned to Violet. "You're married. Tell me."

Lily was relieved that she wasn't the one asked to explain.

While a pink-cheeked Judith learned the facts from Violet, Rose flipped pages in the book. "Here's another one for women to sing," she said when Violet was finished. "'A Tenement to Let.'"

Lily set the book back up on the harpsichord and began to play.

> *"I have a tenement to let,*
> *I hope will please you all—*
> *And if you'd know the name of it,*
> *'Tis calléd Cunny Hall*
>
> *"The place is very dark by night*
> *And so it is by day:*
> *But when you once are entered in,*
> *You cannot lose your way.*
>
> *"And when you're in, go boldly on,*
> *As far as e'er you can:*
> *And if you reach to the house-top*
> *You'll be where ne'er was a man!"*

Even Judith understood that one, as her rapidly reddening cheeks proved. While Rose started turning pages again, Judith sipped more wine. "'Tom Tinker,'" she said, staying Rose's hand. "That one sounds good."

"Innocent, you mean?" Violet's brown eyes sparkled behind her spectacles. "I can promise you, it isn't."

This time, they all sang together.

> *"Tom Tinker's my true-love, and I am his dear,*
> *and I will go with him, his toolkit to bear.*
> *He calls me his jewel, his delicate duck,*
> *And then he will take up my chemise to—"*

"That's ever so—" Judith interrupted loudly, then seemed unable to continue.

Lily stopped playing and looked up into her friend's bright red face. "What's your problem *this* time, Judith?" Despite everything, she was beginning to have fun. Perhaps it was the wine. Or the companionship. Or perhaps one could be woebegone, as Violet had put it, for only so long before needing to forget for a spell—even if only a very short one. "That's ever so *what*?"

"That word there that's missing—the one that rhymes with 'duck.' Why, I do believe…" Judith trailed off, her face turning even redder.

"Yes," Violet said dryly. "The word begins with *f* and we all know what it is now, don't we? But the point, dear Judith, is that it *is* missing. See here, the last printed word is 'to,' and after that comes the chorus."

Judith gulped more wine, clearly getting a little tipsy. "You said that so matter-of-factly," she observed, admiration lacing her voice. "You're so practical and calm, even discussing…"

"Lovemaking?" Rose finished for her with a grin. "That comes of being an old married lady."

"I am *not* old!" Violet protested, reaching to shove Rose's shoulder. But Rose just laughed and launched into the chorus. The others joined, even Lily, even though she couldn't carry a tune. Tonight that didn't seem to matter.

> *"This way, that way, which way you will,*

I am sure I say nothing that you can take ill!"

"See?" Violet said while Lily continued playing. "We're all proper ladies, aren't we? We'd never say a word that could be taken ill!"

Amid laughter, they kept singing.

> *"Tom Tinker I say was a jolly stout lad,*
> *He tickled young Nancy and made her stark mad*
> *To play a new game with him on the grass,*
> *By reason she knew that he had a good—"*

"Ass!" Judith crowed, filling in the word they all thought even though it wasn't meant to be sung.

> *"This way, that way, which way you will,*
> *I am sure I say nothing. . ."*

FIFTY-FIVE

"... *T*HAT **YOU** can take ill!" Chrystabel sang under her breath.

Stretched out beside her on their bed, Joseph couldn't hear the words filtering through the thick stone walls. "What's that, Chrysanthemum?"

"Nothing, darling. I was just talking to myself." She sipped from her goblet of wine. "I'm so happy that Lily is enjoying herself."

He drank with one hand while inching his other fingers beneath her nightgown. "What are they singing?"

"Oh, I cannot make out the tunes." He'd die if he knew. Joseph liked to think his daughters were much too ladylike for bawdy fun, and she wouldn't be the one to disabuse him of the notion. "I'm sure the others are just trying to cheer Lily up. And doing an excellent job, from the sound of it."

She stifled a laugh as she heard them rhyme *five* with the supposed-to-be-unspoken *swive*, and then launch into "This way, that way" again. "It was good of Rose to plan the sleeping party. Thoughtful, don't you think?"

Setting down his empty goblet, Joseph nodded. "Perhaps Rose has finally grown up."

"Perhaps she has." Chrystabel finished her own wine and sighed. "Our children are *all* growing up."

"Too fast," he agreed. His hand on her body stilled as his green eyes turned troubled. He hesitated. "About Lily—"

"I'm concerned, yes. Worried sick, truth be told. Should Rand not find a way out of this, Lily will be left devastated."

"And perhaps with child," he added in a rush.

"Oh, Lily isn't with child." Turning to face him, she reached to caress one whisker-roughened cheek. "I suppose I should have told you, but it never occurred to me that you would worry." She always expected him to be oblivious to such things, like other men. But sometimes he surprised her. And he did love his children very much.

That was only one of the many reasons she loved *him* so very much.

"You're still convinced they haven't shared a bed?" He frowned. "How do you know? A mother's intuition? Because I've told you before, my love, you cannot tell these things just by looking—"

She laughed, a sound of amusement mixed with relief. "I know because Lily's maid told me her courses are upon her."

"Oh." He reddened, as he usually did when confronted by womanly things. But she felt his body relax into the mattress.

"I do think, though," she continued, "that perhaps it isn't such a good idea, after all, to allow young people such privacy. No matter how perfect they are for each other. If things had gone differently, we might have had a disaster on our hands. I…well, in plotting the best way to match Lily and Rand, I think in this one matter I may have been wrong."

"Wrong? You were *wrong*?" His mouth dropped open.

Before he had a chance to close it and elaborate on her innocent miscalculation, she rushed to cover it with a kiss.

To her vast relief—and delight—nothing more was said that night.

FIFTY-SIX

*H*ALFWAY TO Oxford, rain had begun falling, turning the roads to mush and Rand's journey to a snail-paced nightmare. He'd arrived home and trudged through the empty house to the one furnished room, his bedchamber, where he'd promptly fallen into bed and passed a restless night.

Morning found him in a foul mood. Another day gone and no closer to finding a solution. He scrubbed up and pulled on some clothes, then opened his door, intending to inspect the house.

A measuring tape in one hand, Kit stopped and turned. "Rand. When did you get home?"

"Last night. Late." Rand rubbed his aching head. "How is the job progressing?"

"Haven't you noticed? It's all but done."

"Is it?" He followed Kit along the corridor, peeking into beautifully finished rooms. "My apologies. You've worked wonders."

"I've been here since you left. Amazing how a few days onsite will motivate craftsmen to work." He grinned, then suddenly frowned. "Hey, Rand, you're going to break your teeth."

Rand consciously relaxed his jaw, which had been clenched to the point of pain.

"What's got your dander up?" Kit asked.

"The mental image of my father at Hawkridge, planning a wedding for five days hence."

"I thought you wanted to get married."

"To Lily, not Margery Maybanks."

"Margery?" Kit's green-brown eyes widened. "Margery! Why the hell would he want you to marry Margery?"

Rand sighed. "It's a long story."

"Best told over a tankard of ale, I'd guess. Come along. It's a bit early yet, but the King's Arms is always open."

~

"*C*HIN UP, DEAR," Lily's father bellowed across the table.

"You cannot give up hope," her mother added more gently, pointedly handing Lily a spoon. "There must be something that can be done."

"Rand. Rand will have to come up with something." Unable to eat, Lily pushed her dinner around on her plate and sighed.

Rand was her only hope.

The lighthearted camaraderie of last night was gone. In the wee hours of the morning, the young women had all giggled their way upstairs to share Lily's big bed. It had been a tight fit with four instead of three, but worth it for the comfort she'd felt, surrounded by people who cared.

Today she could find no comfort. They'd awakened too late for breakfast and spent most of dinner revisiting all their useless suggestions, reviewing them with Father and Mum. No one had any new ideas to contribute, and Lily's predicament seemed more hopeless than ever.

"Violet? Are you ready to come home?" They all looked over

to see Ford had appeared in the doorway. "Did you have a fine time?"

Violet gave him a wan smile. "We did last night." She pushed back her chair and rose. "While I go get my things, Lily will fill you in on what's happened. Perhaps you'll see a solution we haven't."

But brilliant as Ford was, he had no solution to offer, either. No new plan to change Lord Hawkridge's mind.

They would have to prove Bennett's innocence.

"Maybe one of the other hunters witnessed it," he suggested. "Or someone else. Just because no one's come forward—"

"Rand is planning to interview everyone in the vicinity." Lily bit her lip. "But I'm afraid if anyone knew anything, they'd have come forward long before now."

Ford looked thoughtful. "Not if they were afraid of facing the marquess's wrath. He clearly doesn't want to hear his son was at fault."

"That's true," she said, reluctant to succumb to the thread of hope that suddenly tugged at her heart. "A different way to look at this. He did, after all, offer an enormous reward for information that would prove Lord Armstrong guilty. Perhaps people are reluctant to approach him with anything that would prove the opposite."

Her father nodded sagely. "It's wise to keep on top of it."

Judith reached for more bread. "She said 'the opposite,' Lord Trentingham. Someone could be frightened to bring Lord Hawkridge evidence that proves the opposite."

"Eh?"

Evidently giving up, Judith slathered butter on the bread. "You must trust Rand, then," she told Lily, taking a big bite. The solemn atmosphere had failed to curb her appetite. "You love him, and you have to believe he'll find proof."

Yes, Rand had promised they would find a way. After giving Judith a shaky smile, Lily turned to Ford. "Thank you. You've given me hope."

"It was nothing. Just another way to look at a solution that had already been offered—nothing has changed."

While that was true, Lily was holding as tight as she could to that thin thread of hope. For the first time since she'd awakened this morning, she felt able to breathe.

Violet returned, her satchel in one hand and *An Antidote Against Melancholy* in the other. "I'm ready."

"Why did you want that book?" Ford asked.

As her gaze flicked to their parents, Violet flushed a delicate pink. "Oh, I just thought it might help Lily." She took his arm. "Come along. I cannot wait to see Nicky and the twins."

"What's the book called?" Mum asked.

Having failed to escape, Violet forced a smile. "*An Antidote Against Melancholy*. Lily was feeling a bit melancholy last night, you see, and—"

"Oh, then would you mind leaving it here? I expect she may feel a bit melancholy again the next few days."

"We already read the whole thing," Violet said, clutching the book possessively.

"Well, then." Mum was nothing if not persistent. "Leave it here for me. I adore helping people, as you know, and it seems to me I could learn a lot from a book called *An Antidote Against Melancholy*."

Lily suspected Mum would learn more than she anticipated. In specific, she'd learn her daughters weren't quite the innocents she imagined. And if she could judge by her sister's face, Violet was thinking much the same.

Looking amused, Ford pried the book from his wife's hands and set it on the table. "Here," he told his mother-in-law with a grin that would do the devil proud. "I hope you and Lord Trentingham will enjoy it."

As Chrystabel smiled and reached for it, he hustled Violet from the room, laughingly ignoring her protests.

"Come upstairs, Joseph," Chrystabel purred in her husband's ear. "We can read this educational book together."

FIFTY-SEVEN

*B*Y THE TIME Rand told the whole story, he and Kit had long since finished dinner and were nursing tankards of ale.

Last night's rain had ceased, but the day had dawned depressingly gray. The dark paneling inside the King's Arms made it dreary, and the crackling fire near their table did little to warm the room or lighten Rand's mood.

"Of all the rotten things your father has ever done to you, this wins the prize." Kit shook his head. "Margery. Is she all grown-up, then?"

"Very much so at twenty-one, and she's a beautiful woman, too. But I cannot imagine myself married to her."

"For all intents and purposes, she's your little sister." Looking thoughtful, Kit signaled for another round. "Margery was always very sweet."

"I'd say you're welcome to her, but I'm afraid Bennett Armstrong would have something to say about that. Especially considering she's carrying his child."

Kit blinked. "On top of everything else, she's with child?"

"Yes, and she's asked me to raise the babe as my own."

"You will, of course, should it come to that." Kit knew Rand inside out. "But we must find a way to fix this." He paused, musing as he drained his tankard. "Skinny old Bennett, huh?"

Despite the gravity of his situation, a ghost of a grin materialized on Rand's face. Bennett *had* been rather scrawny when they were all lads. "He's not skinny anymore. I wouldn't challenge him were I you. Remember, he's killed once already, even if it was in self-defense."

"True, but the man he killed was Alban. He did the world a favor." A serving maid set down two fresh tankards, and Kit flipped her a coin. "Some of my most amusing childhood memories are of Alban's fury whenever you deciphered his diary."

"It was never amusing when my father found out." Rand took a deep swallow; then his mouth dropped open as his tankard hit the table. "That's it!"

"Pardon?"

"The evidence I've been looking for to prove Bennett Armstrong's innocence. Alban's diary."

Kit frowned. "I must've had one ale too many. What evidence?"

Ales notwithstanding, quite suddenly Rand's head felt crystal clear. "You know that Alban always kept a diary—he was obsessed with putting his thoughts on paper. If he'd planned to kill Armstrong, there's an excellent chance he'd have recorded that fact. The marquess cannot refute proof written in Alban's own hand. All I have to do is find it."

"*All* you have to do is find it? That could turn out to be a tall order, my friend."

"It's my only hope." He drained his ale and stood, a new energy singing through his veins. "I must collect some things, talk to some people. I'll leave for Hawkridge at dawn."

Kit rose, too. "I'm coming with you. Your house can wait."

FIFTY-EIGHT

"**I'M WORRIED.**" Chrystabel sighed as she shut the bedchamber door. "After all I did to push Lily and Rand together, it's frustrating to find them in this predicament with seemingly nothing we can do to help."

Joseph sat in a chair and set *An Antidote Against Melancholy* on his lap. "You cannot fix everything wrong with the world, my Chrysanthemum. If they're meant to be together, Rand will find a solution."

"Oh, I suppose you're right." She started toward him. "But as a mother, it's hard to stand by and watch our Lily suffer."

"I hurt for our daughter, too, but the boy will come through." Looking down, he opened the book. "You picked a bright one in Rand."

"I intend for all of our girls to wed highly intelligent men."

"Our girls…" His head jerked up. "Our girls were reading *this*?"

"Certainly not," she fibbed, closing the distance between them to distract him with a kiss. "They barely glanced at it. Didn't you hear Violet say they misunderstood what *An Antidote Against Melancholy* was about? They took the title to mean it was a treatise on how to cheer a poor girl like Lily. When they found otherwise, they shut the book immediately."

He looked puzzled. "I didn't hear this."

"So sad that you cannot hear better." She sighed prettily and sat herself on his lap, turning to run her fingernails down his shirtfront. "Will you sing me one of these songs? I do imagine it could put me in the mood."

"In the middle of the afternoon?" He laughed, reaching around her to flip the pages. "I shall sing, then, yes indeed."

Watching his eyes widen as he read some lyrics to himself, she smiled. "I've been thinking, darling."

"Hmm?" He turned another page, humming a tune under his breath.

"I'm thinking we must keep Rand and Lily apart. They shouldn't be allowed alone together, not until after they're wed. You were right to be relieved she's not with child, and we must take steps to see that doesn't happen." Her sigh this time was heartfelt. "I was so certain they would end up together, but heaven only knows how all of this will work out. Joseph, are you listening?"

He looked up, his lips curving as his gaze trailed toward the bed. "Of course, my love, whatever you say."

Raising the book, he cleared his throat and began to sing.

FIFTY-NINE

*R*AND SHOWED UP in Trentingham's entry hall days before Lily thought he would, and the moment she saw his face, she knew he had a new plan. Even from the top of the stairs, she could see hope shining in his eyes.

Her heart leapt in response. Without a thought for her sister standing beside her, she lifted her skirts and ran down and into his arms. "You've thought of something, haven't you?"

"I have, yes." He kissed her exuberantly before continuing. "There's no guarantee, of course, that it will work out, or that even if it does, the evidence will convince the marquess, but—"

"Bloody hell," Kit Martyn interrupted from the doorway. "Tell her your idea already."

"Yes," Rose yelled down the stairs. "Go on, tell us." She began walking down to meet them. "I'm likely to die of curiosity. We've all been wracking our brains for a solution—Lily and I, Violet and our friend Judith—and I want to hear what you've come up with that our superior female minds missed."

Rand laughed. "It's Alban's diary."

"Pardon?" Lily and Rose said together.

"As long as I knew him, Alban always kept a journal detailing all his nefarious doings. If he continued the habit, all I have to do is find it, and I'd wager his plans to kill Bennett Armstrong will be written there in his own hand. No matter how much the marquess wants to believe in his innocence, it will be impossible to refute that."

"If Bennett is telling the truth," Rose put in.

Yes, if, Lily thought. But he'd seemed so sincere. And she had to believe him, because proving his innocence was the only chance she and Rand had.

"Finding the diary could work against you instead of helping," Rose pointed out. "If it's found and there's no mention of ill will towards the man, the marquess will consider that to be proof Alban was innocent. Even should witnesses come forward, he'll disbelieve them and insist on hanging Bennett—and Rand will have to marry Margery to save her love's life."

It was an intelligent observation. Annoyingly intelligent. And depressingly true, but Lily couldn't think about that now.

Hope had taken flight and refused to be grounded.

She clutched Rand's arm. "Do you really think you can find Alban's journal?"

"For all we know, it could be sitting in plain view in his bedchamber." Rand crossed his fingers. "If not, I'll turn the house upside down if need be."

"And inside out," Kit added. "I'm going along to help."

"Thank you," Lily said, impulsively giving him a hug. "I'm going, too."

"Lily." Rand stared at the oak-planked floor for a moment, then raised his eyes to meet hers. "I came to tell you my plans as I had promised, not to take you with me. Before I left, the marquess specifically instructed me not to bring you back."

Although she wasn't really surprised, Lily felt crushed. Had the man hated her that much?

"Nonsense," said Rose. "The Ashcroft motto is Question Convention, and Lily will do as she likes. You cannot leave her here languishing while you men have all the fun. Besides, she could very well notice something you miss. Women's minds work in different ways than men's."

"Truer words were never spoken," Kit put in dryly, but Lily noticed that he looked toward Rose with approval. "She's right, Rand. Lily should come along. We'll need all the help we can get."

"But I never—" Rand started.

"Never say never." Kit raised a dark, meaningful brow. "Didn't you declare your father was done dictating your life? Fourteen years ago."

Rand's shoulders went back. "My concern is Lily, not myself. She's going to receive a rather chilly welcome."

"Then I'd best fetch my cloak," she said, smiling when Rose laughed.

"Wait!" Mum appeared out of nowhere as usual. "Where do you suppose you're off to?"

"Hawkridge Hall. Rand has a plan, and—"

"Not overnight. I want you back here to sleep, Lily."

Lily frowned. Her mother had never cared about such things before.

"I know Lord Hawkridge will be less than welcoming," Mum explained rather unconvincingly. "I'd as soon not have to worry about you all the night long."

"I'll bring her home," Rand promised, and Rose began telling Mum about Rand's idea, and the awkward moment passed.

Regardless of her mother's odd change of heart, Lily couldn't wait to leave. Even knowing the marquess would be furious to see her. It felt good to do what was right instead of what was nice.

And it felt even better to be doing something to remedy her situation instead of sitting here feeling frustrated while the hour moved ever closer to Rand and Margery's wedding.

SIXTY

*J*HE THREE OF them decided that, rather than take a carriage, they'd ride horseback to save time. Lily quickly changed her gown for her blue riding habit, and an hour and a half later, they arrived at Hawkridge Hall.

As they rode up the path from the river, Lily stared at the massive mansion. "It doesn't *look* evil," she said thoughtfully.

Rand leaned from the saddle to smooth her hair. "It won't be," he promised, "just as soon as we've exposed Alban for what he was."

"Goodness, I hope we can find that diary."

"We will. We have to."

The stables were around the back. As they headed in that direction, past the dog enclosure, Lily gasped.

"Oh, my God!" She slid from the saddle and hit the grass running. "Rex!"

Gaping, Rand watched her scale the fence. By the time he dismounted and caught up with her, she was kneeling in the dirt, her hands on either side of one very agitated mastiff's head.

"Hold him like this," she ordered without looking up. Rand leaned down to comply, not a simple task since the animal was violently pawing at its face. It gasped and gulped, its stomach pumping as though it was trying to vomit.

Lily reached for the dog's mouth and pried it open, ignoring all the foamy saliva that dripped from the canine's black lips. Rand struggled to hold the animal still while she pulled out its long tongue.

"Up!" she yelled, her fingers moving the tongue this way and that. "I need to see!" Kit leapt to help, angling the mastiff's head toward the sun while Lily peered down its throat. "I knew it!" she ground out through gritted teeth, calm and determined although she was clearly furious.

Heedless of the animal's sharp teeth, she reached back into its mouth. But she couldn't grasp whatever was choking the poor creature.

Only a whimper betrayed Lily's distress. After that, she was all action. She stood and, leaving the dog's front paws on the ground, went around to lift him from behind. Though the canine was easily twice her weight, she managed to raise both his legs. But she was too short to get them up high.

Rand and Kit both jumped to help, taking one hind leg each while Lily knelt again by the dog's head. "Come on, Rex," she pleaded. "Cough it up. Shake him!" she told the men.

They did, holding him up like a wheelbarrow, but though the dog jerked and made choking sounds, the object still remained lodged.

"Dear God," Lily moaned, panting as though she could breathe precious air for the animal. "Set him back down."

With the flat of her hand, she administered three sharp blows between the huge creature's shoulder blades, but nothing happened. Finally she leaned over its back, wrapped her arms around its middle, and squeezed so hard her face turned red, pressing up on its belly with both fists.

All at once, a slobbery red apple came shooting out of its mouth.

"Oh, Rex!" The dog collapsed to the ground, and she hugged

him around the neck, laying her cheek against his sweaty coat. Tears poured down her face. "I thought we were going to lose you!"

The other dogs came closer to investigate, barking loudly and poking at Rex with their noses. Though he was clearly exhausted, Rex turned his head and licked Lily's face, a big wet swath of love.

She laughed, and Rand smiled, his own eyes embarrassingly damp. His legs felt shaky, as if he'd run miles. He was speechless.

Kit spoke for them both. "That was incredible, Lily."

She hugged Rex even harder. "It was only what had to be done."

"No," came another voice, one filled with admiration. "It was an amazing display of quick thinking." Rand turned to see his father unlocking the gate. The man walked right over to Lily and reached down a hand. "Thank you for saving Attila. I need to get rid of that apple tree."

Lily was too nice to say she'd told him so, but her lips curved in a smile that melted Rand's heart. She unwound her arms from the hound's neck and allowed the marquess to help her rise.

As soon as she moved away, the other dogs pressed even closer. Lily brushed at her less-than-pristine riding habit. "Perhaps, my lord, you should take him into the house for a while. He needs some time to recover, and out here he will get no rest."

"My dogs are not allowed in—" the marquess started, then apparently had second thoughts. "An excellent suggestion, Lady Lily. Will you come with us and help me get him settled?"

Rand watched, aghast, as his father and Lily headed for the house, the dog walking gingerly between them.

After a moment, he and Kit exchanged glances and began following. "He didn't even ask what she was doing here," Rand whispered.

"He didn't notice me at all," Kit said dryly. "He had eyes only for your lady."

"He's grateful at the moment. It won't last."

Kit shook his head. "She's won him over."

"Perhaps," Rand conceded, although it seemed more likely his father was temporarily bewitched. Lily, after all, was very good at casting spells, especially where Nesbitt men were concerned.

But regardless, he'd best not forget that nothing had really changed. "This doesn't mean he'll assent to my wedding Lily instead of Margery."

"No," Kit agreed. "We still need to find that diary."

In the back parlor, Lily settled Rex-Attila by the fireplace and requested a blanket. Without questioning her, the marquess rang for a footman and asked for one to be brought. Lily knelt by the dog, murmuring soothing nonsense while the marquess looked on, a bemused expression on his face.

When he finally looked up, his features hardened. "Christopher," he said, apparently noticing Kit for the first time. "It's been years."

Kit nodded an acknowledgment. "Since Rand left for Oxford."

"What brings you here now?" the marquess asked rather suspiciously.

Before Kit or Rand could answer, Lily spoke up from where she knelt on the floor. "We've come to find Alban's diary," she said clearly, although they had all agreed they would claim they'd come to discuss Rand's marriage and then perform their search on the sly. "Rand is of the opinion that it could clear Lord Armstrong's name."

To Rand's surprise, the man didn't respond with one of his characteristic explosions. "My son hadn't kept a diary in years."

Rand's heart dropped to somewhere in the vicinity of his knees, but Lily seemed undaunted. "Are you certain, my lord?"

"I knew my son," he said shortly.

Rubbing his dog's back, she gave a graceful shrug. "Well, it couldn't hurt for us to look, could it? You wouldn't mind, would you?"

Her tone could melt butter in a snowstorm, not to mention a man's heart. In his current mood, Rand's father was no exception. "Go ahead," he said. "But it's a waste of time. Even should you find my son's writings, I'm certain there will be nothing in them that would exonerate Margery's lover." His gaze on Lily was almost apologetic. "My lady, I appreciate your care for my dog, but you cannot marry my heir."

"I understand, my lord," she said softly. But as she rose to join Rand and Kit near the door, her eyes looked as determined as ever.

Rand appreciated that determination more than words could say. As they turned to leave, he took her arm. "We'll get Margery to help, too."

"She's not here," came his father's voice behind him.

More than a little concerned, Rand swung back. "Where is she?"

The marquess waved a hand, apparently unaware that his son had assumed the worst. "In Windsor, with Etta. They went to choose fabric for her wedding gown."

As the vision faded of Margery locked in a dank dungeon somewhere—not that Hawkridge Hall had one—Rand's shoulders slumped with relief. "They'll return soon, then?"

"First thing tomorrow morning."

"They're staying overnight to choose fabric?"

"And fittings or some such. They were to visit a seamstress. I gave them leave to stay the night at an inn, since they seemed to think it would be dark by the time they finished. I know nothing of these womanly things."

The man knew nothing of Margery at all, Rand thought incredulously. His foster daughter wouldn't care what she wore to be wed against her will. Rand would lay odds Margery was spending the night with Bennett Armstrong—and he wasn't surprised her old nurse had conspired to arrange it. The two had always been thick as thieves, females in a household run by men. In fact, Margery was likely the reason Etta had decided to stay after her nursemaid days were finished.

The men standing guard over Bennett had all been at Hawkridge for years, and Rand imagined they were as loyal to Margery as Etta. While they wouldn't go so far as to allow an escape—they'd doubtless face death for a betrayal of that magnitude—he suspected they'd turn a blind eye to an overnight visit.

By all appearances blissfully unaware, his father stroked the dog's head. "Now be about your business. The sooner you give up on finding this diary, the better. You need to prepare for your wedding. To Margery," he added with a glare.

Refusing to rise to that bait, Rand turned and walked away. There was no point in arguing now.

When he'd found what he was looking for, it would be a different story.

SIXTY-ONE

*T*HE MOST logical place to start, of course, was Alban's suite.

Unlike the single small chamber that had been Rand's refuge during his childhood, the marquess's heir had had three rooms to call his own. They began in his bedchamber proper, a darkly paneled room that sat between the other two and provided entrance to them all.

"Cluttered as ever," Kit remarked when they walked in.

"Nothing's been touched." Rand paused on the threshold. "It's as though he still lives here."

"He hasn't been gone that long," Lily said gently. She skimmed a hand thoughtfully over the unmade bed. "Perhaps his death is still too fresh for the housekeeper to deal with."

"I doubt that." Rand crossed to his brother's dressing table and opened a drawer. "I cannot believe Alban changed enough to ingratiate himself with the staff, even in fourteen years. He was ruthless in both his expectations and treatment of them. I suspect they're as relieved to have him gone as I." Finding nothing but a neatly folded stack of cravats in the drawer, he slid it closed and opened another. "If this room is undisturbed, it's my father's doing."

Ignoring a frisson of unease, Lily inspected a pile of books on Alban's night table. "What did his diaries look like?"

"Nothing in particular, at least back in the day. Whatever blank books he could find."

All the books on the table had titles on their spines, so Lily assumed they weren't journals. Just to make sure, she began opening them.

"I remember this," Rand breathed, pulling something sparkly from a drawer full of stockings. "My mother wore it all the time."

Lily moved closer to see. It was a beautiful oval pendant made of white gold, with many small diamonds set into a delicate filigree design accented with black enamel. "Goodness, it's really quite lovely. Do you think your father gave it to her?"

"Maybe," Rand said as he slipped it into a pocket. "I wonder if he knows Alban had it."

Rather than checking the obvious places, Kit lay down on the floor and stuck his head beneath the red brocade bed skirt. "There's a box under here," he said, pulling it out.

It was long, large, and shallow, made of wood with a heavy, locked hasp. "The diary must be in there," Lily said, amazed that they'd found it so easily. "Where do you suppose we can find the key?"

"Where would you keep a key?" Rand asked, almost to himself. Or perhaps he was addressing his brother's ghost.

"Behind the headboard?" Lily suggested.

Rising to his feet, Kit rubbed the back of his neck. "Maybe under the mattress."

"No," Rand said. "Alban was more clever than that. It will be in this room, but not anywhere that typical."

He began methodically lifting objects while Lily checked the headboard and Kit looked for a key tucked into the ropes that supported the mattress. Both of those places revealed nothing.

"Aha!" Rand set down a Blue Willow jar that he'd found on

the mantel. He held a wad of cotton that had concealed the key inside.

His fingers shook as he worked the lock.

Please, Lily prayed silently, let this be it.

But when Rand raised the lid, the box wasn't filled with books. Instead it held an astonishing array of various knives.

Lily stared in horror. "Some of them have dried blood on them."

"Alban never was very tidy." Rand's gesture encompassed the general condition of the room. "Frightening, isn't it?"

Lily nodded and swallowed hard, her gaze still fixed on the jumble of sharpened steel. Curved blades and straight, serrated and smooth, double-edged and honed to a deadly point. "Perhaps we have no need to find the diary now. This should convince your father that his eldest son had no good in mind."

A short, harsh laugh rent the air. Kit's. "I expect not. Alban's love of hunting was well known."

Rand nodded. "He rarely carried a firearm, either. Alban liked to kill with his hands. I'm surprised he even tried to shoot Bennett, although I suppose that goes to show his desperation to see the man dead." He released a pent-up breath. "No, I'm afraid this proves nothing except that my brother was fascinated with knives. I doubt the marquess will find that to be startling news."

"It seems he was fascinated with killing, too." Lily shivered, imagining all the creatures that had died at his hands. While she'd never objected to hunting for food, somehow she knew he'd had other reasons. She looked up and met Rand's eyes. "I believe Bennett. The man who owned this collection wouldn't hesitate to murder."

"We still must find his journal to prove it."

But a careful, exhaustive search of the bedchamber revealed nothing. They spent an hour combing Alban's dressing room—reaching into his pockets made Lily's skin crawl—and another turning his sitting room upside down.

Nothing.

Kit plopped into a red-and-gold-striped chair. "We're missing something."

"There's no desk in here," Lily said. "Where did he write?"

Rand began pacing. "In his bedchamber. At his dressing table. Didn't you see the quill and ink?"

"But the drawers there were filled with accessories, not paper."

"Alban didn't write letters," Rand said peevishly. "He wrote only in his journal."

"No," Kit disagreed. "I think Lily is on to something. Perhaps at sixteen, when you left home, Alban wrote only in his journal. But he died at thirty. Surely he was handling some of the estate work by then. Did he not have a study?"

Rand gave a weak shrug—a shrug that alarmed Lily, because it suggested he might have given up. Could Lord Hawkridge have been right that Alban had stopped keeping a diary? The thought was so disturbing she was afraid to voice it aloud.

"This is the sum total of Alban's rooms," Rand said dully. "Perhaps he shared the marquess's study."

But Rand's father was *in* his study when they went there to search. He looked up from his paperwork, impatiently tapping his quill on the desk as he swept all three of them with a cold gray gaze. "I can assure you," he said curtly, "you will find nothing of Alban's in here."

Lily deliberately smiled, a smile she suspected would have done Rose proud. "My lord, I'm certain that your son, as your heir, would have assisted you in the task of running your estate—"

"Of course he did. He was never a man to shirk his duties." Lord Hawkridge's eyes swung toward Rand, as though to say he *was* one to shirk.

Lily felt her hackles rise. Rand had had no choice but to make his own life—not if he'd wished to survive. And though his life would be changing now, he certainly deserved time to grow accustomed to the idea.

Besides, she could see no need to rush. Lord Hawkridge appeared almost indecently healthy for a man of his age, not that he was elderly to begin with. Fifty-two, Rand had said. And for all they knew, he could live to be a *hundred* and two.

She forced her lips to remain curved in that smile. "Did Alban do that sort of work with you here in this study?"

"Of course not. I told you, there's nothing of Alban's in here. He converted part of the library into a study for himself." With that, he looked down and scribbled something on one of the papers in front of him.

"Converted part of the library," Rand muttered as they trooped upstairs. "I suppose his own three rooms weren't large enough."

Their footsteps sounded muffled on the woven rush matting that covered the floor of the long gallery. Gilt-framed family portraits lined the lengthy chamber, hung on dark, gilt-trimmed panel walls. Noticing one in particular, Lily stopped.

The painting showed a younger Lord Hawkridge standing behind his seated lady, who held a white kitten on her lap. Her blue eyes looked kind, and Lily liked her on sight. The marquess's eyes looked...happy, she decided in surprise.

He must have been very much in love.

Lady Hawkridge wore a lovely pink dress and the beautiful diamond pendant Rand now had in his pocket. "I see your mother did love that necklace," Lily said with a soft smile.

Rand nodded. "Maybe this picture is why I still remember it."

Beside that portrait, another young man gazed from a canvas, a man Lily guessed to be Alban. He resembled Rand, except his hair was darker, his expression cooler. His eyes, however, of indeterminate color, looked so cold as to make his smile seem warm in comparison.

There was, of course, no portrait of Rand.

"Professors do not rate paintings," Rand said dryly beside her, apparently reading her mind.

She looked back to the picture of his parents. She could almost see the woman's graceful fingers stroking the silky, purring cat. "She looks very loving," she said of his mother.

"She was. The only love I ever received."

"Not the only," Lily said quietly, and Rand squeezed her around the shoulders.

Kit had gone ahead through the library and into a small room beyond, where a massive desk took up most of the space. Upon entering, Rand immediately moved behind the desk and began opening drawers.

Kit was already pulling books off the shelves. "These are deep," he said. "There's another row of books behind the first." He gestured to the opposite wall. "Lily, you can start over there, and we'll meet in the mid—"

She was heading over to do as he suggested when she heard his indrawn breath. She swung back. "Have you found them?"

"I think so."

Behind the books he'd removed sat a long row of multicolored spines, none of them marked with titles. As he drew one out and opened it, a grin spread on his face.

"Yes, this is a diary. An older one, from 1664. Now we just need the most recent."

Her heart racing with renewed hope, Lily pulled out another and flipped open the cover. "I cannot read it."

"It's in code," Rand told her, standing over her shoulder.

"Oh, now I remember." The dates, at least, weren't encrypted. She turned pages, noting this one ran from mid-1668 to early 1669. "You got in trouble for breaking the codes, didn't you?"

"Did he ever," Kit confirmed with a wry grin.

"When I translate the latest diary," Rand said, "it will get us *out* of trouble. Let's find it."

But though thirty-odd journals crowded the shelf, none of them were the most recent. They looked behind the books on all the other shelves, floor to ceiling, but there were no more journals to be found.

An hour later, when they'd closed the last cover of the last book in the small room, Lily dropped onto a chair. "What now?"

Rand's jaw set. "We search the rest of the house."

"It's gigantic! And one small diary could be anywhere...if it even exists."

"It exists," Rand forced through gritted teeth. "My brother didn't record his life for twenty-nine years and then suddenly stop."

Lily felt as though her emotions were on a swing. Down and then up. Up and then down. Dejection settled in for now. "It could take days. We could still be searching when the priest shows up to marry you."

"Lily." Rand came over and took her face in both hands, raising it for a soft kiss. "We will find it, and *we* will be the two who are married." He looked to Kit. "We may as well start here in the main library."

That lofty, two-story chamber was easily eight times the size of Alban's study. Lily took one look at the endless shelves and felt like weeping.

This would never do. She had to regain her spirits, had to do her share of this enormous task. Rand wasn't giving up, and she couldn't, either.

But after the excitement of the discovery and the disappointment that had followed, she couldn't face starting over just yet. "I'm going to check on Rex," she told the men. "I'll be right back."

Downstairs, she hugged the huge mastiff around his neck, tight, as though she could draw strength from his big, warm body. After all, he'd survived a harrowing ordeal and, from the looks of it, come out none the worse for wear. When he licked a slobbery path across her face, she laughed. "All right, then. I'm going to find that diary."

Feeling immeasurably better, she rose, then froze, staring at the dog. "I wonder..." she whispered, then took off at a run, heading back to the library.

SIXTY-TWO

*E*TTA IN TOW, Margery ran into Bennett's study and smiled when he bolted up from his desk. "What are you doing here?" he gasped.

They met halfway, his mouth dear on hers, the kiss wild despite her old nurse's presence. Her fingers twined into his long dark hair, and his arms went around her to clutch her close. When he finally broke the kiss, she was breathless. "I told you I'd come to you again, didn't I?"

"Well, yes, but—"

"I've been combing the countryside for witnesses. Rand had promised to do that, but then he took off for Oxford and has yet to return." She ran her hands up and down Bennett's back, frantic to touch him, to feel the strong muscles beneath his thin shirt, to convince herself he was here, he was real, he wouldn't die, that somehow they'd end up together. "I cannot just sit in my uncle's house and pray anymore. I have to *do* something. I have to find someone who saw Alban come after you."

His hands clenched on her waist. "I feel so helpless, stuck here in this house. All I can do is write letters." His gaze flicked to the papers littering his desk. "Letters and more letters," he said, looking back to her, his green eyes laced with despair. "But I know no one with influence greater than the marquess's. No one who can save me."

"Did you get *my* letter? The one where I explained Uncle William's promise to spare your life if I marry Rand?"

The look in his eyes—misery—told her he had. "Do you suppose you could come to love him?" he asked, his voice so harsh she pictured each word being forced through his throat.

"Not like this. He's my brother—"

"Then you cannot do it. I won't allow you to sacrifice your life for mine. You'll be unhappy all your days."

"Not as unhappy as if you were *dead*." She wasn't going to let him argue this point. "I'm going back out—I just stopped here to tell you what I'm doing. God willing, I'll find someone able to vouch for your innocence in this matter. Either way, I'll be back tonight."

"Tonight?" She saw his heart leap into his eyes.

Her own heart pounded at the thought of a night in each other's arms. One precious night. She'd never thought to feel like this, hadn't considered herself a woman driven by lust. Until Bennett.

"Yes, tonight." She nodded toward Etta. "Uncle William thinks we're staying overnight in Windsor. Ordering a wedding gown—as though I would care what I wore to wed Rand. Sackcloth would do." She snorted. "For all his power, sometimes my uncle can be blind to a woman's wiles."

"He's a man," Etta put in with a nod of her curly gray head. "His wife could outwit him just as easily. A crafty woman she was, although she loved him too much to play him the fool very often."

Margery had seen a loving side of Uncle William in the past, but right now she found it hard to summon loyalty. "Am I wrong, Bennett, for going behind his back?"

She'd warred with herself for days. Perhaps Rand's mother

had been the crafty sort, but Margery had always prided herself on her honesty.

Until now.

Now she was hiding a pregnancy and sneaking off to meet her lover, and she couldn't find it in herself to feel guilt for either dishonest action. But she was also contemplating ruining two other lives to save Bennett's, dooming both Rand and Lily to loveless futures…and that sparked enough guilt to make a nun dread the Day of Judgment.

One of her hands left Bennett's body and went to her own belly as she prayed her child wouldn't suffer for the sins of its mother.

Bennett's gaze dropped to her middle, then flicked toward Etta.

"She knows," Margery said. "She guessed."

Etta's big green eyes took on that wise-old-nurse look. "There are signs. Another woman would know."

Bennett nodded. "No, you're not wrong," he murmured in answer to Margery's earlier question. "The marquess is being unreasonable. He claims to love you, yet he plots to deprive your child of its father."

One of his hands slipped from her waist to cover her fingers. She wished he could feel their child move, but even she hadn't felt that yet. It was too early. Were it not for the signs Etta had mentioned, she'd have a hard time believing she even carried a babe.

And yet she knew in her bones that Bennett's child grew under her heart. And she could only be joyful for it.

"Uncle William doesn't know I'm with child," she said softly. "Because it wouldn't make a difference. And should the unthinkable happen, I would want him to believe the child is Rand's."

The last word was said with a sob—a sob Bennett smothered with his mouth. Heedless of Etta watching, they both poured themselves into the kiss.

It wouldn't be their last, Margery consoled herself when they finally parted. They still had tonight.

But what of the days and nights after that?

SIXTY-THREE

"I HAVE AN idea!" Lily shouted as she burst back into the library. "Maybe Rex can find the diary."

Up on a ladder, Rand turned to look down at her. "Rex? You mean Rex the dog, otherwise known as Attila?"

"Yes, Rex the dog. And no, I haven't gone mad. Animals have a keen sense of smell, you know."

Kit's lips twitched. "I didn't realize journals were smelly."

Lily was so hopeful, she only laughed. "Alban's diary would carry a specific scent. Come, let me show you what I mean."

Rand and Kit exchanged a dubious glance but followed her out of the library.

On their way through the long gallery, Lily glared at Alban's image. He wasn't going to come between her and Rand and their happiness. Rex wouldn't let her down.

Downstairs in the back parlor, Lord Hawkridge was examining the mastiff. When they walked in, he looked up from where he was kneeling—a very unlikely position for such a dignified man.

Lily liked him the better for it. There was always hope for a man who loved animals.

He smiled, an expression that sat rather oddly on his face.

"Attila appears to have fully recovered, Lady Lily. I'm very grateful. My thanks to you."

"I would do my best for any living creature, but you're quite welcome. He's a special dog. In fact, I'm wondering if I might borrow him for a while."

He rose to his feet. "Gratitude extends only so far, my lady. Attila lives here."

Rand spoke up. "She doesn't mean to take him away. Only to use him to help find the diary."

"He's a fighter, not a hunter." A more skeptical look had never graced a man's face. "And there's no diary to be found."

Rand crossed his arms, appearing ready to do battle, but Kit cleared his throat. "It's a harmless enough request from one who has done you such a favor. Attila will stay in the house. The exercise will do him good after his ordeal."

"Exercise is all he'll get—he won't be finding any diary. But I suppose it's harmless enough. So long as he stays indoors. I plan to keep him inside overnight."

Lily beamed. "A kind and wise decision, my lord." She snapped her fingers. "Rex, follow me."

"His name is Attila," the marquess called after them.

She led Rand, Kit, and the dog across the marble-floored great hall and through to Alban's suite. Once there, she patted the bed. "Up!" she commanded, and the huge animal landed where she wanted—with a leap that made the bed ropes groan.

Rand grinned. "My father would kill you if he saw this."

"Nonsense. Your father adores me. I saved his favorite dog." She grinned in return, stroking the animal's stiff fur. "Kit, would you run to the kitchen and fetch some meat? Cut into cubes, if possible."

He made her a mock bow. "By all means. Even the exalted marquess believes you walk on water, so your wish is my command."

As he marched to do her bidding, she giggled. In spite of

everything, she giggled. "This is going to work, Rand. I know it."

Holding one bedpost, he leaned to press a kiss to her lips. "Don't get your hopes up, will you? Even if we find a recent journal, I'll have to translate it, and we'll have to hope it turns out to be incriminating. And *then* we'll have to convince the marquess it says what I claim it does—unlikely to be a simple task—and that such evidence merits freeing Bennett and allowing Margery to wed him. We're a long way from victory, sweetheart."

"But we're about to take the first step. I feel it."

When Kit returned with a bowl of meat, she took Alban's fancy silver inkwell and held it to Rex's nose. "Diary," she said clearly.

"That's not a diary—" Rand started.

"Hush. I'm going to have him smell diaries, too, and I don't want to confuse him. One word for a scent is enough." She fed the dog a piece of meat, then waved the inkwell beneath his nose again. "Diary. Diary." She fed him more meat, then snapped her fingers. "Down. Come along. You, too," she said to the men.

Rand barked, eliciting a hoot of laughter from Kit as they followed her.

She hurried back upstairs to the library and through to the small room beyond, Rex trotting by her side. Once there, she took down a stack of Alban's journals. "Sniff, Rex. Diary." She opened one and held it under his nose, then another and another. Each time he sniffed a page, she fed him another reward. "Diary. Diary."

Kit and Rand just looked at each other and shrugged.

After the dog had sniffed a dozen different journals and received a dozen treats, Lily leaned to look into his eyes. "Diary. Find another diary. Now, Rex. Go."

Without hesitation, the mastiff bolted from the room.

They all ran after him.

Back downstairs, through the great hall, into Alban's

bedchamber. By the time they caught up, the three of them were panting harder than the dog.

"Diary," Lily reminded him.

He went straight to the silver inkwell.

She released a strangled laugh. "Good, Rex." She fed him a piece of meat, holding the inkwell out to Rand. "Will you take this out of here? He'll never find anything else with this in the room. It smells too strong."

"Does it?" Kit wondered.

Rand waved the inkwell beneath his friend's nose.

"Whew." Kit blinked. "It does stink."

Rand smelled it himself. "Tannin, and something else I cannot identify. Alban always mixed his own ink. Plain lamp-black and linseed oil wouldn't do for him."

He set the inkwell outside the room, shutting the door for good measure when the mastiff looked after it longingly.

The three of them watched him sniff all around the chamber.

"This isn't going to work," Kit said. "There isn't an inch of this room we haven't looked in or over or under."

"Give him a chance," Lily said. She set the bowl of meat on the mantel. "Diary, Rex. Find a diary."

Rand gestured toward the night table. "He hasn't noticed all those books."

"He's not searching for books. He's searching for a scent. Those books weren't handwritten by Alban, so they don't smell of his ink."

Rex trotted into the sitting room, sniffed around there, and came back.

"Perhaps," Rand said, "we should lead him to some other chambers. Ones we haven't searched yet."

"Give him a chance," Lily said.

Rex sniffed all around the bedchamber again, jumping on and off the bed twice in the process. The coverlet slid to the floor, and Kit bent to pick it up. "He's—"

"Give him a chance," Lily said.

Rex checked out the dressing room. Thoroughly. Lily walked to the doorway and watched. "Diary. Diary. Rex, find another diary."

Back in the bedchamber, the dog sniffed around once more. Then he stopped before the marble fireplace and sat on his haunches, gazing into it.

He barked once.

The three humans looked at each other.

"He's done," Kit said. "He didn't find it."

Refusing to believe that, Lily knelt by Rex's head. He licked her cheek, then looked back at the fireplace and barked.

"He thinks it's there," she said. "In the fireplace."

Rand lifted a poker and stirred the cold ashes. "Nothing. There's nothing here."

"Maybe Alban burned it," Lily whispered, afraid that if she said the words out loud, she might somehow make them true.

"Maybe." Rand set the poker back in its wrought iron stand with a final-sounding *clunk*. "I suppose he might have, if he were worried enough that someone might find it."

Disappointment fisted Lily's heart. She stepped toward Rand, toward the comforting heat of his body, the comforting circle of his arms.

Would this be the last day she ever felt that comfort?

Rex barked again. And again. And again, gazing at Lily as though he was trying to tell her something but didn't have the words.

"He thinks it's in there," she said with a sigh. "It must have burned."

"No." Kit walked across the room, then back, staring at the fireplace. He poked his head into the sitting room, then looked again at the fireplace. "There's space behind there."

"What do you mean?" Lily asked.

"Empty space. Maybe a hiding place. I cannot believe I failed to notice it immediately. Can't you see the proportions are off, in both this room and the next?"

"We're not architects," Rand said dryly, but with a fresh note of hope in his voice. "How do we get to this space?"

Kit started feeling around the paneling above the mantel-piece. "There has to be a latch, or a lever, or something…" He moved to the side, running his hands down the wood to the floor.

And there it was. A little *snick* reverberated in the room, and a panel swung open.

Lily stepped in first.

A secret room. No, a space. It was tall as a man but no more than three feet deep. Just wide enough to step into and access the area behind the fireplace, a nook so dark she couldn't see her own hand in front of her face.

She heard the soft hiss of a flame being struck. Rand stepped in holding a candle, illuminating the hidden space and its shelves.

Shutting her eyes in horror, Lily turned away.

But she'd seen what was on the shelves. Traps of all sizes, some with steel teeth large enough to capture a man. A bloody saw. Well-used rope. Cuffs. Whips.

And a lone, leather-bound journal.

Rand reached for it and hurried her out, closing the door with a *bang*.

Taking the candle from Rand, Kit reopened the panel, peeked in, and slammed it shut again.

Lily's limbs shook. "What—what were all those things for, Rand?"

"I'm not certain I want to know. But I imagine this diary will reveal all."

"Will you show your father that space?"

He was silent a long moment. "No. Not unless I have to. Not unless the diary fails to reveal Alban's plan to kill Bennett, or the marquess refuses to believe my translation."

She nodded. It was a sound decision. The marquess had

clearly loved Alban, and there was no sense disillusioning him more than was necessary. After all, Alban was already dead.

Never had Lily, nice Lily, thought she'd be glad for a man's demise. "Never say never," she whispered.

Rand slanted her a glance, then slowly opened the journal and flipped to the final entry. "'Nineteenth of August, 1677,'" he read aloud before looking up. "The day Alban died."

"We've got him," Kit said with a smile.

Lily dropped to her knees and buried her face in Rex's neck, wetting his fur with her tears. After a long moment, she got to her feet, reached for the bowl of meat, and set it on the floor.

"Thank you," she murmured.

SIXTY-FOUR

$\mathcal{A}$LL THE WAY back to Trentingham, Lily and Rand and Kit reminded one another that the diary might not reveal anything incriminating.

But they couldn't help but believe that it would.

It was late when they arrived, and Lily was exhausted. She'd hardly slept a wink those long nights waiting for word from Rand.

The rest of the family were already abed. After a yawning Parkinson let them in, Rand drew Lily close and dropped a kiss on the top of her head. "Go to sleep," he told her. "You cannot help with this, anyway. In the morning you'll feel better, and with luck I'll have good news."

She nodded and took herself off to her room.

Parkinson led the way up to the library, then lit a few candles and went back to bed himself. Rand and Kit settled at a round wooden table to decipher the diary.

No sooner had Rand opened the cover than Rose walked in, carrying another candle and wearing nothing but a white night-gown with a red wrapper tied over it. Although the garments were concealing, their effect was undeniably intimate. She set down the candle and rubbed her eyes. "You found the journal?"

"We did," Kit said. "Would you like to help us decode it?"

Rand opened his mouth to protest, but before he could, she took a chair. "Of course. Lily asked me to help, because I'm good at that sort of thing."

She *was* good at that sort of thing. Inside of an hour, they had Alban's final entry translated, Rand and Rose doing most of the work while Kit sat back and watched.

Rand noticed that Kit mostly watched Rose, not the diary.

"What does it say?" Kit asked.

"'I'm going to do it,'" Rose quoted. "'The time has come.'"

"It's not enough." Rand rubbed the back of his neck. "We need to find something that clearly implies murder. The rest of this entry's no more than a recitation of his day."

"Then we do the one before it," Kit said.

Rand sent him a wry glance. "We?"

"Hey, we all do what we can. I found the thing, didn't I?"

"With Rex's help," Rand conceded.

Rose went to a cabinet and poured them each a measure of Madeira, herself included. Then they went back to work.

Another hour passed, an hour of slow but steady progress.

"We're going to find the evidence," Rose said, adding to the ever-growing column of words they'd managed to decipher. "It's here. I know it." She looked up. "He was a wicked man, wasn't he, your brother?"

Rand nodded, afraid to be optimistic, but feeling Rose was right. They were going to find their proof. Then he'd just need to convince his father.

They puzzled out a few more words of an entry dealing with the sale of some cattle. "You're going to take care of my sister," Rose said while scribbling some notes. "And I expect you to be kind to her all your days."

He looked up. "I'll cherish her like no man has ever cherished a woman."

"You'd better," she said darkly, then jotted another word.

A smile on his face, Kit watched her and sipped his Madeira.

"'The date draws near,'" Rand read when the entry was complete. "'If she is to be mine, steps must be taken.'"

"Not enough," Kit said. "He could be talking about a horse."

"But he isn't." Rose reached to refill his goblet. "He's talking about murder. Another entry. Let's get back to work."

She seemed tireless, and Rand was rarely tempted to sleep when faced with a puzzle. Especially one this important.

"Lady Rose," Kit started.

"Hmm?" She crossed out a word and wrote another.

"Rand led me to believe you were, ah, a mite antagonistic concerning his relationship with your sister."

"Well, that," she said, "was before I got to know the man properly. I didn't feel he was good enough for her at first. But now…"

Her soft smile said it all. Although she'd had other reasons to oppose the match than those she was willing to admit, Rand knew her new attitude was genuine. Miraculously, she seemed truly happy for him and Lily. And approving.

It would be an enormous relief for Lily, he knew, and for him as well. And now, when it seemed everything might work out after all, that seemed more important than ever.

Several hours and four entries later, at last they hit gold.

Rand sat back, staring at the page.

"Read it," Kit said.

"'Margery begged and begged,'" Rose read softly, "'but Hawkridge refused as always.'" She paused, glancing up at Rand. "He called your father Hawkridge?"

Rand shrugged. "Ours is not a warm family."

"You'll be warm now," she warned, "with my sister. Or—"

"Peace, Rose. I love Lily more than my life. Read the rest, will you?"

Kit laughed. At a time like this, he laughed. If Rand hadn't been so tense, he'd have reached over and slapped him. But in his present mood, he feared he might do his old friend permanent damage.

"'Hawkridge refused as always,'" Rose continued slowly. "'I followed Margery to Armstrong's place, her sobbing all the way. And there, they plotted to elope.'" She reached for her Madeira and took a swallow. "Here," she said, handing Rand their notes. "You read the rest."

He took a deep breath before reading, for the first time, the individual words they'd translated, all pieced together. "'When I overheard their plans, I felt I couldn't draw air. My heart swelled to such a size it filled my chest, squeezing my lungs, robbing me of sustenance. I cannot allow this to happen. Margery will be mine. They leave in a week, and before that, I must kill him.'"

"There it is," Kit said admiringly.

"Yes, there it is," Rose echoed with a satisfied sigh.

"Thank God." Rand sent a quick thanks to heaven. "And both of you. If—when—Lily and I wed, I'll be silently thanking you as we recite our vows."

Dawn was breaking when they left the library. Rose had made peace with the fact that he'd chosen Lily over her, and amazingly, she and Rand were friends. But Kit, Rand was sure, wanted to be more than friends with Rose.

A shame she hadn't seemed to really notice him.

"Go to Lily," she told Rand. "Go tell her what we've found."

"Go to her in her chamber? You…you'll come along, won't you?"

"No." She flashed the sort of smile that only Rose could flash. "But if you're not out in five minutes, I'm coming in. Even you, Rand Nesbitt, cannot ravish a woman in five minutes flat."

Rand didn't need a second invitation.

Lily looked like an angel, her hair a dark halo on her pillow. But her mouth was turned down in a frown. Her dreams, he knew, weren't sweet.

He leaned down and pressed a kiss to those pouting lips. They curved up, and her arms rose to wrap around his neck.

She smelled of sleep and lilies. "Rand?"

"Yes, sweetheart. I'm here." Was it silly of him to be so glad she hadn't called another man's name? He knew she was his, knew it as well as he knew which English words came from Latin.

Her eyes slid languidly open. "Could you read the diary?"

He smiled and sat beside her on the bed, his fingers playing idly in her hair. "Alban Nesbitt," he said, "has never contrived a code I couldn't decipher."

She sat up, suddenly wide awake. "What did it say, Rand?" Her hands twisted together in her lap, her fingers rubbing the faint scars. "What did it say?"

"It said he planned to murder Bennett. I love you, Lily Ashcroft, and we're going to be married."

He would make it so. He hadn't come this far to fail now.

Before Lily rose for breakfast, he was riding hard for Hawkridge, the diary and notes in one hand.

SIXTY-FIVE

*R*AND ARRIVED at Hawkridge to find the marquess and Margery at breakfast, sullen and silent.

His arrival took care of that.

"It's here," he said, striding in and waving the diary and some papers. "In Alban's own hand. His plans to kill Bennett Armstrong, here in black and white."

Margery's face lit like a full moon on a cloudless night. The marquess took one look at her and frowned. "Sit down, Randal. I haven't finished my breakfast."

Rand took some spice bread and a bowl of meat pottage from the leather-topped sideboard and carried them to the table. He sat and spread his evidence on the cedarwood surface.

The marquess deliberately looked away, focusing on his food.

Margery pushed her pottage around in her bowl, evidently too excited to eat. "What did you find, Rand?"

"The diary ended on the day of Alban's death." Ignoring the marquess's wince, Rand took a big bite of the fruited spice bread. He'd been awake twenty-six hours without taking any time to eat. "Here"—he rustled through the papers with one hand—"here's the crucial passage." He held out a page to Margery.

Her hand shook as she took it. Although it was a translation, not Alban's writing, the words on the paper were his.

As she scanned down the page, a soft gasp escaped her lips. Rand's father looked annoyed before she even started reading. "'I cannot allow this to happen. Margery will be mine. They leave in a week, and before that, I must kill him.'"

The marquess snatched the sheet from her hand. His eyes narrowed before his gaze shifted to Rand. "This isn't Alban's hand. It's yours."

"Actually, that's Rose Ashcroft's writing." Rand wasn't at all surprised the man didn't recognize his own son's hand. The marquess had never bothered to look at any of his lessons. "Her writing is much tidier than mine."

With a flick of his still-supple wrist, his father tossed the paper onto the table. "I'll never believe that's what the diary says. Do you think me a fool? You'd claim anything in order to wed that Ashcroft chit." He looked back down to his food, cutting a bite of ham with a fitful, cross motion. "Those aren't Alban's words. I know—I *knew*—my son."

Rand struggled for calm. "No, Father, you didn't."

The man's gaze jerked up from his breakfast. Rand hadn't called him Father in twenty years or more. Staring at Rand, he stabbed blindly with his fork.

"You didn't know him," Rand repeated. "You knew the son you wished he was."

"Hogwash." Having managed to spear some ham, he stuck it in his mouth, taking his time to chew and swallow before continuing. "My son was incapable of premeditated murder."

"Are you aware that your son kept knives under his bed? A collection to rival a museum's. Most of them stained with blood."

If Rand could judge from his expression, the man hadn't known. "There have been no murders in this district other than Alban's."

"Not of people," Rand agreed. "But I'd wager animals have been found senselessly slaughtered."

From the look on his father's face, he'd hit home. "What of it? It's no crime."

"It could be a small leap from beasts to humankind."

The marquess pursed his lips and shook his head, but his armor had cracked. Rand could see it in his eyes. He pressed his sudden advantage. "Come to Alban's chambers. I'll show you the blades. After you see the evidence, your imagination will fill in the rest." With that, he rose and strode out of the room, trusting his father would follow.

When he heard an additional set of footsteps as they crossed the great hall, he glanced over his shoulder. "Wait in the dining room, Margery. This isn't fit for a lady's eyes."

Lily had seen the knives—and worse, to Rand's regret. He had no intention of allowing another woman to witness his brother's depravity.

But Margery lifted her chin. "I'm no lady, as your father often reminds me. Only a mere miss. And seeing as I was supposed to wed the man, I feel entitled to view what I escaped."

By the time she finished her brave speech, they were all standing in Alban's bedchamber. Rand sighed and gave up.

"Where?" the marquess asked, clearly discomfited in the disarray that made it seem as though his eldest son were still alive. "I see no knives."

"They're under the bed." Rand stooped to pull out the box. They'd left it unlocked. He lifted the lid.

"Dear heavens," Margery whispered, looking away.

Her hand went protectively to her abdomen, and Rand winced, hoping his father wouldn't notice the telltale gesture. He went to wrap an arm around her shoulders. "He's dead," he said softly. "He cannot hurt you now."

"Or anyone else." He felt her shudder, then straighten. "Or any*thing* else."

He looked to the marquess. "Well?"

The man's jaw looked tense enough to crack walnuts. "This proves nothing. Alban was an avid hunter, as you well know."

Margery's mouth dropped open. "Uncle William, those aren't hunting knives."

The marquess bent and drew one out. "This one is."

Was the man that blinded by stubborn pride? Rand felt anger boiling up from his gut, choking him. In frustration, he yanked the knife from his father's hand and tossed it back into the box. "Were you aware there's a secret space off this chamber?" he asked in a tight voice.

The one thing he'd vowed to avoid bringing into this. And in front of Margery, no less. But had he any choice? Better shocked and disgusted than married to the wrong man.

"Of course I know that," his father scoffed. "I built the place."

Though the room was flooded with daylight, Rand lit a candle. "Then I suppose you also know what's in it?"

"No, I don't. What Alban kept in his chambers was his concern alone." Though the marquess sounded adamant, trepidation laced his voice. His gaze flickered to the fireplace. "Will you never learn that a man is entitled to privacy, Randal? How many times did I tell you not to snoop in your brother's diaries?"

Halfway to the fireplace, Rand whirled. "How many times did you beat me for it?"

"Too many to count," the man snapped.

"Yes, too many times I tried to prove your son was evil and still you continued to deny it." Shoving the candle into his father's hand, Rand knelt to work the latch near the floor. "Here, at last, is your proof," he gritted out. "Try to tell me I'm mistranslating *this* to my advantage."

He stood and swung open the panel.

The marquess stepped into the small space. And his face went white.

As though in a daze, Margery moved closer.

"No!" Rand reached to stop her and turned her into his chest.

His arms went around her protectively. "Take a good look," he told his father over his shoulder. "Perhaps there have been no murders in the vicinity, but that only means he stopped short of killing. You won't convince me all those implements were meant for hunting. Or even animals."

Silence settled over the chamber, so profound Rand could hear both his own heart and Margery's. And the marquess's harsh breathing. Despite his convictions, the man was clearly shaken.

Suddenly he stepped back and slammed the panel, the sound shattering the stillness. For a moment, he just stood in place, swaying on his feet as an odd sort of calmness settled over him. "This doesn't prove Alban meant to kill Bennett Armstrong."

"No," Rand agreed. "It only goes to show he was capable. His diary is the proof."

"I cannot read it. And I refuse to—"

"To take my word as to its translation? I'm not surprised, since you never have. But this time, I'm prepared to sit with you, for *days* if necessary, and demonstrate, step-by-step, how the code was broken and exactly what that journal says." To Rand's mortification, his voice broke. "You owe me the chance to do that, Father. All my life you've dismissed me, and you've already admitted that was a mistake on your part. *You owe me.*"

It didn't take days.

Four hours later, his father slumped in his chair and buried his face in his hands.

SIXTY-SIX

STANDING IN HER mother's perfumery, Lily gazed out the window and squinted into the distance. "Where on earth is he?"

On another day, Rose might have laughed, but she didn't. "Poor Lily. Give him time." She chose several cheerful yellow daffodils and added them to an arrangement. "He had to ride there and convince his father and then come all the way back… why, he likely won't be here for hours."

Mum plucked rose petals, tossing them into the clear glass bulb of the fancy distillery Ford had made for her while courting Violet. "Your sister's right, dear. Come and help me. It will take your mind off the waiting."

With a sigh, Lily walked to the table and idly picked up a rose. "I know Rand will convince his father," she said, as much to assure herself as them.

"Of course he will," Rose said. "If you'd seen that translation, you'd be even more certain. Rand's brother intended murder. Their father won't be able to deny it."

"But that doesn't mean he'll allow us to wed."

That statement was met with silence, because, unfortunately, there was no arguing with it. No guarantees that proof of Alban's intent would lead to the marquess changing his mind.

"Tell me about Hawkridge," Rose said at last. "Is it beautiful?"

"Very." Lily absently plucked rose petals. "Much newer than Trentingham—Rand's father built it just before the war—and every room is exquisite." Except for Rand's, which was rather plain, but she didn't feel up to explaining that. "Why, the dining room even has *leather* on the walls, with designs stamped in pure gold. But the place is eerie, I think. Or perhaps it's just cold. It feels as though no one there has been happy for a long, long time."

"Perhaps they haven't," Mum suggested. "But that will change, of course. You and Rand will be happy indeed, and your happiness will rub off on everyone else. And I imagine that after you move there you'll be able to make improvements, make Hawkridge Hall feel warmer and more like home. If you cannot redecorate the whole house, you should at least have a say in the rooms assigned to you and Rand."

Picturing Rand's tiny chamber, Lily sighed. Maybe— assuming they were allowed to marry—they could occupy Alban's suite of rooms instead. But if that were the case, a complete overhaul would be necessary before she'd agree to sleep there even once.

Rose added several carnations to the colorful spray she was creating. "Will you live at Hawkridge all the time, then? Will Rand have to give up his post at Oxford?"

"I don't know. He and his father have yet to discuss any details like that." She tossed the last of the rose petals into the glass bulb. "All of their energies have been focused on the marquess's insistence that Rand wed Margery."

Mum fitted the lid on the distillery. "Has Rand resigned himself to leaving his position?"

"I don't think he's had enough time to think about it. But I doubt he'll be happy leaving Oxford." Lily hoped he'd be happy just being with her. Whether at Oxford or Hawkridge or somewhere else entirely. But she knew better. "He worked very hard to attain that professorship. And he enjoys that life. He's never fancied himself an earl, let alone a marquess."

Finished, Rose stepped back to eye her masterpiece. "I shouldn't think *that* would be hard to get used to."

Rose might have mellowed a bit, but she was still Rose.

"How about you?" Mum asked. "Will you be happy at Hawkridge?"

"I'll be happy wherever Rand is," she said, knowing it was true. "I'll have him, and my animals…"

Her voice trailed off.

Mum looked up sharply. "What is it, dear? Are you afraid Lord Hawkridge won't approve of your menagerie?"

"No," she said slowly. "He loves animals—more than people, truth be told. He raises mastiffs."

Mum smiled. "Well, then, it sounds like Hawkridge will be the perfect place to build your animal home."

Rose tweaked a few flowers, balancing the arrangement. "I imagine Hawkridge has plenty of space."

"No. I mean, yes, there are acres and acres of land." Lily took a deep breath and decided to come out with it. "You might as well know that if the marquess blesses this marriage, it will be with the stipulation that my inheritance goes to him."

Rose gasped. "How dare he demand such a thing!"

"There was no demand. I offered of my own free will. Hawkridge was mortgaged during the war, you see, to provide funds for King Charles. The marquess was on the verge of losing it when Margery was dropped in his lap, along with her considerable fortune. Hawkridge would face bankruptcy without her land and money."

"Or *your* money," Rose said darkly.

"Exactly. Don't look so sour, Rose. It was my idea to offer my inheritance in exchange for the right to wed Rand, and I'll gladly do so, if only the marquess will allow it."

Rose plucked a daisy from the vase and pointed it at Lily. "All your life, you've dreamed of nothing but building a home for your strays." She shook the flower, emphasizing her words. "Maybe sometimes I've laughed at that, but I know how important it is to you. How can you give that up so cavalierly?"

"I'm in love," Lily said simply.

But she caught Mum's gaze on her and knew her mother hadn't missed the wistfulness in her voice.

SIXTY-SEVEN

ℕOT THE SORT of man to indulge in self-pity for long, nor to accept blame, the marquess had made an excuse and gone off to his study. Half an hour later, when Rand and Margery asked to talk to him, he readily—if gruffly—invited them in.

They sat in two chairs facing him, gazing up at him seated behind his desk on the raised dais. A few awkward moments passed before Rand cleared his throat.

"Father," he began, hoping calling him such might mellow the man, "we would like your assurance that, under the circumstances, you will no longer pursue the conviction of Bennett Armstrong for murder."

"Of course I won't. I'm a reasonable man when presented with persuasive evidence."

"Well, then, Margery respectfully requests permission to marry him."

"Does she?" the marquess asked with a raised brow. He shifted his gaze to his ward. "I haven't heard such a respectful request."

"Uncle William..." Margery's voice shook, and she paused to control it. "May I *please* wed Bennett?"

"No," the man snapped. "I didn't agree before Alban's death, and nothing has changed between then and now. Marriage is primarily a business arrangement, and an alliance of Hawkridge with the Maybanks estates is best for both parties."

"You mean Hawkridge requires Margery's money," Rand said, struggling to remain calm. "As I've told you, Lily has ten thousand pounds that she's willing to invest in Hawkridge's future. Added to her dowry of three thousand, it should be a sufficient sum."

At Lily's name, his father's eyes had softened. It was amazing how much the man had apparently come to like her. He almost looked wistful.

But his expression swiftly hardened again. "I vowed on Simon Maybanks's deathbed that his daughter would wed my heir. Lady Lily's inheritance does nothing to mitigate that."

"Uncle William." Margery rose and walked over to him, stepping up onto the raised dais. She placed her palms on his desk and leaned toward him, her eyes pleading. "I was an infant when my father claimed that boon, and he was only attempting to provide for my future the best that he knew how. Don't you think he would have been thrilled to marry me to a baron with Bennett's vast lands and income? Most especially because I love Bennett so very much, and he loves me in return. You must agree that if my father had had any way of foreseeing such an opportunity, he would have given his blessing freely."

In the silence that followed, Margery backed down the step and returned to her seat. She folded her hands in her black-skirted lap. A clock ticked on the mantel, unnaturally loud in the stillness. The marquess blinked but said nothing.

"Father," Rand pressed, hoping the man's lack of response meant he was considering Margery's words, "you've told me that your treatment of me, in years gone past, was because you blamed me for my mother's death."

The marquess's lips thinned. "I've also told you I'm sorry."

"And I've accepted your apology—and your explanation."

Saying the words, Rand suddenly realized he had. "But what I'm wondering now, or perhaps I should say what I'm assuming, is that you loved her very much."

"Of course I did," his father said, looking bewildered. "I loved her with all my heart."

"Well, then, if you loved her enough to blame me, whyever would you wish to deprive your son and foster daughter of that same sort of love?"

The marquess blinked some more. Margery's hands clenched in her lap. The clock kept ticking. Rand prayed silently, harder than he'd ever prayed in his life.

"Marry whom you wish," his father said at last with a sigh.

Margery leapt up and rounded the desk to hug him. "Thank you, Uncle William, thank you! You've always been so kind to me, I knew in the end you'd choose for my happiness."

Rand's father just grunted.

Rand sat immobile, his entire body seemingly gone boneless.

He'd done it.

He was going to marry Lily.

"I must go tell Bennett."

Rand had never seen Margery's eyes look so green, her face look so flushed. He smiled, picturing Lily looking that happy.

"I'll take you to him," he said, "on my way back to Trentingham. Lily will be anxious to hear this news, too."

"I'm going with you," his father said.

Halfway to rising, Rand dropped back onto his chair. "Pardon?"

"What sort of a man do you take me for?" the marquess asked, then apparently decided he'd best not wait for an answer. "Not only has your Lily saved my dog's life, she is also about to save Hawkridge from ruin. The least I can do is welcome her into our family."

Rand wasn't sure he was ready to think of himself and his father as a family—he suspected they might never truly be friends. But he grudgingly admitted that it seemed the man's heart might be in the right place.

Or getting there, anyway.

SIXTY-EIGHT

*W*HILE THE marquess rode around Armstrong House dismissing all the guards, Rand dismounted and walked Margery to the door. The butler answered and showed them both into a sitting room, then went to fetch Lord Armstrong.

Rand sat on a red velvet chair watching Margery walk aimlessly around the chamber, bouncing a little on the balls of her feet. She'd be happy here, he thought. Though the house was centuries older and much smaller than Hawkridge, it was well kept and richly appointed. Besides, he knew Margery would be happy anywhere so long as she was with Bennett.

It was the same for him and Lily. Home would be where Lily lived, even if that was Hawkridge.

"Margery!" Bennett rushed into the room, then stopped short when he saw Rand.

Rand rose from the chair. "She's yours, Armstrong."

Long-lost hope leapt into the man's eyes. "You mean..."

"Yes. My father has agreed to your marriage."

"How—why—"

"Margery will explain," Rand said. "Later."

She'd stopped roaming. Now she seemed simply frozen in

place, gazing at Bennett as though she couldn't believe he would be hers. When he took a step toward her, she came to life and rushed into his arms.

Their lips met, and Rand smiled. That would be he and Lily soon, and he was sure their reunion would be even better. In fact, he couldn't imagine why he was standing here watching the two lovers kiss when he could be kissing his own love himself.

"I'm leaving," he announced.

With a heartfelt sigh, Margery drew her mouth from Bennett's. "Goodbye, Randy," she said, gazing into the other man's eyes.

"I'm leaving you two alone."

"I know," she murmured, her words directed to Bennett along with a wide smile.

"Be good," Rand said, knowing they wouldn't.

～

*L*ILY'S FINGERS ran over the harpsichord keys in an unceasing pattern. "What time is it?" she asked.

"About five minutes after the last time I told you." Rose didn't bother to look at a clock. "I thought you found music calming."

"Well, today it's not."

"Perhaps it would help if you'd play something besides scales." Rose set down her needlework and pulled a droopy bloom from the flower arrangement beside her. "You're making *me* nervous."

"Sorry." The music stopped abruptly as Lily folded her hands in her lap. She closed her eyes, willing herself to be patient. "That it's taking this long, it's a good sign, it that not so?" She heard her sister rise and walk across the drawing room. "It must mean his father is listening."

"It must," Rose said in a soothing way.

But Lily heard laughter bubbling underneath. Her eyes

popped open. "This isn't easy, you know. My entire life is hanging in the balance."

"Of course it's not easy." Rose plucked three browning leaves off some flowers on the wide windowsill. "But surely not your entire life. If it all ends badly, you'll go on—"

"You've never been in love," Lily said.

The leaves crunched in her sister's fisted hand. "No," she admitted, "I haven't. And given what you're going through, I believe that's just as well."

"You're wrong." Lily's voice came a whisper. "I wouldn't trade love for tranquility."

"Some of us," Rose said, "don't seem to have a choice."

"Oh, Rose." Lily's eyes met her sister's dark ones. "Someday…"

You'll find someone.

The words hung between them, unsaid, until Rose looked away and out the window. "Someone's riding up the road, Lily."

"Rand!" Lily jumped up and brushed at her sky blue skirts.

Rose frowned. "No, two someones. I wonder who they could be?"

"Two?" Lily pulled a few curls forward to frame her face. "How do I look?"

"He's not going to care," said the sister that took the most care with her own appearance. "Go to him, Lily."

As she hurried to the entry hall, Lily wondered if one of the riders was indeed Rand. After all, there were two, and he'd set out for Hawkridge Hall alone. As Parkinson opened the door, she braced herself for disappointment.

Rand stood on the other side, a wide smile on his face. Her heart leapt—until she looked beyond him.

"Lord Hawkridge. How, um, how very nice to see you."

"Lady Lily." Rand's father bowed, for once looking at a loss for words.

"Rand," her mother said warmly, glossing over the awkward moment as she appeared from seemingly nowhere. "Come in, please. And you," she said to Lord Hawkridge, "must be this young man's father. The resemblance is unmistakable."

Rand didn't look particularly pleased at that observation. Lily stared at him, caught in his compelling gray gaze, wondering...

"And you must be Lady Trentingham. I'm pleased to make your acquaintance," the marquess told her mother. "I've come to welcome your daughter into my family."

It took a moment for Lily to register those words, and when she did, she was embarrassed to feel tears spring to her eyes.

"Rand," she whispered.

His gaze flicked over to his father, then her mother, and finally Rose standing at the bottom of Trentingham's wide staircase. He stepped forward to take Lily's hand.

"Come," he said, "I feel a need to take a run." He glanced at her fashionable heeled shoes. "I mean a walk."

That old, rude habit, but Lily didn't care, so long as he wanted her with him this time. Her mother and the marquess would do fine—Rand's father might be on the curmudgeonly side, but Mum had never met a man she couldn't wrap around her finger.

Without saying a word, Rand hurried her through the house, out the back into the gardens, and along the paths to the summerhouse. He dropped her hand long enough to shut the door behind them, enclosing them in the cool dimness of the small, round brick building. Then he turned and gathered her into his arms.

"Rand, how did you convince—"

"Hush," he said as his mouth crushed down on hers.

She was hushed, very effectively, by a kiss so intense it rattled her to her toes. His lips slanted over hers again and again until she couldn't tell where his mouth stopped and hers started, until her knees were so weak she needed his arms to hold her up.

"When can we marry?" he asked, dropping little kisses on

her nose, her cheeks, her chin. His mouth trailed down the side of her throat. "When? Today?"

"No." She laughed, arching her neck to allow him better access. He felt so very *good*—especially knowing that finally, miraculously, he was going to be hers.

"Tomorrow?" he asked, his lips dancing over her skin.

"Not tomorrow."

"The next day, then. Or the day after that. Saturday. A perfect day for a wedding."

"No." She shivered, and not only from his sensual assault. "You and Margery were supposed to marry on Saturday."

"Her birthday. The day she'll wed Bennett." He worked his way back toward her mouth.

"Oh," she breathed, "they must be so happy."

"Mmm." His agreement was muffled by his lips claiming hers, his tongue meeting hers in a heady swirl of sensation. He tasted divine. "Margery will want us at her wedding," he murmured against her mouth. "So ours will have to be the day after that."

"No." Pulling back, she laughed again. "Two weeks. When Violet and Ford wished to marry in a rush, Mum insisted on two weeks to plan the wedding."

"Two weeks?" he said on a groan. "After all we've gone through, two more weeks seems a lifetime."

She smiled softly, basking in those heartfelt words. "Two weeks is entirely survivable."

"As long as we don't have to wait for the wedding night," he said, his fingers moving to the tabs on her stomacher.

His eyes smoldered, and something inside her responded to that heat. But something else held her back. She reached to still his hands. "Rand."

"Hmm?" He kissed her again, nearly melting her resolve.

But she'd thought about this. "I want to wait. Until we're married. Until you're mine, heart, body, and soul, and no one can threaten otherwise."

The heat in his eyes transformed to disbelief. "Nothing can threaten us, Lily. *Nothing.* We've been to hell and back again, and there is *nothing* I will allow to come between us."

Under the force of his gaze, she was weakening. She'd already given herself to this man, and she hadn't been sorry, and more than anything, she burned to share that again.

But it was hard to believe that all would be well. There had been too many hours and days when she'd thought he was lost to her.

"Nothing," he repeated, and the earnestness in his voice went a long way toward breaking her will. "Fate may send us dragons, but I'll slay them for you, fair Lily. Nothing will steal you from my side."

Watching her closely, he pulled something from his pocket.

His mother's pendant, on a delicate white gold chain.

"I've learned that my father gave this to my mother on their wedding day. I was planning to save it for our own wedding day, but I want you to have it now."

"Oh, Rand."

If this wasn't proof that he was certain they'd stay together, she didn't know what was. Her heart seemed to melt as he clasped the chain around her neck. Looking down, she lifted the necklace, admiring all the diamonds and the beautiful enameled filigree design.

Her throat closed with emotion. "I'll cherish it always," she whispered.

It was all she could manage.

Still...when he reached for her stomacher tabs again, she pushed at his hands. "Not here," she said, not an outright rejection nor an unreasonable one, either. The summerhouse had a brick floor and only the narrowest of wooden benches. "This is all so sudden and unbelievable to me, Rand. I want to hear how you convinced your father."

He drew a deep breath, clearly struggling for control,

glancing around as though he felt trapped. "All right, then. But let's walk."

They strolled across the wide lawn and over the bridge and along the Thames. As his story poured out, Lily felt his hand in hers slowly relax.

"You were brilliant," she said when he'd told her everything.

"I was desperate." He squeezed her hand and smiled.

"And how has your father taken it?"

"We spent over an hour riding here—maybe the longest time alone together ever. He expressed regret that he'd never seen Alban for the evil man he was. He seems...repentant."

"You like him more than you thought."

"I wouldn't go so far as to say *like*. We've a long history between us. But the idea of living with him isn't nearly as repugnant as I would have thought last month."

"Will we have to? Live with him, I mean?"

He seemed surprised by the question. "Do you imagine we have a choice? He's certainly assuming we will. Hawkridge will someday be mine, and I've a lot to learn about handling it."

"Oh, Rand, you can handle anything you put your mind to. Your father has years left to live. Why should you give up the life you love now?"

He looked as though he wanted to believe her—but couldn't. "It's a matter of responsibility. Once I would have agreed with you, but now that I've been home...well, there's Margery—"

"Margery will be with Bennett."

"There's Etta and all the others. They're depending on me, and I cannot let them down. Oxford..." His voice turned wistful for a moment before he straightened his shoulders, his hand gripping hers tighter. "This is the way it must be."

"But your professorship, your house."

"There's nothing for it. I'll have to sell the house."

"After you worked months designing it with Kit? The two of you put your hearts and souls into that house."

He gave her a wan smile. "Kit liked some of my ideas so much, he's planning changes to his own home in Windsor."

"You cannot just sell it, Rand."

"Well, it makes no sense to keep it if I'll never be using it, does it? I can put the money into Hawkridge, help it recover from the loss of Margery's land that much sooner. Or...wait..."

A light had entered his intense gray eyes. "What?" Lily asked.

"The money can be *yours*," he said softly, looking pleased with himself. "For your animal home."

It would mean she'd have the best of both worlds—Rand *and* her dream—but she said, "No."

"Yes." He nodded emphatically. "It's my house, after all, built with income that had nothing to do with Hawkridge. My father and the estate have no claim on it whatsoever."

"No, Rand." She wouldn't—couldn't—let him give up his house in Oxford—and the life he'd made for himself there—for an old childhood dream. "I won't hear of it."

It was a silly dream, anyway, a childish dream for a child. Her strays had no need of a fancy, custom-built home and a staff of trained caretakers. She'd done just fine by them so far, all by herself with makeshift pens in a corner of a barn, and surely the marquess would have no objection to her doing the same at Hawkridge.

True, she dreamed of helping more animals—hundreds more, possibly even in several homes spread across the country—but who knew if she'd ever find such a large number of needful creatures? Her strays had always found *her*.

They'd reached the woods, and Rand apparently decided not to argue, instead pulling her into his arms. "Are you *really* going to make me wait two weeks for you?" he asked. "I'm burning for you, Lily. All these days and hours..."

She was burning for him, too. He felt so warm and solid against her body, she could almost believe they really would stay together forever.

She sighed against his mouth. "Let's go back," she said. "There's much to settle. Our wedding date, for one."

"And then?"

"And then maybe I'll believe it."

"If you don't," he warned playfully, "I'll wear you down anyway."

Since that wasn't an altogether unpleasing idea, she let it slide by without a retort.

SIXTY-NINE

$\mathcal{T}$HE NEGOTIATIONS took place over a dinner that had gone cold while waiting for their return.

"Two weeks," Lily told her mother.

"Two weeks! I cannot plan a wedding in two weeks."

"You did for Violet and Ford," Lily reminded her, and that was that.

Looking victorious, Lily turned to Rand's father. "Now I would like to discuss our living arrangements."

His gaze landed on the diamond pendant she wore. Though he'd granted Rand permission to give it to her, Rand still held his breath, waiting for a reaction.

At last the marquess nodded his approval, a small smile curving his lips. "I realize Randal's chamber is small," he told her. "Perhaps we can refurbish—"

"That would be nice, but I meant where we will live and when."

The man picked up his fork, his smile becoming a slight frown. "You'll live at Hawkridge, of course. Where did you think you would live?"

"Oxford, at least part of the year. Rand's position there is important to him. The research—"

"Lily," Rand started.

"He can research at home," his father cut in. "He'll be the marquess someday, which means he has responsibilities."

She smiled sweetly. "Certainly he does—"

"Lily," Rand interrupted.

"—but that doesn't mean he must be at Hawkridge all the time. Many men own more than one estate, and a man cannot be two or three places at once. Why, Father visits Tremayne but once a year, and it thrives quite well without his constant presence."

"Lily," Rand tried to put in.

But she wasn't finished. "Oxford has three terms a year of eight weeks each. Twenty-four weeks out of fifty-two. There are long breaks between those terms and the whole summer free…if Rand agrees to spend the remaining twenty-eight weeks at Hawkridge learning his responsibilities, surely you can survive without him during term times."

"Lily—"

"Just until he's needed at Hawkridge year-round," she said by way of conclusion. "But given your excellent state of health, we're both hoping that won't be for a long, long time."

She topped off her arguments with a sweet smile that the marquess apparently found bemusing, given he seemed to be frozen in place with his fork halfway to his mouth.

But Rand was not similarly charmed. "Lily," he repeated and paused for a moment, expecting her to interrupt. When she didn't, he sighed. "I truly want to sell my house so you'll have the money for your animal home. It's the least I can do after you so generously offered to save my family."

Rose clapped. Lady Trentingham smiled.

The marquess came to life. "Animal home?"

"Lily's childhood dream," Lily's mother explained. "She's rather fond of animals—"

"This isn't news to me," the man said with a grin that looked out of place on his face.

"And she had planned, upon coming into her inheritance, to build a home where strays could be sheltered and, if necessary, nursed to health."

"With a staff," Lily added. "But truly, my lord, I don't mind investing in Hawkridge instead. It will be my children's legacy, after all. And I especially don't want Rand to sell his Oxford house. As proud as you are of building Hawkridge, he feels the same of his home. And—"

"Enough." The marquess waved his fork. "You will talk my ear off, child. Randal shall keep his house, and if his responsibilities at Oxford can be fulfilled in twenty-four weeks a year, they may have him for that time. But I get him the rest," he warned.

"Of course."

His jaw set, Rand shook his head. "No. I said—"

"She shall have her animal home," the marquess interrupted, "at Hawkridge. I have staff enough to spare, and if nothing else, it will ensure you two stay there on a regular basis. Now, if everyone's concerns have been addressed to their satisfaction, I need to go home. Margery's wedding day approaches, and although it surely won't be the extravaganza Lady Trentingham has in mind for yours, there are details to which I must attend."

Half an hour later, Rand found himself dragged out of the house, drafted into helping his father, since, as Lily's mother pointed out, it wasn't term time at Oxford.

No sooner was he riding away than Chrystabel started a guest list.

～

"*W*ELL, DARLING," Joseph said that night, "that was very cleanly done, although I suspect the poor lad might die of longing if there were such a disease. And I don't expect our daughter was very happy, either."

"Nonsense," Chrystabel said as she climbed into bed. "They can survive two weeks."

"I feel for the boy. Before, you were only too happy to push them together, and—"

"There was good reason then. Lily was all too concerned about Rose, and—"

"But they've already been together—"

"That doesn't matter. I won't make the mistake again of allowing our children to risk conception before they're safely wed."

"The date has been set, so this makes no sense, my pretty Chrysanthemum. But not to worry, I love you anyway." He kissed her soundly; then his lips trailed lower, tasting the skin revealed by her nightgown's low neckline. "I shudder to think of that boy alone in his bed tonight," he added, his breath warm on her breast where he'd pushed the fabric down farther. "And I thank God I'm not in that same place."

As his mouth closed over her, Chrystabel thanked God, too... and not only because her daughter's happiness was finally secured.

SEVENTY

"SOON," RAND whispered, "it will be *our* turn."

Lily watched the starry-eyed bride and groom exit Hawkridge's grand red-and-gold private chapel as though they were walking on air. Tears had welled in her eyes more than once during the romantic ceremony. "I cannot wait," she whispered back, reaching up to touch the pendant Rand had given her.

The past few days without him had felt so empty.

Holding his hand, she walked sedately from the chapel, following the other guests to the great hall. Once there, she rushed to hug her soon-to-be sister-in-law. "The wedding was beautiful! You both look so happy."

"We are," Margery and Bennett said together, sharing a joyful smile.

Rand hugged Margery, too, while Lily watched, not at all jealous this time.

"Your gown is gorgeous," she told her.

"Thank you." Margery's fingers skimmed the pearls and embroidery that covered her pale green satin overskirt. "It's my best."

Standing nearby, the marquess narrowed his eyes. "What happened to the gown you ordered in Windsor?"

"Oh." Color flooded her cheeks. "Well. I—I…it wasn't quite ready, after all. You didn't give the seamstress much time, Uncle William."

"Hmmph," he said and walked away.

Rand waited until the man was out of earshot and then grinned at his foster sister. "You never ordered a wedding gown, did you? I suspected you were with Bennett that night."

"It's the vows that count," she said evasively. "Not the clothes."

Her groom laughed and gave her a kiss. As other guests pressed close to offer felicitations, Rand turned to Lily, a silvery glint in his eyes. "Come. I have something to show you."

He led her from the great hall, grabbing a pewter goblet off a sideboard and handing it to her as they went.

She sipped, then smiled when she tasted what was in it. "Your father poured the champagne my parents brought."

"He likes your parents." His shrug encompassed all the bafflement she knew he felt at his father's recent behavior. Beatrix appeared and padded at their heels as Rand entered the corridor that led to his room. But instead of turning left, he walked straight ahead into Alban's bedchamber.

Only it wasn't Alban's bedchamber anymore. It wasn't a bedchamber at all.

She stared. "What happened?"

"You'll be living here the week after next. I told my father we needed more room. He didn't argue, so I sent a message to Kit. The day after that, a crew of men showed up to begin the remodel. They'll resume tomorrow, once all the wedding guests go home."

The dark paneling had been stripped and was half refinished in a warm, honey tone that lightened the whole chamber. The door to the secret space stood open, and she could see it had been emptied. The rest of the room was empty, too.

"Even the bed is gone," she said.

"This will be our sitting room." The drapes had been removed, and soft summer rain blew against the naked windows. Taking her hand, Rand drew her into Alban's old sitting room, now dominated by a huge four-poster bed draped in yellow silk. "I had it brought from another chamber. Just until you choose a new one. Something without a history. I thought we could go to London, and—"

"Thank you," she whispered past a sudden lump in her throat. She knew Rand didn't care whether he slept in the same room that Alban had, or even in the same bed. He'd done this for *her*. "Where are Alban's things?"

"I had them sent to a foundling home. Every last item. I asked Father, and he didn't say yes, but he didn't say no, either. I think he wants to forget that Alban ever existed. He even had his portrait removed from the long gallery."

In an effort to steady herself, she took a sip of champagne. "Did he send that to the foundling home, too?"

"No." Again, that baffled shrug. "He burned it."

"Maybe he'll have one painted of you to replace it."

"I wouldn't go so far as to assume that." He gave a strangled laugh. "But I'm not dreading living here half the year quite as much as I thought I would."

Beatrix followed them back through the sitting room and into Alban's old dressing room, and it was empty, too. The clothes presses were gone, the walls stripped and waiting to be finished. "Kit is arranging for someone to build cabinets." Rand took the goblet from Lily's hand. "Newfangled ones with drawers."

She turned to him. "It all sounds wonderful. I love you."

"And I love you." A smile lit his eyes as he sipped, regarding her over the rim. Without swallowing, he bent and put his mouth to hers, giving her a sweet, cold, sparkly kiss as he shared the bubbly beverage.

She swallowed and laughed. "Eleven more days and we'll be together for good."

"Too long." He took another sip and gave her another effervescent kiss, the champagne still fizzing in her mouth when he pulled back to skim his knuckles along her cheek. "You're not going to make me wait that long, are you?"

She remembered, vaguely, that she'd decided they really should wait. But the kiss had made her light-headed, and her skin tingled wherever he touched, so she couldn't remember why.

When Beatrix began hiccuping, Lily leaned to pick her up, cradling the cat in her arms. Protection from Rand and her own weakening resolve. She mustered a teasing smile. "Did you bring me in here to show me the renovations or to get me into that big yellow bed?"

"Both," he answered with a grin. He took another sip and leaned over Beatrix, meeting Lily's lips once again. The bubbles tickled her throat as Rand tickled her senses.

The idea of making love right now was absurd, but she sighed longingly as she licked the remnants of champagne off her lips. Delicious. Rand's kisses were delicious.

"Not here, during the wedding."

"Here. Now." He didn't look at all concerned with propriety. "The wedding is over."

"But not the wedding supper. There are guests in the house," she reminded him, the protest faint to her own ears.

"We're in here. The guests are out there." His voice was husky and low, filled with the pent-up frustration of desire unfulfilled. "Eleven more days, Lily...and all the days before now..."

His words made heat shimmer through her. What he was proposing was surely wicked, here at a wedding.

Wickedly tempting.

And a weakness in Lily's knees told her she was all too close to surrendering.

It had been so long. So many days of yearning need...so many nights living with that low-burning heat...lying chastely with him here at Hawkridge and then alone in her bed at Trentingham...

When she swayed toward him involuntarily, he laughed and swung her up into his arms.

"Rand!" she squealed, barely holding on to the cat. "We cannot!"

"Oh, I think we can," he said, striding into the sitting room.

Beatrix leapt to the floor as Rand kicked the door shut and set Lily on her feet. "See?" He threw the bolt. "There are no guests in here."

He was impossible. And irresistible. His mouth covered hers, and despite her misgivings, her arms wound around his neck. Now-familiar feelings began coursing through her, building a heat centered low in her middle. She pressed herself close, wishing desperately that she and Rand weren't wearing so many clothes.

A small sound of satisfaction rose from his throat. "I knew I could wear you down."

"A kiss," she said with mock indignation. "I've only assented to a kiss."

Beatrix hiccuped louder, rubbing against Lily's skirts.

"A kiss, hmm?" Rand started easing her into the bedchamber, working the tabs on her stomacher as he went, and she couldn't find it in herself to protest. Her legs felt shaky, and when the backs of them hit the high, silk-draped mattress, she reclined onto it with a sigh, using her arms locked behind Rand to bring him down with her.

Beatrix suddenly began meowing emphatically.

"Ignore her," they whispered together.

Meow...

Lily melted into Rand's embrace. His kisses tasted of champagne and desire, and excitement built inside her, coupled with wonder that he would be hers. Not only today, but forever. Seeing Margery wed Bennett had really driven that home.

Her own wedding was next.

Meow, meow...

The mere thought made her giddy, made her senses spin with delight. She pressed her lips tighter to Rand's, tilting her head until their mouths fit perfectly.

Meow, meow, meeeooow...

A knock came at the door. "Lily? Rand? Are you in there?"

"Goodness! It's Mum!" Lily bolted upright on the bed, her heart pounding not with arousal now, but with something more akin to panic. She rushed to refasten her stomacher.

Still fully clothed, Rand calmly rose to his feet.

"She was trying to warn us!" Lily whispered.

"Your mother?"

"Beatrix!"

More knocking. "Lily? Are you in there?"

Amusement lit Rand's eyes. "I'll get the door."

"Not yet!" Her fingers fumbled on the stomacher's tabs.

"Are you in there, dear?"

Rand walked into the sitting room to answer the door, and Lily scrambled to join him, doing her best to look composed. He pulled back the bolt, at the same time reaching to tweak her stomacher straight. As the door swung open, revealing her parents, she plastered on a smile.

Mum's gaze flicked to Lily's bodice before settling on her face. "There you are!" she said brightly.

Too brightly.

"I was just showing Lily the rooms we'll be using when we live here," Rand said unconvincingly.

"We'd love to see them, too," her mother said and walked straight into the bedchamber.

As her parents passed, Lily looked down, mortified to find one of her stomacher tabs unattached. She whirled away, fastening it surreptitiously before joining them in the other room. Her heart seized when she noticed the rumpled counterpane on the bed.

"This entire home is magnificent." Mum crossed to a wall

and ran a hand down the newly stripped paneling. "The grain is lovely."

"I thought to paint it white for Lily," Rand said while Lily inched over to the bed to smooth the yellow silk. "But Kit suggested a pale stain might look nicer on this wood."

Mum nodded her approval. "What kind is it?"

Her husband pulled out his pocket watch and flipped open the lid. "Half past three."

"Cedar," Rand said, clearly suppressing a laugh. Lily wondered which he found amusing, her father's misunderstanding or her own red-faced embarrassment.

Probably both.

Father snapped the pocket watch shut, nodding vaguely at Rand. "I expect you'll be staying here the next week or so to supervise finishing this?"

Rand raised his voice. "The house in Oxford needs my attention, too, Lord Trentingham. Perhaps I can bring Lily along—"

"I think not," her mother interrupted. "Lily will be at home, busy with the wedding plans."

Lily stopped smoothing. "Mum, I think—"

"You'll be busy," she repeated. "If you weren't insisting on marrying so quickly, it might be a different matter. But I'll need your help. Now, I imagine Margery and Bennett are missing us, so our little tour of the house is over."

As they all returned to the great hall together, Lily exchanged a frustrated glance with Rand.

"Elizabeth!" Mum cried, waving to a neighbor and dragging Father in her direction. "I've found the perfect man for your daughter."

No sooner had her parents walked off than Rand swung Lily to face him. "Margery wasn't missing us." He aimed a pointed look to where his baby sister was half entwined with Bennett, blissfully unaware of any of the guests.

Lily nodded. "Mum is trying to keep us apart."

"And your father is cooperating."

"I cannot figure why. They've left us alone before—"

"Does it matter why? They intend to make certain we don't see each other again until the day of our wedding."

A maid came by with fresh goblets of champagne. Rand took one and a bottle, too, meeting Lily's eyes in a way that made her certain he had an idea that involved the sparkling wine.

An idea her parents wouldn't approve.

Lily's lips—and other places—tingled at the thought. She took the goblet from him and downed a bracing swallow.

"They won't succeed in this," Rand warned, sounding as though he'd just assigned himself a mission. He cast a glance to Lily's parents and, seeing their backs momentarily turned, grabbed her hand. "Come along."

He hurried her into the adjoining dining room, where footmen were setting the long gatelegged table with Delftware dishes for the wedding supper. Lily glanced back into the great hall. "They'll just find us again."

"I wouldn't bet on that," he advised her, taking the goblet from her hand and setting it on the leather-topped sideboard. Still carrying the bottle, he led her into the next room.

His father's chamber. She stopped short and gaped at the tall, heavy oak bed.

"Not in here!"

Laughing, Rand leaned a hand on the wall.

Lily was astonished to see a panel swing open. They slipped beyond it, and Rand closed it quietly.

"A secret passage?" she said in wonder.

"Not secret." Calmer now but no less determined, he guided her through a windowless corridor lit by plain lanterns mounted on walls painted a simple pale gray. "The house has these passages all through it," he explained, guiding her around a corner. Here, a longer hallway bustled with servants carrying dishes and linen. "Father didn't want the staff walking through one chamber to get to another, so corridors run behind. That way, they can duck in and out of rooms unobtrusively."

The floors were not painstakingly polished here, but covered with long rush mats instead. With no fire to warm it, the passage was chilly. "Do all the rooms have secret doors?"

"Most of them, but the doors aren't secret, either. They're designed not to be obvious, but you just have to look for them."

Lily shivered. "If there's a door into our suite, I want it sealed."

She thought Rand smiled beside her, but the corridor was too dim to tell for sure. Rows of leather fire buckets hung overhead, making her think they must be near the kitchen. "Where are we going?"

"Out. Through the servants' entrance."

"Out? You mean outside? Into the rain?"

His hand squeezed hers. "No one will be coming out in the rain to look for us, will they?"

The way he said that made a shiver of another sort run through her.

Summer rain blew in when he pushed open the door. They made a run for it, Rand holding Lily with one hand and the champagne bottle with the other. After crossing the courtyard to the outbuildings, they finally ducked into the dairy.

Though Rand shut the door against the rain, it still pattered on the roof and slashed against the dairy's diamond-paned windows. Lily remembered peeking in here once and seeing a dairymaid with a pockmarked face and a pretty, shy smile.

She glanced around the small room. "Where is everyone?"

"Inside, helping with the wedding. No one will interrupt us." He grinned. "Even Beatrix failed to make it out here."

The walls were plain and whitewashed. Lily turned in a slow circle, her shoes leaving wet prints on the red tile floor. Pails, pans, and strainers sat on a wide marble counter supported on legs that ended in cows' hooves. She hugged herself, smiling at the whimsy.

"Cold?" Rand asked.

"A little. There's no fire."

"I'll warm you up," he said, the tone of his voice leaving no doubt how he planned to accomplish that end. He set the champagne bottle on the marble surface with a definitive *clunk*.

A nervous laugh bubbled out of her. "I hope you're not planning to warm me up too effectively. There's no bed, either."

"I plan to warm you effectively indeed." Both hands on her waist, he lifted her to sit on the counter. "And we've no need of a bed."

The marble felt cold beneath her skirts, but Rand's fingers felt warm on her shoulders as he maneuvered himself closer, working his way between her knees. When he looked pointedly down, her gaze followed, her heart hitching as she saw how it could work.

"I guess we *don't* need a bed," she whispered as his mouth descended on hers.

His lips were gentle and cherishing, and when he coaxed her mouth open, his tongue was gentle, too, exploring as though he had all the time in the world, as though he wanted nothing more than to taste her thoroughly, to commit her texture to memory.

She felt drugged. The pitter-pat of rain blended with her breathy sighs, blocking out the rest of the world. Here and now, it seemed there was only she and Rand and their love.

Easing away, he took her hands and raised them to his lips. Slowly he kissed the palms and the backs and the fine white scars.

"Don't flinch," he murmured when she did. Looking down, he traced the webbed patterns with a fingertip. "They're beautiful, because they're part of you."

Her throat closed with emotion, but she managed a shaky smile. "They remind me that I'm imperfect, which I suppose is not such a bad thing."

"It's a good thing you have one flaw." He kissed her nose and then her mouth, tiny damp kisses. "I'd feel damned inferior living with perfection."

Something twisted in her heart. "There were times when I feared you'd never be living with me at all."

"Never say never," he murmured, reaching for the champagne bottle. He tipped his head back and took a sip, then bent to nuzzle her throat. The wine fizzed in the hollow beneath her chin. She arched her neck, the combination of cold, bubbly liquid and warm, soft mouth sending shivers rippling through her.

As he nibbled his way up to her ear and drew the tender lobe between his teeth, she threaded her fingers into his hair. A soft groan rose from his chest, and suddenly he was kissing her again, more demanding now, nipping on her bottom lip before his mouth crushed hot against hers.

Instantly a matching heat flared up inside her. It had been there, building all day, and now it flamed to life. Her heart thundering, she gave as much as she took, a reckless meshing of lips and tongues and teeth that made her blood race with excitement. When he finally broke away, she was breathless.

She worked her hands beneath his surcoat as he flicked open the tabs that attached her stomacher. He dropped frantic kisses on her cheeks, her chin, her neck, and the expanse of trembling skin afforded him by the wide, low neckline of her saffron gown. With her stomacher removed, he loosened her laces and spread her bodice. Hooking the lacy edge of her chemise with a finger, he dragged it down, exposing her breasts to his hungry gaze.

Once more he reached for the champagne, tilting his head back to take a mouthful. Then he leaned forward and fastened his mouth on a sensitive peak.

The wine was cold and tingly, his mouth hot and emphatic. The combination robbed her of thought. Her senses reeled wildly as drops of champagne trickled free and he followed them with his tongue, leaving warm trails of sensation. She trembled with need, an urgent ache growing within her.

"Now," she breathed, and he shot her a wicked smile, reaching down to ruck up her skirts. His fingers danced up her legs, grazing the delicate skin on her inner thighs. The ache grew unbearable, and she gripped his shoulders. "Rand, we've waited long enough, days and days—"

"Hush," he whispered, reaching higher, brushing against where she ached. Then stroking, over and over, slipping a finger inside and back out to stroke more. His mouth slanted against hers again and again as his hands worked magic. Her eyes drifted shut, and she locked her arms behind his neck, tremors shimmering through her. The sweet torture continued until she was certain one more velvet stroke would be her undoing.

"Rand!" she cried out.

Suddenly their four hands were tearing at the laces that secured his breeches. And at long last he pulled her close and buried himself inside her.

Her arms and legs went around him, welcoming, squeezing tight. It had felt like forever, all those days they couldn't be together. Tears welled in her eyes at the sheer joy of him finally filling her, making her complete.

Their mouths met, hot and wet as he rocked up against her, as they rocked together, an exquisite rhythm that built and built until she came undone with a little cry that was swallowed by his own deep moan of pleasure.

"Oh, my God," she whispered after she caught her breath. "That was one perfect moment."

One perfect moment of euphoria.

"We'll have more," he murmured, pulling back to wipe traces of tears from her cheeks. With one gentle finger, he touched the dent in her chin. "A lifetime together."

Nothing would ever come between them again.

⁓

FOR A LONG time Lily stayed wrapped around Rand, and he held her close, cradling her head against his chest, his gaze drifting out the window. Rain pattered softly against the leaded panes. Beyond the glass, tall old trees danced in the blustery breeze, bright green against the dark gray sky, and farther beyond that, the red brick of Hawkridge Hall loomed majestically.

This, Rand thought—all of it—would someday be his. And he belonged here, as much as he belonged in a lecture hall or huddled over a cryptic passage of ancient text.

As a lad, he'd sought acceptance from a father who couldn't stand the sight of him and a brother who'd hated him since birth. Alban was dead now, his evil laid to rest. And as for the marquess...maybe now he would finally offer that approval that had been so elusive.

But to Rand it didn't really matter anymore. Because now he had Lily.

A contented sigh drifted from her, and he raised her face for his kiss. He would never get enough of her, he thought as he grazed her eyes and her cheeks and her lips, settling there to savor her sweet mouth. A kiss as gentle as the summer rain, a kiss for them both to melt into, a kiss to meld bodies and souls. And then another kiss. And another.

And another, until they heard a scratch and a peck and a tap against one of the dairy's windows.

∼

DEAR READER,

Before I receive a bunch of letters claiming that mastiffs are gentle, protective, indoor, family-type dogs, I want to say that all of that is true—for today's mastiffs. But in days gone by, the mastiff was known as a fighting dog. Caesar mentioned mastiffs in his account of invading Britain in 55 B.C., describing the huge British dogs that fought beside their masters. Soon afterward, mastiffs were bought back to Rome, where they saw combat at the Circus, matched against not only other dogs but also bulls, bears, lions, tigers, and human gladiators. Marco Polo wrote of Kubla Khan, who owned five thousand mastiffs used for hunting and war. Henry VIII gifted Charles V of Spain with four hundred mastiffs intended for use in battle.

However, by the 1920s, mastiffs were disappearing from England. During World War I, people thought it unpatriotic to keep dogs alive that ate as much in a day as a soldier. By World War II, they were nearly extinct in England, but afterward, mastiffs were imported from Canada and the United States to start new kennels. Now they are well established again, but with a change: modern breeders have bred the mastiff for gentleness and companionship rather than fighting. In his *Knight's Tale*, Chaucer described mastiffs as large as steer, which sounds unbelievable until we remember that cattle were much smaller in those days. Today's mastiffs are the same massive size, but they're loving and sociable pets.

In 1680, Irish scientist Robert Boyle began selling coarse sheets of paper coated with phosphorus and wooden sticks with sulfur. A stick drawn through a fold of the paper would burst into flames. This device was the first chemical "match" and ultimately led to what we think of as matches today. In 1855, the first red phosphorus "safety" matches were introduced in Sweden, and paper "match books" were invented in the United States in 1889.

Bawdy songs have always been popular, and in the seventeenth century the English were more comfortable singing such verse than they tend to be today. They relished the ribald and didn't take pains to disguise sex as love. Cromwell's Puritan Protectorate may have driven lusty singing underground, but with the Restoration, the ballad sellers returned. These early entrepreneurs sold single-sheet songs on the street, cheaply printed overnight to gain the most profit from each newly written piece.

In 1661, publisher and composer John Playford put together a collection of these songs and ballads and called it *An Antidote Against Melancholy*. In 1682, his son Henry expanded the collection and published it as *Wit and Mirth: An Antidote Against Melancholy*. By 1698, the book was so popular that Henry expanded it again, this time sold as *Wit and Mirth, or Pills to Purge Melancholy*. It proved so successful that after Henry's death it was published by others, and five further volumes were eventually added. By the time Thomas D'Urfey edited the final edition in 1720, the six-volume set contained more than a thousand bawdy songs.

Most of the homes in my books are inspired by real places you can visit. Trentingham Manor came to life after I saw The Vyne, a National Trust property in Hampshire. Built in the early sixteenth century for Lord Sandys, Henry VIII's Lord Chamberlain, the house acquired a classical portico in the mid-seventeenth century (the first of its kind in England) and contains a grand Palladian staircase, a wealth of old paneling and fine furniture, and a fascinating Tudor chapel with Renaissance glass.

The Vyne and its extensive gardens are open for visits April through October.

Hawkridge Hall was modeled on Ham House, another National Trust property. Known as the most well-preserved Stuart home in England, Ham House was built in 1610 and enlarged in the 1670s. The building has survived virtually unchanged since then, and it still retains most of the furniture from that period. The house and gardens are open daily from April through October. Ham House was owned by the Lauderdales, one of the most powerful families in Restoration England, and a visit gives a wonderful picture of seventeenth-century aristocratic life.

Rand's house in Oxford was inspired by the house Edmond Halley (1656-1742) lived in while he held the post of Oxford's Savilian Professor of Geometry. If you visit Oxford, look for the house in New College Lane near the Bridge of Sighs. The building isn't open to tourists, but you can see the outside, including the rooftop observatory Halley added (although he never saw Halley's Comet from it, since it made no appearance during the years he lived in the house).

I hope you enjoyed *The Scandal of Lord Randal!* If you'd like to revisit Lily and Rand, check out my next novel, *A Gentleman's Plot to Tie the Knot*. Please read on for an excerpt!

Always,

Lauren Royal

Read on for an excerpt from

A Gentleman's *Plot* to Tie the *Knot*

Book 7 of the
Chase Family Series
by Lauren Royal

Determined to land a wealthy, titled husband, Rose
Ashcroft heads off to Charles II's court to find love. And runs
smack dab into Christopher "Kit" Martyn, the one man who
could ruin all her plans.

∾

Trentingham Manor, the South of England
September 1677

STANDING IN her family's small, crowded chapel, Rose
Ashcroft shifted on her high Louis-heeled shoes, wishing she
were in a cathedral so there would be somewhere to sit.

Wishing she were *anywhere* but here watching her sister get
married.

"Randal John Charles, Earl of Newcliffe, wilt thou have this
woman to thy wedded wife, to live together after God's ordi-
nance in the holy estate of matrimony? Wilt thou love her,
comfort her, honor, and keep her in sickness and in health; and,
forsaking all others, keep thee only unto her, so long as ye both
shall live?"

"I will." The confident words boomed through the magnificent oak-paneled chamber, binding Rand to Rose's sister Lily.

But Rose wasn't listening to the ceremony. Instead she heard
twenty-one, twenty-one, twenty-one running through her head.
Twenty-one and a lonely spinster...while both her sisters had
found love.

Happy tears brightened their mother's brown eyes. She
leaned close, bumping against Rose's left side. "They're perfect
together, aren't they?" she whispered.

Rose could only nod dumbly, staring at her sister's petite
form laced into a gorgeous pale blue satin wedding dress
embroidered with gleaming silver thread. Lily's hair, the same
rich sable as Rose's, cascaded to her shoulders in glossy ringlets.

Beside her, Rand beamed a smile, looking tall and utterly hand-some in dark blue velvet, his gray gaze steady and adoring.

The two were so clearly in love, Rose knew they belonged together—and truly, she was happy for her sister.

If only Lily weren't her *younger* sister.

The priest cleared his throat and looked back down at his *Book of Common Prayer*. "Lady Lily Ashcroft, wilt thou have this man to thy wedded husband…"

Standing on Rose's right, her older sister Violet shifted one of her twin babies on her hip and gazed up at her husband of four years, Ford. Sun streamed through the stained-glass windows, glinting off her spectacles. "Oh, isn't this romantic?" she sighed.

Holding their other infant, Ford squeezed Violet around the shoulders. Seated cross-legged at their feet, their two-year-old son Nicky traced a finger over the patterns in the colorful glazed tile floor, obliviously happy.

Rose gritted her teeth.

Her friend Judith Carrington poked her from behind. "I cannot believe Lily's wedding is happening before mine," she whispered in a tone laced with dismay. "*I* was betrothed first!"

Rose couldn't believe Lily and Judith would *both* be married before she even received a proposal.

"…so long as ye both shall live?" the priest concluded expectantly.

In the hush that followed, even knowing it wasn't kind of her, Rose half wished Lily would fail to reply.

But Lily didn't, of course. "I will," she pledged, her voice as sweet as she was, ringing clear and true.

A few more words, a family heirloom ring slid onto her finger, and Lily was clearly and truly wed now, the new Countess of Newcliffe.

And Rose was clearly and truly miserable.

When Rand lowered his lips to meet Lily's, Rose turned away. Behind her, Judith was grinning up at her own betrothed —although only a little way up, since his stature was less than impressive. Lord Grenville was five-and-thirty to Judith's twenty, and his pale brown hair was thinning on top, but Rose imagined that the way Judith looked at him made him feel like a king. And he looked down on her in a way that surely made pretty, plump Judith feel like a queen.

Rose wanted someone who'd make her feel like a queen. Good God, a duchess or countess would do. Or even a lowly baroness...

As the years crawled by without a husband on the horizon, she was getting less picky. So long as the man was titled, handsome, rich, and powerful, most anyone was acceptable.

The guests parted as Lily and Rand began making their way from the chapel. They'd taken but a few steps when a cat, a squirrel, and a chirping sparrow came to join them.

Rose moved to hug her sister. "It was beautiful," she murmured. "I'm so happy for you."

She was. Truly she was.

Lily leaned down to pick up the cat, straightening with a brilliant smile. "Your turn next."

A hurt retort came to Rose's mind, but she wouldn't snap at her sister on her wedding day.

"I'm happy for you, too, Rand," she said instead, rising on her toes to give her sister's new husband a kiss on the cheek. But not too far up on her toes, because Rose was a tall woman. Too tall, perhaps, or too slim, or too quick-tongued...or too *something*.

There had to be some reason she had yet to find love.

Too intelligent, most likely. At one point, she'd thought Rand might be the man for her. Handsome, titled, and a professor of linguistics at Oxford—surely a good match for Rose, given her own exceptional command of foreign languages. But he'd chosen her little sister.

"I'm the luckiest man in the world," he said now, making Rose feel the unluckiest woman.

She'd had better days.

Lily must have noticed her dejected expression, because her fingers stopped stroking the cat's striped fur. Concern clouded her lovely blue eyes. "You *will* be next," she said quietly.

"Undoubtedly so, since I'm the only one left," Rose quipped. "Unless, that is, Rowan manages to find himself a bride before I find a groom."

They both swung to look at their eleven-year-old brother where he stood with Violet's young niece, Jewel, their dark heads close together as they whispered animatedly.

"He may have found himself a bride already," Rose added dryly.

Lily's laughter rang through the chapel, echoing off the molded dome ceiling. "Surely someone will claim you long before Rowan gets it in his head to wed. Why, you're the most beautiful of all of us, Rose!"

Rose had always thought Lily the *most* beautiful, but she knew she was beautiful, too. Yet beauty, she'd learned, was not enough to hook a husband.

Well-wishers pressed closer. Rose began moving toward the drawing room and found Judith by her side. Forsaking her betrothed, Judith clutched Rose's arm. "Who is *that* handsome fellow?" she whispered conspiratorially.

Rose slid a glance to the man in question, a friend of Rand's whose gaze suddenly met hers, then skimmed her body in a way that might have made her heart pound...if she were at all interested. "That's Mr. Christopher Martyn— Rand calls him Kit. He's an architect," she added dismissively.

"Christopher Martyn, the architect?" Awe hushed Judith's voice. "Hasn't King Charles recently awarded him a contract to renovate Whitehall Palace?"

"Along with Windsor Castle and Hampton Court."

"Ah, a man of intelligence to complement yours." Clearly Judith considered the man's lack of a title no impediment. "No need for you to play the featherbrained coquette for him."

"I've no interest in him. And I've never acted feather-brained." But perhaps now was the time to start.

On her sisters' advice, Rose had tried to win Rand by appealing to his intellect, but that hadn't worked at all. Never again would she attempt to attract a man by flaunting her brains. No matter what her family or Judith said, she knew there were better ways to entice gentlemen.

Unfortunately, where Rand was concerned, she'd come to that conclusion too late. To her intense embarrassment, she'd stooped to propositioning him in her family's summerhouse, and when that hadn't worked, desperation had driven her to attempt bribery and trickery of the worst kind.

She couldn't imagine what had come over her that day and had feared she'd never be able to look Rand in the face again. But to her utter relief he seemed at ease with her, as though he'd graciously forgotten that humiliating episode.

"You cannot tell me," Judith whispered, dragging Rose back to the present, "that you don't find Mr. Martyn attractive."

Rose slanted Kit another covert look. Dressed in forest-toned velvet, he was tall and lean, his hair dark as jet, his eyes a startling mix of brown and green. She dredged up a wry smile. "I'd have to be blind to claim that."

"And he looks ever so nice. Do you think he's nice?"

"He's nice enough." Except for those unusual eyes, which were decidedly *not* nice. *Wicked* would be a better description.

"And good Lord, he's building things for the king! I'm certain he has money—"

"Money," Rose interrupted pointedly, "does not make up for lack of a title."

Her sister Violet walked up, sans children for once. "Who needs a title?"

Judith crossed her arms. "Lady Rose apparently wishes to become Lady Something-Higher."

"Oh, well." Violet sent Rose an indulgent smile. "That's only because she has yet to fall in love."

Rose smiled in return. "And given that it's as easy to fall in love with a titled man as one without, I've decided to concentrate on the former."

Violet and Judith exchanged a glance that set Rose's teeth on edge, then left her, to return to their respective men.

Since Lily had given their mother barely two weeks to plan the event, the wedding party was small. Still, there were more than enough guests to fill the drawing room and spill out onto the Palladian portico and into the exquisite gardens. Trentingham Manor was known for its gardens, thanks to Rose's father and his passion for flowers and plants.

But it was a warm, sunny day, and Rose feared for her creamy complexion, so she opted to stay indoors. She wandered the crowded drawing room, sipping from a goblet of the new and frightfully expensive champagne her parents favored for celebrations. Although she enjoyed sharing a word or two with various relatives and neighbors, she was generally feeling at loose ends, not quite sure what to do with herself.

Until, that was, she heard her father's voice and turned to see him addressing Kit Martyn.

"...one of those newfangled greenhouses," Father was saying. "On the east side of the house, I'm thinking, to catch the morning sun. Since autumn is nearly upon us, I'd be much obliged if you could start it immediately."

Rose couldn't believe her ears. It was the second time her father had asked the esteemed architect to build him a lowly greenhouse.

Half tempted to ball up the lacy handkerchief she had tucked in her sleeve and stuff it into her father's mouth, she hurried to join them. "Mr. Martyn builds things for the *king*, Father! Palaces, for heaven's sake. He hasn't—"

"Well, not quite palaces," Kit corrected her. "Renovations to palaces, additions to palaces, but I've yet to build an entire—"

"See?" Rose met her father's deep green eyes, speaking loudly and slowly to make sure he could hear her over the hubbub of the celebration. "Palaces. He hasn't the time to build you a greenhouse."

Kit sipped from his own goblet of champagne, then grinned at Rose's father. "Oh, I think I might find the time," he disagreed, his words infused with a hint of laughter. "In exchange for a dance with your beautiful daughter."

He shifted to look at Rose, making it clear which daughter he meant. His green-brown gaze swept her lazily, almost as though he were mentally undressing her…and if his expression was any indication, he plainly liked the results.

Lord Trentingham frowned. "My bountiful bother?"

Kit looked confused, and Rose knew she should remind him that her father was hard of hearing at the best of times—and in a crowded room, he was all but deaf.

But she couldn't seem to speak. The audacity of the man, thinking he could trade a building for her company. Surely her father would never—

"I'll be most pleased to build your greenhouse," Kit reiterated, "if your lovely daughter will oblige me with a dance."

"Oblige you with advance?"

Understanding dawned in Kit's eyes. "A dance," he shouted. "May I have the honor of a dance with Lady Rose?"

"Oh, yes. Of course," her father said. "Now, about that greenhouse—"

"I'll do a preliminary design before I leave," Kit all but bellowed.

"Excellent." Lord Trentingham turned a vague smile in Rose's direction. "Run along, dear. Enjoy yourself."

Her mouth dropped open, then shut when she found herself propelled from the drawing room by a warm hand at her back. Then she was stepping out onto the covered portico, which had been pressed into service as a dance floor.

Three musicians in one corner were playing a minuet, a graceful dance that facilitated conversation. The wedding guests chatted and flirted, their shoes brushing the brick paving in unison. Though the dance was already in progress, Kit handed both their champagne goblets to a passing maid, took Rose's hands, and swept her into the throng.

She'd never touched him—certainly not skin to skin—and the contact reminded her just how attractive she'd thought him the first time they met. The mere sight of him had set her blood to singing inside her. But that, of course, had been before she'd discovered he was a plain mister. Since then, seeing him had had no effect on her at all.

So it was disconcerting to find that touching him now seemed to make the champagne bubbles dance in her stomach.

"Lovely Corinthian capitals on the columns and pilasters," Kit noted, ever the architect. "Do you know who carved them?"

She pliéd and stepped forward with her right foot at the same time she finally found her tongue. "Edward Marshall, who also carved the Ashcroft family arms in the pediment. And in future, please keep in mind that there's no need to ask my father's permission for a dance. Ashcroft women make their own decisions."

"So Rand has told me," Kit said, breezing over the implication that she might have refused him.

They rose on their toes, and when he pulled her closer, she caught a whiff of his scent. A woodsy fragrance with a base of frankincense and myrrh. It smelled nice, she thought, wondering if she could duplicate it in her mother's perfumery.

"Your family is an odd one," he said. "I don't allow my sister to make her own decisions. Not the important ones, in any case."

She felt sorry for his sister. "Our family motto is *Interroga Conformationem*."

He looked at her blankly.

"Question Convention," she translated. What sort of educated man didn't know Latin? Certainly not one she'd ever consider husband material.

It was a good thing he wasn't in the running.

They dropped hands to turn in place, then he grasped her

fingers again. "Is it true, as Rand said, that your father allows his daughters to choose their own husbands as well?"

She noticed Lily and Rand dancing together—much closer than the dance required. Surprisingly, envy didn't clutch at her heart this time. She only smiled. "Yes."

"In future, I'll keep *that* in mind," Kit responded with a disarming grin.

Ignoring his impertinence, Rose gazed across the wide daisy-strewn lawn toward the Thames. Just then, her brother Rowan raced onto the portico, looking like a miniature version of their father in a burgundy suit, his long midnight hair streaming behind him.

A quite ordinary-looking man followed more sedately, but as he wore red and white—the king's livery—he attracted more attention.

The musicians stopped playing, and the dancers ground to a halt.

"There he is," Rowan said, pointing to Kit in the sudden silence. "Mr. Christopher Martyn, the man you seek."

"IF I MAY speak with you in private, sir," the messenger said. "I bring word from His Majesty."

Kit nodded and stepped off the portico, silently leading the way to the summerhouse he'd spotted earlier. He felt the eyes of the other wedding guests following him and heard their speculative murmurs, but the sudden appearance of the king's man didn't intrigue him as it did them. He was, after all, completing several royal projects. Likely Charles simply wanted a change.

As Kit crossed Lord Trentingham's celebrated gardens, he thought instead of Rose, vaguely wondering where he'd found the nerve to imply he might be interested in marriage. He'd been drawn to her when they first met, but quickly dismissed it when she failed to respond to his advances. He figured there were plenty of splendid women in the world—which meant there was no sense pursuing one who wasn't attainable.

But today she'd sipped champagne, and he'd noticed her lips were made for kissing. And he'd taken her hands and felt something like a punch to his gut. And she'd challenged him verbally, and those words had jumped out of his mouth.

Ludicrous words. As a man who'd never wanted for female attention, he was frustrated by Lady Rose's obvious disinterest, but deep down he knew that pursuing her was an absurd waste of time. Although he thought her lovely and intelligent—he'd watched her decipher a coded diary weeks earlier and been nothing short of astonished—he had no illusions of winning Lady Rose. Or, for that matter, any lady at all. He knew his place in the world.

Commoner, through and through.

His best friend might be an earl who'd grown up in a mansion, but Kit had been raised in a single-room cottage. No Martyn had ever borne a title. Before him, he doubted any Martyn had ever even considered the possibility.

He knew that, social perceptions aside, he was damn well as good as anyone else. But he was also well aware that he wasn't considered good enough for the Earl of Trentingham's daughter. And wishing things were different would never make them so.

At least, not in the near future.

The circular redbrick summerhouse was a small building with classic Palladian lines. He ushered the king's man inside. Owing to the admirable design—large arched windows over each of the four doors—it was bright beneath the cool, shaded dome.

Bright enough to make out the seriousness in the messenger's eyes.

Apprehension soured the champagne in Kit's stomach. "Yes?" he asked.

The man's words were anything but reassuring. "This

concerns one of your projects. I've been sent to advise you that the ceiling at Windsor Castle is falling—"

"Falling? Has anyone been hurt?"

"I should say chunks of plaster have fallen—not the ceiling itself. But it's sagging, and there are many cracks. There have been no injuries, but His Majesty wanted you to know—"

"I understand." Kit understood Charles's underlying message all too well. If he failed to complete this project on time and satisfactorily, his dream of being appointed Deputy Surveyor—a step toward someday becoming Surveyor General of the King's Works, the official royal architect—would be as good as dead.

And without that, the rest of his dreams—his plans to obtain a title for himself and marry his sister Ellen to a peer of the realm —would die along with it.

He yanked the door back open. "I shall depart for Windsor posthaste."

"Sir." The man bowed and preceded him outside.

Back at the house, Kit looked around for Rand, but his friend was nowhere to be found. He went instead to give his apologies to his hostess. "Forgive me, Lady Trentingham, but I must take my leave. There's a problem at Windsor Castle. I cannot seem to locate Rand—"

"He and Lily have a habit of disappearing," she told him with a suggestive twinkle in her eye that took him by surprise. She was, after all, the girl's mother. But then her brown eyes turned sympathetic. "I'll explain," she added. "He'll understand."

In no time at all, Kit was settled in his carriage, rubbing the back of his neck as the vehicle lumbered its way toward Windsor.

Could he possibly have made an error in designing Windsor's new dining room? Had a flaw in the plans gone unnoticed? He unrolled the extra set he always carried, spreading the linen they were drawn on over his lap. But he couldn't seem to concentrate.

Especially when his carriage jostled past the village of Hawkridge, where he'd grown up.

Toying with the small, worn chunk of brick he carried in his pocket—a chip off his first building—he found himself gazing out the window as memories assaulted him. Nights whiled away in his family's snug cottage, he and Ellen playing on the floor while their mother read by the fire. Days spent with his father, learning carpentry and building. Afternoons fishing with the local nobleman's son, Lord Randal Nesbitt, both of them starved for companionship their age.

That felt like a lifetime ago. Rand was married now, a man who declared himself in love. As for Kit, love wasn't high on his list of priorities.

A luxury, love was, and one Kit felt quite capable of living without. After all, love had done his parents no favors. They'd been happy together, content with their simple lot in life—and both ended up in early graves.

That wasn't going to happen to Kit or his sister.

For twelve years—through school, university, and a quickly rising reputation—he had dedicated himself to one goal. The Deputy Surveyor post was almost within his grasp.

He couldn't fail now.

"YOU LOOK melancholy," Rose's mother said later that evening. Standing with Rose in her perfumery, Chrystabel picked over the many flower arrangements on her large wooden worktable, plucking out the marigolds. "Why the long face, dear? Are you sad to see your creations destroyed?"

"Of course not." Rose added a purple aster to a pile of flowers and some ivy to a bunch of greens. She looked up and forced what she hoped sounded like a romantic sigh. "The wedding was beautiful, wasn't it?"

"Made more so by your lovely flowers." Rose had filled the house with towering creations made of posies cut from her father's gardens. "Which is why," her mother added, "I thought—"

"I don't care what becomes of my flower arrangements. Honestly, Mum, it makes no sense to let the blooms wither and die when we can turn them into essential oils for your perfumes. I don't mind in the least." With a bit more force than was necessary, Rose tugged two lilies from the vases and tossed them onto the table. "Whatever happened to Kit Martyn, do you know?" she asked in an attempt to change the subject.

"That messenger brought news of a problem with one of his projects. He had to leave."

"Which project?" Rose asked.

"He didn't say. Or perhaps I don't remember." Mum fixed her with a piercing gaze. A motherly gaze. "Does it matter?"

"Of course not. It was only idle curiosity." A headache threatened, pulsing in Rose's temples. "Why should I care what happens to the man's projects?"

"You danced with him—"

"Father traded that dance for a greenhouse. It meant nothing."

Her mother nodded thoughtfully, beginning to pluck petals from a bunch of striped snapdragons. "You just look melancholy."

If Rose weren't already suffering from a headache, that swift change back to the original subject might have prompted one. She lifted the lid off the gleaming glass and metal distillery that Ford had made for her mother while he was courting Violet. "It's nothing, Mum."

"It doesn't bother you that your younger sister is wed?"

"Why shouldn't I wish her happy?" She was chagrined to hear her voice crack. "I do, Mum, I vow and swear it."

"It's no failing of yours, dear, that Lily found love first."

"Stuck as we are in the countryside, it's a wonder she found a man at all, whether she loves him or not." It was an ancient complaint, but in her present mood Rose had no compunctions against dragging it out again. "We hardly ever get to London, or anywhere else we might meet eligible—"

"You have a point," Mum interrupted.

"Pardon?" Rose blinked.

"You heard me. You haven't much opportunity here to meet men." Mum tossed the pink petals into the distillery's large glass bulb. "I'm thinking that we—you and I—should attend court."

"Court?" Rose decided she couldn't be hearing right. One of them had clearly drunk too much champagne. "As in King Charles's court?"

"I believe they're at Windsor now—they do move around, as you may know."

"What I *know* is that you and Father have always claimed court is no place for proper young ladies."

"Well, you're not so young anymore," Mum said, then came to wrap an arm around Rose when she winced. "I didn't mean it that way, dear. But you're one-and-twenty now, a woman grown. And I *will* be there to chaperone. It's perfectly acceptable."

It was more than acceptable, Rose knew—girls as young as fifteen went to court, many of them *un*chaperoned. And she also knew the licentious men there treated them like full-grown women. Violet had been to court with Ford, and she'd come back with stories that had made Rose's eyes widen.

A little part of her wondered if this was really such a grand idea.

But she wasn't going to argue when faced with such surprising good fortune. "Gemini, I'd best go talk to Harriet. She'll doubtless need to alter some of my gowns, and it will take me hours to decide what to take before she can even begin."

"There's no time for alterations, dear." In opposition to Rose, whose stomach was churning with excitement, Mum calmly plucked petals. "I mean to leave tomorrow."

"Tomorrow!" Rose dropped the stem in her hand. "Tomorrow?"

"There's no time like the present," her mother said with an enigmatic smile.

Normally, Rose might have been vexed at the implication that she was getting more spinsterish as the days sped by. But this was no time to be touchy.

No, it was time to prepare.

She was going to court! Leaving her flowers on the table, she rushed to her chamber to pack.

"WHAT A DAY." Chrystabel slipped beneath the counterpane to join her husband in bed, sinking into the mattress as she relaxed for the first time in what seemed like weeks. "Thank God they're married at last."

"I suspect you're really thanking God they can no longer create a child out of wedlock," Joseph teased, leaning up to kiss her lightly on the lips. He lowered himself onto an elbow, smiling into her eyes, his own a deep, sparkling green.

She pushed a lock of dark hair off his forehead. "Well, there is that," she admitted. When Lily and Rand's marriage plans had been threatened by Rand's father, she'd been mortified to realize she'd allowed them to share a bed before her daughter was safely wed. It had seemed a fine idea at the time, but it wouldn't be happening again with Rose—or Rowan, for that matter.

Chrystabel reckoned she could learn from her mistakes.

"But mostly," she added, "I'm just gladdened to see them happy at last. Everything worked out."

"It usually does," said her ever-practical husband.

She released a contented sigh. "Another wedding."

"Another wedding night," he responded with a lustful grin.

A tradition, their wedding nights. That was one of the reasons she so loved arranging other people's marriages. Not that either of them needed an excuse to make love, but there was something thrilling about watching a wedding while anticipating their own wedding night to come.

She smiled as he kissed her again, then moaned when he slipped a hand beneath her nightgown's neckline to caress a sensitive breast. For long minutes they said nothing, their breathing growing louder and more ragged in the stillness of their thick-walled room.

Here, in their quiet, private chamber, her Joseph could hear whatever she said. Every word, those spoken as well as the silent ones that passed between two as attuned as they.

But they didn't need words now. Actions would do. A brush of lips, warm skimming hands. Bodies coming together, creating a thrill that the years had done nothing to dim. Soft cries filled the chamber, matched by a low groan of pleasure that echoed into the night.

When their hearts had calmed, when Joseph leaned away to blow out the single remaining candle, Chrystabel sighed. "I'll miss you."

"Where are you going?" The words vibrated against her throat where he'd settled back into her arms.

"I'm thinking to take Rose to court at Windsor. With your permission, of course," she rushed to add, knowing he would never deny her.

"Court? Do you expect that's wise? The men there—"

"I'll watch her like a hawk. And rest assured, there's not a man at court I want for Rose. She belongs with Kit Martyn. He's at Windsor as we sleep, checking on a project—"

"Kit Martyn? Chrysanthemum my love, I know you fancy yourself a matchmaker, but Rose has shown no interest—"

"Which is exactly why he's the perfect man for her."

Joseph lifted his head and searched her eyes in the dim, flickering light from the fire. "Come again?"

"You know how she is. As soon as she sets her sights on a man, the act begins. The flirting. The flattering. Don't you see? She has a much better chance of winning a man she thinks she doesn't want. With Kit she'll be herself. Charming, intelligent, sharp-witted….why, he cannot fail but fall in love with her."

"I suspect he's taken with her already," Joseph said dryly. "But what good will that do if she doesn't fall for him? We've promised her she can choose her own husband."

"Making her fall," Chrystabel said, "will be Kit's problem, and I've no doubt he's up to the task. I need only provide the opportunity."

"You cannot push, Chrysanthemum."

Her laugh tinkled through the darkness. "I would never. I know full well our daughters pledged to avoid me arranging their marriages. Yet I managed to match both Violet and Lily without either being the wiser, didn't I? Have no fear, darling—Rose's romance will follow suit. And she'll have no idea I was behind it."

∽

AVAILABLE NOW!
Learn more about *A Gentleman's Plot to Tie the Knot* at
www.LaurenRoyal.com

ENTER FOR A CHANCE TO WIN
a sterling silver replica of the pendant Rand gives Lily in this book!*

Visit the Contest page on Lauren's website
at www.LaurenRoyal.com
and answer a question to be
entered in the monthly drawing.

No purchase necessary. See complete rules on the site.

*Please note: Depending on when you enter, the prize may be another piece of jewelry associated with one of Lauren's books. The author reserves the right to discontinue this promotion at any time.

ABOUT LAUREN ROYAL

LAUREN ROYAL is a *New York Times* and *USA Today* bestselling author of humorous historical romance. Her "truly enchanting" novels have won many awards including *Booklist*'s "Top 10 Romance of the Year" and earned raves from reviewers including *Publishers Weekly*, who calls her "an impressive talent."

All of Lauren's books are complete, stand-alone stories, and yet they are also all connected—because they all feature her beloved "outrageously funny, loyal, compassionate, and unconventional" Chase family.

Lauren writes steamy historical romance on her own and sweet/clean historical romance with her daughter, Devon Royal. She lives in Southern California with her family, their constantly shedding cat, and a stupendous collection of fuzzy socks. When she's not busy writing, she enjoys singing along (off-key) to Hamilton, dancing (badly), and (wasting time) watching HGTV.

ACKNOWLEDGMENTS

~

MY HEARTFELT THANKS:

To Ayn Rand, for the concepts behind Violet's philosophical musings on love at first sight.

To all the honorary Chase cousins in my Chase Family Readers Group, for their enthusiastic support.

And, last but certainly not least, to all my wonderful readers, especially those of you who send emails and post about my books on Twitter and Facebook.

Thank you, one and all!

CONTACT INFORMATION

Lauren's Newsletter

littl.ink/LaurensNews

Facebook Readers Group

facebook.com/groups/ChaseFamilyReaders

Facebook Page

facebook.com/LaurenRoyal

Website

www.LaurenRoyal.com